Darkhaven

A.F.E. Smith is an editor of academic texts by day and a fantasy writer by night. She lives with her husband and their two young children in a house that was apparently built to be as creaky as possible. She can be found on Twitter @afesmith and online at www.afesmith.com

Darkhaven

A.F.E. SMITH

Book One of The Darkhaven Novels

with very best wishes

A.F.E.Smith

HARPER
Voyager

Harper*Voyager*
An imprint of HarperCollins*Publishers* Ltd
1 London Bridge Street
London SE1 9GF

www.harpervoyagerbooks.co.uk

This Paperback Original 2016

First published in Great Britain in ebook format by Harper*Voyager* 2015

A catalogue record for this book
is available from the British Library

ISBN: 978-0-00-812073-3

Set in Sabon by Born Group using Atomik ePublisher from Easypress

Printed and bound in Great Britain

ONE

It had been weeks since Ayla last felt a breeze touch her face. As she slipped through the door into the shadows of the square, the scents of a summer night caressed her with their familiarity: aromatic pine, horse manure, the dragonlilies that grew outside the tower. Above her, the patterns of the stars were unchanged. She hadn't been locked up that long, after all. It just felt like forever.

There will be no-one patrolling the square. She repeated her brother's words to herself. *Go straight across. The postern will be open, and you'll find supplies there to help you. After that I can do no more.*

She hesitated, skin crawling with tiny spiders of unease. The darkness on the far side of the square was too heavy for the moonlight to penetrate; anything could be waiting for her. Yet Myrren's instructions hadn't failed her so far. When she'd tried the door of her cell at the seventh bell, it had been unlocked just as he'd promised. And the two men in the guardroom had been deep in the oblivion of sleep, not stirring even when she crept past them to climb the flight of steps that was the only way out. Her brother's words were her compass. She had to trust them.

Straightening her spine, she stepped into the illuminated patch at the centre of the square, forcing herself to walk as though she were unafraid. Her ears rang with the silence, straining to hear any sounds of pursuit; her muscles quivered with the need to flee. She didn't think she could bear another day trapped in that tiny room with its one barred window, where desperation bled from the walls like damp. If they found her now it would be better to run, to Change, to fight until they had to kill her to subdue her … yet no-one came. The shadows on the far side of the square reached out to enfold her, wrapping her in darkness once more – and then she was standing in front of the postern gate.

Quite calm now, floating in a numb place beyond fear, she lifted the latch. The gate creaked softly as it swung open; she glanced back over her shoulder, fighting to control the harsh gasps of her breath. But the square remained empty, and no vengeful light flared in the windows of the tower. After a long, frozen moment, Ayla stepped through the gate and pulled it closed behind her.

She hadn't gone far when her foot caught on something, sending her stumbling forward. Heart racing so fast it made her dizzy, she crouched down and searched through the charcoal shadows at her feet until her hands brushed rough fabric. A sack, tucked into the space between gate and wall: it must be the supplies Myrren had promised her. She picked it up and hurried away down the hill towards the city, navigating each bump and hollow by the light of the waxing moon. That same light had poured in through the windows of Darkhaven, the night they arrested her. A whole month. Had it really been that long? In her cell, with no daily routine to cling to, it had been hard to tell. Time had stretched to eternity one moment and shrunk to an instant the next, leaving her adrift.

Leaving her with nothing to do but replay, in a futile loop, the events that had brought her there.

As was fast becoming their habit, she and her father had started that evening by arguing. They'd always argued, of course, but not like this. Not as if each would rather kill the other than concede the fight. Ayla knew she couldn't beat Florentyn in a real fight, either in human or in creature form, but she hoped this battle of words would be different. Her father probably wouldn't go so far as to physically chastise his wayward daughter.

Probably.

She had to keep trying, anyway, for Myrren's sake.

'You can't do that to him,' she said for the tenth time in as many days. 'He is your true heir, your pure-blood son. I'm only half a Nightshade.'

On the other side of the desk, her father sat motion-less and in shadow; no need for light when only Changers were present in the room. Ayla resented the fact that he'd summoned her into the library as if he had every right to control her movements. That he'd made her stand in front of his desk like a stripling awaiting punishment, not a fully grown woman. She resented a lot of things. But she had to concentrate on the one that mattered.

'You can Change.' Florentyn's face showed no more emotion than the ancestral busts adorning the bookcases to either side of him. 'Myrren cannot. I have no choice but to disinherit him.'

'I won't take his birthright away from him, Father.' She lifted her chin, but he was as impervious to her defiance as his Firedrake form was to steel.

'You will start accompanying me on state visits. It's time you began to learn what is required of Darkhaven's overlord.'

3

Ayla bit her lip. Always he dangled that in front of her: the chance to meet people, different people, not just her family and the Helm. To see and be seen, rather than be kept hidden away like a secret. She yearned for that. She could almost taste the tang of it. But she had her brother to think of.

'Myrren is your heir,' she repeated. Then, knowing she'd sound like a child, but unable to help herself, 'It's not fair.'

Abruptly, Florentyn pushed his chair back and stood. Palms flat on the desk, he leaned forward, towering over her. For an instant she saw Myrren in him – all Nightshades looked alike, hair the colour of a moonless night and eyes like deep pools of spilled ink. But her father's face was far crueller than her brother's.

'Fair? Fair has nothing to do with it,' he said, every word as sharp-edged and clear as broken glass. 'Else I'd have two true-blooded children, not one who Changes into some mongrel creature no-one's ever seen before and one who is incapable of Changing at all.'

Ayla's hands curled into taut fists. She was all too aware that her creature-self was an unusual one, not one of the pure forms of power her ancestors had taken – Firedrake or Griffin, Phoenix, Hydra or Unicorn. Her mother had been an ordinary woman, a common girl from the city; no doubt that blood had weakened the Nightshade strain. Yet the knowledge didn't make the contempt in Florentyn's words hurt any less.

She wanted to retreat. She wanted to seek comfort with her brother, who at least loved her wholeheartedly. But instead she gripped the desk herself, matching Florentyn's stance.

'You married outside the bloodline after Myrren's mother died,' she said in a voice that shook. 'If you don't like what I am, you have only yourself to blame.'

She heard the crack of his hand across her face before she felt the sting. Belatedly she stumbled backwards a few steps, fingers pressed to her cheek. *Guess I was wrong about the physical chastisement.*

'I had no choice.' Her father's demeanour hadn't changed; it seemed hitting her was of no more import to him than swatting a troublesome fly. 'Otherwise you can be sure I wouldn't have done it.'

That hurt worse than the slap. 'But you loved my mother,' Ayla said desperately.

'Love?' A shrug disposed of that. 'Had I known what you and Myrren would become ... but no matter. Without a Changer at its head, the Nightshade line will lose its grip on this country. And so in the absence of a real Changer, you will have to do.'

At the undercurrent of venom in his words, Ayla finally understood. Florentyn was doing what he considered to be right for his country, but he hated it. More than that: he hated her, for being the only logical choice. For forcing him to pass on his legacy to a half-blood freak.

In the crackling silence that had fallen between them, the sudden pounding at the door made them both start.

'My lord!' The deep male voice was muffled by the door, but the urgency in it was clear. Florentyn remained frozen in position a moment longer, gaze fixed on Ayla's face. Then he straightened up from the desk and clicked his fingers, bringing the oil lamp on the desk to sputtering life.

'Enter,' he snapped.

Ayla turned to see four men of the Helm marching into the room, solemn-faced and self-important with news. They threw her sly glances, but she paid them no heed. She knew how little some of the Helm respected her; they looked at her and saw her mother, her tainted lineage. Even more than the Nightshades themselves, the Helm were obsessed with protecting the bloodline's power. That was why they'd let her mother go to her death without lifting a finger to prevent it.

'My lord, last night a priestess was set upon in one of the sixth-ring temples,' the foremost Helmsman said to Florentyn. 'She passed out during the attack, but before that ...' His gaze rolled to Ayla. 'She claims she saw a creature, all shadows and fire.'

What? Ayla opened her mouth to speak, then closed it again as Florentyn turned on her. His voice burned with righteous ire, but underlying it was an unsettling hint of satisfaction. 'Did you do this, Ayla?'

'Of course not. I wouldn't do something like that.'

'Not even to show me how unfit you are to rule?' Red light flared briefly in his eyes, the Firedrake within him stirring. 'Or perhaps it wasn't deliberate. Perhaps that travesty of a creature you turn into is uncontrollable. Either way, you'd better be put somewhere safe until we get to the bottom of this.'

'No!' Ayla glared at him. 'If you want to punish me then at least be honest about it. Don't use some trumped-up charge without a shred of proof –'

'I will ask you the question one final time, Ayla,' Florentyn interrupted. 'Will you do what's best for Mirrorvale?'

She hesitated. The choice was clear: obey him, or be arrested like a common criminal. She didn't want to think how long he'd let her cool her heels in the cells – and even once he released her, it would only be to offer her the same bargain. In the end, she'd have to give in.

But Myrren deserved better.

'I won't betray my brother,' she said softly. 'Darkhaven's throne is his by right, and I will not take it.'

'In that case,' Florentyn replied, 'this crime must be investigated to the fullest extent of my power.'

He held up a hand, and the Helm hustled her away to the cells.

At first she attempted to measure the passing time by counting the meals she was given, but the food was always the same; no indication whether it was intended as an evening meal or the breaking of her fast. Bathwater and clean clothes were brought to her at apparently random intervals. Sleep was no better as a guide, since each time she woke she had no way of knowing whether she had lost days or moments. When the wind was in the right quarter she could hear the bells chiming the changes in the sixth ring of Arkannen: *one*, night's end, the beginning of a new day; *two*, time to start the morning's lessons; *five*, her father and brother would be sitting down for their evening meal. Once she had understood her life by the ringing of those bells, but now they meant nothing. Slowly but surely, she began to lose her grip on reality.

Then Myrren came to her. It was the first time since her arrest that she'd set eyes on any member of her family; seeing her brother in the doorway of her cell sent her giddy with relief.

'Myrren!' She jumped to her feet and ran to him. 'What's happening? How much longer do I have to stay in here?'

'Little sister …' His taut grip on her hands told her far more than his carefully controlled expression. 'Please, just do as he asks. You have the gift. I don't. It's really that simple.'

She shook her head stubbornly. 'No. I won't do it. He can't bully us any more, Myrren. This nonsense about an attacked priestess –'

'But it isn't nonsense. That's the trouble. There really was an attack, and all the evidence points to a Changer creature.'

A.F.E. Smith

'What?' She closed her eyes for a moment as the world seemed to sway around her. 'But I didn't do it!'

'I believe you,' Myrren said. 'But except for Father himself, there is no other possible culprit. And since you will not cooperate with him ...' His fingers tightened still further on hers. 'He has set the trial for two days' time, Ayla. And he is going to find you guilty.'

'What is the penalty?' she whispered.

'Incarceration.' A hint of pain clenched his jaw. 'You will never be allowed to Change again.'

No. No no no – Ayla swallowed, fighting to remain on her feet until the dizzy ringing in her ears subsided. When she spoke, she was proud that her voice remained steady.

'I will claim the right to die at my own hand. It will be better that way.'

'Ayla, no!' A sudden fierce intensity in his eyes, Myrren drew her closer. 'It won't come to that. If you really are determined not to give in to Father, there is an alternative.'

'What alternative?'

'You hide for a while. Go into Arkannen, conceal yourself there. I'll try to make Father see reason.'

She lifted her shoulders in a shrug, infuriated by her own helplessness. 'But how can I get out of here? He'll know if I Change.'

'I'll help you,' Myrren told her. 'But you must do exactly as I say ...'

And so she had, and here she was: walking down the hill to her freedom. Ayla just wished she'd been able to thank him properly. There was no way of knowing when she would see him again.

When she was far enough away to believe herself safe, halfway between the tower and the wall that separated it from the city, she stepped aside into the cover of some thorn bushes and tipped out the sack's contents. First was a thick woollen cloak, with a hood to conceal the telltale black of her hair. Wrapped in the cloak were a serviceable knife and a pouch containing a few coins. There was also a smaller bag that held food and water.

Don't forget. Myrren's final words lingered at the forefront of her mind. *Once outside these walls, you can no longer be Ayla, royal daughter of Darkhaven. You must be a shadow, a whisper, a breath of air. Any more than that, and they'll find you and lock you up for good.* His hand had brushed over her hair, a feather-light touch, before he turned away. *Be careful, little sister. I'll send word when it's safe to return.*

Ayla pulled the cloak tight around herself, lifting the hood to cover her head. She added the knife and money-pouch to her belt, then swung the bag of food onto her back. Her chest ached with the knowledge that it might be a long time before she could return to her other form, but she ignored it. Better to be an ordinary woman and free than a Changer in a cage.

She glanced back at Darkhaven, looming against the moon. A shiver ran across her skin, as though she had been brushed from head to toe by a cold, invisible hand. It was the sensation she felt when her father Changed, an awareness of the family gift that all the Nightshade line possessed – the reason she couldn't Change now herself if she wanted to avoid discovery. Fearful, she gazed at the sky above the tower, half expecting her father to come bursting out in his Firedrake form and roar after her; yet all remained dark and quiet, only the stars awake.

Lifting her chin, she started down the slope towards the seventh gate, and Arkannen.

*

Myrren was awoken from an uneasy dream by the sudden clangour of bells. With a gasp, he sat bolt upright, tilting his head in search of the sound. It wasn't the temples in the city; it was nearer and louder, an erratic jangling that cut right through him. The old warning bell, proclaiming disaster.

Ayla.

The thought sent him stumbling out of bed, to push aside the heavy curtain that barely stirred in the breeze from the open window. A relieved sigh escaped him at the glimmer of daylight on the horizon. The new day had begun; Ayla ought to be well away by now. The noise must be because the Helm had discovered her escape. He should speak to his father before they did, confess what he'd done. The idea made him more nervous than a grown man had any right to be, but better that than be discovered in a lie.

He turned away from the window, then wavered as dizziness swept over him. It hardly felt as if he'd slept at all. No doubt part of him had been awake all night, fretting about Ayla, hoping she was safe. He knew how much it meant to her to be able to Change; he couldn't bear the idea that she might be denied her gift for good. If he could Change, he would hate to be locked up more than anything … but he pushed that thought aside. Some things were too sour to linger over.

With the prospective visit to his father in mind, he dressed with especial care. Florentyn would never look on him with approval, but at least he could present the appearance of a true Changer child. So he put on his best pair of breeches, a snowy white shirt, a black coat slashed with inky dark blue the exact shade of his eyes – all the while rehearsing what he was going to tell his father. Excuses and explanations wouldn't be acceptable, he knew that. He'd just have to state the facts and take the consequences.

'My lord Myrren!' The knock at his door came just as he was pulling on his boots, startling all his carefully planned words out of his head like so many butterflies. Why had anyone come to him? It was his father who should be informed of Ayla's escape.

Unless Florentyn had learned of his part in the matter, and sent the Helm to arrest him in her place …

In two quick strides, he was at the door and yanking it open; better to pull the splinter than to let it fester. The Helmsman on the other side was pale, his forehead glistening with a sheen of sweat. Myrren's guts clenched in painful anticipation. Perhaps it wasn't Ayla's escape that had set the warning bell ringing. Perhaps it was something far worse.

'My lord,' the man said again, staring through Myrren as if seeing a series of images sent straight from his darkest nightmares. 'Your father.' He passed a shaking hand over his face, then took a deep breath and looked Myrren in the eye. 'He's dead.'

TWO

The first thing they must have seen when they broke down Florentyn Nightshade's door was the blood. Spattered across the walls, pooling on the polished wooden floorboards, dyeing the sheets to deep crimson: it didn't seem possible for all that blood to have come from a single man. Not that there was much left in him. He lay sprawled on his back, bleached to bone white like driftwood left too long in the sun. The only colour in him was the night-dark hair that proclaimed his lineage, and the gaping hole where his throat had been.

Myrren stopped just inside the door, pressing the back of one hand to his mouth in a vain attempt to suppress the bile rising in his throat. The thick, metallic odour in the room was horribly familiar, but for a moment he couldn't place it – and then when he did, he wished he hadn't. It was the smell of the slaughterhouse.

He turned his head, searching the faces of the three or four Helmsmen crowding the doorway behind him.

'Where is Captain Travers?' he asked stupidly, as if that were the most important question. But he wanted Travers to be there. Travers was in charge of the Helm, and the Helm had clearly failed in their duty.

'Called away to the cells, my lord,' one of the men said
– which reminded Myrren all over again of Ayla. No doubt
Travers was currently learning of her escape. Yet now all
Myrren's anguish over that seemed trivial and irrelevant.

'Then you tell me, please,' he said. 'W-what happened?'

'We don't know, my lord.' Myrren couldn't put a name
to the speaker; the watching Helmsmen were all alike with
fear. 'A maidservant tried to deliver his breakfast, but found
the door locked. She knocked and got no answer. And then
...' He swallowed. 'And then she noticed the smell.'

Myrren nodded. 'So she sent for you. I see.'

His gaze settled briefly on his father's body, then shied
away again. It was a good thing he hadn't eaten this morning;
as it was, the scant contents of his stomach were rapidly
congealing into something cold and nauseous.

'Did – did anyone try to revive him?' It was another stupid
question, given the state of the body, but it had to be asked.

'I checked his pulse,' a different man said. His striped sleeve
was stained with a rust-dark smear, as though he had wiped
his bloody hand on it. 'But there was nothing ...'

'No. Indeed.' Myrren could hear his own voice becoming
ever more clipped and precise, a counterbalance for the tumult
of emotion inside him. 'So, then – so –'

'We've had the physician to him, my lord.' One of the Helm
came to his aid. 'He thinks it happened between seventh and
eighth bell yesterday.'

Seventh bell ... A presentiment formed at the edge of
Myrren's thoughts, but he pushed it away.

'So someone broke into Darkhaven last night,' he said.
'Crept to my father's room, picked the lock, then relocked
the door behind him after doing his murderous business – all
without being seen by any of you?'

'No, my lord,' the Helmsman said. 'He couldn't have left through the door. Not with it locked from the inside.' He hesitated, glancing at his fellows, then added, 'We found this on the floor by the bed.'

Automatically, Myrren held out his hand to take what was being passed to him: a black disc, shiny, ever so slightly concave. It felt cool and hard, like something made from metal. An armour link, perhaps, or a scale from a Hydra – though no Hydra had been seen in the Nightshade line for generations. One side was still encrusted with a dull residue of blood.

Slipping the disc into his pocket, Myrren looked over at the splintered door and saw that the man was right: the key still dangled from the now-useless lock. It wasn't possible that anyone could have left that way. His presentiment growing stronger, he scanned the room, trying to look beyond the gore. The scuffling feet of the Helm had obscured any prints the intruder might have left, but across the room a window was open, the shutters banging in the breeze. Whoever had done this must have entered and departed through it: a window set in a sheer stone wall, five storeys from the ground. No man alive could have scaled that wall.

No man could have done it … but a Changer could.

Myrren closed his eyes as the sick knowledge lodged itself in his throat. He couldn't bring himself to speak it aloud in case he made it true. Instead, he stood there in his murdered father's bedroom and listened to the whispers of the men in the doorway.

'Must have been a wild animal, come in through the window.'

'Or an assassin, sent from Sol Kardis or Parovia. I heard as how a Kardise assassin can climb any wall, however steep, and fit through any gap, however narrow.'

'Idiots! This is the old Firedrake we're talking about. You think any man or beast coulda got the better of him?'

The talk went on, growing wilder and wilder. Because they were right: Florentyn in creature form had been well-nigh indestructible, and even as a man he'd been more powerful than most. Changers weren't quite human; they were stronger, faster, *better*. Even ambushed in sleep, Florentyn would have been able to fight off a mere wild animal or knife-wielding assassin. Yet what other possibilities were there? Everyone knew Myrren had been born without the gift, and Ayla … well, Ayla was locked in prison, accused of attacking a priestess.

Or at least, she would have been if Myrren hadn't let her out the night before.

It was with a sense of inevitability that he heard a new voice, cutting through the others in the sharp tones of command.

'My lord!'

He turned to see Owen Travers, Captain of the Helm, making his way past the ranks of suddenly silent men. The captain's words dropped like pebbles into the still pool of the room, sending ripples in all directions.

'My lord, I regret to inform you that your sister Ayla is missing.' Travers spared a single withering glance for his underlings. 'She must have escaped last night, but it wasn't until the second bell that any of the lackwits in my employ noticed she was gone.'

His face was smoothly professional, but the slight flare of his nostrils spoke of excitement. He recognised, just as well as Myrren, the implications of the night's events. The Helm couldn't be expected to protect the Nightshade line from itself. Here, finally, was indubitable proof that Ayla was dangerous – that a half-blood Changer was something to be deplored.

Guilt flooding through him, Myrren bowed his head. He couldn't look at his father's drained corpse. As talk burst out again in the doorway, louder and more vehement than before, he addressed Florentyn in a whisper no-one but the two of them could possibly hear.

'I'm sorry, Father. This is all my fault.'

Later that morning, as news of Florentyn's death spread out from the tower, through the rings of Arkannen and into the country beyond, Myrren sat in his room and stared at the contents of his cupped hands: a small black disc, stained with blood. If he hadn't been born with that one unforgivable, fundamental flaw then maybe his father would still be alive.

They did spring up in the royal line from time to time, children without the ability to Change. Usually they were younger siblings, able to be kept out of sight. They were sent off as ambassadors to the Ingal States or Sol Kardis, or given command of a merchant train: important tasks, but tasks that kept them away from the city and away from Darkhaven. With Myrren, however, it hadn't been that simple. He was his father's heir, the only child of his first marriage. It had been a source of great shame to Florentyn that he couldn't hide his Changeless child away – and it was that shame, in the end, that led him to disinherit Myrren and give his half-Nightshade daughter the throne instead.

Still, it couldn't have been an easy decision to make. An ungifted child of the blood or a half-blood child with the gift: neither was the heir Florentyn would have chosen to succeed him. And Ayla's refusal had only exacerbated the situation. Myrren had accepted his disinheritance with the vague despondent feeling that it was what he deserved, but Ayla had been outraged on his behalf. The fighting had raged for weeks, two strong wills colliding in an explosion of fury, while Myrren stayed quiet in the background. He had told Ayla from the start that he was willing to abide by his father's choice, but she hadn't listened. She, just like Florentyn, was determined to get her own way.

And then she had been accused of a mindless attack, an assault on a priestess of the sixth ring. Myrren hadn't believed it, not for a moment. He'd thought the priestess must have been mistaken – that Florentyn was using the tale as an excuse to punish Ayla for her disobedience. As a result, he'd seen no alternative but to let her out. She was a Changer. She wasn't meant to be caged. She'd made it very clear that she'd rather die than be locked up forever.

So would Myrren, for that matter.

Yet now, he wasn't so sure he'd done the right thing. He had released his sister, and on the very same night their father had been killed. Whether or not it was coincidence, one thing was certain: he needed to find her again. But how? If she was guilty then sending out a public message would only drive her further into hiding. He needed to find her and question her, in secret, before Travers and the Helm could get to her. He needed to learn the truth.

Myrren turned the bloodstained disc over and over in his fingers. His father was dead, unable to attest to what he'd experienced in the last moments of his life. Yet there was another possible witness: the priestess who'd made the original accusation against Ayla. Myrren couldn't believe that Arkannen was home to two rogue Changer creatures, so if her story was true then she was the only living person who had seen his father's killer. He would go to her, and perhaps she would lead him to what he sought.

Perhaps she would lead him to Ayla.

*

17

'There's a man here to see you, Sister.' The acolyte dropped a curtsey, then looked up with wide eyes. 'It's the old Changer's son.'

'Thank you.' Serenna rose from her chair by the window, trying not to wince as her feet touched the floor. It had been weeks, but her right ankle in its brace still ached. She was lucky they'd been able to rebuild the shattered bone at all.

The child fidgeted in the doorway as Serenna took a shawl from her armoire and wrapped it around her shoulders. She had been expecting this visit. Official word from the Helm stated only that Florentyn had died without warning, but rumour was happy to supply far more in the way of detail. It said he'd been murdered by a Changer, perhaps the same creature that had attacked her. And if that was true, the inhabitants of Darkhaven were bound to have questions for her.

'Show him into the little room off the west walk,' she told the acolyte. 'I will follow.'

As the child sped off on her errand, Serenna picked up her slender walking cane from the corner where it was propped. She didn't like to use it; it spoke of weakness, and of age. She worried that people would look at her, a girl in her twenties, and see a crone hunched over a stick. But such thoughts were arrant vanity, unbefitting a woman in her position, and so she forced herself to use the cane whenever she needed to walk more than a few steps around the temple – particularly if she had visitors. Aside from the spiritual good it did her, there was no denying that having something to lean on eased the throbbing ache in her foot.

She made her slow way out of the priestesses' quarters and along the west walk to the room where the man was waiting. He turned as she entered, giving her a short bow that was carefully calculated to convey both respect and authority. *Calculated* was the right word, she decided. Everything about him was controlled: the straight-backed stance, the impassive expression, the slight tilt of the head as he regarded her. If he felt any emotion, it was held in check behind a sober face and a steady hand.

'Sister Serenna.' He touched his fingers to hers in greeting. 'I am Myrren Nightshade, overlord of Darkhaven.'

She looked up into his dark blue eyes. It must be difficult being born without the family gift. Everyone had always referred to Florentyn as *the old Changer*; with Myrren, they mumbled and stammered before settling on *the old Changer's son*. It was as though his lack of power left him without identity, a bare shadow of his Firedrake father.

'My lord Myrren,' she said, offering him a calm smile. 'I was sorry to hear of your father's death.'

'Were you?' The blue eyes assessed her. 'You were, perhaps, the only one outside Darkhaven. Most people seem to believe that without a Changer to rule them –' his voice didn't alter, remaining cool and even, but his teeth showed briefly in a grimace – 'the more stringent laws of Mirrorvale need no longer be kept.'

Serenna revised her first impression; beneath the man's solemn demeanour lay something altogether fiercer. 'But surely the Helm –'

'The Helm are men, and restricted largely to Darkhaven. A creature of power …' Myrren's shoulders lifted in a rueful shrug. 'My father the Firedrake could travel from here to the Kardise border within the space of a day. Nothing keeps people honest like the fear of a fire-breathing lizard turning up on their doorstep.'

His self-possession was absolute, but Serenna caught the hint of a smile at the corners of his mouth. Next moment it was gone, and he was regarding her gravely.

19

'Sister Serenna ... I expect you have some idea why I'm here.'

She nodded. 'You believe the creature that attacked me may be the same one that killed your father.'

'Rumour has wings in this city.' Myrren's voice was dry. 'Then I daresay you're also aware that my half-sister Ayla is the only Changer still living, in Arkannen or anywhere else.'

'Is it possible there could be another?' Serenna asked. He shook his head.

'The gift has never appeared outside our bloodline. Ayla and I are the only living Nightshades.'

'Forgive me.' She watched his face carefully. 'But ... is it possible you're not?'

He froze, staring at her, then released his breath in something that wasn't quite a laugh. 'You have interesting ideas for a priestess.'

She was quiet, and after a moment he went on.

'Yes, I suppose it's possible. But if Florentyn did have another child, it must have been before I was born. My mother died giving birth to me, and it didn't take long after that for him to meet and wed his second wife. He was ... devoted to her, to Ayla's mother, in a way he never was to his own kin. I don't think he would have looked at another woman once he had her.'

'She died too, though, didn't she? Five years ago. Perhaps after that ...'

'No.' Myrren's response was swift. 'The child would be too young. The gift doesn't manifest itself before the age of fourteen. No, if there was another child, he or she must be older than me. A full-grown adult by now.' A frown disturbed the composed gravity of his face. 'I'd like to believe it. Better that than Ayla ...'

'Tell me,' Serenna said, 'what is it that Ayla Changes into?'

'I have no name for it.' He sighed. 'My grandfather was a Phoenix, swift and bright. And his mother's sister was a Unicorn, loyal and fierce. Ayla … she is neither one nor the other. She Changes into a golden horse, with a spiral horn and wings like flame.'

Serenna called up a mental image, her memory from the night of the attack. The shrine, lit by a hundred flickering tapers. Herself, kneeling at the altar. A shadow falling across her face, cutting out the light. She had turned, and seen – what? It had been such a brief impression. Something dark, that gleamed in the candlelight. It rushed towards her, and there was fire –

'It burnt me,' she said aloud. 'The creature that attacked me. I fell down, and it trampled me. My ankle was crushed.' She indicated her brace. 'I saw it only for an instant, my lord, but I don't believe it was a winged horse.'

He frowned. 'Then why didn't you say so, when you reported the incident?'

'I did. Both to the guard who came originally, and to the Helmsman who turned up when it became clear what sort of crime they were dealing with. I told them everything I could remember.' She watched hope and scepticism brighten and dim his eyes, and added, 'I don't think it meant to hurt me, either.'

His eyebrows lifted. 'It burnt you and trampled you, but it didn't mean to hurt you?'

'I know it sounds silly.' She maintained her equanimity. 'But the creature seemed … lost. It didn't know its own strength; the harm it caused me was accidental. I don't think it came looking for me. Why should it?'

'That's a lot to see in an instant,' Myrren said. 'And even if you're right, it certainly meant to hurt my father.'

In the silence that followed, Serenna suppressed the questions she longed to ask: intrusive, shameful questions that were none of her business. *Is it true his throat was ripped out? That there was so much blood it leaked under the door? Do you really believe your own sister could have done such a thing?*

As if her restraint had reassured him, Myrren gave her a direct look; not Darkhaven overlord to sixth-ring priestess, but one person to another.

'Serenna ... will you help me with this? Help me find the truth? Because until I do, my sister is condemned to a life in exile from Darkhaven, and I ...' His shoulders lifted in a weary shrug. 'I am forced to live in uncertainty.'

'Surely the Helm ...' she faltered, but he shook his head.

'They have never liked Ayla – for being a half-blood, for having the gift that should be mine. Indeed, it sounds as though they reported the attack on you in such a way that it made my father suspect her. I'm afraid of what they might do if they find her before I get to the bottom of this.'

Serenna studied him. It seemed crazy that he should ask for her aid. She had seen the creature only once, and that by candlelight; really she had no more knowledge of it than anyone else. She opened her mouth to say as much, but he forestalled her.

'The priestesses of the sixth ring are renowned for their wisdom, Sister Serenna. I need wisdom more than anything, now. And besides ... my father was a creature of Flame, just as you are its avatar. No-one can doubt your commitment to uncovering the truth.' Almost to himself, he added, 'Even Captain Travers will have to respect that.'

Serenna wavered a moment longer. Surely there must be someone better he could choose ... But the directness was still in his eyes, in the honesty of his face; it compelled her.

'All right,' she said. 'I'll help you, if I can.' And she touched her fingertips to his to seal the bargain.

THREE

Tomas Caraway was just sober enough to know he was very drunk indeed. The world around him had blurred into a pleasantly indistinct haze, through which faces and voices loomed and receded like shapes in the mist. Yet despite his extreme inebriation, a small, detached corner of his mind watched his antics and mocked him for what he had become.

It was, he thought with a self-pitying glance at his empty mug, the tragedy of his life. No matter how hard he tried to drown his memories in a pitcher of best Ingalese ale, a part of him always remembered. He'd have been better off saving his coin and getting himself a decent meal for once.

Still, now he'd started on the path of self-deconstruction he might as well see it through. A few more drinks and with any luck he'd be unconscious.

'Hey, barkeep!' He waved his mug at the man on the other side of the counter, nearly falling off his stool in the process. ''M empty. D'you think y'could remedy the situation?'

The man gave him an appraising look. 'Got any more money?'

'Well …' Caraway fumbled in all his pockets, then offered his best smile. 'You find me temporarily unfunded. Better put it on my account.'

23

'Sorry.' The bartender folded his arms. 'No coin, no service.'

'But I've been comin' in here for weeks!' Caraway protested.

'And that's exactly why I'm not going to serve you. Be reasonable, Tomas. We can't give credit to a man who has no hope of paying his debts.'

'Oh, pour him a drink, why don't you,' the mocking edge of another voice cut in. A hand slapped two copper coins down on the counter. 'After all, he doesn't have many pleasures left in life.'

Tensing at the familiar tone, Caraway twisted in his seat. The man standing at his left shoulder was tall and blond, his pale eyes dancing with malicious amusement. Caraway looked from his multicoloured striped coat to the slim-bladed sword at his hip, and felt a heavy stone lodge itself in his guts. Quickly he turned back to the bartender.

'I've changed my mind,' he said with as much dignity as he could muster. 'I no longer have need of refreshment.'

'Then I'll have it myself.' The note of amusement in the supercilious voice remained unchanged. As the bartender went to fetch the ale, the new arrival leaned one elbow on the counter and regarded Caraway through narrowed eyes.

'So how are you, Breakblade? Still drinking yourself into a stupor, I take it.'

Caraway forced himself not to react to the name, though the ale surging through his blood made him long to throw a punch.

'What d'you want, Travers?' he muttered.

'Captain Travers.' The correction was prompt. 'I'm still commander of the Helm, remember? Whereas you are just a civilian.'

Caraway flushed. 'This is Arkannen, not Darkhaven. You have no authority here.'

'Not as yet,' Travers agreed. 'But that will change. Didn't you hear? The old Firedrake is dead. And his heir is much more … persuadable.'

'Florentyn Nightshade is dead?' Caraway rubbed his eyes, trying to clear his head. He squinted at Travers with intense dislike, but his desire for information was even stronger than his hatred. 'When? How?'

'Last night. He was murdered.' A smile twisted the corners of the captain's mouth. 'By his daughter, no less.'

'Liar.' Caraway was off his stool in an instant, glaring into the other man's face. 'Lady Ayla would never –'

'She killed her own father and went on the run,' Travers said, still smiling. 'No more than you'd expect from a half-blood, I suppose.'

Caraway's hand fell to the hilt of the sword at his belt, a mirror image of the other man's. Travers tracked the motion with his eyes, then looked up with eyebrows raised, satirical.

'Why does it matter to you?' he drawled. 'It's a well-known fact you cared little enough for her mother.'

Caraway's remaining rationality dissolved in a dark rush of anger. For one hot, crazy instant he forgot everything except the habits that had once been drilled into him; with a scrape of metal he drew his sword, dropping into a defensive position.

There was silence.

Caraway's gaze travelled slowly up his own arm, over his hand holding the sword hilt and the span of jagged steel that was all that remained of the blade, and beyond to the captain's laughing face.

'Why on earth do you still carry that thing, Breakblade?' Travers lingered over the hated name as though he knew how much it hurt. 'It's completely useless.'

'By the elements, you're absolutely right.' With a sweet smile, Caraway pushed his broken sword back into its scabbard. Then he did what he'd wanted to do all along, and punched Travers in the face.

His head was still swimming with ale; the blow didn't land square on the other man's nose as intended, but on the side of his mouth, sending him staggering backwards. Travers regained his balance with an effort, turning his head aside to spit a mouthful of bloody saliva onto the floor. His scarlet-edged teeth showed in a snarl.

'That was stupid, Caraway. Just one more stupid thing to add to the list.'

Caraway shrugged, massaging his stinging right hand. Already he was beginning to regret his hasty reaction. What did it matter if Travers mocked and insulted him? He had already lost everything that was important to him, through negligence and his own conceit. After five years, it shouldn't hurt so much.

It shouldn't, but it did.

'And now you wish you hadn't done it.' Travers was watching him with contempt in his eyes. 'Always the same, with you: the thought arrives long after the deed. What insane whim ever led me to admit you into the Helm, I'll never know.'

'You're right.' Caraway hung his head, staring at the worn leather of his boots. 'I'm a drunkard wasting his life away in a second-rate alehouse.' He looked up, meeting the other man's gaze. 'Still, at least I'm not a vindictive bastard like you, Travers. 'Cos if I was, I'd probably do this.'

With that, he flung himself at Travers, bearing him to the floor. He got in one good punch before he was dragged away by the two slabs of muscle who guarded the entrance to the alehouse: enough to give Travers a bloody nose to match his swollen lip. After that, they just held his arms and let Travers beat him. The ale wasn't much help; the effects had begun to fade by then. Caraway sagged between his two captors, a crooked grin on his face, absorbing the pain. Maybe if he endured it for long enough, Travers would hit him with sufficient force to knock the memories right out of him.

Unfortunately, he passed out before they got that far.

When he came round, it was to a familiar stench of unwashed bodies and filth: he was in one of Arkannen's jails. He turned his head, licking dry lips, then winced as pain skewered his skull. His entire body felt like a giant bruise, all his limbs aching in unison. Travers had certainly got his own back.

He forced himself to sit up, though the effort made him want to vomit. Once his head stopped spinning, he examined his surroundings through swollen eyes. There wasn't much to see: four stone walls, a small barred door, a ledge lined with straw from which came the occasional suspicious rustle. The city watch had taken his boots and his broken blade, for all the good it would do them. No doubt he'd get them back in the morning, with a stern word about the perils of drinking alcohol and picking fights with the Helm. Until then, he was stuck with his nauseous stomach and his uncomfortably persistent thoughts.

He lay back on the rat-infested straw, and gave in to memory.

It had happened five years ago. He'd been a young man, fresh out of training, new to the Helm. And he'd been given the task of guarding Florentyn's second wife, Ayla's mother, as she walked in the forest north of Arkannen.

They said the old Changer had married for love, the second time. He had done his duty, begetting a Nightshade heir on his cousin, but when she died in childbirth he didn't hesitate to take a second wife. Her name was Kati: a blonde-haired, green-eyed sprite of a woman who brought light and laughter into the solemn walls of Darkhaven. Barely two years after Myrren's birth, she gave Florentyn his second child, Ayla – a girl who bore all the hallmarks of a Nightshade, except for the hint of green in her eyes. And for the next thirteen years after that, they were happy.

Yet Darkhaven was not an easy place to live in, especially for one who had grown up unconstrained by its walls. Kati yearned for freedom, for fresh air and growing things and open spaces. Submitting to her persuasions, Florentyn allowed her to go walking outside the city, always accompanied by at least one of the Helm. She was never in any danger ... until they put her in the care of young Tomas Caraway.

'Let's follow the river today, Tomas,' she said, eyes alight with the prospect. 'See if we can spot any fisher-birds, or maybe a golden trout.'

'Yes, my lady.' He bowed with one hand on the hilt of his sword, a callow fool replete with self-importance. They took a balloon to the edge of the forest, setting down where the river entered the shadow of the trees. He followed Kati as she wandered along the bank, turning his head at every splash and leafy rustle, taking pride in his own alertness.

'This is a good place.' She stopped when the forest began to climb into the mountains, on a flat rock overlooking the water. By then the river gorge was narrow, the banks steep on either side.

'Be careful, my lady.' He took her arm. 'Don't go too close to the edge.'

28

Kati laughed at him. 'It's fine, Tomas. I'll sit here, look, and watch for birds. I'll be quite safe.'

She settled down on the rock, some distance from that vertiginous drop. Caraway stood two paces behind her and kept his futile lookout.

'Oh, do go away,' she told him after a while. 'You're scaring the birds.'

'As you wish, my lady. I'll be over here if you want me.'

With another bow, he retreated to the treeline and sat down with his back against a sturdy trunk. Kati's golden hair glinted in the sunlight; she didn't turn her head in his direction, all her attention fixed on the opposite bank and the holes where the fisher-birds nested. The air was warm, with a gentle breeze that did little to relieve the stuffiness of his new striped coat. He tried to make himself as still and quiet as she was, listening to the sounds of insects chirping and the water running by.

He closed his eyes.

Some time later, he drifted back into consciousness with the guilty realisation that he'd been asleep. Something had woken him, a sound that seemed to linger just beyond the edge of hearing. The light had faded. He got to his feet, rubbing his eyes – and then he saw it. An invisible monster had taken a giant bite out of the bank; earth and rock had vanished into the gorge, leaving only a crumbling lip. The ground was all cracked and torn around it, tumbled by a mighty force.

Landslide.

For a sick, frozen instant he stared, unable to take it in. Then he ran forward, shouting Kati's name, searching for her. Any moment now, he told himself, she would appear from the shelter of the forest and laugh at him for being so silly. He kept on trying to convince himself of that, right up until he dropped to his knees at the edge of the crumbling bank and gazed down at the slowly eroding mound of debris in the river below – at the pile of rock and earth not quite concealing the splash of bright red that was Kati's skirt.

Red had always been her favourite colour.

Caraway pressed the heels of his hands to his eyes, desperate to block out that final, fatal image. After he'd returned to the tower alone, incoherent with shock and grief – after a search party had recovered her body – they'd taken his coat and broken his sword. They'd banished him from Darkhaven and even from his old training grounds, confining him to the lower rings of the city where he belonged. But no punishment they dealt him could have been worse than the knowledge of his failure. He had been given a duty to perform, and he hadn't been able to perform it. In the end, his devotion to the Nightshade family hadn't been enough.

Of course, there had been whispers about him after it happened. People said he hated Kati for being an ordinary woman, that he was a fanatic who thought the royal line should remain pure. They implied that the accident wasn't an accident at all, that he'd pushed her into the gorge and sent the rocks down after her. He didn't blame them. After all, if it weren't for him she'd still be alive. The guilt of it gnawed at him every day, a constant unforgiving presence.

And now, five years later, Kati's daughter was being accused of murdering her own father. Caraway couldn't believe that was true. He had always loved Ayla the best of her family: her mercurial moods, her ready wit, the way her face seemed to glow when she was excited. He would have been willing to lay down his life for her – for all of them, but for her most of all. It just wasn't possible that the girl he'd known could have turned into a killer.

The alcohol had worn off by now, leaving a pounding headache and a faint bilious haze in its wake. Caraway turned onto his side, curling around his tender stomach. There was nothing he could do about any of it, anyway.

He'd be much better off trying to work out where to get the money for more ale.

FOUR

Ayla was lost. She had never ventured into the lower rings of the city before; her human life had been spent within Darkhaven's walls, save the occasional visit to one temple or another on celebration days. Her father had always claimed that this restriction was imposed with her own welfare in mind. *Too many dangers wait in the world for an unprotected girl,* he'd say. *After what happened to your mother …* Yet in creature form Ayla was equally limited, allowed only brief flights to the deserted country north of Arkannen – and even that at night, when she'd be no more than a shadow against the moon. Florentyn might have called that solicitude, but she knew it was shame.

It had taken her a full day to descend from the seventh ring to the fourth. Getting out of the seventh ring had been easy enough; it was the job of the two guards at the Gate of Death to watch for intruders from the city below, not fugitives from within the grounds of Darkhaven. And it had still been dark when she passed the temples of the sixth ring, their delicate spires and gleaming rooftops concealed by shadow. She had identified each one by sound alone: the gentle ticking of the Temple of Time, with its thousand clocks of different sizes; the spine-chilling moan of the wind caressing the Spire of Air, a needle-thin shard of glass that reached higher than anything in Arkannen save Darkhaven itself; the soft, rippling murmur of water flowing endlessly through the many wheels of the Water Garden; the whispering and rustling of the Cathedral of Trees. Only the Shrine of the Moon had been awake, its priestesses raising silver voices in homage to the eternal power of night.

The fifth ring, her first step into unfamiliar territory, had been harder. It was the training ground of weaponmasters, warriors, the Helm: anyone involved in the subtle arts of combat. Even with dawn no more than a faint smear on the horizon, people had been up and walking the streets. And these were men and women with hard eyes and purposeful gaits, conditioned by years of experience to notice anything unusual. Ayla had hurried along with head bowed, sure that at any moment she would hear her name spoken or feel a hand close around her wrist. As the sun rose higher in the sky, prying into the shade of her hood with bright inquisitive fingers, she had slipped into the narrow gap between a duelling room and a weaponry. There she'd squatted in an unsettled half-doze, waiting for her chance.

Finally, as the light began to fade once more, she'd used a taciturn group of mercenaries as cover to escape through the Gate of Steel into the fourth ring, the residential ring where most of the citizens of Arkannen lived. The onset of evening meant many were returning home after a day at work, whilst others were venturing out; the streets were full of horses, carriages, hurrying pedestrians, crossing-sweepers, dogs and the occasional mechanical cycle. Overwhelmed by the sheer number of people – more than she'd seen in the previous eighteen years of her life put together – Ayla had wandered along for some time before admitting to herself that she had no idea where to go. She knew from her lessons that the fourth ring was divided into sixteen Quarters, each named after one of the semi-precious stones mined in the mountains to the north of Mirrorvale, but that dry fact couldn't possibly have prepared her for the reality.

The largest and most attractive dwellings may be found in Charoite, home to Arkannen's oldest and wealthiest families. She found herself silently reciting her tutor's words, trying to make sense of it all. *Airmen and their families live in Angelite, while traders and merchants from the land caravans make their homes in the Serpentine Quarter. Those who migrate to Arkannen from elsewhere in Mirrorvale, or from one of its neighbouring countries, tend initially to move into Elbaite. The crowded streets of the Dravide Quarter are home to the city's labourers and sewerers, while plumbers and gas suppliers live in the slightly more spacious Larimar. And so it goes, with each Quarter having its own character and inhabitants.*

She was so intent on trying to remember the lesson that she walked straight into a heavyset man in worker's overalls, who swore at her with incomprehensible vigour.

'... Watch where yer goin', girlie!'

She tensed in expectation of being recognised, but his gaze skated over her for an indifferent instant before he moved away. Her apparent anonymity gave her enough courage to call after him.

'Wait! I'm trying to find the Gate of Wood. Can you –'

'You want blue.' As she stared at him, trying to get some meaning out of the words, he puffed out an impatient breath. 'Follow the pale blue line 'til you reach the Angelite Quarter.' His finger stabbed downwards at the stretch of road between them. 'Then keep going 'til you see the gate.'

'Thank you,' she muttered, but he had already rushed on. She looked down at the stripes of different colours that paved the street. It hadn't occurred to her earlier, but presumably they represented the sixteen Quarters of the fourth ring. Follow the pale blue stripe to the Angelite Quarter, he'd said; it made sense, because airmen would want to live near the gate to the third ring where they plied their trade. But how would she know the Angelite Quarter when she reached it?

As it turned out, it was as straightforward as the stranger had made it sound. When the blue stripe stopped, Ayla raised her head to see that the roofs and window frames of the houses around her were the same shade of blue. She kept going along the main street, and soon enough the gate came into view. The third ring. One step further away from captivity. Already she felt as if she'd been on an epic journey, full of colours and textures and scents she had never previously experienced. Darkhaven was built on stark lines and silence. Who could have guessed there were so many different shapes and sounds in the world?

She spent the night in the shadow of a tethered airship, listening to the cables creak and strain in the breeze, thankful it was summer and the air was mild. Despite her exhaustion, it was impossible to sleep. Her mind was brimming over with everything she had seen: the buildings, the people, the noise. By the time her second day of freedom dawned, her eyes were grainy, her head as light and bobbing as the balloons that were taking up their first passengers of the day around her. Yet she had to keep going. The sooner she could bury herself in the obscurity of the first ring, the safer she'd be.

She descended a short flight of steps cut into a sheer rock face, and found herself on a ledge overlooking the lower rings of the city. Tiered roofs stretched down and out, red tiles and golden wood and grey-blue slate. She identified the dark smoke rising from the factories, as well as several lighter puffs of steam – travelling fast – which must be the trams that partly circled the lower rings. Even from here, with four rings behind her and only two ahead, the city merged into the horizon. She couldn't make out where Arkannen ended and the rest of Mirrorvale began.

Of course, she had seen the city many times from the air, at night, but the sheer scale of it had never impressed itself upon her as it did now. From above, Arkannen was orderly and structured, seven neat rings descending in sequence. She hadn't realised how much bigger and more complicated it would appear when she was actually in it. It was daunting, but it was also encouraging. As long as she was careful and didn't draw attention to herself, she didn't see how anyone would ever find her.

Dragging herself away from the view, she plunged into the darkness of the narrow passage that cut into the rock behind her. She emerged into a spacious, paved square with various streets and staircases joining it on three sides. On the fourth side stood a high-arched gateway, the sole route into the second ring: the Gate of Wind. Although each of the gates Ayla had passed through so far had been impressive, she thought this one might be the most spectacular of all. The arch was carved from pale, translucent marble, a series of abstract curved shapes swirling around each other like the patterns of the breeze; in every gap hung delicate crystals that tinkled with the slightest movement of the air, so that the gate was never silent. In the centre of the square, a three-bladed sail on a long pole turned with the currents, marking wind speed and direction for the captains of the airships.

None of the other gates had posed a problem, but even so, Ayla pulled her hood forward to hide her face before she joined the workers who were converging on the gate from all directions. It was even busier down here than it had been in the higher rings. An elbow caught her in the ribs; she stumbled, and someone trod on her foot. Then, as she passed under the archway itself in a squeeze of tight-knit crowd, she overheard a snippet of conversation.

'Murdered in his bed ... the old Changer ...'

In an instant, the press of people around her – their heat and smell – became unbearable. She tried to keep up with the two men who were talking, but they were borne away from her like twigs in the relentless current. The many voices of the crowd became a tumult, a hundred different words competing for attention. Ayla snatched at one sentence, then another, letting each one slip away as she became aware of the next. But she heard nothing more about her father. Perhaps her overwhelmed brain had conjured up a phantom.

Once through the gate she could breathe again, but the half-heard sentence still niggled at her. As she hesitated at the top of the steps that led down into the second ring, buffeted and jostled on all sides by people passing to and fro, she heard a shout like an echo of her thoughts.

'News-up! News-up! Git yer news here!'

A boy stood at the foot of the stair, catching at the sleeves of the crowd as they passed by. It was his voice that had cut through the sounds of the city like diamond through glass. Ayla descended the steps and offered him one of her few coins, keeping her head down and her eyes averted. In exchange, he pressed a sheet of green-tinged paper into her hand with a mumbled 'Thank you, ma'am.' As his calls

37

started up again, Ayla retreated to a quiet spot by the wall and unfolded whatever it was he had given her.

The first thing she saw was her father's face: a smudged line drawing, perhaps printed from a woodcut, but recognisable nonetheless. Above it, large bold letters shouted *FIREDRAKE DEAD*. Her pulse accelerated, the flimsy paper damp beneath her fingers as she scanned the rest of the story. *Florentyn Nightshade ... unexpected death ...* Her gaze snagged on her brother's name. *No information has been provided by the new overlord of Darkhaven, Myrren Nightshade, concerning the manner of his father's demise. However, it is rumoured on the streets of Arkannen that this was no natural death but a murder of the foulest and most vicious kind.*

The paper crumpled in Ayla's hand.

Her father was dead. Someone had killed him.

Shock washed through her in a cold wave, leaving her gasping and close to tears. It was too large a thing to comprehend all at once; maybe that was why she felt so hollow. Yet as the treacherous waters of emotion subsided, they threw up a sneaking small relief. She didn't need to be here after all. She could go back home without being imprisoned. Maybe there, in the safety of solitude, she'd find a decent way to mourn the father who had always viewed her as a source of humiliation ...

Though the news-sheet hadn't mentioned her escape.

Another wave broke, drowning relief in breathless fear. She smoothed out the paper, scanning the article again. Florentyn had died the night before last – the same night she'd left Darkhaven – yet there was no mention of her disappearance. If the Helm hadn't put the word out, it could mean only one thing: they thought she'd done it. They thought she'd murdered her own father, and they planned on giving her no warning whilst they searched for her. Far from being safe to return home, she was in even greater danger.

Myrren must think she was a murderer as well. That realisation hit Ayla harder still. If he'd believed her innocent then he would have sent messengers to find her, as he'd promised he would. Which meant she couldn't Change; Myrren might not have the gift, but – like all the Nightshade line – he could sense the transformation in others. She was stuck in the city, perhaps for good, never able to show her face for fear of discovery, living always cloaked and shadowed …

No, she told herself sternly. *It won't be like that. I'll find a way to prove I didn't do it.* The prospect was daunting; she swallowed over a dry throat, her stomach suddenly tight with anxiety. *Or if not, I'll stow away on an airship or a goods barge and escape to another country. The Helm can't pursue me over the border.*

Yet even as she thought it, she knew she wouldn't go through with it. Fleeing Mirrorvale was too much like professing her guilt. She didn't want to be an exile the rest of her life; though she might have railed against her lack of freedom, the austere walls of Darkhaven were her home. And besides, where else in the world would her Changer abilities be accepted? What was considered a gift in her own land might be deemed an unnatural curse elsewhere. No, she would be better off staying in Arkannen and maybe, just maybe, finding a way to prove her innocence.

Stuffing the news-sheet into the pocket of her cloak, she squared her shoulders. She had to get down into the first ring, as far away from Darkhaven as possible. She had to find a place to hide. Only then could she work out how to make things right.

FIVE

The priestess was an attractive woman. Myrren eyed her
sideways as they walked together through the corridors of
Darkhaven, their pace slow and steady to make allowance
for her injured ankle. Despite the thin veil covering her head
– required costume for a priestess outside her own temple
– her hair shone like polished bronze in the light from the
gas lamps. He couldn't make out the freckles that he knew
were scattered across the bridge of her nose like seeds on
a fresh-baked roll, but the curves of her body were clear
enough through her high-necked gown. There were very few
women in Darkhaven; it was a place for men, hard-eyed and
dour. Serenna was like a bright bird caught within its walls,
something vibrant and incongruous.

As though sensing his hungry stare, she turned her head
to look at him. Quickly, he averted his gaze. During their
previous conversation, her frank grey eyes had met his
without any hint of judgement. He had liked that; he was
used to people judging him. He didn't want to spoil it by
making her uncomfortable.

'I hope I haven't caused you too much inconvenience by
asking you to come here, Sister Serenna,' he said. 'The high

priestess seemed happy enough when I spoke to her, but I know how these things can be.'

'No inconvenience, my lord.' Her voice rose and fell in measured cadences, like the bells of her temple; he'd noted that about her on their first meeting. 'The Altar of Flame is always open to those who seek advice – though admittedly, it's rare for us to leave the temple in order to give it. The high priestess was glad to be of service to Darkhaven.'

'You can stay in Ayla's room,' Myrren said. 'I hope that will be all right. Our guest rooms are really not in a usable state.' He shot her another sideways glance. 'The Nightshade line doesn't receive many visitors. I can't think why.'

He saw the lifted curve of her cheek; she was smiling beneath the flimsy veil. But her voice remained as cool and even as always.

'I assure you, Ayla's room will be more than sufficient. I am used to far more ascetic surroundings.' She stopped, leaning on her cane. 'But first, I think it would be a good idea for me to see your father's body.'

Surprised and rather dismayed, Myrren tried to make out her expression beneath the veil. 'Are you sure that's –'

'If I am to help you, I need to know as much as possible,' she said. 'And that includes seeing with my own eyes how your father died.'

She was right, of course. It had been presumptuous of him to solicit her aid at all, but now he'd done it, there was no purpose in keeping anything from her. Still, something in him shrank from the idea of showing her exactly what Ayla had done. Except she didn't think it was Ayla, did she? She'd suggested that the creature she had seen might have been something else altogether. Maybe if she saw the body, those suspicions would be confirmed. Hope rising in him, Myrren nodded.

'Very well. I'll take you to him.'

Florentyn's body had been carried to the vault beneath the tower, to lie for the requisite number of days in the unlocked antechamber before being moved into the vault itself. The tradition dated back centuries, to a distant Changer ancestor who, it was said, had been discovered lying still and cold in his bed. Believing him dead, his family laid him to rest in the vault; a day later, he awoke and found himself trapped. Unable to wrench the door open or make anyone hear him, he Changed and came bursting out of the vault in his Hydra form – after which, driven half mad by the experience, he refused to return to his human shape until his real death several years later. The precaution was hardly necessary in this case, Myrren thought; there was no way his father could still be alive, not after losing that much blood. Still, tradition was there to be followed.

He showed Serenna into the antechamber, closing the door behind them so they wouldn't be disturbed. His father's body lay on a marble slab in the centre of the room. It had been washed and dressed in good clothes, but the ugly wound at the throat was undisguisable. Above it, Florentyn's face looked waxy and stiff, like an ill-fitting mask over the head of a completely different man. Nauseous again, Myrren lingered by the door as Serenna approached the body, pushing her veil back from her face with steady hands. A contemplative silence fell, during which Myrren closed his eyes and tried to think about something different. After a time, Serenna's cool voice recalled him to the present.

'Have you examined these wounds yourself?'

'Not closely.' He opened his eyes again, fixing his gaze on her glossy hair rather than the body on the slab. 'I – I couldn't bring myself to –'

He choked back the rest of what he had been about to say. He'd already revealed more of himself to the priestess than perhaps was wise; showing the extent of his weakness could only be dangerous. No need to tell her that the sight of blood made him weak and squeamish inside.

'I asked the physician to make a report,' he said, trying to sound firm and competent. 'He concluded that no man could have made those wounds. It must have been a creature both fierce and powerful.'

'He was right about that.' Serenna glanced over her shoulder at him. 'Come and see.'

Reluctantly Myrren approached the body. Serenna moved closer, her arm brushing his as her slender fingers hovered over the throat wound, gesturing in time to her words.

'See here, and here? Those are tooth marks. Something seized his throat in its jaws and ripped it out as easily as tearing paper.'

'Mmm.' Myrren's stomach roiled, and he swallowed. He couldn't be sick; it would be too humiliating. 'I see.'

'I'm not sure you do, my lord!' Her face was animated with discovery. He concentrated on that, on the way her grey eyes lost their habitual serenity as she talked. 'The form Ayla takes – does it have teeth?'

He frowned, belatedly understanding what she was getting at. 'Yes … but not that powerful. A horse can deliver a nasty bite, but it can't rip a man's throat out. A Unicorn's main weapon is its horn.'

'Exactly! If Ayla had killed your father, I would expect to see stab wounds all over the body. Unless …' She bit her lip, studying him as though trying to work something out. 'Is it possible for a Changer to take more than one animal form?'

'Not that I know of. A Changer's other form is like an expression of identity. It is unique.'

'Then Ayla must be innocent.' Serenna gave him a decisive nod. He smiled at her, forgetting his discomfort.

'You're right. I can send messengers into the city, call Ayla back to Darkhaven ...' His excitement faded just as swiftly as it had flared. 'But no. I can't.'

'Why not?'

'Two reasons.' Myrren turned his back on Florentyn's body, folding his arms. 'First, we have no solid proof. Unless we can locate the real culprit, Ayla will be found guilty by default. With my father's death, she is the only known Changer in Mirrorvale – and no-one has ever seen her other form except Florentyn and myself.'

He paused. Serenna's grey eyes searched his face.

'And the second reason?'

'The second reason follows from the first,' Myrren said. 'If Ayla is innocent then there must be another Changer in Mirrorvale. Perhaps an illegitimate child of my father's.' He still found that hard to believe. 'If so, any public message intended for Ayla will also send a message to the murderer: it will tell him I have guessed his existence. No, if we're to have any chance of catching this criminal, we have to let him think he's still safe, still unknown.'

'Then how do you suggest we go about finding him?'

'I'm not sure.' Myrren frowned, thinking it through. 'We know a little about the creature he Changes into. You've seen it, albeit briefly. And –' He felt in his pocket for the black disc he had carried everywhere since Florentyn's death. 'This was found beside my father's bed. We're looking for a Hydra, or perhaps – since it's a half-blood we're dealing with – a hybrid creature like Ayla's.'

Serenna took the scale and turned it over in her fingers, examining it closely.

'But as for the man himself, we know nothing about him at all ... and I say "man" for no good reason, since the killer could just as well be a female Changer.' Myrren shrugged, allowing temporary defeat. 'I really don't know where to start.'

'Have you searched your father's room?' Serenna suggested, handing the disc back to him. 'If he did have an affair then he may have kept some token that would give us a clue as to the identity of the mother. And once we find her, it should be relatively easy to find the child.'

'True. My father wasn't a sentimental man, but it's possible there is something.' Myrren slipped the scale back into his pocket, then bent to kiss her hand. 'I am most grateful for all the help you have given me, Sister Serenna.'

'I must admit, I am anxious to catch this criminal on my own behalf.' She gave him a cool smile, extricating her fingers from his grasp in one graceful movement. 'Being trampled by the creature hasn't given me much liking for it.'

Her earlier vivacity, ignited by the joy of discovery, was gone. She was all priestess now, and both gesture and tone of voice were telling him to keep his distance. Myrren answered her smile with a grave one of his own, showing that he understood; in return, her expression warmed just a fraction.

'I will search through my father's possessions when I have the chance,' he told her, handing her the cane she'd abandoned on the floor whilst examining the body. 'In the meantime, allow me to show you to my sister's room. I will have someone bring you refreshment.'

Ayla's room was a large one, the furnishings heavy and elaborate. Serenna sat at the table by the window, enjoying a glass of Parovian wine and a plateful of sweet cakes – neither of which came her way very often in the Altar of Flame. She was trying to forget the sensation that had stirred in her when Myrren kissed her hand, something strong and animal that she was sure was inappropriate for a priestess to feel. Perhaps she shouldn't have ventured outside the walls of her temple.

The temples of the sixth ring celebrated the elements and life in all its forms. That was the Mirrorvalese way. The lower rings were scattered with shrines to the lesser powers, available day and night for prayers of thanks or supplication. But the great temples of the sixth ring did more: they kept the balance of nature. It was widely believed that if a temple were ever to fall, that power would fail in the world, leaving utter chaos in its wake. And so the people made offerings to their favourites, and gave thanks on appropriate days – and revered the priestesses of the sixth ring, who maintained the balance.

To that end, a priestess was expected to take on the qualities of the power she served. In that sense, Myrren should count himself lucky the rogue creature had attacked Serenna and not a priestess of Winter or Steel. As she'd told him, the priestesses of Flame were used to giving advice and resolving disputes amongst the populace, so it hadn't been such a stretch for the high priestess to let her go. Flame was quick and warm and bright. Flame was welcoming. And so unlike the colder temples, the Altar of Flame stayed open to the inhabitants of Arkannen on all but the most sacred days.

Yet despite that, Serenna still had rules to follow – particularly when it came to the relationships she was allowed to forge. Her temple was her family, and she was forbidden any other. As for the physical side … well, the Altar of Flame might not be one of the most severe, but nor was it as lenient as the Temple of Procreation, where on certain days the priestesses opened their doors to all comers for an orgy of satisfaction and the conception of new life. A priestess of Flame was expected to remain devoted to her element above all things, playing her small part in maintaining the balance of the world. She had to remain detached from everyday concerns, and she couldn't do that if distracted by desire. And she could certainly never give in to her body's impulsive urges. Like her sisters, Serenna had sworn to remain chaste: an untouched vessel for the power she served. Break that vow, and her future at the temple would be in grave doubt. She'd certainly never be high priestess, as it was already rumoured she would be one day.

Still, Myrren had accepted her unspoken warning, remaining solemn and formal throughout the walk from the vault to Ayla's room. No doubt his gesture had been a courtly one, not meant to convey anything other than gratitude. There was no danger he would lead her into anything she might later regret.

Darkhaven was lit by gas lamps, but Serenna had asked for a candle, which had been brought to her along with the food and drink. Now she pushed her plate aside and set the candle holder in the centre of the table. Gazing into the flame, she took a deep breath, allowing the flickering orange light to become the focus of her entire body. She had always been attracted to fire above all the other powers: its fluidity, its changeability, its heat. Letting it fill her vision, she became one with the flame.

Later, the candle guttered and Serenna realised her muscles were stiff with sitting still. After blowing the candle out, she got up from the table and went to turn the lamps back to their full brightness, stopping halfway across the floor to yawn and stretch. Her mind's eye still brimmed with firelight, reassuring her that she was doing the right thing. It was as Myrren had told her, at their first meeting: the old Firedrake, Florentyn, had belonged to flame more than to any other element. Whatever this creature was that had killed him and attacked her, she owed it a debt of vengeance.

Besides, the freedom of an innocent girl was at stake.

Hoping to get a sense of what Ayla was like, she looked around the room, taking in the details that earlier had been swamped by embarrassment and confusion. In the middle was an imposing bed, its four posts carved with the shapes of powerful creatures. The covers were neatly folded, the pillows arranged square upon the bolster. On one side of the bed was the window, with the table and chair that Serenna had been using earlier. On the other side was a large wardrobe, and beyond that a cabinet with a basin embedded into its surface. Serenna went over and turned on the long-necked tap; it coughed and spluttered, having sat unused for some time, but finally spat out a thin stream of water. She trailed her hand through it, then turned the tap off again. So they had plumbing in Darkhaven. In the Altar of Flame, water for washing and drinking was still drawn from the central well.

She opened the wardrobe and ran her fingers over the heavy fabrics within: velvet, brocade, silk, all far richer than anything she was used to. What happened to a Changer's clothes when he took animal form? Did they go through the transition too, becoming hide and hair, then reclothe the wearer when he turned back? Or were they discarded, leaving the Changer in an uncomfortable state of nakedness when he became human once more? Perhaps she would ask Myrren ... or perhaps not. Based on her earlier misgivings, it was the kind of subject she should probably avoid.

A drawer at the bottom of the wardrobe turned out to hold underclothes; the cabinet beneath the basin gave up a toothbrush, a bar of soap, a facecloth. Serenna sat on the bed and stared around at the dark wooden furniture. There was nothing here that could tell her anything about Ayla – no books or ornaments, no pictures on the walls. Either Ayla was a very secretive girl, or she must have been bored and lonely. Even Serenna's simple room in the temple revealed more of herself than these luxurious, empty surroundings.

A memory slipped into Serenna's mind: Myrren talking about his father. *He was devoted to her, to Ayla's mother, in a way he never was to his own kin.* Members of the Nightshade line intermarried, to keep the gift of their bloodline strong. Ayla and Myrren were destined for each other; even if Ayla were convicted of her father's murder, she would be kept alive to bear Nightshade heirs.

Serenna shivered, the wide walls and high ceiling closing in on her where she sat. Ayla had spent her whole life in this room, knowing she was obliged to marry her own brother, her only escape the ability to Change into a creature her father disapproved of. Yet now, despite the difficult circumstances, she had tasted freedom …

Serenna sighed. Perhaps she and Myrren would be able to prove Ayla's innocence beyond doubt. But by then, would Ayla even want to come home?

SIX

They let Caraway out at first light, bundling his possessions into his arms and shoving him through the door without even giving him the chance to put his boots back on. As he sat outside the jail and tugged them over his much-darned socks, the bustle of the city held as little promise for him as the four walls of the cell in which he'd spent the night. The grey morning was reflected in the windows of the buildings and the eyes of the people, making everything dull and dreary. He couldn't begin to comprehend what he should do next. It was tempting to turn around and walk straight back inside. Perhaps if he punched the duty guard in the face they'd lock him up again until tomorrow.

For five years he'd been living like this, doing odd jobs to earn the coin he needed to rent a room, clothe himself, buy food and drink – mostly drink, of late. He knew it was only a matter of time before the alcohol dissolved his brain and he became one of the old drunks he saw wandering the streets at night, with a web of red veins across his cheeks and a purple nose and wet, gummy eyes that forever gazed upon a vision of the past. Soon he'd lose even his current small room above the tanner's yard, forced to sleep in doorways and under bridges with only cheap spirits to keep him company.

In the cold light of day, he knew it; yet already he was wondering when he'd next be able to buy ale.

You're not going to drink today, he told himself. *You're going to go and find work. Rent's due in a few days and there's nothing to pay it with.*

In response his craving tugged harder at him, setting his guts lurching with the need for a liquid something to see him through the day. Trying to ignore it, he set off down the street at a brisk pace, though his head swam with every jolting step. He would go to the second ring and see if the smelters or smiths were looking to take anyone on. Casual labour was usually available for anyone who didn't mind working a long, hot, noisy day; perhaps he could sweat the desire for alcohol out of his skin.

His resolve lasted nearly all the way to the Gate of Flame – lasted, in fact, until he spotted a scuffed silver coin lying at the side of the path. He snatched it up and scrutinised the markings, chewing on his lower lip. One donol: a tenth of his weekly rent. Enough to buy a good meal at a cookstand that would keep him going until the evening, and still leave plenty of change for more food over the next few days.

Or the exact amount needed to obtain a pitcher of ale in the Wyvern, just a few short streets away ...

'You bastard,' he whispered to the coin, before pocketing it and turning in the direction of the inn.

It was noon before Caraway emerged from the Wyvern, floating in a world that seemed altogether more pleasant than it had that morning. He considered going on to the second ring as he'd planned, but just as quickly dismissed the idea.

The day was half over; better to rest this afternoon and go tomorrow. Guilt stirred in his chest, but he smothered it. It was up to him how he spent his time.

His way home took him through the nearby bazaar, a rather disreputable centre of trade on the edge of the Night Quarter. The booths lining the streets offered an array of imported goods, some rare, some specialist and all on the verge of being illegal. Caraway stopped to look at a gigantic snakeskin draped over one counter, its mottled pattern faded yet still discernible. Ahead of him, a girl in a hooded cloak was examining what looked like a large hookah pipe.

'You want some?' The man on the other side of the counter from Caraway held up a little bottle, tilting it enticingly. 'Powdered skin of the Kardise cobra. Most powerful aphrodisiac in the world. One pinch of that'll keep you up all night, know what I'm sayin'?'

He offered a suggestive wink, extending his hand for Caraway to take the bottle. A breeze caught the skin, making it rustle like dead leaves. Discomfited, Caraway shook his head; his voice came out too loud.

'No, thank you.'

The girl in the cloak glanced over her shoulder, and Caraway caught a glimpse of blue eyes beneath the hood. His heart gave one sudden thump, pure shock cutting through his clouded brain. He would know Ayla Nightshade anywhere. What in the name of the elements was she doing in the first ring?

Leaving the snakeskin booth behind, he trailed after her as she walked on down the street. His gaze was so firmly fixed on her that twice he bumped into passers-by, murmuring absent-minded apologies without ever looking to see who he'd trodden on. Then Ayla turned the corner, heading deeper into the Night Quarter, and Caraway quickened his pace.

Whatever she was doing here, it wasn't safe. And if one of the Helm caught her, they'd have her back in Darkhaven and on trial for her father's murder before she even had the chance to cry for help.

At the corner he stopped, peering down the street towards the lavishly decorated brothels, his pulse quickening as he realised he'd lost her. He started forward, searching in vain for the slight figure with its hood of dusky grey – and then a blade pricked him in the small of the back. Her voice was low and determined.

'Who are you and why are you following me?'

'I just wanted to make sure you were all right.' Caraway didn't turn, although he could have had the knife from her in an instant. His reflexes still worked, even after five years spent deadening them. 'I spotted you further up the street. My lady Ayla.'

'I don't know what you're talking about.' The blade pushed harder, piercing the thin fabric of his clothing; he had to suppress a yelp. 'My name isn't Ayla. I think you've made a mistake.'

'I recognised you as soon as I saw you.' He kept his voice even. 'I understand you must be nervous. But I'm not here to hurt you or to turn you in.' A sudden ache constricted his throat as he added, 'I believe you're innocent.'

'Why?' She was trying to sound defiant, but the word cracked as she said it. 'Why should you? You don't know me.'

'I do.' The pressure of the knife at his back had slackened; he risked taking a step away, turning around slowly, hands spread. Ayla was there in the shadow of a doorway, hair tucked beneath the hood. The blade glinted in her taut fist.

'I know you,' he said again, and watched recognition spark in her eyes.

'You,' she breathed. 'You were in the Helm ... five years ago ...' Her face changed as though the blood in her veins had congealed into ice. The knife lifted, forming a barrier between them. 'You killed my mother.'

So she did remember him.

Caraway didn't try to refute the accusation, just stood still and kept his gaze on hers. The hint of green in her eyes was stronger in the dim light, a wash of turquoise over the Nightshade blue. He had always liked that in her, that one echo of her mother. It made her more human.

'What do you want?' she demanded.

'To help you.' He offered her a hopeful smile, then winced as her nose wrinkled in disgust.

'Of all the people in the world, Tomas Caraway, you're the very last one I'd want to help me.' Her contemptuous gaze raked him from stubbled chin to scuffed boots. 'You look as if you haven't washed for days. You stink of cheap ale. And in case you've forgotten –' the knife blade stabbed towards him, a vehement statement – 'you let my mother die, and I hate you for it.'

'No more than I hate myself,' he mumbled. 'Lady Ayla ... you're in danger out here alone. You need help.'

She shook her head. 'Not from you.'

'Please ...' He reached out to her. 'For your mother's sake ...'

Ayla's whole body tensed like an arrow poised on the string. Her free hand caught him square across the cheekbone, the full weight of her arm behind it. The sound of the slap reverberated in the confined space.

'How dare you? You piece of filth, how dare you ask me to do anything in my mother's name?'

Flushed with anger and embarrassment, Caraway grabbed her wrist and twisted it until she dropped the knife. Then he gripped her by the shoulders and gave her a shake, desperate to make her understand.

'You can't stay out here alone, Ayla! If I let you go there'll be two deaths on my head, not one!'

'Get off me!' She struggled in his grasp, kicking at his shins. 'Get off me, you murdering bastard!'

At the last two words he released her, stung by instant remorse and an intense sense of his own worthlessness. Momentary anger fading into melancholy, he bent down to retrieve her knife for her. She snatched it out of his hand, glaring. Her fingers brushed fastidiously across her cloak as though she wanted to remove all traces of his touch.

'Good luck, Ayla,' he told her, and stepped out of her way. She marched past without looking in his direction, her jaw still set with fury.

When she'd put a little distance between them, he called after her, 'You know, I could help you find out who did it ...'

She came to an abrupt halt. Then, slowly, she turned on the spot. 'What?'

'You want to prove your innocence, don't you?' He was making it up as he went along, seeking anything that would keep her there beside him. 'Find out who really killed your father? Well, I can do things you can't – visit places where you'd be caught.'

'True.' She fixed him with the narrow-eyed stare of a gluemaker sizing up an old nag. 'You're expendable.'

'I can give you a place to stay. Feed you. And to be honest, my lady ... I'm the best you're going to get. I'm the only person in this city who's going to believe you didn't do it.'

Ayla didn't reply, but nor did she leave. Caraway kept his gaze pinned on the ground, not wanting to look her in the eye in case he antagonised her further. After a while her shoes came into view, stopping just over an arm's length away. He looked up.

'All right.' She was pale and fierce, as if she had reached an uneasy compromise between morality and expediency. 'I accept your offer. But it doesn't mean I have to like you. And it certainly doesn't make up for what you did.'

'I know.'

'Fine. Then let's go.' She turned on her heel again, then looked back at him, pure hatred narrowing her eyes. 'But I'm warning you: if you ever touch me again, I'll kill you.'

The room her mother's murderer led her to was small, and stank of the unpleasant ingredients being used in the tanner's yard outside. Ayla glanced around it with her nose wrinkled in disdain, noting the empty bottles stacked beneath the bed and the mould growing on the windowsill. He deserved to live in a place like this; she just wished she wasn't forced by circumstance to share it with him, even if only for a short space of time.

She turned. He was watching her from the doorway, a hopeful expression on his face. What did he expect her to say? That it was a lovely room and she was very grateful for his hospitality? Being in his presence made her want to scream. She had only taken him up on his offer because she knew it would be difficult to discover anything on her own without being caught by the Helm. If anyone was going to be caught, let it be him. He owed her.

'I need some water,' she said. 'Do you have any?'

'There's a pump downstairs.' He brushed past her to fetch a rusty bucket from the corner of the room. She looked at it, then silently held out her water bottle as he came back past. He took it from her, hesitating as if he wanted to say something; then he gave a quick nod and left the room. Good. Whatever he had to say, she had no desire to hear it.

In one swift movement she stepped over to the bed and stripped the tattered blankets from it, kicking them into the corner of the room, then wiped her hands on her skirt, shuddering. The mattress was old and stained; she'd have to sleep wrapped in the cloak. It would be more comfortable than sleeping on the floor, she told herself, and tried not to think about the possibility of fleas.

Apart from the bed, the only item of furniture in the room was a battered wooden chest. With a glance over her shoulder, she knelt down and began to rifle through the contents. They didn't amount to much: a shirt that looked just as threadbare as the one Caraway was wearing, a lamp without any oil, some worn eating utensils. At the very bottom lay something small and oval; she explored it with her fingertips, finding the cool gloss of glass and a raised rim. A picture frame. She pulled it out, tipping it face upwards. It was her mother.

Ayla sat back on her heels. She remembered the portrait: it belonged on the sideboard in the dining hall, one of a collection of miniatures. Clearly no-one in Darkhaven had noticed its absence, these five long years. Why had he taken it? Did it make him happy, to look at it and remind himself how he had rid the Nightshade line of its impurity?

A footstep sounded outside the room, and Ayla realised her jaw was clenched tight with fury. She turned as Caraway entered, carrying the full bucket and her water bottle. His hair was dripping and his shirt was damp, as though he'd stuck his head under the pump too. The smell of alcohol no longer lingered about him.

'Why do you have this?' she demanded, brandishing the picture frame at him. 'Did you steal it?'

A complex expression passed across his face, half guilt, half anger.

'You shouldn't have gone through my things, Lady Ayla.' He put the bucket down and stepped towards her, holding his hand out for the miniature. Reflexively her fingers closed around it.

'You have no right to this. You have no right.'

He let his hand fall, his shoulders lifting in a weary shrug. Eyes downcast, he gathered up the blankets she'd dumped in the corner and began to lay them out on the far side of the room.

'I think about her every day.' His mutter was barely audible. Ayla released her breath in a bitter laugh.

'Why? Because you're sorry for what you did?'

It was intended sarcastically, but he nodded as if he hadn't heard her tone of voice.

'Of course. If I could go back and change what happened, I would. I'd willingly fling myself beneath the landslide if it would save her life.' He looked up, his gaze meeting hers. 'I loved your mother, Ayla. She was a ray of light in a dark place.'

How could he tell so many lies? She scrutinised his face, but found no trace of mockery or deceit. After a moment it became too much to bear; she turned her back on him, looking out of the window so she wouldn't have to see him any longer.

'If you'd loved her, you wouldn't have let her die.'

He made no reply. Ayla traced a finger along the curve of her mother's painted face, her heart contracting with a pain that felt as fresh as it had been five years ago. Outside, men moved through the yard, going home for the day.

'Anyway,' she flung over her shoulder, 'what makes you so special? All the Helm despised her – and me – for not being pure-blood Nightshade. They were glad when she died. And once they've got me locked up they won't have anything more to worry about.'

'I never despised her.' His voice was low. 'Or you.'

The edge of the picture frame dug into Ayla's palms. She would have believed him, once. There had been a time when she saw a difference in young Tomas Caraway, the Helmsman who looked at her with respect in his eyes. He wasn't like the others; he had engaged her in conversation, smiled when he passed her in the corridor, attended her with eagerness instead of boredom. If she was honest, he'd been the first man she was ever attracted to. A young, brave warrior – what better subject for an adolescent's romantic dreams?

When she'd found out he was the one to blame for Kati's death, a part of her had died too.

'It doesn't matter what you say,' she snapped. Outside, night was falling; her eyes adjusted automatically to the change in light, but she closed them against the distraction. 'If it wasn't for you, my mother would still be alive.'

'True enough.' Just two words, but they contained a world of wistful sadness. Ayla was horrified to feel a tiny stirring of pity, for him and for what his life had become. She squashed it, keeping her back resolutely turned. When at last she did look round, he was lying on the folded blankets; she couldn't see his face.

Pulling her cloak tight around her, she lay down on the bed. She was still thirsty, but she didn't know where the water bottle was and couldn't bring herself to ask. Clutching her mother's portrait to her chest, she closed her eyes and tried to find refuge in sleep; but it was a long time coming.

SEVEN

'Captain Travers, sir!' The Helmsmen on either side of the door saluted, straightening, as Travers approached the interrogation room. He returned each of them a nod.

'Thank you, men. You may stand down.'

Inside, a scruffy urchin was sitting at the table, fists propping up his chin, surveying his surroundings with wide-eyed interest. When Travers entered the room, the boy greeted him with a lopsided grin that didn't quite conceal his nerves.

'Nice place you got 'ere, guv'nor.'

'You may address me as *Sir* or *Captain*.' Travers took a seat opposite his latest informant, regarding him with bored disdain. The Helm had made no public announcement of their search for Ayla, not wanting to scare her into fleeing the city, but they had circulated the word amongst their usual network of spies, who in turn had made a few discreet enquiries in the right places. Of course, that meant there had been plenty of false leads to follow. At times like this, it seemed every common muckspreader and his dog thought he'd seen or heard something important; sifting the gems from the dross was a time-consuming process, and a frustrating one.

'Well?' he asked the boy. 'What is it you want to tell me?'

'I 'eard from an associate of mine as 'ow you was lookin' for a girl wiv black hair an' blue eyes,' the urchin explained. 'An' I seen one.'

'Really.' Travers gave him a sceptical look. 'And when did this fascinating occurrence take place?'

'Yesterday.' The boy shrugged. 'I was sellin' news-sheets at the Gate o' Wind. She come an' had one off of me. Just 'fore second bell, I think, or coulda been just after …'

Travers waved a hand in the air. 'Get to it! What did she look like?'

'I only saw 'er for a moment.' It was a sullen mumble. 'She was wearin' a hood. Dark hair underneath, if not black then dark brown. Just like a Changer, 'cept for the eyes.'

Travers leaned forward. 'What about the eyes?'

'I dunno.' The boy frowned. 'They was blue, like the man said you was lookin' for, but when she looked up and they caught the light, they was greenish.'

Travers nodded, careful not to give anything away, although his concentration had doubled. Plenty of people had come forward with information, reciting stories about black-haired, blue-eyed maidens, but none of them had mentioned the one distinguishing feature that would give the ring of truth to their words – until now.

'You begin to interest me,' he said. 'What did she do, this girl?'

'I told you.' The urchin rolled his eyes. 'She bought a sheet. Took it over to the wall to read. After a bit she crumpled it in 'er 'and like this –' he clenched his fist, staring off into the distance – 'an' looked like she was gonna cry. But then she smoothed it out and read some more, an' put it in 'er pocket and went off.'

'You didn't see where she went?' Travers asked, and the boy shook his head.

'Nah. Not back through the gate, though. She musta headed into the second ring.'

'I see.' Travers sat for a moment, deep in thought. It sounded as though the girl in question had indeed been Ayla – and now he had Helmsmen watching each gate, she wouldn't be able to get back through without detection. So she had to be somewhere within the first two rings of Arkannen. Of course, that still left a wide area to cover, but at least he knew where to concentrate the search. Before, he'd wondered whether she might have taken sanctuary in one of the sixth-ring temples, or found a home in the fourth ring to hide in.

'You've been very helpful,' he told the boy, taking a silver donol from his pocket. 'This is for your trouble.'

'Thank you, sir!' The sight of the money made the child more respectful than he had been throughout the interview. Travers flicked the coin across the table to him.

'Good. Now be off with you.'

He banged on the door, and the two Helmsmen came in to escort the boy back down into the city. Travers remained at the table, considering his options.

He knew Myrren must have let Ayla out on the night of the murder; questioning the men on duty that night had revealed as much. The knowledge made him reluctant to keep Myrren informed of his progress with the investigation, aware that the man's loyalty lay more with his sister than with his dead father. As far as Travers was concerned, Myrren and Ayla were as bad as each other: neither was a true Changer child. And it was to the Nightshade line that Travers had sworn his allegiance, not to any particular member of it. He would do

62

everything he could to preserve it, even if Florentyn himself had failed to do so.

While the old Firedrake's marriage to a common girl after his first wife died had been deplorable, it had also been unavoidable. At the time, he and Myrren had been the only Nightshades left, so Florentyn had taken the necessary steps to get a daughter. Yet when Ayla hadn't been followed swiftly by other children, the responsible course of action would have been to set Kati aside and turn elsewhere. After all, Florentyn himself had bemoaned Darkhaven's emptiness often enough.

How the Nightshade line has dwindled, he would say. *Once there were thirty, forty, fifty Changers living in these halls. And what has it come to?*

He was right, of course. He and Myrren's mother – Florentyn's cousin – had been the only Nightshades of their generation, just as Myrren and Ayla were of theirs. The once-flourishing family tree had withered to a single branch. Yet Florentyn had done nothing to remedy the situation. He had pinned all his slender hopes on his two children, assuming that his full-blooded son would be as powerful as he was and that his half-blooded daughter would be sufficient to bear heirs. True, he couldn't possibly have predicted the utter failure that was Myrren – but all the same, it had been an uncharacteristically imprudent path to take, and all because he didn't want to hurt his common little second wife.

Yes: whatever Florentyn might have claimed in the bitter aftermath of her death, love had made a fool of him.

Yet despite all that, he had been the last real Changer. And thus, whatever Myrren said, Travers would continue to follow the orders the old Firedrake had left before he died.

Ayla must be kept alive to bear children, but she can't be trusted, Florentyn had said just a week ago. *This accusation means she must be sentenced to permanent incarceration. Myrren will be my heir after all, if only in name. It pains me to think of an ungifted boy taking my seat, but we may never come to that. If their children breed truer ...* He'd looked up, blue eyes darkened almost to black by the intensity of his thought. *Or, of course, there is always the alternative. You must keep an eye on it for me. If necessary, I may call upon you to implement it.*

Of course, Florentyn hadn't known he would be murdered just a few days after giving those instructions, but all the same Travers intended to obey them to the best of his ability. When his search for Ayla succeeded, he would have her brought back to Darkhaven and chained in the windowless room beneath the tower, next to the family vault that would be her father's final resting place. If she struggled, he would have her drugged into submission; she didn't need to be in her right mind in order to breed. And if, while she was locked down there alone, he happened to visit her one day and take what he'd wanted ever since she was twelve years old and began to show signs of becoming a woman, who was to know? She was a murderer. She deserved it.

Myrren himself would do perfectly well as a ruler. Unsure of his status, embarrassed by his position as a Nightshade without the gift, he would be easy to manipulate. Travers hoped it would be possible to persuade him into giving back some of the powers the Helm had once possessed, centuries ago. Back then the Helm had been a genuine fighting force, a band of elite warriors honour-sworn to protect the city of Arkannen from its foes. If the borders of Mirrorvale were to fall to one of its neighbours – the Ingal States to the west, Parovia to the east or Sol Kardis to the south – then it was the Helm's task to defend Arkannen from the invaders. In fact, Arkannen itself had been built with that purpose in mind: its seven rings, each with just a single ingress, provided an ideal structure for defence. It would take a besieging army months, if not years, to work its way ring by ring into the heart of the city; and all the while the Helm would be menacing them from the higher rings, and the reigning Changer in creature form would be wreaking as much havoc among them as possible.

In those early days the Helm had power throughout Arkannen, not just within the walls of Darkhaven. Yet as the threat of war lessened and was replaced with an uneasy peace, there was no longer any need for martial law. Several incidents in which the Helm overstepped their authority caused an outcry among the citizens and nearly resulted in the first civil war in Mirrorvale's history. As a result, the Nightshade overlord of the time gave in to the people's demands and removed the Helm from the city, leaving Arkannen subject to the same laws as the rest of the country. The Helm were reduced to a smaller force, taking on the status of bodyguards. They still had the right to come and go freely in Arkannen, to carry messages between Changers and city officials, and to apprehend anyone who was wanted by the Nightshade lords in connection with a criminal charge; but they were no longer above the precepts of the city.

Despite their diminished status, the Helm remained some of the best warriors in the world, chosen for their prowess from the elite training circles of the fifth ring. They were far more capable than the city watch, whose grip on the criminal elements within the city was feeble at best, and whose unwillingness to cooperate with the Helm had meant days had passed before Travers had gained permission to set his own men to watch the gates. *Permission* – when if the

Helm had been in charge, Ayla would never have been able to escape into the city without being caught. Yes, Arkannen was an unruly beast in dire need of taming. But once the Helm had their authority back, they could make sure the Changers were properly feared again, as they should be. They could counteract the inevitable rot that would set in when it became widely known that the newest Nightshade lord was no more of a Changer than were his subjects.

As for the alternative ... Travers frowned. With all the furore over Florentyn's death, he had been unable to check on the alternative for several days. Perhaps it was about time he went back down into Arkannen and continued with the final part of his orders.

'Captain Travers.' A Helmsman stepped into the room, giving a salute. 'Lord Myrren sent me. He wants to consult with you.'

Travers suppressed a sigh. His errand to the city could wait; for now, he would have to go and find out what Myrren wanted.

The old Changer's son was waiting in his room, looking serious and uneasy. Stepping through the doorway, Travers bowed low to hide a smile. Myrren had always been uncomfortable with ordering people around; it would make the forthcoming conversation much easier to steer.

'You sent for me, my lord?' he enquired, straightening up.

'I wanted to talk to you about Ayla,' Myrren said. 'Are you looking for her?'

Travers nodded. 'Of course.'

'Why?'

'My lord ...' Travers spread his hands; surely the reasons were obvious. 'She escaped on the same night your father was murdered, after having been imprisoned for carrying out a previous attack. Do you really need to ask why?'

'I have interviewed the priestess who was attacked, and her description of the creature does not match Ayla's other form.' Myrren gave him a narrow-eyed look. 'As your men knew very well, the night they brought the news of that attack.'

It was an unexpected accusation. Travers shook his head, unsure how to react.

'My lord … there was no deliberate misinformation on the part of the Helm. Lady Ayla was the only Changer in Mirrorvale apart from Florentyn himself. No-one else could have done it.'

'The priestess doesn't think she was attacked by Ayla,' Myrren said stubbornly. 'And if something else attacked her, something else could very well have killed my father.'

Travers shrugged. 'The priestess must be mistaken.'

'Captain Travers, my father was killed by something that ripped his throat out!' Myrren's voice rose in anger. 'The form my sister Changes into couldn't possibly commit such an act.'

'I am sorry, my lord.' Travers deliberately remained calm and reasonable. 'But you are the only person still living who has seen Lady Ayla's other form. She can't be acquitted on your word alone.'

Myrren frowned. 'Acquitted?'

'Before Lord Florentyn died, he informed me that he was going to find his daughter guilty of the attack on the priestess and that I would be required to carry out a sentence of incarceration,' Travers explained. 'He signed and sealed the warrant in my presence. Until it is proven that another person committed these crimes, I am bound by law to uphold your father's judgement.'

'I see.' Myrren folded his arms, looking suddenly weary. 'So no matter what I say to you, you will continue to search for Ayla in order to lock her up.'

'It is my duty to the Nightshade line, my lord.' Their eyes met, and it seemed to Travers that they understood each other. Then Myrren sighed.

'Very well, then. In that case, I have no more to say to you.'

He nodded dismissal, and Travers departed with a feeling of slight surprise. He had met an unexpected adversary in Myrren; it was clear the man believed his sister innocent and would do what he could to prove it, which didn't suit Travers at all. At the very least, it meant he should set a watch on Myrren, just in case he found Ayla before the Helm did. Once Ayla was locked up, in that lightless room with its thick stone walls and its reinforced metal door, there would be nothing anyone could do about it. The room was too small to Change in – intentionally so – and the holder of the single key controlled all access to it.

Travers intended to make sure he was the one who held that key.

EIGHT

Caraway awoke with a dry mouth and a longing for ale. His neck and shoulders ached from lying on the floor all night, though he couldn't remember what he was doing there. He sat up, rubbing his eyes, and saw the cloaked and hooded figure curled up on the bed. In an instant, memory came flooding back: he had offered Ayla Nightshade his help, and she had accepted.

Moving softly, so as not to wake her, he left the room and descended the stairs into the chill air of dawn. Plunging his head under the pump, he gulped down a few mouthfuls of water, then wandered over to the pisspot to relieve himself. At least when you lived above a tanner's yard, your urine didn't go to waste. As he stood there, breathing in the stench of rotting flesh and excrement that characterised the leather-making process, he tried to work out what he should do next. He had no money, lived in what was probably the worst room in Arkannen, and couldn't get through a single day without needing a drink. How in the name of all the elements was he going to help Ayla prove her innocence?

Of course, it didn't aid matters that she hated the very sight of him. He understood that, though it saddened him.

69

It must be difficult for her to accept help from the man who was responsible for her mother's death. And she'd changed: in place of the bright-eyed girl he remembered was a bitter and arrogant young woman who clearly thought he was worth less than the dirt beneath her shoe. He hadn't been able to envisage the old Ayla committing murder, but the new Ayla seemed wholly capable of it. Yet be that as it may, he knew he had to do something to help her – to atone, in however small a way, for his past. After all, if the years since Kati's death had changed her, he had only himself to blame.

These thoughts weren't helping. He tried to push aside recrimination and regret, to think rationally. If Ayla was suspected of her father's murder then he must have been killed in a way that suggested a Changer had done it. In turn, that meant one of two things: either there was a hidden Changer in Mirrorvale, or someone else had committed the crime and made it look like a Changer's handiwork.

Well, actually it meant one of three things. The third possibility was that Ayla really had killed her father. Thinking back over the few words they had exchanged, he couldn't remember her saying outright that she hadn't. Still, he would have to ignore that third option, because if it was true he might as well slit his wrists now and be done with it.

So, two possibilities. He could think of no way to investigate the first with the limited resources at his disposal, but the second struck him as far likelier anyway. Ayla had said the Helm despised her, and to a large extent she was right. Caraway could name several men he'd met during his brief employment in Darkhaven who would have been glad to see the half-blood Changer discredited. Whether they would go as far as killing Florentyn, who was pure blood and a true creature of power besides, he didn't know. But perhaps if they thought he was betraying the Nightshade line in some way, they would have taken the chance to swat two flies with one blow …

He ran his hands under the pump, then hurried back upstairs. Ayla was sitting on his bed, arms folded, the cloak arranged neatly at her side.

'Where have you been?' she demanded as soon as he set foot inside the door, her expression a mixture of suspicion and annoyance. He shook the question off, too intent on deduction to let her hostility affect him.

'Lady Ayla, before your father died, did he do anything … unusual? Anything that might have been seen as a threat to someone who wanted to preserve the purity of the Nightshade bloodline?'

'You mean, like announcing his intention to disinherit Myrren and make me the heir to Darkhaven instead?' Her tone was dry. 'Of course, that was before he decided I was unstable and needed to be locked up for the good of the country.'

Caraway frowned at her. 'He locked you up?'

'About a month ago, a priestess was attacked in the sixth ring,' Ayla said. 'I was the only suspect. Myrren helped me escape on the same night my father was murdered.'

The words held no trace of emotion, and for a moment the third possibility Caraway had considered earlier seemed distinctly the most plausible of the three. Yet looking at her more closely, he could see the tension in her interlocked fingers and her straight-as-steel back. She was frightened and in danger, and it was up to him to protect her as he hadn't protected her mother.

'It's possible both of these attacks were carried out deliberately to implicate you,' he said. 'I think I'd better visit the fifth ring.'

Her lip curled. 'Surely you're not allowed up there any more?'

'I know a man who owes me a favour.' Five years had passed since he left, but he'd never called it in. He'd always been too ashamed to show his face. But now ... he studied Ayla's tight, controlled expression. Now he had something more important than shame.

'I'll go this morning,' he said. 'Just as soon as I've brought you breakfast.' He hesitated, chewing the inside of his lip. 'Um ... do you have any money?'

After dashing off and returning with something he called a *butty* – he produced the thing with a beaming smile, as though he hadn't just bought it with her own coin – Caraway started out for the fifth ring. Ayla sat on his bed and stared at the butty. It appeared to be two thick slices of coarse bread with an unidentifiable chunk of singed meat in between. She had never eaten anything so disgusting in her life, and she didn't fancy starting now.

On the other hand, she'd finished the last of the food from Myrren a full day ago ...

The smell of the meat crept into her nostrils, and her stomach gave an insistent gurgle. Deciding she had to be practical about the situation, she took a tentative bite. A surprisingly short time later, she was left with nothing but grease on her fingers and a longing for more. Interesting. It hadn't been nearly as horrible as it looked. She supposed it was hunger and the stress of her situation that made a cheap piece of meat and some bread taste as good as anything she'd ever eaten in Darkhaven.

Wiping her fingers on a fold of her cloak – if she kept that up, she'd soon fit in here – she gazed around the room. It was just as depressing as it had been the previous evening:

filthy and bare. And she was going to have to spend her days here, relying on Tomas Caraway to exonerate her. At the thought, the food she'd just eaten condensed to a cold lump in her belly. She swallowed, fighting the sudden nausea. If only her Nightshade colouring didn't give her away. If only she wasn't so obviously herself …

She'd left her knife on the windowsill, where she'd be able to reach it in a hurry if Caraway decided to rid the world of another taint to the Nightshade line. Now, without letting her mind dwell on what she was doing, she caught up the heavy fall of her hair in one hand and the knife in the other. Maybe she could make herself look a little less like an inhabitant of Darkhaven.

Her hair was harder to cut than she'd expected; it resisted the blade like a tight-woven rope. Gritting her teeth, she sawed away at it. As each individual strand snapped, there was less and less resistance, but it became increasingly difficult to hold straight and taut. When she finally finished the job, she probed her head with her fingertips: as she'd guessed, she'd cut it crooked. Looking down at the dark locks scattered around her on the bed, she blinked back unexpected tears. She wouldn't cry. Even if her hair seemed a symbol of everything she'd lost, she wouldn't cry. But how in the name of wind and flame was she going to neaten it up without the aid of a mirror?

After hacking at a few odd strands without much success, she gave up and put the knife down. She had become aware of another, more pressing problem: she needed to use the water closet. Only Caraway didn't have a water closet, did he? Where on earth did people like him go to relieve themselves? She paced the floor with increasing urgency, before finally deciding she had no choice but to go out. It was hardly likely the Helm would be looking for her in a tanner's yard, after all. She'd wear her cloak, though, with the hood pulled close over her head. She wasn't altogether convinced by the efficacy of her shortened hair as a disguise.

The door to Caraway's room didn't have a lock on it, of course, so she just pulled it shut behind her and crept down the rickety stairs. At the bottom stood the archway that led out into the yard; she hesitated before walking through, surprised by just how busy it was compared to yesterday evening. Several skins were pegged out in the centre of the open space, the workers leaning over and scraping them with knives. The smell was even worse than it had been indoors; it made her eyes water.

As she watched the scene, unsure where to go, one of the men walked over to a large pot at the side of the yard and started to unbutton his breeches. Feeling her face heat, Ayla averted her eyes. She looked back in time to see him pick up the pot and carry it over to a vat containing more skins, into which he emptied the contents before replacing the now-empty pot beside the wall. So that was how they made leather. Ayla glanced down at her boots and wrinkled her nose. She'd never be able to look at footwear in quite the same way again. And if she had to use that pot ...

Summoning up her courage, she stepped out into the path of two women who were passing the archway with covered baskets in hand.

'Excuse me? Can you tell me where women go to, um, you know ...?' Speechless with embarrassment, she gestured at the pot. One of the women she'd accosted, an improbable redhead, let out a broad chuckle.

'Same as the men, my lovely, only we does it sittin' down.'

Ayla stared at her, aghast. The other woman – brown hair and a missing tooth – shook her head, grinning.

74

'She's just messin' with you, sweetheart. For those of a sensitive disposition, there's a closet t'other side of the yard.'

'Oh.' Limp with relief, Ayla gave them both a nod. 'Thank you.'

She turned to go, only to be stopped by the redhead's voice. 'What's yer name, love?'

'Kati.' Her mother's name fell from her lips before she could stop it. She suppressed a wince, but the two women seemed not to notice.

'Nice to meet you, Kati,' the brown-haired one said. 'Just moved in, then, 'ave you?'

Ayla offered a weak smile. 'I – I'm staying with Tomas Caraway.'

'Ah.' The woman exchanged glances with her friend. 'Well, good for 'im, I say. Been 'ere years, and this is the first time he's 'ad a girl in his room. I was beginnin' to think his interests, well, you know …' She produced a leering wink. 'Lay elsewhere.'

'So.' The redhead leaned in, eyebrows raised suggestively. 'What's he like, Kati? No need to be shy. We're all dyin' to know.'

Fire and blood. They thought she was – that Caraway was – that the two of them were *together*. Ayla opened her mouth to give a swift and unequivocal rebuttal, but before she could speak it occurred to her that denying it would only lead to more questions about who she was and what she was doing there. Though it pained her to let it happen, it would cause less talk all round if they thought she and Caraway were an item. So she forced her jaw closed, gave the two women a tight-lipped smile, and hurried off towards the water closet before they had a chance to ask any more inappropriate questions.

On her way back across the yard, she stopped to wash her face and hands under the pump, wishing she had some of her favourite rosemary soap. She hadn't realised, until she left Darkhaven, how many little everyday indulgences she really depended on – indulgences that hadn't been kept from her even in prison, though they'd been less regular. Like soap. And clean clothes. And a water closet that was more than just a worm-eaten lean-to with several cracks large enough to see out of and thus, by inference, in through …

Ayla shook her head, straightening her shoulders. This was only temporary – she just had to keep telling herself that. And besides, she wasn't a spoilt rich girl who couldn't live without luxury for more than a day. She was a Nightshade, and Nightshades endured.

All the same, she didn't think she'd be filling her water bottle again for a while. The less frequently she had to avail herself of the facilities, the better.

As she walked back towards the archway and Caraway's room, a heavy arm fell across her shoulders. She looked up to see a man grinning down at her, his rough sleeveless vest doing nothing to disguise his muscular build. At the same time, with a horrible plummeting sensation that shot right through her core, she remembered she'd left her knife upstairs. How could she have been so stupid?

'All right, love?' the man said, pushing the hood back from her face with his free hand. 'Gonna introduce yerself?'

'Don't touch me, you big oaf!' Deciding attack was the best form of defence, Ayla slipped out from under his arm and turned to confront him, hands on hips. He frowned at her.

'You better watch yerself, girlie –'

'No, you watch it, Carlo.' The two women she'd met earlier were observing the scene from a little distance away. It was the redhead who'd spoken; she nodded in Ayla's direction. 'She's Caraway's woman.'

'Oh.' Instantly the man's expression turned wary. 'Well, she only had to say so, din't she. I din't mean any harm.'

With that, he shambled off across the yard; Ayla frowned after him before recollecting herself and hurrying back to the safety of the archway. Yet the little scene stayed with her, playing over and over in her mind. Apparently, despite being a drunken idiot and a murderer besides, Caraway had these people's respect. He didn't seem the slightest bit intimidating to her – in fact, he cringed around her like a dog longing for its master's approval – but she supposed he must still have some fighting skills that made ordinary folk keep their distance. Which meant, though she hated the very thought of it, that her continued safety in this place depended on her remaining *Caraway's woman*.

At least for now.

NINE

Myrren stood in his father's bedroom and tried not to shudder. They had stripped the bed, of course, and scrubbed the floor until it shone as bright as it had the day it was laid, but he thought he could still smell the blood: a faint, cloying reek underlying the heat of the gas lamps and the scent of the dragonlilies someone had put in a bowl on the table. Myrren had never liked dragonlilies – their florid purple and red blooms reminded him of an open wound – but in this room they were appropriate enough. He stepped closer to the flowers, breathing their spiced aroma deep into his lungs. The stench of death was replaced by the smell of a Changer creature, cinnamon and heat. His father's smell.

Grief hit him then, hard, in the back of the throat. Yet once it had receded far enough for him to breathe again, he was ashamed to find that it wasn't so much for his father as for Ayla. He didn't know how to mourn Florentyn, didn't know how to reconcile the complex mixture of sorrow and guilt and, yes, relief that gripped him every time he thought of his father's brutal passing. But Ayla was alone, exiled from home and falsely accused of murder. If Myrren gave them both room in his heart, they would overwhelm him – and his sister's life had to take precedence over his father's death.

Of course, not everyone agreed with that assessment. His conversation with Captain Travers still circled in his head, leaving a dull ache of frustration in its wake. He had deliberated for almost an entire bell over whether to inform the Helm of his findings, but in the end he'd decided the evidence of Ayla's innocence was too strong for them to ignore. If he could get them on his side then it would be possible to search Arkannen for the unknown Changer much faster and more thoroughly. Yet it hadn't happened that way. Travers had as good as said that on this matter, he wouldn't defer to Myrren's authority – where Ayla was concerned, Florentyn's word still held sway.

Myrren might have tried to overrule him, were it not for the precarious sense he had of his own position. There was, after all, a good reason his father had wanted to disinherit him: a Nightshade overlord kept his subjects in line largely through fear, and that fear was instilled by his awe-inspiring other form. Myrren had an unpleasant suspicion that if he tried to oppose Travers without that backing, Travers would turn the Helm against him. After all, Travers had a signed warrant for Ayla's incarceration in his possession, stamped with the Changer seal. It wouldn't take much for him to convince his men that Myrren was betraying the Nightshade line by rejecting that warrant. Which meant Myrren and Serenna were on their own, and it was vital that the two of them find the real criminal before the fifty men of the Helm found Ayla. The urgency of it left Myrren in a state of paralysis, the sheer scale of the problem daunting him into inaction.

If he did have an affair then he may have kept some token. He repeated Serenna's words to himself. Never mind that every passing bell stole a fraction more of his precious time, widening the gap between him and the Helm in this fatal race they were caught up in. For now, he had to forget he was in a hurry, and concentrate on finding something in his father's bedroom that might give them a clue.

Unfortunately, though, what he'd told Serenna was true: Florentyn had never been a sentimental man. Nor had he been a hoarder, as popular legend held that a Firedrake should be. His room was neat and bare, and not just because they'd cleaned it after his death; he had never seen the purpose in possessions or displays of material wealth. The idea that somewhere in his bedroom might be hidden a reminder of a love more than twenty years old would have been laughable, if it hadn't been Myrren's only hope of solving the mystery.

He opened the wardrobe. His throat tightened again at the sight of the shirts and coats hanging inside like the shed skins of a snake – a brief flash of memory showed him his father's bleached face and staring eyes – but he gritted his teeth against the renewed surge of emotion and forced himself to push his hands into each empty sleeve and fold, searching. If Florentyn had kept anything important, it would most likely be in a concealed pocket … but there was nothing. At the end of the row Myrren rocked back on his heels, thinking a moment, then opened a drawer in the chest next to the wardrobe. Yet a hunt through his father's breeches and smallclothes bore just as little fruit, as did a comprehensive search among the contents of the shaving stand.

He turned in a slow circle, examining the room, and his gaze fell on the writing desk in the far corner. In a few strides he was there, sitting on the matching chair to fold open the front. The internal compartments revealed themselves in perfect, lifeless order: writing paper, pen and ink, the Nightshade seal. There was nowhere for anything to be hidden, but Myrren rifled through the sheets of paper anyway in case something was caught between them. The drawer underneath the desk held nothing but dust. Three books sat on the shelf above, records of lineage and genealogy: Myrren turned their pages in search of an inserted slip or a handwritten note, then took each one by the spine and gave it a shake. Still nothing. But after all, he had no reason to expect more. Florentyn hadn't even kept a portrait of Kati, the woman he had loved most deeply, in his bedroom; why should he have kept anything to remind him of what must have been a brief and almost certainly casual affair?

As Myrren stood up again, a faint rustling sound came from the padded seat of the chair. At any other time he would have thought nothing of it, but with all his senses set to high alert it immediately claimed his attention. Crouching down beside the chair, he examined the embroidered cushion and found that it was not – as he had thought – attached to the wood. Instead, it was a separate pad set into a recess in the seat. Scrabbling with his fingernails, he succeeded in lifting the cushion out. Beneath was a shallow cavity, and folded within it a single piece of paper.

Myrren stared at the innocuous-looking thing, his pulse racing. All of a sudden, he didn't want to touch it. The very fact that it was there, hidden under a cushion in the seat of a chair, showed it to be something Florentyn had wanted to keep secret. What if it wasn't what they had come up with, he and Serenna? What if it was something far worse, something that would destroy Myrren's opinion of his father for good? Yet he had to look. Ayla's freedom might depend on it. So after a moment, he reached out and smoothed the piece of paper open. It held just a few words, written in Florentyn's heavy black hand.

45 Avenue of Rowans, Ametrine Quarter

Myrren's immediate anxiety faded back into the hollow ache it had been ever since Ayla's escape and his father's murder. The Ametrine Quarter was a residential area in the fourth ring; what he had found was an address in Arkannen. Perhaps Serenna was right, that Florentyn had carried out an affair before Myrren was even born and fathered a Changer child who'd grown up into something mad and terrible. Perhaps the mother of that child still lived there in the Avenue of Rowans. Or perhaps this address had nothing to do with Serenna's theory, but meant something else altogether. Whatever the truth of it, Myrren knew he would have to go there and find out – and he didn't want to go alone.

He slipped the piece of paper into his pocket, and went to see Serenna.

'What do you know about the Ametrine Quarter, Sister Serenna?' Myrren stood in the doorway of her room, his dark gaze fixed on her face. Serenna frowned, trying to think past the mixture of panic and pleasure his unexpected appearance had called up. She'd thought her meditation had laid these feelings to rest, yet as soon as she saw him again her heart had started pounding as though she were a lovesick girl. She wasn't sure whether it made the situation better or worse that Myrren now seemed to be completely oblivious to her; whatever had prompted his question, he was focused on it to the exclusion of all else.

'It's in the fourth ring,' she said, gathering her scattered thoughts with an effort. 'They call it Nightsbane in the lower rings. Members of the city watch live there, law officials, soldiers. Sellswords and bodyguards for hire. Oh, and the wives and children of your Helm.'

'Really?' His eyes narrowed. 'It's where Helm families live?'

She nodded. 'Anyone who has anything to do with law enforcement, I suppose. It must be the least burgled Quarter in the city.'

He was diverted; the intensity of his gaze faded into a quizzical look. 'Once again, you know an awful lot for a priestess.'

'I wasn't born in the temple, Lord Myrren.' Funny, how everyone assumed that just because she was a priestess she must know nothing of the world outside the sixth ring. She'd wager a ranol to an ennol she knew a lot more about Arkannen than Myrren did. 'I lived in the fourth ring, in Carnelian, for twelve years before I took my vows.'

'And what do they call Carnelian in the lower rings?' The nascent smile at the corners of his mouth made her entire body jump and tighten in response. She kept her voice cool, striving for detachment.

'If that is your subtle way of asking what my father does, my lord, he is a professor at the university. Carnelian is the Academics' Quarter.' She shrugged. 'I was the youngest of five. My parents were relieved when I expressed my desire to serve the Altar of Flame.'

'Brothers or sisters?' Myrren asked.

'I'm sorry?'

'You said you were the youngest of five.'

'Oh ... two of each.' She looked past him, a memory suddenly vivid in her mind: a winter day, snow on the ground, covering everything in pristine white. Before the roadsweepers came to clear the streets, she and her siblings had built a Unicorn, the elemental creature of ice. Her older brothers had lifted her onto its back, and she'd sat there proudly as the melting snow seeped through the seat of her dungarees, waving at the people who trudged to and fro. Strange ...

she hadn't thought much about her family for a long time. She'd been homesick, of course, the first few years in the temple; she must have been, it was only natural. But it was ages now since she'd thought of home as anything other than the Altar of Flame.

'That sounds nice,' Myrren said, and the image vanished. She looked back at him, raising her eyebrows in disbelief.

'Nice? Five noisy children crammed into a three-bedroomed house with thin walls and a roof that leaked when it rained?'

'Why not?' He sounded a little defensive now. 'Growing up, I often wished I had a brother. It was lively enough here when Ayla's mother was alive, but after she died ...' He sighed. 'Ayla and I rattled around like two peas in an empty pod.'

Lonely. He didn't say it, but she heard it all the same. She'd only been here two days, and she already knew Darkhaven was a lonely place – even for someone who was used to solitude. She fought the urge to reach out and touch his arm; before she could succumb to it, the smile crept back to the corners of his mouth.

'What's more, Sister Serenna, I defy you to claim that your father – a professor at the university, you say – was anything like as fearsome as mine.'

'I wouldn't dream of it.' She smiled back at him. Then, because they seemed rapidly to be reaching an understanding she wasn't sure it was safe to reach, she hurried to change the subject. 'Anyway, Lord Myrren ... why did you want to know about Ametrine?'

'Because you were right.' The focused expression returned to his face. He reached into his pocket and brought out a piece of paper. 'I found this hidden in my father's room.'

She scanned the address, committing it to memory, then looked up. 'So if there is another Changer child out there, you think the Helm may have some knowledge of it?'

'Yes.' His glance conveyed tacit approval of her swiftness. 'It's very possible. My father trusted the Helm implicitly. If it was a matter concerning the Nightshade bloodline, he wouldn't have hesitated to approach them.'

She read the uncertainty in his eyes. 'But …?'

'It could be nothing.' He took the paper back from her, frowning at it in an abstracted way. 'This could just be a Helmsman's address or the contact details for a sellsword my father wanted to hire for his next trading venture. Of course, I could ask Captain Travers about it, but after what he said earlier I'm not inclined to trust him with this.'

'Then I suppose you have no choice but to go and see for yourself,' Serenna offered, and he nodded.

'Exactly. It's approaching dusk now, but I think we should aim to get there by second bell tomorrow.'

'We?' she echoed, suddenly nervous. She hadn't been down into the fourth ring since she left it to become an acolyte, nine years ago. And being in the company of Myrren Nightshade was hardly an unobtrusive way to pay a visit.

'I hope so.' He looked grave. 'It would be very helpful if you could join me, Serenna. I am not accustomed to navigating the streets of Arkannen alone.'

'All right.' Her heart skipped as she said it; but after all, she had made up her mind to help him, for her own sake and for Ayla's. Cowering in Darkhaven whilst he went out into the city in search of the criminal wasn't going to be of much use. 'Come back here at first bell and we'll go together.'

'Thank you.' He offered her a bow – though this time, she noticed, he didn't venture to touch her – and strode away. Serenna retreated into Ayla's bedroom and prepared herself for bed; she would have to be up early tomorrow. Yet once she was lying under the covers, sleep seemed a distant and unlikely prospect. And no matter how she tried to tell herself it was just her nerves sparking in anticipation of tomorrow's intended trip to the city, she knew that in reality it was fear of an altogether different kind keeping her awake.

TEN

Elisse stood at the window, gazing into the street below. She wasn't supposed to be there, but she didn't think anyone would notice her. The window was swathed in thick lace drapes, veiling everything in a haze of white; and besides, no casual passer-by ever looked up as high as the top floor.

She was bored. She had been provided with books and embroidery, a drawing pad and a spinet: everything a girl could want for entertainment, except company. For a few weeks she'd enjoyed the luxury of it, a life so far removed from her previous one that it might as well have belonged to a different world. She'd been able to get up when she liked, wear what she liked, do what she liked – except go outside. Yet sooner than she would have expected, the novelty of that had begun to wear off. By now, she'd looked at all the books that held any interest for her; she'd set a few crooked stitches in the tambour-frame before putting it aside; her drawing pad was full of abandoned portraits and poorly executed perspective sketches of the rooms that made up her apartment; and she had tired of the sound of her own musical fumblings. She would have swapped all the grandeur around her, the thick rugs and polished wood and scented flowers in vases, for the freedom to walk through the long grass of a meadow with a breeze in her hair. Even all those chores she'd grumbled about had begun to take on a certain nostalgic appeal.

She was almost sure she wished Lord Florentyn had never showed up at her mother's farm at all.

When he'd first arrived, almost a year ago now, she'd been tending to her own little flower garden behind the house. Kneeling in the soil, humming to herself as she pulled up the weeds around a climbing rose, she didn't notice his approach until he was almost upon her. It was the scent she became aware of initially: a hot smell, spicy but not unpleasant, like the iron stove in the kitchen when Mam was baking cinnamon bread. Then a twig cracked, and she looked up to see him striding past the flowerbeds towards her.

'Excuse me.' His voice was deep and smooth. The sun was behind him, leaving Elisse with no more than an impression of a tall figure silhouetted against sky.

'Can I help ya?'

She expected him to ask for directions or offer goods for sale, but he appeared lost for words. When he did speak, it seemed almost at random.

'How old are you, girl?'

She stood up, brushing dirt from her skirt. She could see him more clearly, now: dark hair and blue eyes similar to hers, a long aristocratic nose. Her mother's age, or a little older. This man wouldn't be selling anything; he would have come in a carriage or an airship, sailing on by while the rest of the world trudged. She couldn't think what he would be doing in the isolated countryside of her mother's farm.

'I'm twenny-three,' she said. 'Not a girl.'

'Indeed.' His eyes searched her face as though looking for a hidden message. 'And have you always lived out here in the wilds of Mirrorvale?'

'We moved from the city when I was little.' She wasn't sure why she was answering his questions, except that he was so obviously interested. 'My father died, and Mam bought the farm soon after.'

He gave a slow nod. 'So it's just the two of you.'

'Yeah.' She waited, but when no further comment was forthcoming she said again, 'Can I help ya, sir?'

'What's your name?' he asked abruptly, as if he hadn't heard her. She told him, and he offered her a smile. 'Elisse. That's pretty. Tell me, Elisse, do you look much like your mother?'

She shook her head. 'Mam always says I'm like my father.'

'I see.' The look he gave her was speculative; she didn't altogether understand it. She backed away a few steps.

'Would ya like me ta fetch Mam for ya, sir?'

'No.' With startling suddenness, he bowed. 'I have to go. But I hope I will have the opportunity to pass this way again.'

Elisse snorted. If she'd known then what she knew now, she would have understood just how disingenuous a statement that was. And indeed, over the next weeks he'd turned up several times whilst she was washing clothes in the river or gathering kindling in the south wood or leading the sheep to pasture. They'd talked – or rather, he'd asked her questions and she'd answered them – but all the while, it had felt as if he was watching for something in her to reveal itself. As if he was waiting.

Then came the incident, the one that changed everything. After that, he'd told her the truth about who he was and what he wanted from her. *It's no longer safe for you to stay here,* he'd said. *Every child of Darkhaven should be under the eye of the Helm.* And so she'd packed up her few belongings, despite her mother's protestations, and travelled under armed guard to Arkannen.

Since then, she'd been living in this set of rooms in the fourth ring with only her own thoughts for company. Florentyn had visited her regularly in the early days, spending the whole of the fourth bell with her, but gradually his visits had become shorter and less frequent. Of late, she had hardly seen him at all. Instead, like a punishment for some unspecified crime, she had to endure the visits of his Captain of the Helm.

As if the thought had called it up, she heard a knock at her door. Turning away from the window with a roll of the eyes, she went to open it. She couldn't decide what was worse: being bored or being visited by Owen Travers.

'Lady Elisse.' Sure enough, it was him: sketching a bow, face and voice deferential, but with the snooty look that told her he despised everything about her from her calloused hands to her country twang. 'May I come in?'

She shrugged, ungracious. 'I can't stop ya.'

He walked into her living quarters, glancing around as though he hoped to catch her doing something she shouldn't. Well, he'd be disappointed; she didn't have anything forbidden to do, except go outside – and she didn't quite dare to break that prohibition, not when Florentyn himself had laid it upon her.

She'd asked him about Travers, in the early days when he actually visited her, but he'd shrugged it off. *Travers doesn't approve of half-bloods, Elisse. And indeed, I would prefer a full-blooded heir myself. Sadly, the elements have not seen fit to provide me with one. Ayla, and not Myrren, is my*

Changer child. A scowl had touched his face briefly before he forced it into a smile. *Still, should she prove intractable, you provide me with an alternative.*

Watching Travers now as he prowled through her rooms, Elisse wrapped her arms protectively around herself. Florentyn had found her, had brought her here to Arkannen; no matter how much she longed to return home, she wouldn't show it. She wouldn't let this Helmsman intimidate her. She was better than that.

'Would ya like something ta drink, Captain Travers?' she offered, keeping her voice cool and polite. She might not be a lady, as he saw it, but she could still behave like one.

'No, thank you.' He sat down on her chaise longue, arranging his sword, smoothing imaginary wrinkles out of his multicoloured coat. He seemed oddly ill at ease. 'Elisse, I need to talk to you.'

The look he gave her was almost sympathetic; it scared her.

'Why?' she asked, sinking into a chair opposite him. 'What's happened?'

'It's Lord Florentyn.' Travers glanced down at his interlocked hands, then back at her face. 'He's dead.'

Dead. The world spun around her. She grasped the arms of the chair for support, trying to make sense of something senseless.

'How? He wasn' ill, was he?'

'No, my lady.' Travers' face darkened, and he shot her a glare as if she were responsible. 'He was murdered. By a Changer.'

'A Changer?' Even more incomprehensible. Elisse began to wonder whether she was imagining the whole thing. 'Who?'

'Ayla escaped from Darkhaven on the same night,' Travers said. Then, as though it were the logical continuation of what he was saying, 'I promised Lord Florentyn I'd look after you, Elisse.'

'Yeah – yeah, I know, I –' She couldn't marshal her words into a coherent sentence. 'But – are ya saying it was Lady Ayla who killed him?'

'That's what the Helm believe. After all, she is the only known Changer in Arkannen, though Myrren would have us think otherwise.' He looked up, a warning in his pale eyes. 'They mustn't find out about you, Elisse, either of them. You're a threat to them.'

She nodded, suddenly frightened. 'I know. I won' leave my rooms, I swear.'

'Good.' Travers leaned forward, intent. 'Remember, if Ayla can kill her father in cold blood, then she could kill you just as easily.'

Elisse bit her lip. 'But she doesn' know where I am, does she?'

'No.' Travers gave her a smile that was probably meant to be reassuring. 'And we need to keep it that way. Which is why I've arranged protection for you.'

'Protection?'

'Someone to guard you. Make sure you're safe.'

She suppressed another roll of the eyes; now Florentyn was gone, she'd be depending on Travers to see her through this. Best to keep him sweet. 'I know wha' protection is, Captain Travers. I jus' don' see what a single Helmsman can do against a Changer.'

'The woman I've hired to attend you isn't a Helmsman,' Travers said. 'She has certain ... specialist skills. She's undertaken to act as your personal guard until this situation with Ayla is resolved.'

Personal guard. So did that mean the woman would be her bodyguard, Elisse wondered with dour humour, or her jailer? The way Travers looked at her, she wasn't sure if he was more concerned with keeping her safe or keeping her locked up. And even if the Helm did catch Ayla, would they ever let Elisse go back home? Or would she be stuck in Arkannen for good, forced into complying with the plans Florentyn had set out before his death?

'She'll be here tomorrow,' Travers said. 'In the meantime, you need to stay out of sight. Keep the curtains drawn and the door locked. I'll let you know when there's news.'

'All right.' Elisse was full of questions – *what's this woman like? what's her name? does she know why I'm here?* – but she kept them to herself. She wanted to be alone with her thoughts, which meant the quicker she could get rid of Travers the better. In fact, maybe she could hurry him along a bit. 'But if I'm ta have company, could ya have some Kardise tea sent over? I'm running low.'

'If you wish.' As she'd expected, Travers leapt to his feet as though someone had stuck a pin in his backside. It was the same every time she started asking for things: he ran away before the list got too long. She suspected he found it demeaning to be waiting on a country girl like her – but since she wasn't allowed out, and he and a few trusted Helmsmen were now the only people in Arkannen who knew she was here, he didn't have much choice.

'And some o' them little sweet biscuits,' she added for good measure, offering him a guile-free smile.

'Very well. I'll order them for you.' By now he was at the door. Straightening up from another bow, he fixed her with an intent stare. 'Remember, Elisse, don't let anyone see you. Your colouring alone is enough to get people asking questions, even if they come up with the wrong answers.'

With that, he departed. Once she was certain he'd gone, Elisse tipped her head back in her chair and closed her eyes. She felt drained and tired; she didn't have much energy these days, cooped up within these walls. So she stayed where she was and thought about Florentyn Nightshade: the abrupt way he had come into her life, and the abrupt way he had left it. She knew she ought to be upset, to mourn him; yet now her initial shock had faded, what remained in its place was emptiness. He'd uprooted her, taken her away from her mother and her home, left her drifting and anchorless like a cloud of yellowroot seeds on the wind. She couldn't return to her old life, but as yet she had no idea what the shape of her new life would be. And since it wasn't safe to leave Arkannen, at least not yet, there was nothing to do but wait.

'Looks like we're on our own, kiddo,' she said to the silence of the empty room. 'I guess we'll just have ta make the best of it.'

ELEVEN

As soon as he caught sight of the Gate of Steel in the distance, Caraway came to an abrupt halt. He'd gone the long way round through the fourth ring, avoiding the Ametrine Quarter – today was exactly the wrong day to bump into any of his former colleagues from the Helm – but even so, the gate had crept up on him before he was ready for it. It left a dull ache in his chest, as if he'd been stabbed with a blunt blade and was slowly bleeding to death. He hadn't been up here for five years: not since he stumbled away from Darkhaven with sword and heart both newly broken, knowing he could never return. Now he gazed at the sharp blades that lined the archway like a set of vicious metal teeth, and remembered anew the first time he'd walked through that gate: how proud he'd been finally to be setting foot in the hallowed fifth ring, the training ground he'd dreamed of all his young life.

Still. That was the past, and he'd wallowed in it too many times already. Yes, he'd lost everything. Yes, he could really do with a pitcher of ale right now. But he had a purpose again, and he wasn't going to fail this time. So he squared his shoulders and kept walking. If he ignored the pain for long enough, maybe it would go away.

Technically he shouldn't even have been allowed into the fourth ring; he wasn't a respectable enough citizen to have a home there, and he certainly hadn't been invited in by any of the residents. But the members of the city watch who guarded each of Arkannen's seven gates knew what he'd been, and what he'd become. Their embarrassed eyes slid over him as though they could be infected with his outcast status just by looking at him. As a result, as long as he didn't try to climb too high through the city, he was given the freedom to wander where he liked. It wasn't something he had ever taken much advantage of – all the inns were in the outer rings, after all – but now he was going to put it to the test.

As he approached the gate ahead of him, the two guards straightened up and stepped forward to block his path. Theirs was not just the upright posture of good discipline; it was the rigidity that went with an awkward and potentially unpleasant task.

'Breakblade,' one of them said, his gaze resting on a point somewhere beyond Caraway's left shoulder. 'Can we help you?'

They're not going to let me in. The longing for a drink tingled in Caraway's fingers and toes. He forced himself to speak clearly and calmly, as if his presence at the Gate of Steel were an everyday occurrence. 'I need to see someone in the Warriors' Hall. I'll be there and back before you know it.'

'I'm sorry, Caraway.' The other guard looked directly at him, a hint of sympathy in her eyes. 'You know the rules. You have no business here any more.'

Caraway tried a smile. 'In that case, could one of you please carry a message to my … friend? Once he knows I'm here, I'm sure he'll come out.'

The male guard shook his head. 'I don't think so.'

'Look, Art Bryan owes me a favour, all right?' A headache was gathering behind Caraway's eyes, making his voice uneven. 'And I need to collect it today, so can you please just tell him I want to speak to him?'

The two guards exchanged doubtful glances.

'Art Bryan?' the woman said. 'You mean the weaponmaster?'

Caraway nodded. 'Assistant weaponmaster in my day, but yes. Him.'

She hesitated, then spread her hands in a gesture of resignation. 'I'll let him know you're here.' Then, at a fulminating look from her colleague, 'What's the worst that can happen? Either Bryan'll come out, or he'll tell me to tell Caraway to piss off.' She glanced back at Caraway, eyebrows raised. 'And you will piss off if he asks you to piss off, won't you, Breakblade?'

Caraway shrugged. 'If he won't speak to me, I don't have any reason to be here.'

'Right.' She turned on her heel and walked through the gate, leaving the male guard glowering.

'Quite hot for the time of year,' Caraway offered in what he knew was a pathetic attempt at small talk, and the other man spat at his feet.

'Shut up or I'll make you.'

Fair enough.

As Caraway waited in silence, trying to breathe through the pounding headache now attacking his eyeballs, it occurred to him that the female guard could just lurk out of sight for a while, then come back and tell him Bryan didn't want to see him. And what would he do then? He didn't have any other contacts worth mentioning, other than a large number of innkeepers and bar staff. How would he keep his promise to help Ayla if he couldn't find anything out? He couldn't bear to fail her. He had already hurt her enough.

By the time the female guard came back into view, he'd almost convinced himself she would be alone; it was with considerable surprise that he recognised Art Bryan's hulking form at her heels. Bryan was the sort of man who dominated a room, a sparring ground or even a street simply by virtue of being in it, and not just because he was built like a box full of bricks. He radiated an aura of sheer stubborn will that affected everyone in his path. And yet, although he was one of the most feared figures of the fifth ring, he was also one of the most admired. He didn't take any shit, but nor did he give any; even the hapless apprentices who bore the full brunt of his scorn ended up respecting his fairness.

He was also one to offer credit where it was due – which was why he hadn't hesitated to admit his debt to a young Tomas Caraway, after an incident with a runaway horse that could have ended his career for good if Caraway hadn't been there to stop it. Looking at the glare on his face now, though, Caraway didn't think gratitude was uppermost in his mind.

'By ice and steel, if it isn't my most notorious student.' Bryan stopped a short distance away, eyebrows drawn so close they almost touched. His voice was a penetrating bellow, honed by years of shouting instructions at the recalcitrant youths in his care. 'What in the name of all the powers do you want, Caraway?'

'Six years ago, you said you owed me.' Caraway stood square and took it on the chin, trying not to remember all the times this man had berated him on the training floor, back when they were student and teacher. Back when he had a future. 'I've come to call in the favour.'

'And here was I thinking you'd drowned that memory in ale.' Bryan scowled. 'You've got a bloody nerve.'

'I wouldn't ask if it wasn't important, you know that.'

'Do I?' Bryan folded his arms. 'Seems to me I don't know you at all.'

'You at least know me well enough to be sure I would never intentionally have hurt Kati Nightshade,' Caraway said softly. 'A man can't train a clumsy boy into a half-decent Helmsman without learning what he's capable of, and what he's not. Isn't that what you always said?'

'That's assuming you ever were a half-decent Helmsman,' Bryan replied. 'Sometimes I have my doubts.'

It was like a punch to the guts. Caraway closed his eyes a moment, breathing through the pain. 'Then that's it? You're not going to help me?'

'I didn't say that.' Bryan's voice was gruff. 'Whatever I may think of you, I won't have it said that I don't keep my word.'

That was what Caraway had been counting on: his old mentor's innate sense of honour. He began to stammer out his thanks, only to be stopped by Bryan's upraised hand.

'What is it you want? Make it quick, Caraway. I'm in no mood to linger.'

With a glance over Bryan's shoulder at the two guards, who weren't even trying to conceal how avidly they were listening, Caraway lowered his voice. 'I need some information. I need to know if the Helm have been doing anything out of the ordinary over the last month or so. You're there when they're training, you must hear them talk … has there been anything at all that struck you as unusual?'

Bryan assessed him through narrowed eyes. 'What's this about, Caraway? I swear to you, if I find out you're up to no good I'll –'

'You'll have heard the rumours about Lord Florentyn's death,' Caraway said. 'They're saying Lady Ayla did it. I intend to prove them wrong.'

Bryan's brows quirked upwards. 'So that's what this is? Atonement?' He contemplated that a moment, then sighed. 'I don't see that you stand much chance with that one, boyo. And I don't see what the Helm have to do with it, either. But for what it's worth, there is one thing that might interest you: Owen Travers recently hired a sellsword. And not just any sellsword, either. He hired Naeve Sorrow.'

Now we're getting somewhere. Caraway knew Sorrow, at least by reputation. Who didn't? Eight years ago, when he'd first arrived in the fifth ring, she'd already made a name for herself as a mercenary. It was whispered that no job fell outside her remit, however difficult and however dirty – as long as the price was right.

'Do you know what Travers hired her for?' he asked, hopeful, but Bryan pulled a face and shook his head.

'I only know about it at all because I saw the two of them together in the fifth ring. Travers invited Sorrow to spar with him, and afterwards they talked business.'

Caraway nodded thoughtfully. It wasn't much, yet it fit his suspicions. Travers must have hired the sellsword to carry out the attacks and make it look as though Ayla had done it. The Helm were obsessed with the Nightshade bloodline; Florentyn's decision to raise his half-blood daughter above his pure-blood son must have turned them against him. So they'd had him killed and implicated Ayla in the murder, allowing Myrren to reclaim what they considered to be his rightful position – and, at the same time, the Helm gained more power. *Much more persuadable ...* wasn't that how Travers had described Myrren? Yes, clearly the Helm would prefer it if Myrren inherited his father's seat rather than Ayla.

Coming out of his reverie, Caraway met Bryan's frown

with a tentative smile, more relieved than he could express to have been given something – however small – to go on.

'Thank you, sir.' Reflexively he fired off a military salute, then caught himself doing it and wanted to give himself a good shaking. A bitter edge crept into his voice as he added, 'Consider your debt paid.'

He turned to leave, but was stopped by Bryan saying his name. He looked back over his shoulder; Bryan was watching him from beneath heavy brows.

'When did you last have a drink?'

Not recently enough. Caraway shrugged. 'I don't know. Yesterday. Does it matter?'

'Of course it matters.' Bryan snorted. 'I'm not giving you my hard-earned money just so you can piss it down the drain.'

Caraway stared at him. 'But I didn't ask you for –'

'Are you telling me you don't need it?' Bryan demanded, and Caraway looked down at his feet.

'No, but –'

'Then take it. And don't ever show your face up here again.'

Stomach churning with an uneasy mixture of gratitude and shame, Caraway accepted the handful of coin. 'Thank you,' he muttered. 'I won't spend it on alcohol.'

Bryan nodded. 'I know you won't, boyo. Because if you do, I'll come down to the lower rings and make your hide into a tablecloth.'

Then, without any further words or even so much as a glance, he pivoted on his heel and marched back through the Gate of Steel. Caraway looked at the money in his hand: enough for several pitchers of finest ale. Enough to drink himself unconscious three times over. But Bryan trusted him ... and besides, Ayla must be hungry by now.

*

When he got back to his room with food for both of them, he found Ayla sitting on the bed with her arms wrapped around her knees, looking out of the window. Her hair was short and jagged, falling to just below her ear on one side and halfway down her neck on the other.

'You cut your hair,' he said stupidly.

She didn't bother to respond to that, just kept watching the tanner's yard below as though it fascinated her.

'Where is it?' he asked. At that she did turn her head, fixing him with a cool stare.

'Where is what?'

'The hair. I could get a couple of ranols for that amount of good-quality hair, especially in that colour.'

'It's under the bed.' Her expression told him that she found the whole conversation unspeakably sordid. That she found *him* unspeakably sordid. She watched in silence as he fetched a broom and swept her hair into a pile, knocking a couple of empty bottles over in the process. Clumps of dust clung to it, but it still gleamed blue-black in the fading light. He might even be able to get three ranols, if he haggled properly.

'I'm not going to drink it, you know,' he told her. 'I thought … I thought I could buy you a wig in a different colour. Then you'd be able to leave the room without being spotted. It must be pretty dull for you in here.'

She didn't reply to that either, but her face softened a fraction. As he gathered the hair into a bag she remained silent, but this time it wasn't quite so hostile.

'Now …' When he'd finished, he looked at her rather nervously. 'Would you like me to neaten it up for you?'

She hesitated, then gave a quick nod. 'Yes. That would probably be sensible.'

Taking the proffered knife, Caraway sat down beside her on the bed. He could feel the tension radiating off her like heat, the desire to flee. Her fingers were locked together so tightly they looked bloodless.

'I'm not going to hurt you, Ayla,' he said softly.

'Just get on with it.' She turned her back on him, giving him access to her hair, and added with a note of strain in her voice, 'Please.'

Heartened by the small courtesy, he obeyed, trying not to notice how the ends of her shortened hair brushed against her skin or how the shape of her slender neck was newly exposed.

'I should tell you what I found out,' he said to distract himself as he worked. 'Owen Travers recently hired a notorious sellsword by the name of Naeve Sorrow. It's my belief that Travers arranged your father's murder in order to frame you for the crime. Tomorrow I intend to visit Sorrow's lodgings and see what I can uncover.'

'You know where she lives?' Ayla asked.

'I know where she lived five years ago.' Back then it had been his job to know that kind of thing. 'I'll start there and see how far I get.'

His hands were shaking, the blade veering dangerously close to cutting her; he badly needed a drink. Putting down the knife, he forced a smile into his voice. 'There. Finished.'

'Thank you.' She retrieved the weapon without looking at him, her head bent. 'Did you bring food? I'm hungry.'

'It's here.' Caraway handed her the loosely wrapped package of pastries, then watched as she proceeded to eat her share and most of his as well. For a slender woman, she certainly ate a lot. But the old Changer had been a spare man, and he'd consumed enough food for two as well. Perhaps there was something in their blood that required more fuel: after all, the energy required to Change must be immense.

When she'd finished, Ayla glanced up. 'Aren't you eating?'

He gestured silently at the empty wrappings.

'Oh …' A slight hint of colour touched her cheeks. The look she threw him was half apologetic, half defiant. 'Sorry. But it was my money.'

He didn't bother to tell her that the copper coin she'd given him that morning had all been spent on her breakfast; he just nodded and moved over to refold the blankets on the floor, preparing for sleep. When he straightened up she was still sitting in exactly the same position, head bowed, shoulders tense.

'It'll be all right,' he told her. 'I'll find out the truth, I promise I will.'

'And just exactly how much is your promise worth, Tomas Caraway?' Her voice was low and somehow sad, despite the aggressive words. He shook his head.

'Perhaps very little. But I'm all you've got.'

As they sat in silence in the darkening room, he on his side and she on hers, he suspected the same thought was uppermost in both their minds.

I just hope it's enough.

TWELVE

It was getting dark, and Travers took it personally. Striding through the streets of the first ring, he glared at the descending night with all the frustration of a man thwarted by an intangible enemy. Darkness made it easier for people to hide; it made it easier for Ayla to evade him. Every time he came down into Arkannen he convinced himself he would find her – that he would turn a corner or mount a flight of steps and there she'd be, waiting for him. Waiting to be dragged back to Darkhaven and locked up, under his power. The thought of it made his throat hurt. He had been waiting years for it: six long years, and she'd never so much as glanced his way in all that time. To begin with she had been too busy making eyes at Tomas Caraway; Travers had hated the son of a whore for that, feeling a gleeful satisfaction when Caraway's ill luck or poor judgement resulted in Kati's death and his own demotion from the Helm. Yet even with Caraway gone, Ayla never looked at Travers. Instead she became aloof and cold, an untouchable ice-maiden whose gaze brushed over him as though he were no more than furniture. Travers longed to grab her by the shoulders and shake the disdain right out of her.

She'd been barely more than a child when he began to want her, and a half-blood besides. He'd told himself he shouldn't desire her, that she was flawed by her mother's heritage. He had tried to convince himself that she wasn't a true Nightshade and that he was dishonouring the bloodline with his lust for something impure. Yet with the passing of the years, that belief had mutated. Contempt and longing had fused into a single, burning emotion: the conviction that whatever he did to her, she deserved it, for being a half-blood Changer and for looking at him as if she didn't really see him at all. Since she had murdered her father, the knowledge that he was entitled under law to punish her had gnawed at Travers, a hunger that never went away. And seeing Elisse had only made it worse. Her resemblance to Ayla was superficial, but those blue eyes and that long dark hair had awoken a physical ache in him that wouldn't subside.

Giving in to it, he turned on his heel and made for the nearest brothel.

The brothels of Arkannen were notorious for their ability to cater to every taste, however unusual, but Travers preferred to avoid the more exotic establishments. He had one requirement, and one requirement only. Stepping past the heavyset man at the door with a nod, he paid no attention to the provocatively dressed child offering him refreshment as soon as he entered the vestibule, or the madam of the house murmuring a list of the services her charges could offer. Instead, his practised eye scanned the girls arranged in various poses on the velvet-upholstered furniture until he found what he was looking for. In every brothel in the city, there was always at least one girl with pale skin, dark hair and blue eyes. It was rare colouring, aristocratic colouring; that made it prized, by some. For a short time, with a girl like that, Travers was able to pretend he'd got what he really longed for.

He gestured, and the madam nodded. The girl he had identified came weaving her way across the room, hips swaying in invitation. As she got closer, he saw that her dark hair was the result of imperfectly applied dye; really black hair was hardly ever produced by nature, save in the Nightshade line. Still, she would have to do. Moistening dry lips, he followed her through another door and down a corridor, already groping for the few coins that were the cost of ridding himself of desire, even if just for a night. Once inside the bedroom, he dropped the money onto the ornate table that stood by the door and glanced around. Bed, basin, battered armchair: it was all plain and poorly maintained, inappropriate for a lady of Darkhaven. The table was the only piece of furniture with any quality to it.

The girl had positioned herself on the bed in what was meant to be a seductive manner. Travers looked away from her painted lips and dark-lined eyes; they weren't what he wanted. Ayla never wore cosmetics.

'Come here,' he ordered with an impatient gesture. 'Bend over.'

Without demur she walked over to the table and leant her elbows on it, presenting herself to him. From behind, the dye was more convincing; she was just a slight, dark-haired girl. If he kept his gaze on her and on the carved table beneath her, he could believe he was back in Darkhaven. That he had walked into Ayla's bedroom at night, as he'd imagined so many times in the past, and forced her to submit to him ...

He fumbled with his breeches, fingers made clumsy by anticipation, breath harsh in his throat. Finally he got the fastening undone; lifting her flimsy skirt, he plunged himself in her to the hilt. The sensation was exquisite, almost over-whelming. Gripping her by the hair, he slammed against her again and again, words spilling out of him that belonged in the darkest places of his dreams until, finally, he groaned her name in the tumbling rush of climax.

'Ayla …'

Afterwards, he felt as cold and ashamed as he always did, but at least he was free of it for a while. He bent his head and refastened his breeches, trying not to look at the room. Now, all he wanted was to get out.

'So.' The girl eyed him, cocky, as she collected the scat-tered coins from the table. 'Got a thing for the royal family, 'ave we?' She laughed. 'You'd be surprised 'ow many men come in 'ere askin' for a little bit of Changer magic. Keeps me in business, any rate.'

Travers looked at her sharp, world-weary face and itched to slap her. Already he could feel the hunger starting to build again, the desire for something more than a temporary illu-sion. The desire to have Ayla in his power for good. Without a word he left the room, heading back out to the street.

This obsession is making a fool of you, Owen Travers, he told himself, full of self-disgust. *Get a grip.* But it was no use. Every time he thought he'd managed to put it aside for a while, he remembered that he was now allowed to punish Ayla. That Lord Florentyn had expected him to do it – if not quite in the way he had in mind. That by locking her up, he would be answering both his own desire and his obligations to the Nightshade line. The knowledge made the need to find her burn ever hotter in his veins.

He caught a tram back to the Gate of Flame, then another through the second ring to the Gate of Wind, scanning every face he passed on the lamplit streets for dark blue eyes with a hint of green. He was some way into the third ring when he remembered he was still carrying Elisse's groceries in his pockets, tea and biscuits he'd bought in the first ring earlier. It was too late to have them sent over now; he'd have to take them himself. He sighed. At least the safe house was on his route back to Darkhaven.

There was a short way round and a long way round from the Gate of Wood to the Gate of Steel. Members of the wealthier professions inhabited the more convenient south side of the fourth ring, with the poorer quarters to the north. Once Travers had been a hungry small boy growing up in a one-roomed flat in Larimar, looking after his younger brother and running errands to earn a few extra coins while his father struggled to bring the two of them up alone on a lamplighter's pay. In those days Travers hadn't possessed much in the way of ambition, beyond the desire for a full belly and a bed of his own to sleep in. But that was before the night a gang had broken into the flat and stabbed his father to death, mistaking him for an informant. In an attempt to leave no witnesses, they'd stabbed the two boys as well. Travers had only survived by lying perfectly still and quiet in a pool of his family's mingled blood, watching in mute anguish as the life drained from his brother's eyes.

Once the gang had gone, he'd stumbled south – dizzy from shock and loss of blood – to the Ametrine Quarter. It was a Helmsman who'd found him, a Helmsman who'd taken him in and listened to his story. And it was Florentyn Nightshade himself who'd helped to capture the offenders and oversee their execution. Ever since then, Travers had been driven by a single aim, or perhaps more truthfully two: to serve Florentyn in whatever way he could, and to reinvest the Helm with the power they required to make sure nothing like what had happened to his family would ever happen again. He'd worked hard to learn everything he needed in order to achieve those aims – and he hadn't been back to Larimar since that blood-soaked night. There was nothing left for him there.

He passed the imposing frontages of Charoite and Cerussite with barely a glance, and stepped with an indefinable feeling of relief into Ametrine. Although Darkhaven was his primary home now, he always considered his roots to be here, among the yellow-purple stone of the Ametrine Quarter. The colour reminded him vividly of bruised flesh, appropriate for the houses of Helmsmen and soldiers; he often thought that whoever designed Arkannen's fourth ring must have had a sly sense of humour. Tonight the roads were quiet, only a few pedestrians and the occasional carriage crossing between the pools of light shed by the street lamps. Travers took a deep breath, drawing the mingled scents of sword oil, leather cream and antiseptic into his lungs to overlay the constant undertones of horse manure, lamp fuel and coal smoke that pervaded the city. Take him anywhere in Arkannen, and he'd be able to tell where he was even with his eyes closed.

As he entered the Avenue of Rowans, he became aware of another smell: something singed and acrid. It was out of place, and so he stopped, scanning his surroundings. Fewer lamps lined this street than the main thoroughfare, allowing shadows to pool thick and black in the spaces between them, but nothing appeared to be stirring – in fact, the street was deserted. Maybe someone had burned their evening meal. Travers shrugged off his doubt and carried on walking, but he kept one hand near the hilt of his sword. He had been involved in too many street brawls not to rely on his instincts now.

The burnt smell grew stronger with every pace he took towards his destination. It was almost familiar, though he couldn't place it. Then, from one of the side alleys that branched off the street like capillaries from a vein, he heard a distinct sound: a scraping noise, perhaps a blade coming out of its sheath or a steel-capped boot on stone. Someone was there. His sword was in his hand before he had finished turning to face the alley mouth.

'Who's there?' Moonlight streaked the alley, but the far end was in darkness; he peered into the shadows, fighting the creeping unease that climbed up and down his spine. 'This is Captain Travers of the Helm speaking. Show yourself!'

There was no response, but the scraping grew louder. Now it was accompanied by a rattling hiss, like steam escaping from a valve. Some kind of machinery? The hot smell, the sounds of metal and pressurised steam – it all suggested a manufactory or an ironworks, but of course that made no sense. Travers took a few steps into the alley, blade angled in the direction of the noise.

'Whoever you are and whatever you're doing down there, I advise you to come out before I come in and get you.'

The reply was a low, menacing growl that vibrated through the soles of his feet. It conveyed a message that bypassed his brain and went straight to his gut, leaving him quiveringly certain of one thing: that was no machine. Whatever was down there, it was a living, breathing creature – and it wasn't happy.

On legs that felt suddenly too weak to support him, Travers stumbled backwards, just about managing to keep his sword steady in his hand. At the end of the alley, a dark shape coalesced from the shadows, emerging into the open like a nightmare made flesh. As it stalked towards Travers, it passed in and out of the stripes of moonlight that cut across the alley between the silhouettes of neighbouring roofs, so he saw it in slices: a glint of pointed teeth, a vast clawed foot, a flash of silver on gleaming black scales. No doubt about it: this was the creature that had killed Florentyn Nightshade and attacked a priestess in the sixth ring. Nothing that large, that powerful, could possibly exist without being the product of Changer blood.

'Ayla?' he said, half certain, and was unsurprised to hear the tremor in his own voice. In response, the creature darted forward with a speed that belied its size, the scrape of its claws and the hiss of its scaled tail against the stone providing an eerie counterpoint to the rush of his blood. A jet of flame shot past his head; he felt the scorching heat of it, heard the sizzle as his right eyebrow singed. Travers sidestepped and pivoted, bringing his blade up in defence.

'Come on, then, you bitch,' he flung at the creature, heart pounding, seized by mad exhilaration. 'Come and try me.'

He didn't even have the chance to dodge a second time. The creature came in low, its jaws clamping around his leg and yanking him off his feet with all the force of a team of horses. His head hit the paved surface of the street hard enough that his vision blurred and he almost lost his grip on his sword, but he hung on grimly, gritting his teeth against the searing pain that raced through his body in both directions. Blinking to clear his wavering sight, he twisted his body round and took a wild swing at the creature, aiming for the neck. The steel blade bounced off as though the scaled hide were made of stone, leaving the hilt ringing in his hands; with a curse he dropped it, but it had been enough of a distraction to make the creature's jaws relax in momentary surprise. Travers scrambled free and backed away, his wounded leg buckling under him with each step. This was the trouble with Changers, even the half-blood ones. In animal form, they were virtually indestructible.

He looked around for his lost sword, but it was lying almost under the feet of the creature, and he didn't have any other weapon to hand. He considered running, but he knew he wouldn't get very far with one leg that could barely hold his weight. So, deliberately, he straightened up and gave the creature a long, slow look, taking in wings and scales and claws and teeth, seeing where it was like a Griffin and where like a Hydra, searching for possible weak spots. It might have butchered Florentyn, but there was always a chance it might not do the same to him – and next time, he'd be forewarned.

'You won't kill me, Ayla,' he said, flashing a defiant grin. 'You wouldn't dare. Kill again, and you'll lose all hope of ever being pardoned for your crimes.'

Then the mighty jaws closed over his shoulder, those vicious teeth piercing his flesh, and the white-hot pain of it sent him hurtling into oblivion.

THIRTEEN

He was locked in a metal coffin, trapped between four small walls, and someone was hammering the final nail into the lid. *Thud. Thud. Thud.* Gasping for air, he fought to free himself, struggling against the winding sheet that bound his arms tightly to his sides – and still the pounding continued. *Thud. Thud. Thud.*

With a shuddering breath, Myrren jerked awake. The bedclothes had tangled themselves around his body; he flung them off, panting, and sat up. He felt hot and prickly all over, as though his skin were a size too small.

Thud. Thud. Thud. The noise from his dream still echoed through his head. He rubbed his eyes, disoriented, and realised someone was knocking at his door. The knowledge was like cold water to the face, dashing away the last vestiges of sleep. He swung his legs out of bed and reached for a robe, shivering as the cool breeze from the window brushed over his naked skin. For a moment he was reminded of the morning after his father's death, when he had woken to the sound of the warning bell. He'd slept poorly that night as well, his mind too full of anxiety to switch itself off. He hoped this time it wasn't a presentiment of disaster.

Robe belted tightly around him, he stumbled to the door and opened it. A young Helmsman stood on the other side, his hand already raised to knock again.

'Please, my lord, you have to come quickly,' he said. 'It's Captain Travers.'

Travers was lying on a stretcher in the mess hall, Darkhaven's physician beside him; a huddle of agitated Helmsmen stood off to one side, muttering to each other. As Myrren drew nearer, he saw the vivid scarlet stains on the captain's tattered uniform and felt sinking dread meet rising nausea somewhere at the base of his throat.

'Is he – is he –'

'No, my lord.' The physician looked up with a reassuring smile, responding to the query Myrren had been unable to put into words. 'Just unconscious.'

The heavy doors to the hall creaked again, signalling another arrival, and Myrren turned quickly. To his relief it was Serenna, accompanied by the man he'd sent to fetch her. He started to angle himself so that her view of Travers' bloodied form would be restricted, then remembered how little she had been affected by the sight of his father's corpse. She might be a priestess, but her stomach for unpleasant things was far more robust than his.

'His wounds are less severe than they look,' the physician said, reclaiming Myrren's attention. 'By far the greater effect on his constitution will come from lying undiscovered in the night air for a bell or so after the attack. We're lucky it's summer, my lord, indeed we are. He'll be able to leave his bed after a day or two.'

Lucky wasn't the word Myrren would have used for any of this. He forced himself to ask the question to which he was afraid he already knew the answer. 'What exactly happened to him?'

'Well, my lord ...' Suddenly the physician wasn't looking him in the eye. 'The shape of the wounds is consistent with having been inflicted by the teeth of some, ah, powerful animal.'

'Like the wounds on my father's body,' Myrren said quietly, and the physician gave an uncomfortable nod.

'Quite so, my lord.'

Unable to help himself, Myrren stepped closer. One of Travers' legs and both his forearms were already bandaged, but his torso was yet to be treated. The physician had got as far as cutting his uniform aside to reveal a wound at the join between shoulder and neck, which gleamed wet and red in the light from the windows. Even without any medical training, Myrren could tell it wasn't in the shape of a blade. No, something had very obviously taken a bite out of the man.

'May I see?' Serenna moved nearer, to crouch down beside the physician. *Definitely a stronger stomach for unpleasant things.* Swallowing hard, Myrren turned to the group of Helmsmen waiting by the wall.

'Which of you found him?'

A moment's silence; then one of the older men spoke up with a faint country burr. 'None of us, my lord. It was two o' the watch on their rounds. They sent a message to the fifth ring, and some o' the Helm who were there for the night went down to see what was going on.'

'We thought he'd been stabbed.' A second man took over the narrative. 'Thieves trying to steal his money, or a criminal with a grudge against the Helm ... though as every thug in this city knows, Captain Travers is more than capable of defending himself.'

'In Ametrine as well,' a third Helmsman mumbled. 'With all those fightin' men around, you'd think someone woulda seen somethin'.'

Myrren's eyes narrowed, his attention caught. 'Then it happened in the fourth ring?'

'They found him in the Ametrine Quarter, m'lord.' The man looked nervous beneath the intensity of Myrren's stare. 'Avenue of Rowans.'

That name again. Myrren scanned the faces in front of him, looking for signs that any of them knew more than they were letting on, but the eyes that looked back at him were blank in their honesty. If he wanted any more information, he'd have to get it out of Captain Travers himself – once he came round.

Myrren spun on his heel and walked over to the window, where he stood gazing at the central square beyond without really seeing it. There was something odd about all this, something that nagged at the edges of his mind, but he couldn't grasp even what kind of thing it was, let alone the specifics of it.

'Lord Myrren?' Serenna's quick footsteps crossed the tiled floor towards him. He didn't look round as she joined him at the window.

'The physician is right,' she murmured, keeping her voice low enough that only he would be able to hear her. 'The same creature attacked both your father and Captain Travers.'

The harder Myrren tried to catch the elusive thought, the quicker it slipped away. With a sigh for his own incompetence, he turned and gave Serenna a nod of acknowledgement, inviting her to continue.

'Surely this confirms our suspicions.' The movement of her lips was barely visible beneath the gauzy veil. 'There is

117

another Changer in the city, living at the address you found. Captain Travers has fallen foul of his own secret.'

'The evidence would appear to point that way.'

'But?'

'But ...' Myrren struggled to find the appropriate words, still unsure why he was so uneasy. 'Does it not seem rather a coincidence to you? That I should discover the address, only for an attack to take place there that very night?'

'If the Avenue of Rowans truly is where the rogue Changer is hiding, and if the creature is as unstable as we believe it to be, then it was only a matter of time before an attack took place there,' Serenna said. 'Do you still want to go there today?'

Myrren hesitated, then shook his head. 'The street will be crawling with Helmsmen after last night's attack. And if I give the slightest hint that I suspect something, they'll lose no time in moving their charge elsewhere.'

Serenna's eyebrows lifted under the veil. 'Even when their captain has just been viciously wounded by the creature?'

'Even then.' Myrren shrugged. 'Travers made it clear to me that the Helm are still following my father's orders, despite his demise. If Florentyn told them to keep his third child a secret then that's what they'll do.'

That sense of something wrong, of a piece of the puzzle he hadn't quite slotted into place, still lurked at the edge of his mind; he pushed it away.

'All the same, this attack surely vindicates Ayla. Even if she wanted to hurt Travers, she'd have no way of knowing where to find him.'

'Perhaps.' Serenna's voice was apologetic. 'Unless she caught sight of him in the lower rings and followed him for that very purpose.'

She was right. Myrren's shoulders slumped as he faced, once again, the possibility that Ayla was guilty. But if that were so, what was it the Helm were hiding in the Avenue of Rowans? No, he had to believe she was innocent. Otherwise he'd go mad with the knowledge that by letting her out of prison, he'd killed his own father.

'You know, both the night that Florentyn died and last night, I suffered some very odd nightmares,' he said, to convince himself as much as Serenna. 'I can't help wondering whether that's what it feels like, when this unknown Changer takes his creature form. Maybe his madness makes him feel different to me from how Ayla feels.'

'You sense it, then? When someone else Changes? Even though ...' She stopped, biting her lip.

'Even though I can't Change myself?' he supplied for her. 'Yes. That part of my heritage, at least, I received as I should.' That sounded far too self-pitying; he forced a light-hearted note into his voice. 'Some small consolation for Florentyn, I suppose.'

'Tell me about him,' Serenna said softly.

'Who, my father? He was fully thirty feet long from nose to tail-tip. Scales like polished bronze. Vast wings tipped with spikes, and four sets of truly vicious talons –'

'I meant as a person,' she chided him, though she was smiling. Myrren lifted a shoulder. How could he explain that to him, his father *was* his Firedrake self? That Myrren's personal acquaintance with those talons had made it hard to see beyond them?

In the silence, Serenna's smile faded. 'I hope you don't mind if I ask ... when did you first know for sure that you hadn't inherited the gift?'

Myrren's first impulse was to tell her sharply that he did mind, and that he didn't appreciate her curiosity. That

if she wanted him to keep his distance from her, he had a
right to expect she would do the same for him. Yet although
her voice had been soft, it held no hint of embarrassment,
and in her eyes he saw only frank enquiry. Once again she
offered him neither pity nor judgement, and for that he felt
he owed her something.

'Usually the gift manifests itself when the Changer is fourteen,' he said, looking out of the window to avoid watching
her reactions. 'To begin with my father thought I was a late
developer. He had Changed on his fourteenth birthday, but
my mother was nearly fifteen before she showed her creature-
self for the first time; it was possible I took after her. Yet
fifteen came and went, and still I gave no sign. It frustrated
Florentyn, but Kati – Ayla's mother – used to talk him out
of his anger. *He'll come to it in his own time,* she'd say. *You
can't punish the boy for something he can't help.*

'Then, soon after my fifteenth birthday, Kati died.' Myrren
swallowed, fighting back a surge of remembered emotion.
'Her death destroyed my father. It made him bitter. For a time,
he … focused all his attention on me. He was determined
to rouse the Changer gift in me, by any means necessary.'

Myrren darted a sideways glance at Serenna, but the understanding he saw in her face nearly undid him. He couldn't
tell her about the trials his father had made him undergo:
the half-drowning, the push from a window, the unexpected
attack by ten men of the Helm. All trying to awaken something in him, to surprise him into revealing the gift Florentyn
couldn't believe he didn't have. Until finally, near the end of
it, his father had Changed before turning on him.

Myrren still remembered in vivid detail the gleaming teeth,
the gouts of flame, the rending claws. The description he'd
given Serenna was nothing to the reality of it. He had truly

thought he was going to die, that day. He'd done everything in his power to escape. But the one thing that *hadn't* been in his power, no matter how he willed it, was the only thing that mattered to his father.

After that, Florentyn's attempts to rouse the gift in him had continued more out of dogged determination than any real hope. It was obvious to both of them that if Myrren couldn't be spurred into Changing by the threat of an angry Firedrake, he simply didn't have it in him. And so all those relentless trials had achieved no more for him than an impressive set of scars and an acute sense of his own failure. The old desperate longing to become what his father wanted him to be rose up in his throat, nearly choking him.

'Then, when Ayla turned fourteen, she Changed for the first time,' he said, rushing now, anxious to reach the conclusion as swiftly as possible. 'I was sixteen by then, and it was clear I was never going to Change myself. That, coupled with Ayla's unusual animal form, sent Florentyn into a rage that lasted for days. When he came out of it ...' Myrren shrugged. 'It was as though he'd lost all interest in us as his children. We were just a bad situation he had to make the best of. And the way he eventually chose to do that was to make Ayla his heir instead of me.'

'Until I was attacked, and she was the only possible suspect.' Serenna's voice was soft. 'Then tell me, my lord: if we are able to prove Ayla's innocence, will you stand aside and let her take the throne?'

'She doesn't want it,' Myrren said. 'But I think it would be best for Mirrorvale. What use is a Nightshade overlord without the power to Change?'

Serenna's cool hands came to rest on his, stilling them. He realised he had been turning the bloodstained scale from his pocket over and over in his fingers, displaying his inner agitation to the world. His father would have given him a dressing-down for that. With a quick, blind smile in Serenna's direction, he slipped his hands out from under hers and returned the scale to his pocket.

'Lord Myrren –' she began, but whatever she was about to say was overridden by a call from the physician.

'My lord! I believe he is coming round.'

Leaving the window, Myrren hurried back to the physician's side. Travers was now fully bandaged, and the physician was holding a phial of smelling salts under his nose. Even as Myrren reached them, the captain's eyelids flickered and lifted.

'Captain Travers.' Myrren leaned down to address him. 'How are you feeling?'

An insubordinate gleam entered the pale blue eyes. 'Better than dead, my lord.'

Myrren longed to ask him straight out what he had been doing in the Avenue of Rowans, but of course he couldn't. The Ametrine Quarter was a perfectly normal place for Travers to be, and if Myrren gave any indication that he recognised the significance of the address, he would only warn the Helm that he was on the trail of their secret.

'Can you tell us what happened?' he asked instead.

'She chewed me up and spat me out.' Travers managed a crooked smile, though his face was drawn. 'Got a nasty temper, your half-blood sister.'

Myrren clenched his fists, trying to prevent his rising temper from bursting out of him; it would do him no good to shout at an injured man in front of his loyal followers. 'Please describe what you saw, Captain Travers.'

'It was waiting for me in the shadows,' Travers said, gasping. 'It breathed fire, like Lord Florentyn's Firedrake.

Had wings, too. But the scales and tail were like a Hydra's ... the claws like a Griffin's ...' He closed his eyes for a moment, perhaps seeking strength, then opened them again and said clearly, 'A hybrid creature, my lord. Not one of the true Changer forms. What else could it be but Ayla?'

You tell me. Myrren bit the words back and said, as calmly as he could, 'The creature you have just described does not correspond to the form Ayla takes.'

'With all due respect, my lord –' Travers took in a sharp, pained breath – 'we have only your word for that.'

'Captain Travers, much as it may grieve you to realise it, I am now the overlord of Darkhaven.' Myrren's voice came out loaded with such vehemence that even he was surprised. 'I – not my father, and not the Helm – am in charge here. So if you want to keep the position you so evidently prize, I suggest you stop doubting my word. Immediately.'

There was silence. Myrren looked up: the physician was hovering protectively over his patient, and beyond him the Helmsmen stood pale-faced and wordless. Serenna was still by the window; Myrren couldn't be sure, with the veil concealing her expression, but he thought she looked approving.

'Now, captain,' he said softly, returning his attention to Travers. 'Is there anything you've been keeping from me that you wish to tell me – anything at all?'

Travers stared up at him, a vertical line between his brows as if he was trying to work something out. After a moment he shook his head, the smile returning to his face: a smile that said he knew something Myrren didn't.

'No, my lord,' he answered. 'There's nothing.'

FOURTEEN

It was the middle of the night when Caraway woke up – he could tell by the colour of the sky outside, a smoky blue-grey charcoal lit only by the glow of the city's lamps. For an instant he wasn't sure what had woken him; then he turned his head and saw Ayla. She was sitting upright on the bed, her arms wrapped around her bent knees, her eyes wide in the darkness.

'Lady Ayla?' he whispered.

'I had a bad dream.' She sounded like a little girl, younger even than she'd been when he first met her. 'I thought my father was coming to find me ...' Her voice shook, and he realised she was shivering.

'You're cold,' he said. He tried to think of something to give her for warmth, something more than just her cloak to sleep in, but she'd already rejected the blankets. After a moment's hesitation, he sighed and shrugged off his coat. 'Here.'

She made no objection as he placed it around her shoulders, nor did she resist the pressure of his hand as he eased her back down into a lying position.

'It was exactly how it used to be when he was alive and I felt him Change,' she said, almost to herself. 'Like icy fingers prickling over my skin. Strange – I felt it the night he died.'

Already Caraway could feel her shivers lessening beneath his spread palm, the presence of the extra layer driving out the chill. He crossed back to his side of the room and looked ruefully at the thin blankets on the floor. By now he was familiar with every nail and splinter in the floorboards, and without his coat to protect him he had no doubt that the acquaintance would be furthered considerably.

'Tomas?' Ayla's voice was small and somehow far away, as if she were speaking to him from beyond the threshold of sleep. 'Do you think it's wrong of me to be relieved that he's dead?'

Caraway swallowed over the ache in his throat. 'No, Ayla. I don't.'

She said nothing more, and soon the rhythm of her breathing changed. Caraway lay awake and uncomfortable until dawn, wondering whether it really had been just a nightmare, or whether he should reconsider the possibility he had previously dismissed as too difficult to investigate: the possibility that there was another Changer in Arkannen.

In the morning Ayla handed him his coat without a word, but he saw something in her eyes he hadn't seen before. He thought it might be gratitude, or at least the beginnings of it. Perhaps she was starting to accept that he might not be all bad – in which case, he'd better not say anything about how shaky he was feeling after an entire day without alcohol.

It's pathetic, Caraway, he told himself. *You weren't nearly this desperate even a month ago.* Yet at some point over the last few weeks, he had given up even trying not to succumb to the lure of an ale-cup. Maybe Ayla had re-entered his life just in time.

'I'll get you some breakfast,' he told her, shrugging the coat back on, and she nodded.

'Do you need more money?'

The question was asked in condescending tones, dissolving in an instant the tentative rapport he'd thought was growing between them. Perhaps he had imagined that look in her eyes. Perhaps it had only been wishful thinking.

'I've got enough,' he mumbled. Avoiding her gaze – he just knew she was about to ask where he'd got the money from, and he didn't think what remained of his battered pride could take the admission that it was given to him as an act of charity – he ducked out of the room and went to find food.

Once he'd taken care of Ayla's breakfast, Caraway set off in search of one of Arkannen's most notorious sellswords. Naeve Sorrow didn't live in the fourth ring – or at least, she hadn't five years ago. Instead, like Caraway, she rented a place in the first ring, amongst the frantic and never-ending activity of the city's industry. Unlike Caraway, however, her presence there was through choice rather than necessity. She lived in an expensive suite of rooms overlooking the Floating Gardens, which meant that rather than the stink of animal skins and waste, she woke every morning to birdsong and the scent of rare flowers. As for what she'd done to earn the money she needed to live in a place like that … well, Caraway had heard the rumours, but none of them had ever been substantiated. That was why she could charge so much. All anyone knew was that she'd do anything if she was paid enough, and whether it was legal or not didn't come into the equation. She'd been a thorn in the heel of the Helm for as long as Caraway could remember, which was why it was so odd that Travers should have hired her … unless, of course, the Captain of the Helm was doing something he didn't want anyone else to find out about.

Caraway's route to the Floating Gardens took him through the fashionable shopping district, so he made a brief detour to a high-class perruquier. The painted and perfumed female wig-maker looked at him askance when he walked through the door – a man who needed a good shave and wore a coat with holes in the elbows wouldn't usually be welcome in such an establishment – but as soon as Caraway revealed the glossy strands of Ayla's hair, everything changed. Caraway was offered a glass of fresh pomegranate juice and some ever-so-discreet bartering, before escaping with a blonde wig and two ranols in his pocket. He got the impression that the perruquier didn't care if he'd slaughtered a Nightshade and thrown the body into the river, so long as she got hold of that hair. No doubt some wealthy lady would cause a sensation by wearing it to her next social function.

Swinging the bag containing the new wig, Caraway crossed the Half-Moon Bridge and entered the Floating Gardens. One of Arkannen's most popular attractions, the gardens had been created by deliberately flooding an area of the city beside the river. A series of vast rafts drifted on the surface of the water, a chain of man-made islands linked by wooden walkways. Each raft was layered with enough earth to allow plants and even small trees to take root, and rare specimens had been brought in from every corner of Mirrorvale as well as its neighbouring countries. As a result, the gardens were a haven for waterfowl and other birds; their calls, combined with the splashing of the water over artificial rockeries and miniature waterfalls, made the place seem like a small portion of countryside within the walls of the city. In winter coloured lanterns were hung in the trees, but now – at the height of summer – the air was full of the drone of insects and the warm soft scents of open flowers.

I should bring Ayla here, Caraway thought. *She'd probably like it.* Then he remembered how unlikely he was to do anything of the kind: even if the blonde wig was sufficient disguise for Ayla to visit such a public place, and even if they had the time to spare from the investigation they had undertaken, there was no reason why she would want to go anywhere with him on a social basis. For her, their association was no more than an inconvenient but necessary business arrangement.

Annoyed with himself, he hurried along the walkways without looking too closely at the beauty around him. Sorrow's rooms were on the far side, part of a tall white building that rose up out of the gardens like a ship floating on the surface of the water. Caraway glanced at the double-faced clock set into the upper part of the wall: the hand on the inner dial was pointing to the top left corner, while the hand on the outer dial pointed almost directly right. About halfway through second bell – Sorrow could easily have left for the day by now. Still, there was only one way to find out. He had already decided not to walk up to her front door and start asking her questions; if she was working for Travers, there was no chance she'd answer them. Instead, he positioned himself in the shadow of the floral archway that was the exit closest to the building, and settled down to wait.

He could see why Sorrow chose to live here, if live here she still did: it was a tranquil part of town. The clatter of the trams was never completely inaudible anywhere in the lower rings, but here it faded to a muted rumble like the merest hint of thunder on the horizon. Far clearer was the bird singing somewhere nearby; Caraway thought it was probably a honeyfinch. He closed his eyes as the dappled sunlight danced over his face, a changing pattern created by the leaves of the scarlet creeper overhead as they fluttered in the breeze. For an instant he was a child again, before he left home, before he came to Arkannen to fulfil the single bright dream of his life and saw it crumble into despair. A child in a summer meadow, with all of life's vast possibility ahead of him …

The abrupt whirring of the clock shattered the illusion. Caraway opened his eyes, regrets and pressures settling back on him like a heavy weight, as it chimed the third bell in ragged unison with the more distant clocks throughout the city. At the same time, the front door of the building ahead of him opened and a woman with very short fair hair emerged, carrying a holdall. Caraway didn't need the twin swords strapped to her back or the air of aggression she exuded to tell him this was Naeve Sorrow; she looked exactly the same as she had five years ago. Relief pouring through him – that she still lived here, that she was only just leaving her rooms, that he hadn't missed her by daydreaming – he let her get some way ahead, then left the shelter of the archway and followed her.

Sorrow was of average height and build, for a woman, but her reputation made her seem larger. As she strode through the streets of the first ring, anyone who knew anything about her did their utmost not to get in her way. That meant she was easy to follow – the swathe of bowed heads and averted gazes she left behind her was as conspicuous as the tram tracks that partially encircled the lower rings – but it also made it hard to stay out of sight. Several times Caraway had to turn aside or stay well back for fear of being noticed; after all, his quarry wasn't exactly a novice to this game, and he had no doubt that if she spotted him she would either turn on him or give him the slip – neither of which was a

129

desirable outcome when all he wanted was to find out where she was going.

Once she reached the second ring, Sorrow hopped on a tram and rode it round to the Gate of Wind, which gave Caraway time to relax. He stood at the opposite end of the carriage from her and kept her visible from the corner of his eye, but other than that he was free to let his thoughts wander. Inevitably, they returned to Ayla, where they lingered with a sort of self-indulgent misery. He was almost glad when Sorrow got off the tram and he had to concentrate on following her again, passing through the Gate of Wind and into the third ring. As usual, the ground around the gate was plastered with old news-sheets that people had read and discarded. Caraway looked down and saw Florentyn Nightshade's face staring back at him; he imagined disapproval in the dark eyes and the tight-pressed lips.

I'm doing my best, my lord, he told the old Changer silently. *I won't let your daughter down like I did her mother. I promise.*

He almost lost Sorrow a couple of times in the freight sector of the third ring; several large airships had come in with cargoes, and the unloading areas were bustling with activity. Finally both of them reached the fourth ring, where Sorrow turned left, taking the south road towards the Gate of Steel. Caraway followed with a degree of unease. This way led to the Ametrine Quarter, which meant Helmsmen – and the last thing he wanted was to draw any of his former colleagues' attention to himself. What was more, if it turned out that Sorrow was heading for the fifth ring, he already knew he wouldn't be able to follow her. Of course, she might simply be going for some weapons training or sparring practice: being in the pay of Owen Travers didn't mean that every single thing she did would be on his behalf. Thus for all Caraway knew, this exercise might turn out to be completely pointless. Still, he'd come this far. He didn't want to return to Ayla and tell her he'd given up unless he absolutely had to.

There were fewer crowds up here during the day than there were in the lower rings, which made Caraway feel conspicuous. Eventually he jogged up a side alley until he reached a street that ran parallel to the main road on the inner part of the curve. Once there, the shorter distances made it easy to catch up with Sorrow and then keep her in sight down the alleys that connected the two streets. In that way they passed through Obsidian, Charoite and Cerussite, until finally – in the Ametrine Quarter, the one Caraway had been dreading – Sorrow didn't appear at the end of one of the alleys. Caraway sprinted down it, and caught sight of her going up one of the streets that branched off the opposite side of the road. The Avenue of Rowans. So she was going to visit someone in the Helm.

He reached the near end of the avenue in time to see Sorrow turning left down a side alley. She had quickened her pace, and he could see why. A little further up the road, several Helmsmen were gathered – more than were commonly to be found standing in the street, even in the Ametrine Quarter. A crime scene? Some sort of accident? Caraway didn't stop to wonder any further. He followed in Sorrow's footsteps, only to find that she had paused at the end of the alley and was looking back over her shoulder. He retreated in the direction of the street, pulse racing, wondering if she had seen him. Then he was forced to step aside into the concealment of a doorway as two of the Helm walked past. He stood there hardly daring to breathe, willing them not to look in his direction, but they appeared to be too deep in conversation to notice him.

'... wasn't just an ordinary stabbing or a theft that went wrong?' one of the men was saying. The other shook his head.

'Seems it was the same creature that killed the old Changer. Must've happened late last night ...'

Then they had moved on past, leaving Caraway frowning. Another attack: that would fit with Ayla's nightmare, if such it could be called. The same creature had struck again, and she had felt it Change. Which, as far as he could see, proved two things. First, there was indeed another Changer in Arkannen, making his task both harder and more confusing. If Travers hadn't hired Sorrow to kill Florentyn, it was hard to see where she fitted into the picture – though, of course, it was possible he was about to find out. Second, and far more important, Ayla wasn't guilty of her father's murder. How could she be? She hadn't left the first ring last night. So if the same creature had carried out both attacks, she wasn't responsible for either.

Caraway had never believed her guilty – or at least, he had never wanted to believe it – but all the same, the conclusion made him buoyant. It was all he could do to stop himself whistling as he followed Sorrow through the back alleys to rejoin the Avenue of Rowans a short way beyond the milling Helmsmen. The houses here were in one long terrace, several stories high. Caraway lurked in an alley mouth and watched as Sorrow crossed the street to open one of the front doors, then disappeared inside.

Once he was sure she wasn't going to come back out straight away, he emerged into the middle of the road and stood looking at the house. The windows looked back at him, empty and secretive. An ordinary terraced house of the kind that Helm families often shared. What would Sorrow be doing here? Perhaps he should just walk up to the door and turn the handle, try and find out which flat she had gone into.

He was about to approach it when a flash of movement caught his eye. He froze, staring up at the top floor of the building. If he was seeing what he thought he was seeing, he knew exactly which flat Sorrow had entered.

Because there was a woman at the window. And she looked an awful lot like Ayla.

FIFTEEN

The knock at the door came at the same time as the clock on the mantel chimed the fourth bell, startling Elisse out of a doze. She struggled upright, yawning and rubbing her eyes. Her hair was all rumpled from lying against the cushioned arm of the chaise longue; she smoothed it down before getting to her feet and going to open the door. There was a woman standing on the landing outside, a leather holdall in one hand. She had cropped blonde hair that looked almost white against her honey-coloured skin, and her face was set in a forbidding scowl.

'You shouldn't have answered the door,' she snapped before Elisse could say a word. 'I could have been anyone.'

Elisse's gaze moved from the woman's face to the row of throwing-knives strapped across her chest, and then back up to the twin sword hilts protruding over her shoulders. Since no normal person walked around carrying enough weaponry to sink a merchant barge, this must be the bodyguard Travers had promised. Elisse retreated a few steps as the woman stepped into the hall and closed the door behind her.

'I was expecting ya,' she offered in an attempt at self-defence, but her new bodyguard shrugged it off.

'Doesn't matter. If you want to stay alive, you have to be cautious.'

Leaving her bag lying on the floor as though she expected Elisse to pick it up, she strode into the living room and over to the front window, where she set an eye to the narrow gap between the drapes without actually touching them.

'What –' Elisse began, but the woman waved her to silence.

'On my way here, I suspected I was being followed,' she said, still peering out at the street. 'Now I'm sure of it. There's a man standing outside, watching this house.'

She turned on her heel and marched back to the door, brushing past Elisse, who was still hesitating just inside the room.

'Stay here,' she flung over her shoulder, before leaving as quickly as she had come. Half nervous and half curious, Elisse stole over to the window and peeped through the gap. The bodyguard was right: there was a man standing on the opposite side of the street. Elisse didn't think she recognised him, but it was hard to be sure. She pulled one of the drapes aside ever so slightly, leaning forward in order to see better, then froze.

The man had noticed her.

He was looking directly at her.

She had an instant to take him in: brown hair and skin, an arrested expression on his face. Then he turned and hurried away, slipping down the first side alley he reached. Next moment the blonde woman appeared on the street where he had been, looking left and right with an irritated frown, some kind of black metal device in one hand. Biting her lip, Elisse drew back from the window before she could be seen. She really didn't want her new bodyguard to know that she was the one who had inadvertently scared off the stranger. She had no idea who the man was or what he wanted, but from what she had seen of the two of them, the woman was by far the more intimidating.

By the time the blonde woman walked back into the room, Elisse was at a safe distance from the window and felt able to meet her glower with an enquiring glance. 'Who was it?'

'I don't know. He'd gone before I got down there.'

That metal device was still in her hand. Elisse eyed it with some trepidation as she said, 'Ya didn' tell me ya name.'

The woman flicked her a quick, dismissive look. She was clearly still on the alert, poised on the balls of her feet as she scanned the opulence around her. 'Naeve Sorrow.'

'Sorrow,' Elisse repeated. 'As in sadness?'

'As in Sorrow.' The woman's mouth was an inflexible line, and not even the ghost of a smile appeared in her eyes. Elisse wondered whether she and Owen Travers had been separated at birth.

'I'm Elisse,' she said.

'I know who you are.' Sorrow crossed the room to scrutinise the kitchen, then went over to open the door to the bedroom, still clutching that strange weapon. Elisse stood and watched her, unsettled, but fascinated as well. It was like the time a feral cat had got in through the farmhouse window and prowled stiff-legged around the furniture, suspicion bristling from every hair and very obviously not domesticated.

'I think I would've noticed if there was anyone hiding in here,' she said finally, when Sorrow showed no sign of letting up. 'D'ya want a cuppa?'

Her new bodyguard didn't reply, but her own question reminded her that Owen Travers had never returned with her groceries. Still, she wasn't running as low as she would have had him believe; she'd be all right for a few days yet.

Or rather, *they'd* be all right. Sorrow was now going to be living here too. The thought filled Elisse with dread.

'What kinda weapon is that, anyway?' she asked in a desperate attempt to make some connection with the woman. To her relief, Sorrow stopped pacing and came to stand beside her, holding the black metal object out on the palms of her hands.

'This? It's a pistol.'

She wasn't as tall as she seemed, Elisse realised. Half a head shorter than Elisse herself, in fact, though sturdier and more muscular; it was that aura of coiled aggression that gave her such presence.

'Pistol?'

'The rarest of all weapons.' Everything Sorrow said was produced in the coldest and most factual of tones, as if she were detached from any kind of human emotion, but there was a hint of satisfaction in her face as she looked down at the pistol. 'I had it imported from Sol Kardis. Even there they're scarce.'

Elisse frowned at it. The thing just looked like an elaborate kind of tube with a handle; she couldn't see what would make it so prized. 'What d'ya do with it? Hit people?'

For the first time, the corners of Sorrow's mouth turned up in a smile. 'Allow me to demonstrate.'

She spun round and pointed the device at a stone vase that stood on top of the spinet. Her thumb moved with a metallic click, and then the world exploded in a flash and a deafening bang. With a yelp of surprise, Elisse stumbled backwards until her legs hit the chaise longue and she sat down hard, arms wrapped around herself for protection. The air in the room was hazy with smoke, making her eyes sting and the back of her throat hurt. It was only when she'd got her breath back that she realised the vase was now a shower of stone fragments across the spinet and the floor. She looked at Sorrow, who was watching her calmly with the smoking pistol still in one hand. Her heart was pounding, and she felt as though she ought to be angry, but for some reason what she wanted most was to laugh.

'I've put a dent in your wall,' Sorrow said. 'Sorry about that.'

Elisse shrugged. 'It's not my wall. It belongs ta Captain Travers.'

They stared at each other for a moment. Then the giggle that was dancing in Elisse's stomach came bubbling up in her throat, and she was no longer able to swallow it back. She laughed until she was almost crying, her sides aching with the force of it. When she'd finished, Sorrow came over and sat beside her. The blonde woman's face still gave nothing away, but now there was a hint of interest in her hazel eyes as she looked at Elisse.

'You're not what I expected,' she said.

Elisse took in a shaky breath, still fighting the vestiges of laughter. 'Well, what did ya expect?'

'When Travers hired me, he told me who you are and –' Sorrow made a vague descriptive gesture – 'why you're here. I thought you'd be stupid. Scared. Girly. But maybe you're not.'

Elisse grinned. 'Maybe.'

There was a silence. Then Sorrow tilted the pistol and said, as though it were an apology, 'I won't fire it again unless I have to. It costs me five ranols every time I reload this thing. We don't have the chemicals or the technology to make explosives in Mirrorvale, and there's only one man I know in the whole of Arkannen who's willing to bring Kardise powder into the city.'

Elisse looked doubtfully at the device. 'Is it safe? I mean … it won' blow up or anything?'

'Probably not,' Sorrow said. 'But I'd better get on and clean it. In the meantime, I'd drink that tea now if the offer's still going – unless you've got anything stronger?'

'I think there's some taransey,' Elisse offered. She'd never fancied it herself, but Florentyn had liked a drink when he came to visit her. He'd told her all about it: how the first ring of Arkannen was the only place in the world where it was made, how the Mirrorvalese refused to export it on the grounds that foreigners didn't have the constitution for it, how a vintage keg of taransey could sell for the same price as a piece of antique jewellery or a small house. *Dances on your tastebuds like the sweetest of nectar and hits you with all the force of a steamhammer,* he'd said, but she hadn't been convinced. Now, though, the look on Sorrow's face revealed that Florentyn wasn't the only one with a taste for expensive liquor.

'This might just be the best job ever,' the blonde woman said. 'None of my clients have ever offered me taransey before.'

Elisse shrugged. 'Ya welcome to it.'

As she poured the deep amber liquid into Florentyn's old glass, she watched Sorrow through the open kitchen doorway. The bodyguard was humming to herself as she inserted a long cloth-covered rod into the hollow part of the pistol, a smear of black dirt on her cheek. Elisse had never met any woman who had such short hair, but it looked right on Sorrow. It must be strange, being a female mercenary. Sorrow wasn't much older than she was, yet Elisse didn't see how their lives could be more different.

'So is this what ya normally do?' she asked, carrying the glass through to the living quarters. 'Guard people?'

The twist of Sorrow's mouth suggested a wry smile. 'Not exactly. This is a change for me. Usually ... well, let's just say that usually I'm on the other side.'

'Ya kill people?' The words were out before Elisse could stop them, but Sorrow only shrugged.

'Sometimes. If that's what I'm asked for. Other times, I just threaten.' Her smile changed into something that made Elisse shiver. 'I'm very good at threatening people.'

She took the taransey from Elisse's hand and swallowed it in one quick gulp. Handing back the empty glass, she added, 'But don't worry. I'm being paid good money to protect you. And besides –' her pale eyebrows twitched, as if it was a surprise even to her – 'I like you.'

'There's no need ta sound so horrified by it,' Elisse said tartly, trying to brush over her previous moment of fear. 'People like people all the time.'

Sorrow shook her head. 'I don't.'

She returned to cleaning her pistol, while Elisse retreated to the kitchen. *Doesn' like people,* she thought as she washed up. *What sort o' screwed-up girl doesn' like people?*

Another knock at the door startled her into nearly dropping the glass. Before she could dry her wet hands, Sorrow had extracted a knife from her body-belt and stalked over to open the door. Pushing herself up onto her tiptoes, Elisse peered down the hall and caught the flash of a striped coat over the blonde woman's shoulder: she was talking to one of the Helm. After a short conversation, Sorrow closed the door again and turned around.

'Word from Darkhaven,' she said. 'There's been another attack. On Captain Travers this time.'

Elisse had been about to point out that she could open her own door, thank you very much, but the news drove the complaint back into her throat unvoiced.

'Is he dead?' she whispered, but Sorrow shook her head. 'Only hurt. Apparently it was the same creature that

killed the old Changer. It happened just down the road.'
She shrugged. 'I wondered why I passed so many Helmsmen
on my way here this morning.'

Just down the road. Elisse pressed the back of one hand to
her mouth, suddenly dizzy. It had happened on her doorstep.
Travers must have been returning with her groceries when
he was attacked. He'd said she was in danger, and he'd been
right. What if the creature had been coming for her? What
if it – if *Ayla* – knew where she was?

'Are you all right?' Sorrow asked. Elisse tried to nod,
but the dizziness was increasing, swirling through her head,
covering everything in front of her in a haze of sparks. She
leant on the edge of the sink, bowing her head, taking in a
long, difficult breath. Dimly she was aware of Sorrow crossing
the room towards her.

'I'm sorry.' It was the second time her new bodyguard
had apologised to her, but this time it sounded as though she
meant it. 'I should have thought – in your condition – here,
come and sit down.'

Elisse felt Sorrow's arm encircle her, steering her in the
direction of the living room. Once there, Sorrow sat her in
the nearest chair and fetched her a cup of water.

'Are you all right?' she asked again. Elisse took a sip of
the cold liquid, though her trembling hands chinked the
porcelain against her teeth.

'I'm fine,' she managed. 'It's jus' – Florentyn, and now
Travers –' Her vision was clearing now, her chest loosening.
She looked up at Sorrow, who was watching her with a slight
frown on her face.

'Ya said ya thought I'd be stupid and scared.' Her voice
came out shaky. 'Well, I dunno abou' stupid, but I'm scared
all right. If the Nightshades find out abou' me ...'

'Travers gave me permission to protect you against anyone who tries to harm you,' Sorrow said. '*Anyone*, even a member of the royal family. He said I was immune from prosecution by the Helm. I'm not allowed to kill anyone, but like I said – there's plenty more I can do besides killing.'

Elisse nodded. 'I'm glad ya here, Sorrow, really I am.' And it was true, she realised; somewhere between the firing of the pistol and her dizzy spell, her earlier dread had faded. 'But ... 'scuse me for asking, but wha' can one person do against a Changer?'

'One person, not a lot.' That hint of satisfaction back in her face, Sorrow gestured towards the black metal contraption that still lay in pieces on the table. 'But one person with a pistol ... well, I reckon they can do plenty. Even against a Changer.'

SIXTEEN

Lamp in hand, Serenna pushed open the door to the library. With their trip into the city cancelled, Myrren was attending to some of the business he had neglected these past few days – the country wouldn't run itself, even if he was trying to solve a murder at the same time – and so Serenna had decided it might be a good idea if she did some research. Myrren had assured her that the library wouldn't be in use and that she wouldn't be disturbed; it had always been Florentyn's place, and now he was gone there wasn't a man or woman in Darkhaven who would enter it unless requested.

Setting her lamp down on the desk at the far end, Serenna studied the room. It was large, dark and imposing, like most of Darkhaven, but the indefinable smell of musty paper and old ink put her instantly at ease. With a professor for a father, she had grown up around books; she often thought that if she hadn't joined the Altar of Flame she would have followed in her father's footsteps to become an academic. But her eldest brother had taken that path, and her family couldn't afford to educate more than one child to university level, so here she was: a priestess made nostalgic by the scent of knowledge. She supposed she ought to be grateful that she and her siblings had all been taught to read and write. Not every child in Arkannen had that luxury, even now.

She crossed to the window and pulled back the heavy curtains, sneezing at the dust that billowed from their folds. Even with the daylight spilling in, the room remained dim and forbidding. She'd need the lamp, especially since the one carved chair was set with its back to the window and so she'd be casting her own shadow on every document she tried to read. Perhaps Florentyn had been blessed with unusually good eyesight. She knew all Changers in their creature form possessed certain virtues that made them powerful: heightened senses, unnatural strength and speed, an imperviousness to weaponry. It was possible that to a lesser extent, some of those qualities remained even when the Changer returned to human form. Despite the prying questions she had asked Myrren that morning, it was surprising how little she knew about the gifts of the bloodline that ruled over her and every other person in Mirrorvale.

'Well, that's what I'm here for,' she said aloud, then winced at the sound of her own voice breaking the silence. Another academic habit, that, talking to oneself.

Leaving the lamp on the desk, she scanned the shelves. The books were mainly vast tomes with leather bindings, bearing such enticing titles as *Upon the Principles and Ordinance of Government* and *An Assessment of Trade Relationships Between Mirrorvale and its Neighbours*. No doubt Myrren and Ayla had been forced to read them, but as an ordinary citizen Serenna had absolutely no need to do so. She skipped over them with relief, moving on to a set of slimmer but equally tall books that looked more promising. *The History of the Nightshade Bloodline* ... *Meditations on the Changer Gift* ... then, as she started to lift the *Meditations* down from the shelf – it took both hands – her fingertips brushed against another book that had fallen down behind the others. Intrigued, she fished it out: a small handwritten book with browning edges, entitled *Changer Myths and Truths*. Perfect. Serenna set it on top of the *Meditations* and carried them both back to the desk.

After reading a dry introduction with difficulty and concluding that she probably would have been lost in the world of academia, she skipped on to the chapter of the *Meditations* that talked about Changer forms.

There are five essential elements from which everything of substance is made: flame, ice, wind, wood and steel. Each of the Changer forms is made purely from one of those elements: Firedrake, Unicorn, Griffin, Phoenix and Hydra respectively.

Over the centuries, alloys of these five elements have sprung up from time to time. These forms are not pure and so should be bred out of the bloodline wherever possible.

It seemed the author of the book had thought so little of what he called 'alloys' that he didn't want to say anything more about them; Serenna skimmed the following pages, but couldn't find anything to indicate what sort of creatures they were or how often they appeared. Giving up, she turned to *Changer Myths and Truths*, and was relieved to discover that it contained a set of colour illustrations.

As well as the five singular Changer forms, the cramped handwriting said, *there are many other possible hybrid forms. Here I will document all those that have been seen in the Nightshade line since records began.* Then, on the opposite page, the author had drawn a detailed picture of a winged horse, underneath which was the caption *Alicorn (Unicorn–Phoenix)*. Serenna looked at the illustration, created with meticulous care in coloured inks that glowed with vibrant life in the dim light of the library, and wondered how anyone could claim a thing of such beauty was impure. Then she remembered with a kind of amazement that this was Ayla's form. *A golden horse, with a spiral horn and wings like flame* – that was what Myrren had said, but the description didn't even begin to express the glory of it.

'We won't let them lock you up,' she whispered, reaching out a hand, then snatching it back before her fingers could smudge the ink. 'I swear it.'

She turned the page, and her heart gave a heavy thud. There it was, the creature that had hurt her and that Travers had described: a construct of fire and shadow, all wings and scales and claws. This time it wasn't beauty that awed her, but the sheer sense of power that came crackling from each bold line and dark colour. Underneath it, the author had written *Wyvern (Firedrake–Hydra–Griffin)*.

Serenna sat back in her chair, releasing a long breath. Now she knew what Ayla's creature-self was called, and she could give a name to the animal that had killed Florentyn. Unfortunately, she couldn't see how that would help her to find the missing Changer.

Abandoning the *Meditations* entirely, she turned back to the beginning of *Changer Myths and Truths* and began to read.

For those who seek to understand the nature of the Changer gift, this book sets out some of the most common fallacies that surround it and aims to uncover the truth that lies at the heart of each one, if any. Yet I counsel you to remember, oh traveller in strange lands, that a Changer is nothing if not dangerous. Over countless generations, we of Mirrorvale have grown used to the idea that our country is ruled by men who have the power to become beasts at will. Perhaps we have grown complacent, thinking ourselves safe.

Yet at the heart of every Changer is something fierce and a little cruel. How else, indeed, would they have maintained their ascendancy for so many centuries?

A tale is told of a long-ago Griffin overlord of Darkhaven who returned from a wide-ranging journey to find his wife cavorting in her chamber with another man. In an instant he Changed. Ignoring his wife's screams, he seized the other man in his powerful forearms and soared with him high into the sky above Arkannen. When they were far enough above the city that they could see the seven rings laid out beneath them, the Griffin let go of his captive and became human once more. As the two men plummeted towards the earth, the Changer looked across at his rival and said, 'You sought to take my place, so Change if you can!' Then he reassumed his Griffin form and swooped to safety, whilst the other man's body smashed against the roofs of the city. But his wife he locked up in a chamber beneath the tower, saying she must bear his heirs in darkness lest she be tempted again.

Just a tale, you might think; yet that little incarceration room in the foundations of Darkhaven still exists, and other men have died over the years for far lesser offences than seduction. Like the wild animals they become, our overlords are quick to mete out bloody vengeance to those who oppose them. So, if nothing else, remember my warning: if you have dealings with Changers, you may be many things, but you are certainly not safe.

Serenna massaged her temples, where the first inklings of a headache were beginning to make themselves felt. The warning seemed almost directed at her personally, making her doubt her own judgement in coming to Darkhaven. But having been burnt and trampled by a Changer creature, she knew better than most how unsafe they could be. And although she had glimpsed the fierceness at Myrren's heart, she didn't think he was cruel.

But then, of course, Myrren wasn't a Changer.

After the introduction, the following chapters appeared to be a brief history of the Nightshade line. She skimmed through them until, unexpectedly, the word *murder* caught her eye. Returning to the top of the page, she scanned the text.

Calyst had an especially large family. He had three wives, upon all of whom he fathered children. Once all those children had grown up there were nine Changers in Darkhaven, as well as one who it was rumoured had been born without the gift (though she was never seen outside the walls of the tower). These Changers took all kinds of forms, and at any one time there were often two or three of them to be seen in the skies above Arkannen.

It is rumoured that Calyst planned to use his children to found a Changer army. No longer willing to be squeezed between the Ingal States, Sol Kardis and Parovia, he wanted to prove Mirrorvale's strength. Yet before he could continue with this plan – a foolhardy one, perhaps, with the threat of war so recently averted – a spate of murders in the city changed the direction of his focus. People were dying, and in such a way that it was obvious a Changer was the perpetrator. Rather than give up one of their own to public justice, the Nightshades closed ranks and denied responsibility. Several times the Helm were sent down into Arkannen to quell any threat of protest or rebellion. It was this, in part, that led to the Helm losing much of their power only a few decades later.

Serenna drummed her fingers on the desk, frowning. So there had been murderous Changer creatures around before. It seemed most Changers were no more aggressive in animal form than they were in human form, but occasionally there was one who became really vicious when he or she Changed … or perhaps it was just a reflection of the individual's own nature. After all, there were plenty of ordinary people who did all kinds of terrible things through greed or rage or ambition – or even madness. It was inevitable that the Nightshade line should be prey to the same emotions; it was just that those emotions were all the more terrible when translated into creature form.

She kept turning the pages, lingering over the illustrations again when she reached them. After that she discovered a section called *Unusual Changer Conditions*, which she read quickly, and then again more slowly.

As well as the hybrid forms, both more and less common, there are various other oddities that spring up in the Nightshade line from time to time. For instance, it is true that most Changers have a single creature-self; indeed, for a long time it was thought that nothing else was possible. However, there have been rare instances in which a Changer was able to take on two distinct forms. In some of these cases the Changer was able to choose at will which form to take. In others, he didn't know when he Changed which creature he would end up as. And in a very few cases, the Changer was unaware of his second form, the periods that he spent in it appearing as blanks to his conscious human mind.

Serenna shivered. She had asked Myrren whether that very thing was possible, and he had replied in the negative. *A Changer's other form is like an expression of identity. It is unique.* Yet this book contradicted that. According to this single paragraph, Ayla might be able to Change into both an Alicorn and a Wyvern. Which meant – whether she knew it or not – that she could still be the killer they were looking for.

Serenna didn't relish the prospect of passing the news on to Myrren.

By now her shoulders were aching, and her scalp throbbed from the pins that held her veil in place above her tight braid. She looked up and realised it was getting dark; the lamp on the desk cast a pool of light around her, throwing everything else into shadow. Furtively, she scanned the room, but she was alone with the books – and Myrren had told her she wouldn't be disturbed. With a sigh of relief, she pulled off her veil, sending hairpins skittering across the desk. Then she unwound her hair, separating the braided strands with deft fingers and letting it flow over her hands like a river of flame in the lamplight. Already the pressure in her head was easing. She leant back in her chair and indulged in a luxurious stretch, arching her back, raising her arms as high above her head as they would go. She'd done enough for today. The only question was whether she should tell Myrren what she'd learned – and if so, when.

When she lowered her arms and opened her eyes, she found the man himself standing at the edge of the circle of light.

Immediately she could feel herself blushing. Her chagrin was laced with a strange sense of guilt, as if on some level she had known he was there and had tried to entice him with her ridiculous display, like a stupid heroine from a romance who lounged around in provocative poses and pretended not to realise what she was doing. Yet what made it even worse, somehow, was that Myrren didn't appear to be at all enticed. His mouth was set in an unusually stern line, and he was staring at the floor in front of his feet as though she was making him profoundly uncomfortable. With trembling hands, Serenna snatched up her veil and pinned it as fast as she could over her hair.

'Good evening, Lord Myrren,' she said with an attempt at her usual cool smile.

'Good evening, Sister Serenna.' His voice held the clipped tone that she had come to realise meant he was concealing some strong emotion. 'Have you found what you were looking for?'

'I'm not sure.' She couldn't tell him about her suspicions – not now, when she was still striving to suppress the tremors of nervous embarrassment. 'I've certainly learned a lot about the Nightshade line.'

'You probably know more than me.' Myrren glanced around at the shelves full of books. 'My father tried so hard to drum our ancestral history into my head that I think he must have drummed it right out again.'

He was endeavouring to put her at her ease, Serenna realised, but the knowledge only set her more on edge. She swept her remaining hairpins into her hand and stood up. 'Well, I must get some rest if we're to visit the city tomorrow.'

He turned back towards her. 'Serenna –'

'Good night, Lord Myrren,' she said, and fled.

SEVENTEEN

Another day trapped in Caraway's room, and by fourth bell Ayla thought she might go mad with boredom. If only she had a book to read, or a sketchpad for drawing – even a page of mathematical problems, which she'd always hated being set by her tutor, would afford some relief from this mind-numbingly slow passing of time.

It's no worse than being locked in Darkhaven's cells, she told herself. *Better, in fact, since you're free to walk through the door.* She'd never expected to escape one jail only to end up in a different one, but at least here there was some prospect of getting out in the near future. If Caraway kept his word and brought her a wig, she might be able to emerge into the relatively fresh air beyond the tanner's yard as soon as this evening. She just had to be patient until then. Yet the longer she sat here, the more other things began to break through her boredom, like jagged rocks just below the surface of a sluggish stream. Her father's death and all the complicated feelings that went with it. How much she missed home – because she hadn't realised, until she left it, how lost she'd feel outside the only place she really belonged; the place that had formed the backdrop to every happy memory she'd ever made. How much she missed *Myrren*. How, more than anything, she longed to take her other form and fly …

In the end, she filled the rusty bucket from the pump downstairs and attempted to scrub the mould off the window-sill. From there, it was a short step to cleaning the grimy windowpane, then sweeping the floor and stacking the empty bottles in a neat array. She was just about to fetch another bucketful of water to try washing the blankets when she heard the footsteps out on the landing.

'Like I told y'all,' a woman's voice said. 'I saw 'er yesterday. Dark hair all ragged like someone 'acked it off wiv a rusty blade. Those blue eyes an' all.'

Fire and blood. One of the women she'd met the day before had informed on her. Whatever reward the Helm were offering through their spy network, it clearly outweighed even the local people's respect for Caraway. Ayla looked wildly around the barren room for somewhere to hide, and failing that, something better than a knife to defend herself with. She found neither, so contented herself with backing up against the far wall, the weapon clutched tightly in both hands. If she had to she would Change. It didn't matter if Myrren sensed it, after all. They already knew where she was.

The door banged open, rattling back on its hinges with a shudder that shook the whole room. Two men dressed in Helm uniform entered, positioning themselves so they completely blocked the doorway.

'Ayla Nightshade,' one of them said, grinning. 'You're wanted back at the tower.'

'You do know what I'm wanted for, don't you?' She was pleased that her voice remained steady; pleased too that her hands didn't shake as she aimed the knife blade at the speaker. 'They say I murdered my father. That I attacked a priestess. If that's so, what's to stop me Changing right now and doing the same thing to you?'

For an instant, a shadow of fear touched his eyes. Then he shook his head as if to dispel a dream, and the moment was gone.

'This room ain't big enough to Change in, sweetheart. You know that as well as I do.'

He was right, curse him. Her creature-self was far too large to be contained in these four drab walls; trying to Change would bring the whole building down around the lot of them. Ayla pressed herself even harder against the peeling plaster as the Helmsmen advanced. It was possible she was stronger than one of them alone; she might be half a Nightshade, but she still had many of the abilities of her bloodline. Yet there were two of them, and they knew what they were doing – whereas Ayla's father had never allowed her to train alongside Myrren. Which meant she was relying on …

Where are you, Caraway? She bit her lip. He should have got back by now. Unless, of course, he'd sent them here. Unless he'd sold her back into captivity in return for reinstatement to the Helm …

'What's goin' on here?' As if her whirling thoughts had produced him out of thin air, Caraway appeared behind the two men. She could only see part of his face in the gap between them, but it was enough to tell her something wasn't right. Then the Helmsmen turned, opening up her view, and she saw the full extent of Caraway's dishevelled state: the tousled hair, the rumpled coat, the way he leaned against the doorframe as though he depended on it to keep him upright. In a heartbeat, relief became sinking cold fury. He was drunk. She was about to be hauled off back to Darkhaven, and he was *drunk*.

'You stay out of this, Breakblade,' one of the Helmsmen said. 'You're lucky we aren't carting you off to jail with her.'

'Dear me.' Caraway blinked at the speaker, apparently having difficulty focusing. 'Whatever for?'

'Concealing a criminal. Obstructing the Helm in their duties. Being a drunken idiot.' The man ticked each of them off on his fingers with a sneer, and Ayla winced at the contempt in his voice. In response, Caraway pushed himself off the wooden frame to stand upright and wavering on his own two feet.

'Then I s'pose I should thank you,' he said brightly. ''Cos the thing about jail is, you see –' losing his balance, stumbling forward into the room – 'the thing about jail is –' catching himself on the nearest Helmsman's arm, and looking into his face with a sweet, absent smile – 'the thing about jail is, I'm really rather fed up with it.'

With that, he straightened and brought his knee up hard and fast into the man's groin in one smooth movement. Then, as the Helmsman doubled over, Caraway spun on his heel and went for the second man, who was in the process of drawing his sword. The Helmsman didn't even have time to finish the move. Caraway grabbed his shirt in two fists, knocking him off balance; at the same time he lowered his head and drove it into the other man's face. Ayla bit back an involuntary cry as the sound of the impact echoed in the tiny room, a sickening thud accompanied by the crunch of the Helmsman's nose breaking. He fell against the wall and slumped to the floor, his face smeared with blood.

Without hesitating, Caraway turned back to the first man and hooked his legs out from under him, dropping him onto his back. Still in pain from the previous blow, the Helmsman didn't react quickly enough; in an instant Caraway was on him, a flurry of punches bouncing his head off the floor-boards. The other man tried to fight back, his hands stabbing at Caraway's throat and eyes, but then Caraway's fist caught him directly beneath the jaw and he went limp. In the ringing silence that followed, Ayla could distinctly hear her own heart pounding beneath her ribcage.

Caraway got to his feet, breathing hard, but with no trace left of his apparent intoxication. 'Are you all right?'

'I – I –' Ayla couldn't get the words out. She was still gripping the knife, her hands shaking with the tension that held her entire body locked in position. Dizzy with shock, she gulped in air and tried again. 'You're not drunk,' she said, and detected a suspicious quaver in her own voice.

'No.' Caraway reached out to take the knife from her rigid grasp. His anxious brown eyes examined her face. 'Ayla, are you sure –?'

She shook her head, blinded by the tears that were welling in her own eyes. Then, somehow, her cheek was pressed against his shoulder and his arms were around her. It had been a long time since anyone had touched her like that, in a simple gesture of comfort. Maybe not since her mother died …

The thought hit her like a cascade of freezing water, returning her to full awareness of where she was and who she was with. Wriggling backwards out of his embrace, she wiped each eye in turn with the back of her hand.

'We should go,' she said, not looking at him. 'Before they come round.' She didn't ask how likely it was that the two injured Helmsmen would ever come round; she wasn't sure she wanted to know.

'You're right.' Caraway reached into the bag that had contained her hair and drew out a blonde wig, which he handed to her. 'Here, put this on.'

Skirting the unconscious men on the floor, he walked over to the chest in the corner of the room and began throwing its contents into the now-empty bag. Still shaky, Ayla dipped her head and tugged the wig into place, tucking as much of her hair as she could underneath it. The wig's inner layer of fabric was something coarse and prickly; it made her head itch.

'Ready?' Caraway returned to her side, bulging bag over one shoulder. He studied her for a moment. 'It's on a bit crooked – let me –' He reached out to adjust the wig, pushing a few errant strands of her hair into place, then nodded.

'All right, here's what we're going to do. These men came here in a carriage so they could take you back to Darkhaven. There are two more of the Helm waiting outside with it – I saw them on my way in, though I didn't let them see me. You need to leave first: wear your cloak, it's good and nondescript, but keep your hood down so the wig shows. They aren't looking for a blonde, so it'll fool them at a casual glance – there are plenty of rooms in this building you could be coming from. I'll follow you and provide a distraction if necessary.'

He paused, and Ayla saw something akin to pain flash across his face. Then it was gone, and he looked down at her with a rueful smile.

'Me, they will recognise. And they'll probably want to talk to me. So I'll do whatever is required to keep them occupied for as long as it takes you to get away. Whatever you hear, don't look back; just keep walking until you reach the corner of the street where the slaughterhouse is, and wait out of sight. If they arrest me, or if anything goes wrong –' he shrugged – 'just run as fast as you can.'

He was suddenly very much in control of the situation, and Ayla wasn't going to argue with him. It hadn't even occurred to her that there would be more of the Helm outside, whereas

Caraway seemed to know exactly what he was talking about – and after all, this was why she had agreed to let him help her. So she nodded a silent assent.

'Good,' Caraway said. 'Then I'll keep this, if you don't mind.' He lifted a hand, and Ayla realised he still had her knife. That hint of pain was in his face again as he added, 'It'll be more useful than my own blade.'

She looked down at the hilt of his sword, then back up at him. 'Why don't you just throw it away?'

'I'm not ready for that yet.' His voice was soft enough that she wasn't quite sure she'd heard him correctly. She wanted to say something else, though she didn't know what, but then he was moving towards the door and the moment was lost.

'Come on, then,' he said over his shoulder. 'Let's get out there before they break the door down looking for us.'

Without a word, she followed him onto the dingy landing and down the stairs. At the bottom of the steps, Caraway gave her an encouraging nod and stood aside to let her pass him. She hesitated, scanning the yard outside for any sign of the Helm.

'I'll be right behind you,' Caraway murmured, and she threw him a narrow-eyed glare. He'd better not think she was scared. She was just … preparing herself.

After a final calming breath, she stepped through the archway and set off across the yard towards the exit, keeping her shoulders back and her pace unhurried. When she neared the wide gateway that led onto the street, she saw Caraway had been right: a carriage was waiting outside the yard, with one Helmsman leaning against it and another sitting up on the driver's box. Ayla's pulse quickened, her veins humming with the giddy urge to run, but she forced herself to maintain an even speed. As she passed the carriage, she was aware that the Helmsman leaning against it was sending an idle glance her way, but she didn't look at him; she fixed her gaze on the street corner and kept walking. Out of the corner of her eye she saw him straighten up.

'Excuse me? Miss?'

She froze – and then, to her relief, she heard Caraway's voice.

'Ah, two more of Darkhaven's finest! Good day to you both!'

He was playing the drunk again, and she had to admit it was very convincing. If she hadn't heard him speak with sober intensity just a moment ago, she'd have believed it herself. She kept moving, but more slowly, anxious to hear the outcome of the conversation.

'Breakblade?' That was the man on the driver's box, a sharp edge to his voice. 'What's going on? What are you doing out here?'

'Your esteemed colleagues sent me out,' Caraway slurred. 'They wanted a lil' bit of time alone with Ayla Nightshade. Teach her a lesson's what they said.'

The driver swore. 'They're not supposed to be doing that. Captain Travers doesn't want her hurt.'

That was news to Ayla. She didn't dare glance back the way she had come, but she heard a creak and then the impact of two feet hitting the ground. The driver must have jumped down from the carriage.

'What are you doing?' the other Helmsman asked.

'I'm going to tell those two to bloody well stop amusing themselves and bring the girl out here. The sooner we get her back to Darkhaven, the better.'

Ayla bit her lip: that wasn't good. If he went inside, he'd find the two injured men and raise the alarm. Caraway obviously realised it too, because a note of urgency crept into his voice.

'Well, now, hold on just a moment. There's somethin' I need to tell you first. A message they sent for you.'

'Oh yes?' The driver sounded suspicious. 'And what's that?'

Ayla couldn't stand it any longer. She turned to see what was happening, just as Caraway straightened up from his conspiratorial incline towards the other man and felled him with a precise kick to the side of the knee that left him writhing on the ground in agony. The Helmsman who had been leaning against the carriage started forward, sword in hand; Caraway took a wary step backwards.

'This really isn't going to do you any good, Tomas,' the Helmsman said, continuing to advance. Caraway shrugged.

'What have I got to lose?'

'Your life, for a start.'

'To be honest, I won't miss it all that much,' Caraway said. His gaze met Ayla's over the Helmsman's shoulder, and she could see the message in his eyes: *Run.* Instead, she took a deep breath and spoke as loudly as she could.

'Are you looking for me?'

Reflexively, the Helmsman's head turned part of the way in her direction. As she'd hoped, the moment's distraction was all the opening Caraway required. The knife flashed in his hand; the Helmsman folded like a punctured balloon, his sword clattering to the ground as he clutched at the blood that was spilling through his fingers. Straight away Caraway set off at a sprint, grabbing Ayla's wrist as he passed her and pulling her along after him. He didn't stop until they'd turned the corner at the end of the street and were some way down the road. Then he jerked her to an abrupt halt, facing her with fury in his eyes.

'You were supposed to run!'

She couldn't bear to tell him that she'd wanted to see if he would be all right, so she just lifted a dismissive shoulder. 'I helped, though, didn't I?'

'I mean it, Ayla!' His hands clamped down on her shoulders, giving her a little shake. 'If you're not going to take my advice on these things, then –'

'I told you never to touch me.' She put all the ice she could into her voice, and it worked; he snatched his hands away as though she had stung him. Ignoring a sneaking feeling of guilt – the man had just saved her from a fate worse than death – she folded her arms and scowled at him. 'What's your problem, anyway?'

He sighed, all his anger burnt out in an instant: a swift, hot flame that had consumed itself and then died. 'That Helmsman, the one I stabbed … he was my friend, once. We trained together in the fifth ring. He learned the same thing I did: if your opponent has a sword and you don't, your only hope is to disable him fast and thoroughly enough that he doesn't get the chance to use it. But I just …' He scrubbed his fingers through his hair, and finished in a low voice, 'I just hope he's all right. That I haven't killed him.'

Oh. For the second time that afternoon, Ayla wanted to say something but couldn't find the words. After a moment Caraway let out another long breath, adjusted the bag on his shoulder, and turned away from her.

'All right, Lady Ayla. Let's go and find a new place to stay.'

EIGHTEEN

From his seat in the musty darkness of the Nightshade carriage, Myrren listened to the wheels rattling and creaking over the paved streets of the fourth ring, and hoped the whole thing wouldn't fall apart before it reached its destination. His father had never set foot in it, or any other method of transport for that matter, preferring to travel to even the most formal state occasions in his Firedrake shape. Many a time he had landed outside some great house or governor's palace, Changing with a swirl of black dust into his human form in full view of everyone before striding up the steps with no care for his nakedness, swinging the embroidered robe he had carried with him around his shoulders. *Keeps them on their toes,* he used to say with a ferocious smile. *Lets them know what they're dealing with.* Myrren also suspected that Florentyn had simply enjoyed the thrill of it. Why chug along in a slow, ponderous airship, surrounded by the noise of the engine and the stench of burning coal, when you could have the freedom of the empty air and your own swift wings?

With a sigh, Myrren looked at Serenna, who was sitting opposite. She was peeking through the curtains that covered the window, perhaps reacquainting herself with the streets she had grown up in. Her veil was heavier today, as befitted such a public excursion, but she had swept it back from her face in order to see better; a lock of flame-bright hair had escaped from its confines and was brushing her cheek. Idly he imagined pulling the veil off her head altogether and burying his fingers in that glorious hair, letting it fall free as it had last night in the library ... which of course led to tightening his grip and tilting her face upwards, the better to access the soft curve of her mouth ...

As if she could hear what he was thinking, she turned away from the window, her grey eyes searching his face. To cover his confusion, he hurried into speech.

'I must apologise for the state of this carriage, Sister Serenna.' Using her title calmed him: it reminded him that she was a priestess and therefore untouchable. 'As you can probably tell, it is little used.'

She shrugged. 'It's nice not to have to walk. And this way they won't see us coming.'

'You don't think the carriage is too conspicuous?' Myrren pressed on, fully aware that he was recrossing old ground, but still trying to distract himself. Without a hint of impatience, Serenna gave him the same answer as before.

'Plenty of people in the fourth ring have private carriages, Lord Myrren. And since you've covered the crest on the door of this one, there isn't any way it can be recognised.' She frowned at him. 'Are you all right?'

'Yes. Fine.' He looked away, satisfying himself again that he had everything he might need: a length of thin, strong rope in case they found the rogue Changer and needed to restrain him to get him back to Darkhaven; a hood to cover the Changer's head and conceal that distinctive colouring from the curious eyes of the neighbourhood; his own sword, in case he needed to defend himself. Though, rationally, he would prefer it not to come to fighting, a small part of him hoped it might. It would be the perfect way to work out some of his frustration.

'Probably won't find anything,' he muttered, and didn't even realise he'd spoken aloud until he heard Serenna's reply.

'Have faith, my lord. I'm sure we will discover something useful, even if it's not what we're expecting.'

Looking up, he gave her a rueful smile. 'I wish I had your optimism. I almost don't want to get there, in case it turns out to be a dead end.'

As if to flout his wishes, a few moments later the carriage came to a jerky stop: they had reached the Avenue of Rowans. Obeying Myrren's earlier instructions, the driver didn't get down to open the door as he normally would; instead Myrren let himself out, then turned to help Serenna down after him. The two of them stood on the street, scanning the buildings in front of them. Number 45 was an imposing four-storey house in a terraced row of similar houses, their well-kept facades and neatly curtained windows giving an impression of restrained wealth. Myrren was conscious of a nervous ache in the pit of his stomach, but he suppressed it sternly.

'Please stay behind me, Sister Serenna,' he said, trying to project an aura of composed control. 'Unless you'd rather wait in the carriage –?'

'I won't do much good there.' Serenna had pulled the veil back over her face, and her voice was muffled through the thick fabric, but even so he could tell she was amused. 'And I hardly think the creature will attack us in broad daylight.'

Resisting the impulse to order her to keep out of harm's way, Myrren nodded. They approached the front door together, but before he could knock Serenna reached out and turned the handle. The door swung open, revealing a hallway that led to another door on the ground floor and a staircase leading upwards.

'Divided into apartments,' Serenna said. 'Probably one on each floor.' She took a step towards the closed door ahead of them, glancing over her shoulder at Myrren. 'If you start at the top and work down, my lord, I'll start here and meet you halfway. It takes me longer to climb stairs than it used to.'

'You think we should just knock on each door in turn?' Myrren asked. 'What will you say when someone answers?'

She shrugged. 'I'll lie my way in. And if they won't let me in, it may mean they're hiding something.' That tone entered her voice again, the light-tinted one that meant her lips were curving upwards. 'Don't tell me – I have some interesting ideas, for a priestess.'

'Quite frankly, I don't think you're a priestess at all,' he said, and she laughed.

'Of course, you won't need to do anything other than show them that well-known Nightshade countenance. If they turn pale and run, that's a good sign we've got our man.'

'Right.' Myrren wanted to tell her to be careful, but in the end he just said, 'Shout if you need me.'

Before he could change his mind, he took the first flight of stairs two at a time. The landing above was exactly the same as the hall below; it reminded him of a nightmare he'd once had in which he was trying to escape from something, but no matter how fast he ran he always ended up back where he'd started. Shaking off the uneasy thought, he kept going up the next flight and the next, and was relieved to find that he had definitely reached the top of the building. The door that confronted him was identical to the other three he'd

passed, save only for the design painted on the jamb around
the ornate number '4'. At the sight of that design, Myrren's
focus tightened. To most people it would look like an abstract
pattern, but he was familiar enough with the Helm's system
of coded symbols to recognise it as something more. There
were two codewords in the design, one that meant *a building
to be guarded* – that one usually referred to Darkhaven – and
another that meant something like *safety* or *protection*. A
safe house. This must be the right place.

Breathing deeply to slow his racing pulse, Myrren
knocked and then waited, one hand ready near the hilt of
his sword, the other fiddling with the length of thin rope
in his pocket. After a while he raised his sword hand to
knock again, but the door jerked open abruptly even as his
knuckles grazed the wood. On the other side was a woman
with short blonde hair, who fixed him with a flat, narrow-
eyed look. And beyond her – Myrren's chest tightened. Ayla.
He'd found her. He took a half-step forward, opening his
mouth to say something without really knowing what, but
then the girl backed away into a bright beam of daylight
and he realised it wasn't Ayla after all. It was a stranger, a
dark-haired blue-eyed woman a few years older than him.
His father's secret daughter. So Serenna had been right
about everything.

'You know who I am, I take it,' he said to the Changer girl
over the blonde woman's shoulder. 'In which case, you know
why I'm here. I'm looking for a child of Florentyn Nightshade.'

In the silence that followed, as the rush of discovery faded,
Myrren became aware of two things that perhaps should
have been obvious before.

One, the dark-haired girl who was staring at him with
blind terror in her eyes was clearly and heavily pregnant.

Two, the blonde-haired woman who stood between them had a weapon pressed against his stomach, and unless he was much mistaken it was a Kardise pistol.

'We both know who you are, Lord Myrren,' the blonde said. 'So unless you want to be laid up for months, recovering from a painful injury your physicians don't know how to treat, I suggest you turn around and go back where you came from.'

Myrren had never used a pistol, but he'd seen one once before – the Helm had brought it up to Darkhaven after it was confiscated from a weapons dealer. It had punched a hole in a plate of armour. He wasn't sure exactly what would happen to him if the trigger were pulled, but it wasn't an experiment he was keen to try.

'I don't mean either of you any harm,' he said, making no move that could be interpreted as threatening, but standing his ground. 'I just need to know the truth.'

In response the pistol drew back a short way, enough so it was no longer digging into him. That was a good start.

'I need you to accompany me to Darkhaven.' Again he spoke directly to the girl who, unbelievable as it seemed, must be his half-sister – and a murderer to boot. 'I have some questions I want to ask you.'

'Don't ignore me, *my lord*.' The blonde woman's voice was as intent as a whetted blade; the pistol jabbed at his guts. 'I'm her protector, and she doesn't go anywhere without my say-so.'

Myrren gave her a conciliatory nod, though frustration was boiling up inside him. It was becoming increasingly apparent how impossible it was, as an ordinary man, to get anything done. His father had possessed both the Nightshade gift and the backing of the Helm; Myrren had neither. Without the ability to Change or the power of well-trained soldiers behind him, he had no way of coercing this woman into obedience.

He sighed, shifting his stance. A headache was beginning behind his eyes, reminding him uncomfortably of the nightmares he had been suffering from these past few days. He blinked a couple of times, trying to will it away, but an insidious dizziness was creeping up on him –

'What's going on?' With startling suddenness, Serenna arrived in the doorway beside him. He hadn't heard her footsteps on the stairs, and it seemed that neither had the blonde woman; eyebrows lifting a fraction in surprise, she moved the pistol in Serenna's direction. Next moment she had corrected herself, and was returning it to point at Myrren, but the fleeting waver was enough. Brushing aside his instant of weakness, Myrren caught her wrists, trying to angle the weapon away from himself, and Serenna, and the pregnant girl who was still watching with wide eyes from deeper inside the apartment – angle it, in fact, so that it couldn't do any harm to anyone.

'Stay back, Serenna!' he snapped over his shoulder, and felt rather than saw her retreat around the corner of the doorframe. The blonde woman moved sharply backwards, trying to yank her wrists out of his grasp; he went with her, refusing to let go, one hand moving up to prise her fingers open. He'd expected it to be easy enough – she was both smaller and lighter than him – but she was surprisingly strong. Locked together, they staggered down the hallway, slamming against the walls as they strove to break each other's hold. Then Myrren stumbled into a small table, reducing an ornamental bowl to a shower of broken glass, and his grip loosened temporarily. Taking immediate advantage of the situation, the woman forced the pistol down until it was pointing into his face. He heard the click as she prepared to fire.

'Give it up, my lord.' She sounded out of breath – that was something, at least. 'Let go or I pull the trigger.'

'If you were going to kill me you would have done it already.' Myrren watched her eyes as he said the words, reading the flicker in them that confirmed he was telling the truth. Despite everything, he was still a Nightshade and overlord of Darkhaven; it would take a rare kind of mad courage to attempt to kill him, especially with other people watching. Even by threatening him, this woman was asking for severe punishment.

Then he remembered it must have taken that same mad courage to kill his father, and wrenched the pistol upwards with all his strength as her finger tightened on the trigger. There was a bang that reverberated off the walls, and flakes of plaster rained down on their heads like a localised snow-storm. Letting the weapon slip from her grasp, the blonde woman backed away through the haze of smoke. She was saying something, but Myrren couldn't make it out through the ringing in his ears. Then she drew one of her swords.

Anger washed through Myrren in a hot rush and then drained away, leaving him calm and detached. He'd given her every chance to end this without violence. She had no respect for him or his position. She'd tried to kill him. And now she'd see exactly what she was dealing with.

Drawing his own sword, he advanced on her. She grinned at him, bringing her blade round in the classic Breeze over Water opening: the sort of move a weaponmaster would use on the training ground to test the abilities of a new recruit. Myrren countered with the Mountain guard, then turned it into a sweeping Cascade of Ice. The blonde woman skipped nimbly back, her widening eyes the only sign of her shock. Her smile gone, she gave him the nod of one equal to another before snatching the second sword from her back and dropping into a defensive stance. Myrren eyed the twin blades, rapidly reformulating his plan of attack. Facing two swords required a different set of moves, but it wasn't beyond his capabilities.

Before she could try him again, he went for her with a Firestorm followed by a Steel Kiss, aiming to nullify the threat of the dual weapon by relieving her of at least one blade. She returned an effective Double Whirlwind, but he saw the narrowing of her eyes as the awkward foot positioning set her momentarily off balance. Before she could recover, he came in with another Firestorm and caught her second sword low on the blade, sending it clattering out of her reach. Pressing home his advantage, he used an unusual twist on the Bird's Wing attack to drive her across the floor until the backs of her legs hit a low stool. Intent on protecting herself from his bladework, she hadn't noticed the obstacle: she tripped and fell backwards, her other sword falling from her hand. He followed her, kicking the weapon clear, and menaced her with his own blade as she tried to scramble free. She froze, staring up at him with chest heaving and what appeared to be reluctant admiration in her eyes.

'You're good at this, my lord.'

Keeping her in place with the tip of his blade to her throat, Myrren gave her a fierce smile. He might not be able to Change – he might not have the loyalty of the Helm or the respect of his subjects – but he was still a bloody brilliant swordsman. He ought to be. He'd learned from the best weaponmasters the fifth ring had to offer. His muscles tensed as he prepared to drive the blade home.

'Don't kill her!' Serenna's voice recalled him to himself. He looked up: she was standing in the hallway, watching him.

He couldn't see her face behind the veil – couldn't tell how much of the fight she had witnessed – but of course she was right. He hadn't come here to kill anyone.

'Turn over,' he ordered the blonde, accompanying the words with tiny jerks of the blade. Without a word she wriggled onto her front, allowing him to place a knee in the small of her back and tie her wrists and ankles with the rope he'd brought. A clean handkerchief from his pocket served as a gag; she struggled at that, but he pushed his knee harder into her back and she subsided. She should count herself lucky. He would have been within his rights to have her whipped.

He went to the hall to retrieve the pistol, offering Serenna a reassuring smile on the way, then turned back into the apartment. The Changer girl was still standing in the doorway to an inner room, but now she held a kitchen knife in one white-knuckled hand. The other arm was wrapped protectively around herself, cradling the curve of her pregnant belly. As Myrren's gaze settled on her, she lifted her chin in a brave attempt at defiance.

'Leave me alone.'

Looking at her, Myrren found it hard to believe she could have Changed into a creature that had killed their father and seriously wounded Travers ... but no harder to believe than that Ayla had done it.

'You know I can't do that.' He raised the pistol, hoping she wouldn't know that it was of little use now it had been fired. 'Please, just come quietly.'

She scowled, though there was still a quaver in her voice. 'Ya have ta reload that thing before ya can use it again. D'ya think I don' know that?'

They didn't have time for this. For all Myrren knew, the Helm had already been alerted to his presence here, and he didn't want to confront Travers or anyone else with this matter until the girl was safely back in Darkhaven. He drew the hood from his inner pocket and walked towards her, ignoring the faltering knife.

'I'm sorry about this,' he told her. 'But it can't be helped.'

Dodging the ineffectual swipe she made at him, he grabbed her wrist and wrenched her arm up behind her back. Instantly her fingers loosened, letting him take the knife from her hand and put it aside. Still holding her in a position just short of painful, he tugged the hood down over her head one-handed. She kicked and swore at him, her voice muffled by the fabric; he pulled her arm up a fraction higher and she fell silent, though the set of her shoulders suggested mutiny.

Myrren glanced at the glowering blonde woman on the floor. Ideally he'd take her back to the tower as well, find out exactly what she'd been employed to do and by whom. Yet he wasn't convinced that he and Serenna could manage two rebellious captives by themselves – not without making a scene on the street, at least, which was the one thing he most wanted to avoid – and the Changer girl obviously had to take priority.

Damn you, Travers. If you'd just do your job properly – but Myrren swallowed his anger. Right now, the need to leave swiftly and without fuss overruled all other considerations.

'If I ever see your face again I'll have you locked up,' he told the blonde. Then he picked up her pistol once more – there was no way he was going to leave a weapon like that in her hands – and hustled what he hoped was his father's murderer out of the room. The sooner they got back to Darkhaven, the better.

NINETEEN

By the time he reached the fourth ring, Caraway was
exhausted. He hadn't realised quite how nerve-racking it
would be, escorting Ayla Nightshade through Arkannen.
He'd been tense the whole way, attempting to keep her
from becoming the target of hawkers, pickpockets,
conmen and beggars whilst at the same time doing his
best to look in multiple directions at once for any sign
of the Helm. Ayla herself hadn't helped; she'd tried to
assume an air of unconcern, but the wide-eyed looks she
kept throwing at the most everyday things stated more
clearly than a written placard that she was new to city
life. Her prohibition on being touched meant he'd almost
lost her in the second ring, where they'd been separated
by two men carrying a vast and intricately shaped glass
bottle across the street, and again in the third ring, where
they'd got caught in a press of people who had gathered
to see the newest airship go up for the first time. By now
he was longing to grab her by the elbow and march her
straight back the way they'd come. But she'd insisted on
accompanying him, and she'd made it clear he had no
right to stop her.

'Have you thought what we'll do when we get to the house?' she asked now. 'Surely, if what you say is true, the Helm will have this girl well guarded.'

Caraway looked sideways at her. She was wearing the blonde wig again; it made her both familiar and strange, like a person in a dream. Beneath it, despite her cautious words, her face was bright with excitement. He knew it had frustrated her, to sit tight whilst he carried out investigations on her behalf – though he suspected a large part of that frustration had sprung from the belief that she could have done the job better herself.

'I don't think most of the Helm are involved,' he told her. 'I think this is Travers' little secret. Else why hire Sorrow?'

'Mmm. I suppose … And you're sure the girl you saw was of Nightshade blood?'

Caraway shrugged. 'She looked pretty like it. Anyway, it makes sense. This new attack the night before last – your nightmare the same night – all that points to the existence of another Changer in the city.'

He'd told her what he'd found out and what he suspected the previous evening, once they'd found a new place to stay. Feeling flush with the money he'd earned from selling Ayla's hair, Caraway had plumped for a two-roomed apartment with a communal kitchen facility and an indoor latrine, paid up for a week in advance. There was a bed and a chaise longue, meaning they both had somewhere to sleep. There was a lock on the door. Best of all, there was a perfectly respectable corn mill outside instead of a tanner's yard. Ayla had said she supposed it would have to do, but to Caraway it was luxury. Of course, he'd run out of money soon enough, but he hoped by then he would have cleared Ayla's name. He hadn't thought much about his future beyond that point.

'I can't make it fit, though,' Ayla said now, and he frowned. 'What do you mean?'

'I can't believe my father would have had a child with another woman *before* he had Myrren. It's not the Nightshade way. We breed with our own blood, first and foremost, to keep the gift strong.' Her lips twisted. 'At least, that's the theory.'

The words held a dull resentment that was worse than anger. Caraway had always shied away from wondering what Ayla thought about being intended for her brother; now, all of a sudden, her feelings were painfully clear. Knowing that curiosity and sympathy would be equally unwelcome, he just nodded.

'I only caught a glimpse of her. She could have been between you and Lord Myrren in age. But I suppose we'll find out when we get there.'

This time, now he knew where he was going, he led Ayla along a different route through Ametrine and entered the Avenue of Rowans from the other end, avoiding the crime scene. As he'd hoped, that meant they didn't run into any Helmsmen; he didn't know if they'd still be congregating down there, but it was best not to take any chances. Yet as he and Ayla got closer to the house where he'd seen the dark-haired girl, he realised there was a carriage waiting outside it. Had the girl told Travers or Sorrow that she'd noticed someone watching the house? Were the Helm moving her to a new location?

He felt Ayla stiffen beside him, and glanced at her. She was staring at the house, surprise in every line of her body.

'That's Myrren,' she whispered.

Caraway squinted back down the street, and saw she was right: Myrren and a woman in a veil had just emerged through the front door. Between them was another woman who walked along with her hands locked around her pregnant belly, her bowed head covered with a black hood. The three of them moved at a brisk pace to the carriage. When they reached it, Myrren handed the veiled woman into the carriage and helped the pregnant woman in after her. Then he called an instruction to the driver, before leaping into the carriage himself and swinging the door shut behind them. It had all happened in the space of a few moments.

The driver urged his horses into a trot, starting the carriage swaying down the street towards Caraway and Ayla. To his horror, Caraway saw Ayla begin to step out into its path as though she intended to flag it down. He caught her wrist, yanking her against him; one hand went instinctively to the back of her head, hiding her face against his shoulder. To the occupants of the carriage, they would look like a couple enjoying an embrace at the side of the road. He held her like that until the carriage reached the end of the street and turned in the direction of the fifth gate. Then he allowed her to pull back and deal him a ringing slap across the face.

'What did you do that for?' she demanded, fury sparking in her eyes. Caraway rubbed his cheek and looked at her ruefully.

'I couldn't let them recognise you, Lady Ayla.'

'That was my brother, you idiot! He must have found out about this other Changer and arrested her. If I'd just made myself known to him then, I could have gone back to Darkhaven with him and everything would have been cleared up.'

'You can't be sure of that,' Caraway said. Then, as she opened her mouth for another retort, 'Please, just listen. Assuming the woman in the hood was the woman I saw yesterday, and assuming she is a rogue Changer who has been concealed in the city by Owen Travers for reasons best known to himself, why wasn't she struggling when Myrren came to take her away? And she's expecting a baby, which I didn't realise before. Is it even possible to Change if you're that heavily pregnant?'

Ayla's brows were drawn together in disapproval, but at least she was listening. Before she could interrupt him, Caraway ploughed on.

'And as for the father of the baby ... isn't it possible that the child is Myrren's? That he and this unknown Changer colluded in your father's death so Myrren could regain the throne that was going to be taken from him – and that Myrren let you out on the night of the murder deliberately to cast suspicion on you? In which case, couldn't the hood have been there to conceal the woman's identity, rather than because she was a prisoner?'

By now Ayla was very pale, and there was a stricken look in her eyes. It made Caraway's guts clench, but he couldn't stop until she realised the possible danger she was in. So he folded his arms and raised his eyebrows at her.

'Can you answer any of those questions with absolute certainty, Lady Ayla?'

'No,' she admitted.

'Exactly. Neither can I. And until we can, I don't think it's safe for you to return to Darkhaven. If the explanation is what you think it is, you can go home soon enough. But it's worth waiting until you're absolutely sure.'

There was a tense silence; then she nodded. 'You're right. I'm sorry.'

It was the first heartfelt apology he had ever received from her, but it didn't make him feel any better. Now that the need to make her see sense had faded, the old guilt was creeping back into its place, telling him he should never have raised his voice to her. That he was worthless, and that he needed a drink to make it all go away.

'All right,' he said awkwardly. 'Now I'm going to go into the house and see what I can find out. I suggest you wait here.'

Still unusually meek, Ayla inclined her head in assent, and he headed for the house. It was four stories high, each storey a separate set of rooms; he had seen the girl in a top-floor window, so he climbed all the way up. The door of the apartment was pulled to, but it swung open at his touch. Inside there were signs of a struggle: furniture knocked over, a scattering of plaster across the floor, a lingering smell of something smoky. Caraway walked down the hall into the living room, and stopped. Naeve Sorrow was lying face-down on the ornate rug, a gag in her mouth, wrists and ankles tied behind her and joined with another length of cord. Crouching beside her, Caraway untied the gag; she spat it out as soon as it was loose enough.

'What happened here?' he asked her. She scowled at him.

'You – you followed me yesterday. What do you want?'

'I need to know what happened here,' he repeated. Sorrow's eyes scanned his face, then narrowed.

'I know you,' she said slowly. 'I didn't recognise you before. You were in the Helm, years ago … you're the one who was involved in that scandal. Tomas Caraway.' Her lips tightened. 'I'm not telling you anything.'

'Why are you here?' Caraway flung the questions at her as though they were stones that could knock a response out of her if he tried hard enough. 'Why did Travers hire you? What do you know about the dark-haired girl who was here yesterday? Was it her that was just taken away by Myrren Nightshade?'

To his annoyance, Sorrow only gave him a cool stare and said it again. 'I'm not telling you anything.'

'Fine.' Caraway affected unconcern. He knew she wouldn't be intimidated by a threat of violence, but there were other threats she might respond to. 'Then I'll just leave you tied up here. Who knows how long it'll be before someone else comes visiting?'

She looked defiant. 'I'll free myself.'

'And how long will that take you? By the time you get out of here, it might all be over.' He saw something flicker in her eyes, and pressed the point home. 'You're clearly involved in this situation. No doubt you have something to gain from it. But it's unlikely you'll gain anything if you're stuck here for days.'

'All right,' she snapped at him. 'The girl's name is Elisse. Travers hired me to protect her against the Changer creature that's stalking the streets.'

'Is she a Nightshade?'

'I don't think so.'

'Who's the father of her child?'

'No idea.'

'What did Myrren want with her?'

'Answers to the same questions you're asking.' From her recumbent position, Sorrow gave a kind of half-shrug. 'I don't know any more.'

Caraway studied her face. She was obviously lying – certainly as to the extent of her knowledge, and perhaps in her answers as well – but the set of her chin was obstinate. He was familiar enough with Sorrow to know she wouldn't tell him anything she didn't want to, whatever he did to her. Nor did he much like the idea of torturing a woman when he wasn't even sure what she had done.

'If that's all you've got ...' he said, starting for the door, but was stopped by her raised voice.

'It's all I know, Caraway, I swear! Now please, untie me …'

He turned, eyebrows lifting. 'Never said I would.' Seeing the mute anger in her face, he added, 'Come off it, Sorrow. You'd be after us as soon as I let you go.'

'Us?'

He didn't reply, biting his tongue at the slip. She sighed.

'At least put me into a more comfortable position, Caraway. I can't lie like this for days.' Then, as he hesitated, 'You can sit me on the spinet stool. It's out of sight of the window, so I won't be able to signal for help.'

His first instinct was to say no, to leave straight away. But she did look like she was in pain, and she hadn't done anything to harm him, after all. She'd just got caught in the middle of whatever battle was going on between Owen Travers and Myrren Nightshade.

'Fine,' he said, even as he cursed himself for a soft-hearted fool. 'I'll move you.'

After untying the cord that connected her wrists and ankles, he helped Sorrow hobble over to the stool, then fastened her ankles to one of its legs. The stool was a heavy one, so there wasn't any way she'd be able to drag it with her, but all the same he was conscious of a vague sense of misgiving.

'Just remember,' he said when he'd finished. 'I could have hurt you, but I didn't.'

Her answering smile was satirical. 'I always remember weakness, Tomas Caraway.'

He'd been wavering over whether to fetch her some water before he left, but that remark made the decision easy. Without a word, he turned on his heel and left the room.

As soon as Caraway had gone, Sorrow wriggled around on the stool until her fingers touched cool stone. Perfect. She'd noticed it while she'd been lying on the floor trussed up like a piece of meat: a shard of the vase she'd blown apart, still nestled among the keys of the spinet. Slowly and carefully, she eased it into her hand. Myrren hadn't made the mistake of underestimating her because she was a woman; he'd tied her as tight as he could, ensuring she wouldn't be able to work herself free, which would make what she was about to do all the harder. Gritting her teeth, she pulled her wrists as far apart as they would go and began sawing at the thin rope that bound them.

By the time she had finished she had several nicks and raw patches on her skin, but none of them were serious and she didn't stop to examine them. Having made short work of her ankle binding with one of her knives, she got to her feet and flung a quick glance around the room. Her swords still lay on the floor; she picked them up and returned them to their place on her back. Myrren had taken her pistol, but he'd left behind her bag with the powder and all the other accoutrements, which was something. He clearly didn't know much about firearms. If she could just come up with the right lever to hold him and Travers in balance, she'd be able to get the weapon back and make sure Elisse was all right into the bargain. Not that she had any attachment to the woman; she'd only known her for a day. But it was a matter of professional pride.

Holdall in hand, Sorrow left the room and descended the stairs as fast as she could. She burst out of the front door and onto the street in time to see Caraway and a blonde girl in a cloak turning a corner at the far end. Right. She'd follow them. After all, Caraway had done it to her; it was only fair. Maybe she'd find out why he was so interested in Elisse.

She ran to the top of the street, keeping her footfalls as silent as possible, and saw the two of them ahead. Already she'd caught up to within safe stalking distance, which was considerably closer than Caraway had realised yesterday. But then, she knew more about subterfuge than any Helmsman past or present. She had to, in her profession. And when you were trying not to be noticed, the important thing was not to act stealthy. In general, people had a good sense of when other people were creeping around behind them; follow someone in too suspicious a manner, and they'd be able to pick you out even in a crowd. Yet relax and walk as though you were meant to be there, and chances were you wouldn't even register on their awareness. Dropping into the unhurried saunter she had perfected over the years, Sorrow started after Caraway and his companion.

They'd gone only a short way when a gust of wind caught the girl's blonde hair. She clapped a hand to her head, but not before Sorrow had caught a glimpse of dark hair underneath. A wig. Interesting. Did that mean … Then the girl peered fearfully back over her shoulder, her gaze passing right across the doorway in which Sorrow lounged with careful nonchalance, and her face became visible for the first time. A shiver ran from Sorrow's tailbone to the nape of her neck: the sensation she felt when an unexpected opportunity opened up in front of her.

Ayla Nightshade.

Sorrow's lips curved in a grim smile. No doubt Captain Travers would love to hear about this. And he would hear about it – for a price.

TWENTY

Elisse scowled at the two people sitting across the table from her, trying to hide her fear. When they'd bundled her into the carriage, leaving Sorrow tied and helpless behind them, she'd thought her end had come for certain. If Myrren could defeat Sorrow that easily, he sure as sunrise wouldn't have any trouble finishing off a pregnant woman. As time had passed without any sign that he wanted to kill her, her mind-numbing terror had begun to subside; yet it didn't fade completely. After all, Travers had warned her of the danger she was in, and look what had happened to him.

'What's your name?' Myrren asked her now, fixing her with an intent look. When she folded her arms and pressed her lips together, he exchanged a glance with the veiled woman sitting next to him. Or at least, Elisse thought he did. She couldn't see the woman's eyes through the veil; it was pretty creepy.

As if she could hear Elisse's thoughts, the woman pushed back the heavy fall of fabric to reveal her face. She turned out to be young – younger than Elisse herself – and quite attractive, though her air of cool self-possession made Elisse want to hit her.

'I'm Serenna,' she said. 'I'm a priestess in the sixth ring. And of course you know Lord Myrren. Why don't you tell us who you are?'

Elisse sighed. She couldn't very well keep refusing to give them her name – and she supposed it wasn't so sensible to antagonise a man who might want her dead.

'My name's Elisse,' she mumbled, and Myrren nodded.

'Welcome to Darkhaven, Elisse.'

The words should have carried a certain amount of suppressed glee, or at least a hint of sarcasm, but he appeared to be serious. Repressing an incredulous snort, Elisse looked from him to Serenna. The two of them were so restrained. They were bursting with questions they wanted to ask her, yet they sat there studying her as though she were a rare creature with whom they didn't know quite how to communicate. Well, if they weren't going to ask any questions, she would.

'Wha' did ya do ta Sorrow?'

Myrren frowned. 'What?'

'Naeve Sorrow. My bodyguard.' The woman had promised to protect her, but Elisse couldn't blame her for failing; as it had turned out, even a bodyguard with a pistol hadn't been enough to stand against Myrren Nightshade. 'Wha' did ya do ta her?'

'She'll be all right.' He seemed faintly apologetic. 'You have to understand … it's very important that we talk to you.'

'What about?'

'Well …' Again he hesitated. This time Serenna stepped in to fill the pause.

'We need to ask you … how long have you known you are a Changer?'

A wild gurgle of laughter rose up in Elisse's throat; she pressed the back of her hand to her mouth to stop it, breathing out slowly. 'I think ya got the wrong person.'

'There's no point in denying it.' Myrren's expression was very stern. 'My father was killed, and Serenna and Captain Travers were attacked, by a Changer creature. And other than Ayla and me, you are the only person of Nightshade blood left alive.'

All of a sudden he looked very like his father: the sweep of his hair, the set of his jaw, his fierce blue eyes. It was all Elisse could do not to stare – but she had to answer the preposterous allegation he had just made.

'I'm not o' Nightshade blood,' she said.

'Come on, Elisse.' There was an edge to Myrren's voice now. 'When I said I was looking for a child of Florentyn Nightshade, you were terrified ...'

'O' course!' she snapped. 'I thought ya were there for my baby –'

She pulled herself to a halt, but the words had already been said. The dawning shock on Myrren's face told her everything she needed to know. He hadn't realised. He'd thought she, and not her baby, was Florentyn's child. Would this make him more or less likely to want to dispose of her?

'Your baby,' Serenna said softly, as Myrren seemed unable to speak. 'Florentyn Nightshade was your baby's father?'

Elisse nodded.

'But your colouring ...' Myrren sounded hoarse. 'Even I took you for Ayla, for an instant. Where did you get such colouring, if not from Florentyn?'

Elisse shrugged. 'How should I know? My father was a labourer in the city; Mam always said I take after him.' Irritated, she added tartly, 'It's not impossible for an ordinary person ta look a little like a Nightshade, ya know.'

'Lord Myrren.' Serenna spoke with diffidence. 'Just because the baby is Florentyn's, doesn't mean Elisse can't be of Nightshade blood herself. Would your father have ...'

'No!' It was almost a shout. Myrren's fists came down on the table, making both Elisse and Serenna jump. There was silence. Then Myrren said more quietly, but with just as much vehemence, 'No. I don't believe it. I don't believe any of it.'

Elisse couldn't understand why he was so adamant. She was about to offer a sharp retort when it occurred to her that this must mean Ayla was the killer, just as Travers had suggested. No wonder Myrren didn't want to believe the truth. The knowledge made her soften her tone, albeit slightly.

'Sorry if ya don' like it, but it's true. The only Nightshade blood in me is in the child I'm carrying.'

Myrren's mouth set in a sceptical line. 'So it's just a coincidence, is it? That you look like one of us?'

'O' course not!' Goaded, Elisse bit back at him. 'Ya bloody father chose me so that his bastard child would have the right colouring. I was as close as he could get ta a proper Nightshade – he told me so himself. He would o' taken any girl who looked the leas' little bit like one o' the family, but I'm the one he happened ta stumble across.' She took a long, difficult breath, and aimed every bit of sarcasm she could muster in Myrren's direction. 'Ya can be sure that made me feel really special.'

Myrren said nothing. Glaring across the table at him, she saw his hands shaking before he locked them tightly together. No doubt he was ashamed of his father, and so he should be. Bloody Nightshades! Elisse was sick of the whole cursed lot of them.

She was sick of them, but the child she was carrying tied her to them whether she liked it or not.

'Elisse ...' That was Serenna, offering her a sympathetic smile – though a fat lot she could know about it, being a priestess. 'I'm very sorry, but I think you're going to have to tell us exactly what happened. We ... we need to know what Captain Travers has been hiding all this time.'

Reluctant, Elisse glanced at Myrren, whose face mirrored her own emotion. After a moment, however, he looked up and gave an abrupt nod of agreement. Clearly he didn't want to hear it, but was accepting it as a painful duty. Well, if he thought it was painful for him, how did he think she felt?

There was an expectant pause; they were waiting for her to speak. Fine. She'd tell them the story, and she hoped it choked them.

'Ta start with it was jus' talk,' she said. 'He'd show up now and then, chat ta me as I was doing my chores, asking me all kinds o' questions. I thought it was strange, but ... I s'pose I was flattered, too. I mean, I didn' know who he was in them days – I didn' know how rare my colouring was, ya see – but he was obviously someone important. I thought how nice it was, that a rich man like that found me interesting enough ta chat with.' She felt her lips twist in a caustic smile. 'Then, one day, everything changed.'

It was early autumn, but the air was still thick with summer's heat. She'd been kneeling on the riverbank with her arms immersed up to the elbow, trying to get the stains out of the hem of her best winter dress, when she looked up to see him standing at the treeline on the opposite side of the river.

'Shall I come over, Elisse?' he called to her, gesturing at the stepping stones that lay half-submerged and slippery in a line between them. She straightened up, laughing.

'Better watch ya step, sir!' By then she'd fallen into the habit of thinking of him as a kind of surrogate father; after all, she had almost nothing on which to base her idea of what a father should be. 'Ya wouldn' wan' ta spoil ya nice clothes.'

187

'No chance of that,' he told her, and crossed as nimbly and quickly as if he'd been using that particular set of stepping stones his whole life. Yet when he had nearly reached her, his heel came down on a smooth patch and he wobbled, holding out a pleading hand.

'A little help, my dear?'

Still grinning, she left her laundry weighted down by a couple of rocks in the river and went to steady him. Yet somehow, as her fingers touched his, he moved back and it was she who lost her balance, sliding down the bank into his arms. He caught her against his chest, looking into her face; the sudden intensity in his eyes made her try to pull away, but his grip was unbreakable. Then his mouth came down on hers, hard and aggressive. She didn't like it. She tried again to retreat, and this time he let her.

'What're ya doing?' she gasped, trying to catch her breath.

'What do you think I'm doing?' It was said lightly, but the purpose was still in his face; it made her uneasy. 'You can't tease me all this time, Elisse, and then act so coy now.'

She knew she hadn't been teasing. She should have run. But a moment of self-doubt left her hesitating, and in that moment he reached out again to grasp her shoulders.

'I – I don' think –' she stammered, but he pulled her close.

'Sssh. This is what I'm here for. You know that.'

He kissed her a second time, silencing her incoherent protests. And perhaps she was just being silly, she told herself. Perhaps it had always been obvious what he wanted from her, only she'd been too stupid to see it. After all, she liked him, didn't she? Maybe that was enough. So she didn't resist as he manoeuvred her into a lying position on the bank and slid his hands up her thighs beneath her thin summer skirt. She endured the discomfort as he pushed inside her, grinding the knobs of her spine against the rocky ground beneath. With the prickly softness of grass tickling her outflung hands and the rich smell of crushed earth in her nostrils, she watched his face above her and wondered what it was about this act that was so significant, so essential, that a man like him had to pursue it on a riverbank with a girl like her. And when it was over, he rewarded her with a self-satisfied smile.

'You know, Elisse, in all the time we've known each other you've never once asked me my name.'

It was true: she'd always called him sir. Somehow it had never seemed her place to ask him questions. She mumbled something indistinct, and his smile widened.

'My name is Florentyn Nightshade. And I want you to bear me an heir.'

Florentyn Nightshade. Then this man was the overlord of Darkhaven. This man was a Changer. This man had power over everyone in Mirrorvale; he had power over *her*. Elisse scrambled to her feet, tugging her crumpled skirt down over her bare thighs.

'My lord – I –'

'You may already be quickening,' he said. 'But I'd better visit you several more times, just to be sure.'

'Don't ya have an heir already?' she asked, struggling to understand. A brooding expression settled on his face.

'My existing children are … insufficient. I need an alternative, Elisse. Another chance at producing a true Nightshade child. And lacking any appropriate female of the blood, you're the best I've got.'

Speechless, she stared at him. Gradually his dark look eased and he smiled at her once more.

'Don't worry, my dear. This will all work to your advantage. Once you're carrying my child, I'll give you every luxury you could possibly want. You'll never have to work for a living again. And one day, if it's born with the right gifts, your child might become overlord of Darkhaven. That's a big step up in the world for a girl like you.'

He wasn't saying anything about marriage, Elisse noticed. He seemed to assume that she would treat the whole thing as a business arrangement, for the sake of the advancement it would bring her. That was obviously what he expected of *a girl like her*. And why should he expect any different? She hadn't struggled; she'd let him do what he wanted. Now she had to accept the consequences. With him being who he was, it wasn't as though she had a choice.

'Good,' Florentyn said, correctly interpreting her silence as assent. 'Then I'll see you again very soon, my dear.'

And with that, the course of her life changed for good.

Elisse's lips twisted again as she concluded her recitation. True to his word, Florentyn had come to her repeatedly over the next few weeks, bedding her in a host of awkward places out of sight of the farm. Believing his promises of luxury and grandeur, half convincing herself she was in love with him, she'd allowed it to happen – though she never grew to like it. And as soon as it had become apparent that she was pregnant, he'd bundled her up and carted her off to Arkannen.

'It's no' like he forced it on me,' she told Myrren now. 'I wen' along with it 'cos I thought he'd be able ta give me a better life. O' course, as i' turns out, I preferred the life I already had – but he wasn' ta know that.'

'And Captain Travers?' Myrren asked faintly. 'Where does he come into this?'

Elisse shrugged. 'He's the one who's looked after me, mostly. There's not many people who know I'm here or – or why.' She lifted her head, meeting Myrren's gaze without flinching. 'He's the one who warned me abou' Lady Ayla. Tha' she killed Florentyn, and tha' maybe she'll kill me too.'

'On that front, Travers is sorely mistaken.' Myrren's voice was tight. 'Ayla has no reason to hurt you.'

'With respect, my lord, o' course she has. Both o' ya have.' Elisse sat upright, made defiant by fear now that at last they were getting to the point. 'This baby is Florentyn Nightshade's baby – ya father's baby – and it could grow up ta be a Changer. If it does, it could be a direct challenge ta ya position.'

To her surprise, Myrren's tense face relaxed into a smile. 'Believe me, Elisse, at this moment that's the least of my worries. It will be fourteen years or more before we find out whether your child is a Changer, and longer still before he or she would pose any kind of threat to myself or Ayla.' He exchanged glances with Serenna. 'All the same, from now on I want you to stay here in Darkhaven. The child needs to grow up with its family, to learn about its heritage.'

I'm its family, Elisse thought, but she didn't say it. Instead she asked, just to be sure, 'So – so ya not going ta hurt the baby?'

'There are few enough Nightshades in the world without destroying one of them,' Myrren said. 'I won't hurt you or your baby. I just think it would be safer if you stayed within these walls.'

Yeah, right – but again she suppressed the retort that leapt to her lips. Because the funny thing was, although she had no reason to believe him, she couldn't help but feel that Myrren was telling the truth. That he had no interest in hurting her. In which case, she probably would be safer in Darkhaven than anywhere else.

She just wished it felt less like a prison sentence.

TWENTY-ONE

Captain Travers aimed a razor-sharp glare at the physician who was hovering anxiously beside his bed.

'I don't care what you say,' he announced through gritted teeth. 'I've already lost a day and a half. I'm getting up, and I'm getting dressed, and that's all there is to it.'

'I really wouldn't advise it, captain.' The physician looked distressed. 'You're fit enough, yes, but your stitches –'

'Screw my stitches!' Travers snarled. 'I'm just going to sit at the table and read these reports. I'm not going to sign up for a practice session with a weaponmaster.'

The physician sighed. 'If you're set on it, captain, there's nothing I can do to stop you.'

With an air of slightly offended dignity, he picked up his bag and stalked out. Travers relieved his feelings by throwing a pillow at the closing door, then swung his legs out of bed. His head was fuzzy, as though strands of his fever-soaked dreams still clung to it, but he refused to let that stop him. He was getting up, and the world be damned.

Once he'd washed, shaved and struggled into his uniform, he felt considerably less defiant and considerably more respectful of the physician's opinion. His wounds were throbbing in counterpoint to his heartbeat, which itself was much too fast and erratic. Still, now he was up he might as well see it through. Small sheaf of reports in hand, he staggered over to the table and sat down.

Most of the reports contained standard administrative information, but three were sealed and marked urgent. The first concerned the attack that Travers himself had suffered: the Helm had taken over the investigation from the city watch, but learned nothing of significance. By the time Travers had been found, the creature was long gone; the only traces of its presence were a bloody footprint, several scorch marks and another scale similar to that which had been found beside Florentyn's body. There had been no witnesses to the attack, and no-one in the vicinity had seen or heard anything suspicious. In fact, the report concluded, the captain's own eyewitness account was the single best piece of evidence they had. Travers tossed the folded paper aside with a contemptuous snort. He hadn't expected them to find anything, not when they were dealing with a Changer creature. The only way to catch a Changer was to catch her in human form.

The second report was from one of the Helmsmen he had sent to watch the lower gates. Travers scanned the straggling handwriting, then read it again more slowly and with growing incredulity. Phrase after phrase jumped out at him, each more shocking than the last: *acting upon information laid with us, we attended a room above the tanner's yard ... found Ayla Nightshade in the company of Tomas Caraway ... four Helmsmen were overcome, all injured, two grievously wounded ... have been unable to track the fugitives.* His gaze travelled inexorably back up the page to the name *Tomas Caraway*, and he cursed under his breath. He didn't know what infuriated him most: that the Helm should have come so close to Ayla and let her slip through their fingers, that Ayla should have sought refuge with Caraway – of all people! – or that a man so destitute, so inebriated, so bloody *useless* as Breakblade should have defeated four of the Helm with apparent ease. And now it would be twice as hard to find Ayla, because she would be on her guard.

Travers broke the seal on the next paper, but for some time he couldn't concentrate. Caraway's name kept swimming before his mind's eye, followed by white noise as his brain filled up with swearwords. Finally, however, he managed to banish it long enough to read the third report. It was from the man he had set to watch Myrren, one of the few trusted Helmsmen who knew about Elisse, and it was a couple of lines in a hasty scrawl. *Captain Travers – have to report Lord Myrren visited fourth ring this morning and brought alternative back to Darkhaven. Unable to intervene without calling loyalty of Helm into question. Please advise.*

This time Travers was too stunned even to curse. Myrren had found Elisse. Myrren had brought Elisse to Darkhaven. While he had been lying in his bed recovering from Ayla's bloody attack, his entire world had been falling down around him and any chance of fulfilling Florentyn's last orders had vanished forever. In one fatal blow, he had lost control of the situation. And where had the sellsword he had hired been whilst all this was happening? By the elements! Was everyone under his command an incompetent fool?

But no, this was all Ayla's fault. If she hadn't attacked him, then he would have been there when the Helm went to Caraway's room. He would have killed Caraway and got Ayla under his control. And Myrren would have been too distracted even to think of going into the city. Yes, every little bit of blame in the entire debacle could be laid at Ayla's feet – and Travers would make her pay. Oh yes, he would definitely make her pay. Locking Ayla up was the only act he could still carry out on Florentyn's behalf.

On Florentyn's behalf, and on his own.

As though it had been timed specifically to taunt him with his failure, an abrupt knock sounded at the door. Travers knew even before it swung open that it would be Myrren Nightshade on the other side. The overlord of Darkhaven strode into the room, stopping only a short distance from the table. His expression was grave, perhaps a little sombre; he had the air of a man forced to perform an unpleasant duty.

'The physician told me you were feeling better,' he said. 'I'm glad to know your injuries weren't serious.' There was a pause, before he fixed Travers with a stern look and added, 'I expect you know why I'm here.'

Travers arranged his features into something suitably respectful and repentant. 'You're probably here about Elisse, my lord.'

'Quite so,' Myrren said. 'Didn't I ask you only yesterday morning whether there was anything you wanted to tell me?'

'My lord …' Travers spread his hands. 'You have to understand, I was following your father's orders. He wanted Elisse and the baby to be kept a secret. Even though he is no longer with us, it would have been wrong to break the oath of silence he laid upon me.'

With a resigned sigh, Myrren sat down in the chair on the opposite side of the table.

'I understand why you might have kept the girl hidden,' he said. 'But neither I nor Ayla would ever hurt her. The baby is of our blood, and as such is to be protected. Once it has been born, I want it to be brought up here in Darkhaven.'

Travers said nothing – he could hardly object to that. True, he had lost the advantage that secrecy had conferred on him, but he was willing to play the long game. If, in fourteen years' time, Elisse's child revealed itself to have the Nightshade gift, the Helm would be willing to support its claim over Myrren's. For all Travers knew, Myrren was spineless enough to agree to that himself. The man didn't have the ruthless edge that would lead him to rid the world of anyone who stood as a potential rival to himself and his heirs.

'Where I do take issue is with the guard you set over Elisse,' Myrren said. 'Engaging in a fight with a member of the royal family is little short of treason, and the Helm should be quick to prosecute anyone who dares do such a thing. Yet I must assume the woman was acting under your instruction.'

Travers shook his head – what else could he do? If anyone ever found out that he had told Sorrow she could do whatever it took to keep Myrren and Ayla from getting their hands on Elisse, short of killing them, he'd lose his captaincy for sure and probably his position in the Helm as well. After that, there'd be nothing to choose between him and Tomas Caraway.

'With Lord Florentyn gone, I feared for Elisse's safety,' he said. 'I hired a guard for her only so that she'd have someone with her all the time who could protect her from danger. But if Sorrow fought you, then she was overstepping her authority.' Catching a look of doubt on Myrren's face, he added, 'I will of course have her punished appropriately.'

'Very well.' Myrren ran his hands through his hair, a weary gesture. 'I do wish you'd trusted me with all this, captain. Or that my father had.'

'I daresay he had his reasons,' Travers said. Then, as Myrren got up to leave, 'Forgive the question, my lord, but where does this leave us with the investigation into Lord Florentyn's death?'

Myrren froze, but said nothing. Encouraged, Travers continued.

'Some time ago, you expressed your reservations as to whether Lady Ayla was really guilty of the crime. Perhaps you thought you would uncover an alternative explanation. But as it turns out, you have been chasing a shadow. Elisse and her baby have nothing to do with these vicious attacks. As I have said all along, Lady Ayla is the only possible perpetrator.'

There was a tense silence. Then Myrren said, tight and low, 'I refuse to believe my sister is a murderer, Captain Travers. And when you find her, I insist that you notify me immediately. If I find out you have done anything else, I will personally make sure you are demoted.'

For the space of a heartbeat, Travers made no answer. A wonderful idea had dropped fully formed into his mind, hitting him with the force of a lightning strike.

'Of course, my lord,' he said finally. 'She must be given a fair trial, and any evidence you have that would exonerate her will naturally be taken into account.' He paused, before delivering his master stroke. 'But the latest information we have suggests that she may have left the city. In which case, it's possible we may never find her.'

Myrren flinched as though he'd been slapped, before answering with a stiff nod. 'Thank you, Captain Travers.'

Travers sketched a bow from his seated position and watched the other man leave, continuing to turn the new idea over in his mind. He would find Ayla. He would bring her to Darkhaven, secretly, without the rest of the Helm hearing of it. He would lock her up, and he would keep the key. And if Myrren or anyone else asked if there was any news, he would deny all knowledge of her whereabouts. That way he would be fulfilling Florentyn's orders in every respect. Ayla would be incarcerated, and if Elisse's child turned out to be a Changer, he or she would have no challengers when it came to taking the throne. Everyone would think Ayla had fled the city, and he ... he would have her to himself.

Another knock came at the door, and he looked up as one of the Helm stuck his head into the room. 'Naeve Sorrow to see you, captain. I brought her the back way; Lord Myrren doesn't know she's here.'

Perfect. Travers nodded. 'Show her in. I have some questions to ask her.'

He waited where he was, evaluating his plan from every angle, until Sorrow sauntered in and settled herself in Myrren's recently vacated chair. Travers exchanged nods with the Helmsman accompanying her, who backed out of the room and closed the door after him. Immediately Travers leaned forward, glowering at his visitor.

'You're meant to be the most vicious sellsword in Arkannen,' he flung at her. 'Yet you were defeated at the first test! You lost the woman you were supposed to be protecting to the very man you were supposed to be protecting her against. Is your reputation based on nothing more than boasts and lies?'

'You tell me, Captain Travers.' Sorrow seemed unaffected by his diatribe. Her gaze flickered downwards; he followed it under the table, and his pulse quickened. A blade had sprung out of the toe of her left boot, positioned with exquisite care at the back of his knee. One move she didn't like, and she could sever the tendons and put him out of action for good.

'I was hampered by two factors in the assignment you gave me,' Sorrow said, punctuating her words with little twitches of her toe that kept Travers in a state of permanent tension. 'First, you expressly forbade me to kill a Nightshade, whatever else I did. In a certain type of fight that becomes quite a handicap. Second, and more importantly, Myrren Nightshade knows his way around a sword.'

Travers couldn't help the scepticism that crept into his voice. 'Myrren Nightshade? The man born without the gift every one of his ancestors possessed?'

'I've never fought anyone better,' Sorrow said. 'What made you think he wouldn't be good? Have you ever watched him train?'

Travers was forced to shake his head. She gave him an amused look, stroking the back of his knee with her blade.

'As heir to the throne of Darkhaven, Myrren will have been taught by the best. No doubt his father expected him to excel. And Myrren Nightshade strikes me as a man who has always done everything he could to meet his father's expectations, to make up for that one core failing he can never change. If I were you, I wouldn't underestimate him.'

She withdrew her toe, and there was a metallic sound as the blade retracted inside the sole of her boot. Travers relaxed, breathing a surreptitious sigh of relief. Sorrow smirked at him as though she knew exactly what he was thinking.

'All this is beside the point, Captain Travers. I came here because I've acquired certain information that I think may be of interest to you.'

Travers had been considering having her thrown out – how dare the woman threaten him on his own ground? – but that stayed his hand, at least for now. 'Go on.'

'After Myrren left me, I had a visit from Tomas Caraway.' Her lips quirked at the involuntary clenching of his fists. 'Yes, I thought that might catch your attention. Seems Lord Myrren isn't the only one on your tail.'

'Was Ayla still with him?' Travers demanded. Her eyebrows lifted.

'Ah, so you knew that part already. Yes, Ayla was with him, though he tried to keep it from me. The poor sap couldn't bear to see a woman all tied up and forlorn, so I convinced him to move me somewhere I could free myself. I followed him and Ayla all the way back to the first ring.' Sorrow gave Travers a look that suggested she was well aware of how badly he wanted this information. 'I know where they're staying, and I'll tell you on two conditions.'

'Well, what are they?' he asked with some impatience. She leaned back in her chair, examining her fingernails, deliberately stringing him along.

'One, you tell the Helm to give me the freedom of Darkhaven. Myrren Nightshade took something from me that I want back. I'm going to find it, and I don't want anybody to stop me.' Her gaze flicked up to meet his for the briefest of moments. 'And two, you let me know where Elisse is.'

Alerted by the offhand tone in which she had made her second request, Travers studied her face and felt a smile tugging at the corners of his mouth. 'You like her, don't you? You like the little country girl. I wouldn't have expected her to be to your taste.'

'Don't be ridiculous.' Sorrow's voice was flat, but a telltale hint of colour crept into her cheeks. 'I just want to check that she's all right.'

'I'm sure she's fine,' Travers drawled, resisting the urge to provoke the sellsword further. 'Our noble overlord wouldn't hurt a flea, let alone a woman.'

'Really.' Sorrow raised an eyebrow. 'So I take it you don't class me as a woman.'

'I wouldn't dream of it,' he replied maliciously, and she nodded.

'Funny, that. Because I'd barely class you as a man.' Grinning at his mute fury, she dismissed the subject with a gesture. 'So do you agree to my conditions?'

Travers pretended to mull it over, but the truth was he'd have given Sorrow anything she asked for. She knew where Ayla was, and that overrode all other considerations. Of course, whether he actually kept to the terms of the agreement was another matter altogether.

'All right,' he said. 'I'll let the men know they're not to interfere with you.' He gave her a sapient look. 'Though do bear in mind that I can and will revoke that instruction if you start doing anything I don't like.'

She nodded as though she would have expected nothing less, and Travers continued.

'As for your second condition, Elisse has been put in Ayla's room. She's sharing it with Serenna, the priestess Myrren appears to be using as his personal aide – supposedly for Elisse's protection, though no doubt in reality it's so they can watch her.' He gave Sorrow a rather vindictive smile. 'So you won't be able to see her alone. And anything you say to her will be taken straight back to Myrren.'

'Not a problem.' Apparently Sorrow wasn't going to rise to his bait a second time; she crossed one leg over the other, unruffled. 'So is Myrren sleeping with his priestess? I didn't think priestesses were meant to do that kind of thing.'

'I doubt it. Myrren's not one to break the rules.' With a shrug, Travers set that question aside and moved on to the only thing he was really interested in. 'I've agreed to your conditions, Sorrow. Where is Ayla?'

Her eyebrows twitched. 'You give me directions to Ayla's room, and I'll give you directions to Ayla herself.'

'Fine.' Travers tore a strip of paper off the bottom of one of his reports and made a quick sketch of the route through Darkhaven. In return, Sorrow handed him a folded card that contained an address in the first ring.

'Nice doing business with you,' she said, taking his hasty map and flashing him a smile. 'I'll show myself out. Don't forget to inform the Helm of my presence.'

Travers scowled after her retreating back. She was much too cocky for her own good, that one. Luckily, while they were talking he had come up with a way of turning their agreement to his advantage. What had he told Myrren? That Sorrow had overstepped her authority when she'd engaged him in a fight. And the best way to ensure that Myrren never found out the truth – either about the instructions Travers had really given her, or about his knowledge of Ayla's whereabouts – was to have Sorrow disposed of. She was a criminal, after all. It had gone against his principles to employ her in the first place. He didn't think anyone in the Helm would object if she was put through a quick trial and an even quicker execution.

When the Helmsman who had originally brought her in reappeared, Travers beckoned him closer and lowered his voice to a conspiratorial murmur.

'Naeve Sorrow is currently loose in Darkhaven. I believe she's here to steal something. Have her watched, but make no move to apprehend her until she finds what she's looking for.' He gave the man a significant look. 'After all, we won't have any evidence against her unless we catch her in the act, will we?'

Once the Helmsman had gone, Travers leaned back in his chair and aimed a grin of satisfaction at the ceiling. Everything was falling into place. And this time tomorrow, Ayla Nightshade would be in his power.

TWENTY-TWO

Her arms wrapped around her knees, Ayla huddled in the corner of the chaise longue and watched the flames leaping in the fireplace. Even in the height of summer, when it wasn't needed for practical purposes, it was amazing how comforting a fire could be. That in itself made this place a thousand times better than Caraway's old lodgings, let alone the availability of a proper water closet. She wasn't sure about the communal bathing room, but she supposed she could sneak in there early tomorrow morning before anyone else was around. She couldn't decide whether it would be worse to stay dirty or have someone in the building catch her with no clothes on. Caraway didn't appear to have any such dilemma; he was down there at this very moment having a much-needed wash. This place must be like paradise to him, after what he was used to.

Ayla had to admit that Caraway had been useful to her, much as she longed to despise him. Without his contact in the fifth ring, she never would have found out about the possibility of another Changer in Arkannen. If he hadn't come back in time to help her, she would have been captured by the Helm the day they found her alone. And today, if she'd gone storming up to the fourth ring without him, she could have ended up in even worse trouble than she was in now.

Isn't it possible that the child is Myrren's? His words still whispered in her mind, circling round and round like vultures waiting to swoop down on her weakness. *That he and this unknown Changer colluded in your father's death so Myrren could regain the throne that was going to be taken from him – and that Myrren let you out on the night of the murder deliberately to cast suspicion on you?* She didn't want to believe it. Myrren had always been her friend, the only person she could turn to in the dark days after her mother's death when her father had been too wrapped up in his own grief to concern himself with hers. But she had to allow that it was a possibility.

'Are you all right?'

At the sound of Caraway's voice she looked up, only to find that she was regarding him through a blur of tears. She blinked them away and gave him a curt nod.

'Of course.'

He didn't answer straight away, just stood there looking down at her. His hair was damp from his bath, and he was wearing a clean – though equally worn – shirt in place of his old one. He'd even shaved properly for the first time since he'd found her on the streets of the first ring. If she ignored the new lines at the corners of his eyes, she could almost see him as the same young man she'd admired five years ago.

'You know, I didn't get much out of Sorrow, but one thing that seemed clear was that Lord Myrren is on the same trail we are,' he said finally. 'It seems he went there today looking for answers, just as we did. So all we can do now is wait and hope he finds them.' He sat down at the other end of the chaise longue – tentatively, as though he feared she might tell him to go away – and gave her an apologetic look. 'Which means my speculations earlier today were wrong. I'm sorry.'

I hope so. I really do. Ayla studied his face. 'You're not just saying that to make me feel better?'

'Not at all.' He smiled at her. 'By this time tomorrow, you could be back in Darkhaven.'

She nodded. 'And then you can have your life back.'

'Yes …' A shadow entered his eyes; he turned his head away, gazing into the fire. 'At least … I hope it won't be exactly the same life. There isn't much about the past five years that's worth holding on to.'

Watching his profile, Ayla realised for the first time that her mother's death had had an even greater impact on him than it had on her. She pushed that thought aside; it came dangerously close to sympathy. Really she ought to leave him here and retreat into the bedroom to get some sleep. Yet she wasn't tired. She felt the need for company and conversation, and talking to Caraway didn't seem such a terrible prospect as it once had.

'How did you come to join the Helm in the first place?' she asked him. He glanced her way, eyebrows drawn together in surprise and doubt.

'You really want to know?'

She shrugged. 'Why not?'

'All right.' He addressed his words to the fire, hunching his shoulders as though her sudden interest had made him uncomfortable. 'There's not much to it, really. Being part of the Helm was my childhood dream, my sole ambition. I never had another.' The corners of his lips turned up in a self-deprecating smile. 'At least I achieved it before I threw it away. Not everyone can say that.'

'But why the Helm?' Ayla asked, and the smile became wistful.

'I grew up in a small town to the east of Arkannen. My father wanted me to join the family trade, but I had no aptitude for it. The time I should have spent learning about buying and selling, I spent practising swordplay with a stick, or reading the big book of Changer legends my father kept in his study. I was always fascinated by the Changer gift – it seemed so wonderful that such a thing could exist in the world, that real people could have such awe-inspiring power. I read about Darkhaven and the dedication of the Helm and the prowess of those trained in the fifth ring, and I wanted nothing more than to be part of it all. To serve the very heart of my country. And so, as soon as I was old enough, I left home for the city.'

'And the weaponmasters let you in,' Ayla said. There was no incredulity or sarcasm in the words – they were intended purely to keep the conversation going – but Caraway shot a quick sideways glance in her direction.

'Yes, they let me in,' he agreed. 'All youngsters who arrive at the fifth ring wanting to be trained as warriors – and there are plenty of them – undergo several weeks of testing to determine their aptitude. Boys who wish to join the Helm are also subject to further and more rigorous testing after a year of basic training.' He shrugged. 'It was a hard life, but I loved it. I was fulfilling my dream and I never looked back.'

'You miss it,' she said softly. In response, an expression of such sadness settled over his face that she could hardly bear to look at it.

'Always.'

She said no more, just sat still and watched the memories in his eyes. After a time he took a deep breath, shrugging his shoulders as though to shake off the past, and turned his head to fix her with a steady gaze.

'May I ask you a question in return, Lady Ayla? The Changer gift ... is it as wonderful as I always imagined?'

Swept up in his previous honesty, she answered without stopping to consider her words. 'Sometimes I think it's the only thing in my life that's worth having.' Then she bit her lip, unsure whether she should have said as much; but his face showed no judgement, and so she tried to explain. 'More than anything, the gift is one of freedom. The children of Darkhaven spend their lives within its walls. To have the freedom of the skies ...' She offered him a twisted smile. 'You may have spent your life dreaming of getting into Darkhaven, Tomas, but I've spent mine dreaming of getting out.'

'Then not being able to Change, now ... it must be like losing one of your senses. A fundamental part of your life that's no longer accessible.'

How strange, that he understood that so well. Ayla nodded. 'I was imprisoned for a month before I left Darkhaven, too, so it's been a long time. Though I was never allowed to Change much anyway. My father ...' She looked down at her hands. 'He was ashamed of the form I take. It isn't one of the five elemental creatures. He always used to say that Myrren and I between us barely made half a real Changer.'

'Lord Florentyn was a strong-willed man,' Caraway murmured, and she gave a short, humourless laugh.

'That's one way of putting it. The Nightshade line was everything to him. Certainly much more important than any of the individual people in it. And the Helm ... well, they say the Helm are the mirror of Darkhaven's overlord. I suppose that's why they ended up with a captain like Owen Travers.' She sighed. 'My father and Travers both hated the fact that I and not Myrren was the one to inherit the gift. When my father decided to give me the throne instead of Myrren, it went against both his heart and his will. He knew it would be better for Mirrorvale to have a Changer on the throne – even a hybrid one like me – but he didn't want to do it. I think that's why he was so ready to believe the worst when news came of the attack on that priestess. It gave him an excuse to change his mind and lock me up.'

'Do you really think he would have imprisoned you for good?' Caraway asked.

'I'm not sure.' Ayla realised she was biting her lip again and stopped, not wanting to reveal how much the question agitated her. 'Maybe he would have let me out, once I'd agreed to obey his commands. Because that was the other thing ...' She looked up, forcing herself to meet Caraway's gaze. 'Florentyn was determined that Myrren and I should have children as soon as possible. He hoped our offspring would have the gifts we lacked. We'd resisted it for years, but sooner or later we would have had to give in. Because that's how it works. The Nightshade blood has to be kept strong.'

Caraway said nothing, but the sympathy she saw in his eyes almost made her want to cry again. She looked away, watching shadows and flickering orange light dance across the walls of the room. She had never said so much about her life to anyone before – but after all, it was only Caraway. Soon she'd be going back to Darkhaven, and then she'd never have to see him again. And besides ... it felt good, to talk to someone who listened properly.

'I love Myrren,' she said. 'But he's my brother. Neither of us wanted anything more than that. So we refused to submit to what we knew was inevitable. But once I was incarcerated ...' She swallowed over a suddenly painful throat. 'I wouldn't have had any choice. And who knows how long Myrren would have been able to hold out on his own?'

'Perhaps that's one good thing to have come out of everything that's happened.' Caraway's voice was gentle. 'Once all this is resolved and you return to Darkhaven, you and Myrren will be free to make your own choices. Marry who you want. And if the Helm don't like it ...' He shrugged. 'You control the Helm. They don't control you.'

Ayla looked at him. Firelight had softened his face, making him seem younger and somehow purer, as though she were seeing him as he had been before time and disappointment took their toll. Something like anticipation stirred in the pit of her stomach: a memory, perhaps, from when she was a girl and had fancied herself half in love with him. Yes, a memory. It could be no more than that.

'You may be right,' she said, making her voice cool and even. 'But now, if you don't mind, I'd like to get some sleep.'

He blinked as if she had slapped him, and for a moment she was sorry. But she'd given away too much this evening already. She had to call a halt to it, before she said or did something she might later regret.

'Of course.' He stood up in an awkward flurry of limbs, backing away from the chaise longue. The openness that had blossomed in his face during their conversation was fading, to be replaced by the hangdog expression she was used to seeing on him. 'Have you got everything you need?'

Belatedly Ayla remembered that she was going to be sleeping in the bedroom – that she was the one lingering in his quarters, not the other way around. She scrambled to her feet in turn, a rare blush heating her cheeks.

'I'm sure I will be fine.'

'I'll fetch you a news-sheet in the morning,' Caraway said. 'If the girl we saw in the fourth ring really is the missing Changer and your father's murderer, I'm sure Lord Myrren won't hesitate to make it widely known. Then you'll be certain it's safe to go home.'

'Thank you.' Feeling strangely guilty, as though she'd broken something fragile, Ayla retreated in the direction of the bedroom. When she reached the doorway, she turned – she couldn't help herself. Caraway was still standing by the fire, gazing after her; she couldn't read his expression.

'Thank you for talking to me tonight, Tomas,' she said softly. He nodded.

'You're welcome, Lady Ayla.'

Then she closed the door on him. Yet even as she did so, part of her wished she'd stayed out there; that she hadn't brought their conversation to an abrupt end, but kept going to see where it might lead. Now that she was by herself in a cold bedroom lit only by a single lamp, she felt ... lonely.

That's stupid, she told herself. *It's just because you're in yet another unfamiliar place. Tomorrow night you'll be back in Darkhaven and everything will be fine.* Yet even the thought of returning home didn't make her feel any better. Because the truth was, she had been lonely for years – and although she longed to see Myrren again, she didn't think her old life would be enough. Not any more.

She had almost drifted into uneasy sleep when a light tapping startled her back out of it. Someone was at the door to her bedroom. She sat bolt upright, reaching for her knife – which Caraway had returned to her after they'd escaped the Helm, just in case she needed it – then relaxed when she heard Caraway's whisper. 'Lady Ayla?'

'What is it?' She opened the door a fraction and peered out. Her stomach plummeted: he'd put his coat back on. 'Is there trouble?'

'No. I ...' He looked down at the floor, then back at her face. 'I'm sorry to disturb you. I thought – well, I've been thinking about what you said, and ... I wanted to show you something.'

'Can't it wait until morning?'

'Better at night, I think. Fewer people around.' He held out her cloak and added diffidently, 'I hope you'll trust me, just this once.'

Ayla hesitated. But though it wasn't so long ago that the very idea of trusting him would have been laughable, her opinion on the matter had shifted somewhat. She no longer doubted that he was doing everything he could to keep her safe. So she nodded and took the cloak from him. 'All right. Give me a moment.'

When she was ready, he led her out of the apartment and down the stairs. But rather than head for the main door he kept going, past the communal facilities to another steep flight of steps that descended into the basement. Increasingly hesitant, she followed him down those as well – and as soon as they reached the bottom, the walls opened up around them. They were standing in a vast, cold cellar lit only by a little moonlight that spilled in through a barred window near the ceiling.

Ayla turned to Caraway. His expression was hard to read through the shadows, even with her Nightshade-enhanced sight, but she thought he looked hopeful.

'I don't understand,' she admitted.

'I – I thought it might be big enough,' he said. 'For you to Change.' She made no reply, and after a moment he hurried on. 'I know it's not the same, because you won't be able to fly, but I thought that wouldn't be safe. Even outside the city, someone could see you. But in here ... at least it's private. I'll guard the door. And since we no longer believe

Lord Myrren is working against you, it doesn't matter if he senses you. So ...'

Ayla put a hand on his arm, and the flow of words abruptly ceased. She tried to speak, but she couldn't stop smiling long enough. No-one had ever done anything that nice for her before. And to think it was *him* –

'Thank you,' she managed finally.

'You're welcome, Lady Ayla.' They looked steadily at each other for a long moment through the half-light. Then Caraway ducked his head and said, 'I'll be outside if you need me.'

Once his footsteps had receded up the stairs, Ayla took a long, deep breath and summoned the Change. Myrren had asked her what it felt like, once, and she'd told him: fire and ice. A long, hot-and-cold wave that started at the crown of her head and swept through her bones to the soles of her feet, remaking her in its wake. Yet that description didn't go nearly far enough. It didn't explain the freedom of it, as though she were expanding along with her body to become more than what she'd been before. Her senses heightened still further. Strength flowed through her veins. And oh, that vast and glorious potential for *flight* –

Yet as the prickling sensation faded, she snorted in frustration – because she had nowhere to go. The cellar was only just large enough. The tips of her outstretched wings brushed the walls to either side; though the vaulted ceiling was high, it didn't leave her enough space to rear. What had been a large room to her in human form was almost as bad as a prison now. She was made for swiftness, for soaring high above the world. Though she tried to ignore it, her whole body tingled with the need to fulfil that potential and fly.

Still, it was the most freedom she'd been granted in over a month, and for that she had to be grateful. She took a few steps forward, then a few steps back, relearning her four legs – as awkward as a new colt. The shadows around her held no mystery, now; she could see every corner of the cellar as clear and bright as day. Her ears twitched, catching the sounds that had been too slight for human ears: footsteps in another street, a rat in the walls, the man breathing on the other side of the door. Small things, compared to the wide expanse of the skies, but they were enough for now. They would have to be.

She kept stretching her legs, arching her neck, furling and unfurling her wings – simply inhabiting the second self she had been so often denied – until her night vision gave way to a hint of grey daylight and she could no longer deny that morning was approaching. Then, reluctantly, she Changed back.

Returning to human form always felt so cramped, as if she were squeezing herself into a space that no longer fitted her. Stepping into an outgrown shoe. Her dress and cloak lay on the floor; she put them on hurriedly, fumbling with the buttons. She was small again, and not as strong – but her mind was bright with new memory, and that would be enough to sustain her.

Caraway was standing at the top of the steps that led up from the cellar. He turned at her approach, offering her a hesitant smile. He looked tired. It was with genuine guilt that she realised he had stayed up most of the night for her sake.

They didn't speak or even look at each other as they climbed back up through the brightening building to their apartment. Only when she reached the doorway to her bedroom did Ayla turn to face him.

'Thank you, Tomas,' she said softly.

'You're most welcome, Lady Ayla.' His fingers brushed the back of her hand for the briefest of moments before he turned away. 'Sleep well.'

'You too,' she whispered, and closed the door.

TWENTY-THREE

Sorrow studied the map that Travers had drawn for her. As well as marking Ayla's room, he had helpfully indicated several landmarks along the way, including the mess hall, the prison cells ... and the armoury. Sorrow traced the route to the armoury with a fingertip: it wasn't very far. Myrren Nightshade was a precise sort of man. It seemed likely he'd have put her pistol in what he considered to be its rightful place.

She turned in that direction, throwing a glance over her shoulder as she did so. Travers might have given her the freedom of the tower, but she still felt uneasy. It was probably just habit of thought. She'd never walked through Darkhaven's corridors before; she'd never been welcome in Darkhaven before. Add to that the fact that if Myrren caught her here he'd probably want to clap her in irons, and she had reason enough for her disquiet.

She saw no-one on her way to the armoury, not servant or Helm or Nightshade. That should have been a relief, but it only set her more on edge. She guessed it wasn't much after fifth bell: the sort of time when people moved from one kind of activity to another, from their daily work to the evening meal. Why weren't there more people? It was possible Travers had shown her a route that he knew would be unfrequented at this time of day, but she doubted he would be so considerate – until it occurred to her that he probably had no more desire for her to bump into Myrren than she did herself. It wouldn't take very many questions to reveal how closely Travers was implicated in her actions that morning; his safety depended on her not being caught. Feeling slightly more relaxed, she blew out a long breath. If she'd known how complicated this job would turn out to be, she never would have taken it – no matter how good the money.

The door to the armoury was locked, but Sorrow never went anywhere without a complete set of tools. It was the work of a few moments to pick the lock, slip through the door and close it behind her. Once inside, she glanced around the room, her gaze skimming over the ranks of weapons without interest. This was all bladed weaponry, or ways of countering it; she had quite enough of that already. There was only one weapon she wanted – the future to this room's past – and she couldn't see it anywhere.

A locked cabinet in the corner of the room caught her eye, and she crossed over to examine it. It was a beautiful thing, most likely Parovian in origin: carved out of ebonwood, one of the hardest woods in the world, with elegant legs and a satin finish so smooth that it dimly reflected her face. Sorrow had an ebonwood safe back in her apartment; she knew quite well that it was stronger than metal, as well as far more attractive. She also knew that the multi-dial padlock keeping the cabinet shut would be more difficult to open than a simple door lock. Difficult, but not impossible, for someone who knew how it worked.

Crouching in front of the cabinet, she got her tools out again and manipulated the dials on the padlock, listening for the clicks that would tell her when she'd got the right numbers. On her own safe she'd replaced the standard lock with an Ingalese combination lock, which was meant to be almost impossible to crack; clearly the Helm hadn't felt such a high level of security was necessary in their own stronghold. It took her longer than the armoury door, but soon enough she got all the digits in place and was able to spring the padlock open.

With a smug smile, Sorrow eased the cabinet door back on its hinges. There were two shelves inside, each stacked with a range of fascinating-looking objects, and in the centre of the top shelf was a gleaming black pistol. She picked it up with gentle reverence, turning it over in her hands. It wasn't her own pistol – the barrel was longer, the hammer a slightly different shape – but it would do. It would do very well. Of course, she hadn't learned its idiosyncrasies, as she had with her own pistol, but any firearm was better than none. And there was a certain justice in it: Myrren had taken a pistol from her, and now she was taking one from him.

'Look! What's that?' The man's voice reached her, muffled, through the door of the armoury. Presumably a Helmsman. She sat back on her heels, listening.

'There's someone in the armoury,' a second voice said.

'But isn't it meant to be locked at this time of day?' a third put in.

'Could be an intruder,' the first man agreed. 'Better go and investigate.'

Sorrow closed the cabinet and stuffed the pistol into her bag. She was about to show herself, to tell them she had their captain's permission to be there, but something stopped her. She hadn't left any sign of her break-in. At a casual glance, no-one should be able to tell the door was unlocked – so they must have been watching her to know she was in the armoury at all. If they didn't know she was meant to be there, why hadn't they challenged her sooner?

Unless, of course, what Travers had told them was significantly different from what he'd told her he'd tell them ...

She didn't stop to think through the full implications. As the door to the armoury opened, she grabbed a blackjack off the wall and swung it with her full strength at the first Helmsman who entered. He wasn't expecting the attack; the weapon landed squarely on his forearm, making him howl with pain and drop his sword. Another blow hit his knee, sending him stumbling back into the arms of his colleagues. While they were distracted by that, Sorrow brought the blackjack round in a sweeping arc and caught the second man across the side of the head, suppressing a wince at the sound it made on contact with his skull. She'd chosen the blackjack because she didn't want to kill anyone until she knew what she was dealing with, but she might have misjudged that last blow. He'd certainly dropped as though his strings had been cut.

'Sorrow.' The third Helmsman had struggled free of his wounded fellows and was now advancing on her with sword in hand. He showed no surprise that she was the supposed intruder, which confirmed her apprehension that all wasn't right. She threw the blackjack aside and drew her twin swords in time to catch his blade. This was nothing like fighting Myrren Nightshade; the man was competent enough, but no master. She drove him backwards until his heels came up against one of his fallen colleagues, then took advantage of his momentary stumble to knock the sword out of his grasp. She'd learned that trick off Myrren only that morning.

218

'On your knees,' she ordered the Helmsman, a blade either side of his throat leaving him in no doubt that she meant what she said. Then she circled behind him and put an arm around his neck, applying steady pressure to both sides. His struggles became weaker and weaker until she felt him go limp, at which point she released her chokehold and let him slump to the floor. He'd probably wake up with a headache, but he should be grateful for that. He'd only got away with his life because she preferred not to kill unless she was being paid for it.

Sorrow wiped her forehead with the back of her wrist and studied her fallen attackers, ignoring the whimpers of the one with the smashed kneecap. Only three of them, and they'd thought to capture her when she was trapped in a bloody *armoury*. It was almost insulting. Rolling one of the unconscious men over with scant regard for his dignity, she stripped off his striped coat. He was both taller and broader than she was, which meant his coat covered her bulky knife-belt; with her short hair, she'd look like a Helmsman to anyone who didn't get too close. Her two sheathed swords went into her bag, but she took the time to load the new pistol. Something very strange was going on here, and a single well-placed shot could mean the difference between freedom and capture.

When she was ready, she left the armoury and worked the lock back into place behind her. With any luck, it would be some time before the three men on the other side of that door were found. By now she was pretty sure that Travers was playing a double game, and all her instincts were screaming at her to leave as fast as she could by the nearest exit, but still she hesitated. She wanted to see Elisse. She wanted to confirm with her own eyes that Myrren hadn't hurt the woman. And even though she knew it was probably a bad decision, she couldn't make herself run away.

You're a bloody fool, Naeve Sorrow, she told herself, before turning in the direction of Ayla's room.

She already had the route memorised from Travers' map, and it didn't take her long to get there. From time to time she passed another Helmsman, but she kept her head down and her pistol concealed inside her borrowed coat, and no-one gave her a second look. When she reached Ayla's room, she took a deep breath and knocked on the door. Elisse answered, and for an instant Sorrow was reminded of her own arrival in the fourth ring – was it only yesterday? She'd gone over to the safe house fully expecting to despise Elisse, but instead she'd found something altogether different. As yet, she wasn't ready to explore what that something might be.

'Naeve!' Surprise sparked in Elisse's face, but it quickly turned into a beaming smile. Sorrow didn't think anyone had ever been that pleased to see her before. Nor did people tend to call her by her first name, but for some reason she didn't mind it from Elisse. 'What're ya doing here? Are ya all right? I didn' think they'd let ya see me.'

'I made a deal with Captain Travers.' Whatever that was worth now. Satisfied that Elisse showed no sign of injury – and that she seemed happy enough – Sorrow stepped to one side, trying to peer over the other woman's shoulder into the room beyond. 'Is the priestess there?'

'No. She's with Lord Myrren.'

Interesting. By Sorrow's reckoning, it was well past sixth bell; most people would have sought their beds by now. *Looks like Travers was wrong about her and Myrren.*

'Can I come in?' she asked.

'Sure.' Elisse stood back, letting her into the room. Sorrow closed the door behind her and glanced around: all very old-fashioned and heavy, not the kind of style she admired. She looked back at Elisse, who was watching her expectantly.

'I just wanted to make sure you were all right.' The words sounded lame in her own ears. She tried again. 'I mean, after I failed to stop Myrren from taking you away –'

'I didn' blame ya,' Elisse said firmly. 'Lord Myrren is over-lord o' Darkhaven. Ya couldn' hurt him too much, whatever Travers said.'

Sorrow nodded. The next question came out without any forethought on her part, simply because she wanted to know the answer. 'How much do you trust Owen Travers, Elisse?'

Elisse shrugged. ''Bout as much as I'd trust a hungry wolf.'

'So you wouldn't be surprised if he went back on his sworn word?'

'Not at all.'

'Neither would I.' Sorrow considered it, frowning. 'I think he's trying to pin everything on me. I think he's trying to cover his tracks where you're concerned. But now I know the trap is there, I know how to evade it.'

'What d'ya mean?'

'I mean he's a bastard.' She began pacing the room, assessing it for threats, then caught herself doing it and grinned. 'So did any of his dire warnings come true? Does Myrren mean you any harm?'

Elisse frowned. 'I don' think so. But he wants me ta stay here in Darkhaven. Ta bring the baby up as a Nightshade.'

She didn't look very happy at the prospect. Sorrow raised her eyebrows at her.

'Isn't that what you knew would have to happen, someday?'

'Not exactly.' Elisse sat down in an uncomfortable-looking chair, folding her hands over her bump. 'Florentyn always promised we'd be able ta stay outside the tower, the baby and me. That he'd have a say in its education, bu' he'd only step in ta claim it once it showed signs o' having the gift.'

'Your baby has the blood of royalty in its veins,' Sorrow said. 'Maybe it's better for it to know that as soon as possible.'

'I s'pose so.' Elisse sounded sad. 'I jus' don' want it ta have this life, that's all. All politics and walls and – and loneliness. Now its father's gone, I'm the only parent i' has left. But even if Lord Myrren has the best of intentions, how much involvement d'ya think he'll let me have in my baby's upbringing? I never married Florentyn Nightshade. I'm no-one important. I'm jus' a girl from the country.' She looked up, the knowledge stark in her eyes. 'My opinion won' count for anything at all.'

'Then why don't you just leave?' Sorrow asked, and Elisse shrugged.

'They'd only come after me.'

She looked as if she was about to say something more, but she was interrupted by a knock on the door. Not a polite knock, the priestess announcing her return before walking in on whatever Elisse was doing; an urgent banging. Straight away Sorrow's thoughts leapt to the bargain she had made with Travers. He knew she'd intended to come here. Either he'd already found his men in the armoury, or he was accounting for all possibilities.

Before Sorrow could decide how best to defend herself, Elisse got to her feet, a determined lift to her chin. 'Get in the wardrobe. I'll deal with this.'

Sorrow hesitated – but really, in this situation, hiding was the only sensible option. And besides, she was mildly amused by the way Elisse had taken charge. Without demur, she climbed in amongst the rich fabrics that hung in the wardrobe: presumably Ayla's abandoned clothing. Elisse swung the door shut on her, leaving her surrounded by darkness and the musty smell of brocade. A series of creaks sounded that must be Elisse crossing the floor, followed by a longer creak as she opened the door to the bedroom. Darkhaven was a bloody noisy place.

Sorrow drew the pistol out from the inner pocket of her borrowed coat, just in case. Then she set her ear to the inside of the wardrobe door, listening intently. She heard the rumble of the Helmsman's voice, and the end of his sentence: '... looking for Naeve Sorrow.'

'She's gone,' Elisse said. 'She only stopped by for a moment.'

'Did she say where she was going?'

'No.' Elisse sounded indifferent. 'Ta be honest, I didn' ask. I know Captain Travers thought i' would be a good idea ta hire her, bu' she scared me senseless. I'm glad she's gone.'

Another rumble; Sorrow couldn't make it out, but she caught Elisse's reply.

'All right. I will. Thanks for letting me know.'

Sorrow heard the main door close, and a few moments later the door to the wardrobe swung open. Elisse stood there with one hand on her hip and a grin on her face.

'How was that?'

'Pretty good.' Sorrow jumped down out of the wardrobe, landing lightly on her feet. 'So I scared you senseless, did I?'

'Ta start with,' Elisse admitted. She looked at the weapon that Sorrow was still clutching in one hand. 'Ya got ya pistol back, then?'

Sorrow shook her head. 'This one's from Darkhaven's armoury. I figured Myrren Nightshade owed me.'

'Fair enough.' Elisse's smile was replaced by a troubled frown. 'It's true what ya said, by the way. They are looking for ya. That Helmsman said ya killed a man.'

So that blow to the head had proven fatal after all. Sorrow shrugged, though she wasn't very happy about it. 'If Travers doesn't want his men to get hurt, he shouldn't make bargains he has no intention of keeping.'

'Then it's true?' Elisse asked, wide-eyed.

'Yes. But it was accidental ... sort of. And they were going to arrest me, or maybe kill me ... I don't know.' Seeing the expression on the other woman's face, Sorrow sighed. 'This is what I do, Elisse.'

'I know.' Though Elisse's reply came quickly enough, her eyes still showed a hint of the same uncertainty they'd held back when Sorrow had first arrived at the safe house. It was always the same. There was a reason why people in Sorrow's profession couldn't hold down relationships for long. She picked up her bag.

'Well, I'd better get going.'

'Will ya stay?' The question was tentative. 'It's jus' ... ya the only friend I've got in Arkannen. And I don' like being in this place alone.'

Sorrow hesitated. 'I can't hide in your wardrobe forever, Elisse. If Myrren sees me in Darkhaven he'll want to have me arrested – and I'm beginning to think Travers has the same intention. Between the two of them, I don't stand much chance.'

'I understand.' Elisse didn't look up. 'Well ... i' was nice knowing ya, Sorrow. Thanks for everything.'

Still Sorrow lingered. She should leave, she knew that. Her involvement with this situation had already tangled her life up more than she liked. But, after all, this was the last place either Travers or Myrren would look for her. Myrren had no idea she'd even been in Darkhaven, and Travers wouldn't expect her to have stayed this long. If either of them wanted her, they'd be more likely to send men to her apartment. Which really meant she was safer here than anywhere else.

'All right,' she said. 'I'll stay. If only for tonight.'

TWENTY-FOUR

Serenna lifted her hand to knock on the door, then lowered it again without touching the wood. She still wasn't sure this was a good idea; she had never visited Myrren in his own room before, and certainly not this late at night. Yet she knew without needing to be told that he would want to talk to someone. He would be trying to decide what to do as a result of Elisse's earlier revelations. And of all the people in Darkhaven, Serenna would be the only one he felt he could be honest with.

With a deep breath to ease her nerves, she reached out and rapped on the door before she could think any more about it. Myrren opened it; he looked as grave and calm as ever, but she saw a hint of strain in his eyes before his brows drew together in surprise.

'Serenna! Is everything all right?'

She nodded. 'Can I come in?'

'Of course.' He stood back to admit her. She took a surreptitious glance around the room as she entered it, hoping to find some trace of him, but it was as rich and as empty as Ayla's. The only incongruous object was a picture on the wall: a simple painted thing, showing a flying bird silhouetted against a dawn sky. It didn't fit with its ornate surroundings at all, but the yearning Serenna saw in it brought a lump to her throat.

'My father hated it,' Myrren said, following her gaze. '*Sentimental drivel*, I believe were his exact words.'

She looked sideways at him. 'You painted this?'

'Mmm.' His mouth formed a self-mocking curve. 'You can probably tell by the appalling workmanship. I'm no artist.'

Serenna turned back to the painting. True, it was unmistakably the work of an amateur, but the depth of emotion it conveyed more than made up for any lack of ability.

'I think it's beautiful,' she said.

They looked at each other for a moment without speaking, and Serenna felt something quiver deep inside her. Then Myrren stepped away, gesturing to a nearby chair.

'Please, take a seat.'

She obeyed him, curling her slippered feet up under her skirts and pushing back her veil – he'd seen her face before, after all. There was a small table beside her, and on it was a black metal device she recognised. She frowned at it.

'Isn't that Sorrow's pistol?'

Myrren shrugged. 'I thought it might be useful. But in the rush to get Elisse back to Darkhaven, I didn't think to look for the equipment that goes with it. And there isn't a supply of powder here.' His lips tightened. 'I could ask the Helm where I might procure some, but after the events of the past few days I'm not inclined to trust them more than I have to.'

He walked to the table and picked up the pistol, turning it over in his fingers. For an instant a shadow entered his eyes, as though he saw a future in the weapon that Serenna couldn't see. Then he put it back down, giving her a rueful smile.

'It's a temperamental thing, anyway. Perhaps I'm old-fashioned, but I'd rather stick to the sword. Somehow it's far less ... random.'

Serenna nodded. Having seen him use a sword, she wouldn't have expected anything else. She was still ashamed of the visceral thrill it had given her to watch the short fight in the fourth ring. She'd tried to tell herself that it was simply the pleasure she would feel on seeing any craftsman of such obvious skill wield his tools, but she knew it had been far more primal than that. With a sword in his hands, the precision he brought to everything he did became something far more dangerous, and far more exciting.

'So, then, Sister Serenna.' Myrren crossed to the window, staring out into the impenetrable darkness beyond. 'Was there something you wanted to talk to me about?'

It clearly wasn't going to be easy for him to show how he felt. Serenna kept her voice gentle. 'I came here because I thought maybe you might want to talk to me. About what happened today, and what we learned from Elisse.'

There was a moment of silence in which tension vibrated like a taut string between them. Then Myrren's shoulders slumped, his head drooping. 'She was telling the truth, wasn't she?'

'I think so,' Serenna said. 'Neither her face nor her voice held any hint of a lie.' No, Elisse had been almost brutal in the rawness of her honesty. It was impossible to believe she had been playacting.

'When I first saw her, I thought ...' Myrren sighed. 'But it isn't Elisse who has Changer blood. It is the unborn child she bears.' As if something had been unlocked in him, he began to pace, tracing a well-worn path from window to bed to door and back again. 'Which brings us back to the inescapable fact that Ayla is the only person left in Mirrorvale who can Change.'

Serenna sat still and watched his agitated movements. She wanted desperately to come up with an idea, something that would give him a new path to follow, but her mind was blank. And besides, she was the one who had suggested that Florentyn Nightshade might have had another child. She was the one who had uncovered this little secret.

'Perhaps not,' she said, clutching at slender hope. 'Elisse's existence doesn't rule out the possibility that our original theory was correct. That your father did have an affair before you were born.'

Myrren turned to look at her. The control she had noticed in him earlier was gone, stripped away; his face was naked with doubt. 'Do you really think that's likely?'

The truth was, she didn't – not after what she had read in the library. She still hadn't told him about the precedent she had found: the Changer with two distinct personalities, two different creature-selves. Based on that idea, Ayla could be a murderer and not even realise it, plagued only by a dark shadow that haunted her dreams. But Serenna couldn't bear to say that to Myrren, not when he was so vulnerable.

'I don't see why not,' she said instead. 'In fact, if anything, Elisse's child supports rather than detracts from the theory. If Florentyn could do it once, why not twice?'

'Perhaps you're right.' With a troubled frown, Myrren began pacing again. 'But everything pointed to Elisse. Everything! Without her, we have no more clues.'

'We'll find something,' Serenna said with more confidence than she felt. 'I'm sure we will.' Then, as he passed her chair, she reached out to touch the back of his wrist. 'Myrren, please –'

He came to an abrupt halt, looking down at her. His expression didn't change, but something she saw in the depths of his eyes made her snatch back her fingers as though his skin had burned her. Yet even as she tried to retreat, his hand caught and held hers.

'That's the first time you've ever addressed me without my title.' His voice was almost a whisper. She shook her head, confused.

'I'm sorry – I –'

'I've spent my whole life being judged.' His fingers were warm around hers, sending a flush of heat up her arm and into her chest. 'For what I am, and what I'm not. But you have never judged me, Serenna. Or if you have, it's been on my own merits and not on other people's expectations. Do you know how rare that is?'

Her heart was thudding in her breast, her lungs tight with the need to breathe. Excited and terrified in equal measure, she tried again to pull free of his grasp – and at that he released her, turning away.

'But what am I, after all?' The words were blistering in their self-loathing. 'A lord of Darkhaven without the power to rule his country. Without the Changer gift, a Nightshade is just a man.'

Without any real awareness of what she was doing, driven both by a desire to comfort him and by the heat that was racing through her body, Serenna stood up. 'Myrren –'

With a soft sound of frustration, he spun on his heel. His fingers closed on her upper arms, drawing her close enough that she could feel his heartbeat echoing hers. The hint of fierceness she had always sensed beneath his self-possessed exterior was clearer now, brought to the surface by emotion and by lust. Though she had no experience of such things, she couldn't doubt the lust. She stared at him, knowing this was the last possible moment at which she could draw back, but not knowing whether she wanted to. The vows she had sworn were there in her mind, but so too was he: the shade of his eyes, the shape of his lips, the set of his jaw. She took a deep, uneven breath and tried to move – whether forwards or backwards, she wasn't sure – only to feel Myrren's arms tighten around her.

'I'm sorry,' he breathed. Then his mouth came down on hers, and her body responded as it had longed to since the first day she met him.

She had never done this before – any of this. She had been twelve when she joined the Altar of Flame and consecrated herself to a state of perpetual purity. Yet somehow, it felt entirely natural. The hardness of his body pressed against hers, the texture of his cheek as it grazed her skin, the taste of him – all was as it should be. Briefly she fumbled with the laces on his shirt, but the new urgency that was driving her wouldn't let her linger. Still clothed, they fell tangled together onto the bed, his hands awakening each new part of her in turn. Breasts, belly, hips, thighs: they came alive beneath his touch as though she had never truly been aware of them before. He pushed up her skirts and tugged at her undergarments, and she lifted her hips to help him. Then he was inside her, and her body tensed with a sudden sharp pain that was just as quickly gone.

'Are you –' Myrren whispered, but she pressed her fingers to his lips to silence him, and wrapped her legs around him to urge him deeper. They moved together, and now she could no longer tell where she ended and he began. She was aware of nothing except her own need, her own spiralling climb towards an elusive point. And then she reached it, and she was falling, and it seemed to her that this was flame as much as anything else was – that the heat and the rush of it was just another side of what she had dedicated her life to all along.

Afterwards they lay facing each other in the vast bed, their hands interlocked between them.

'You know this can never happen again,' she said, and he nodded.

'I know. But … thank you, Serenna. For everything.'

She tried to smile, but tears were gathering in her throat and behind her eyes. 'I'm glad I came here. I'm glad I met you.'

'I'm glad I met you too,' he said. Then he drew her tight against him, and she cried a little in the circle of his arms before, unable to resist the warmth of his embrace, she slipped into welcome darkness.

Once Serenna was asleep and breathing deeply, Myrren brushed a kiss across her forehead before getting up and crossing to the window. Pushing it open as wide as it would go, he sat on the sill and gazed out at the full moon high above the city. He was tired – the events of the day would have been enough to drain anybody, mentally and physically – yet he knew he wouldn't be able to rest. There were too many thoughts bouncing off each other in his head for that.

He shouldn't have done what he had with Serenna, he knew that. No matter that she'd been a temptation to him from the moment she stepped within the walls of the tower, he'd had no right to touch her. She was a priestess. He should never have looked at her in that way. And though she'd seemed more than willing, he couldn't see how what he'd done to her was any better than what his father had done to Elisse. The thought made him feel sick and ashamed. Was that what it meant to be a Nightshade? To take what you wanted, and let others suffer the consequences? He couldn't forget the way Serenna had cried in his arms before she drifted off to sleep. Whatever happened, her life had been changed forever. And he, in his arrogance, was the one who had changed it.

Yet despite all that, he couldn't regret it. She was the only good thing that had happened to him since Florentyn's death – in fact, if he were honest, since long before that. Alongside his guilt unfurled a sneaking small hope that when all this was resolved and the elusive killer found, she might leave her temple behind and join him in Darkhaven. He would never ask it of her, of course. It would be unfair to put her in a position where she might feel she had to agree because of who he was and what had happened between them. But if she came to the decision of her own accord – if she cared for him enough to abandon the life she had chosen – he would never want for anything else. He would step down from the position that his father's death had forced on him, letting Ayla take the throne to which her gift entitled her, and devote his life to making Serenna happy.

If, that was, Ayla could ever come back to the tower.

That was the core of his circling thoughts, the crux around which all the rest revolved. Serenna had tried to comfort him, first with her words and then with her body, but still he kept returning to the same cold, unalterable fact: all their work had led nowhere. Elisse had nothing to do with the attacks that had taken place. The killer was still out there somewhere, under the very same moon that Myrren was looking at now. And there was nothing to tell him where, or even what kind of person he was searching for. It was as if he were dealing with a ghost or a shadow, a creature of mist and smoke.

Unless, of course, it had been Ayla all along.

Myrren tipped his head back against the wall, feeling the start of a headache behind his eyes. The Helm believed it. Even Serenna was beginning to believe it, though she'd done her best not to show it. Why look for another explanation when one so obvious was right there in front of him? What evidence did he have to set against it? Only the fact that Ayla's creature-self didn't match any of the witness descriptions, and his own heartfelt belief that his sister couldn't be a murderer. And if somehow it turned out he had been mistaken about the form she took ... why, then all he'd be left with was a feeling. He could just imagine the look on Travers' face if he presented that argument.

'Where do I go from here?' he whispered to the moon. 'Where do I go from here?'

And as if in answer, he felt the unmistakable shiver of a Change happening somewhere in the city. Not the formless nightmare of the unknown Changer, but a far more familiar sensation ...

Ayla.

TWENTY-FIVE

Elisse was startled out of sleep by a sound. Lying still for a moment, she tried to work out what it had been, but it was all mixed up with the dream she'd been having. Something like a nail being hammered into a wall, perhaps, or the metallic clunk a spade made when it hit a rock beneath the surface of the soil …

She struggled into a sitting position, looking around for the source of the noise, and saw the heavy drapes stirring as though caught on a breeze from the open window. She'd never seen such large windows as they had in Darkhaven; it was the one thing she liked about the place. Maybe one of the drapes had knocked something off the table. Could that be what she'd heard?

As her eyes got used to the low level of light in the room, she made out a figure at the foot of the bed. She gasped, clapping a hand to her mouth to stifle the small sound, before realising it was Sorrow. The other woman turned her head, the moonlight glinting off her hair.

'Sssh,' she breathed. 'There's something out there.'

Elisse nodded obedience, her insides cramping with fear. She slid down from the bed, searching through the shadows for something to use as a weapon, but all she could see was the walking cane that the priestess had left propped in the corner by the door. She grabbed it anyway, feeling rather silly, and went to join Sorrow.

'What is it?' she whispered.

'Don't know.' Sorrow gave her a sharp glance, which softened into amusement when she saw the cane. She herself was holding her new pistol; Elisse could see the gleaming metal. 'But maybe –'

Before she could finish her sentence, the moonlight flickered and was gone, hidden by a dark shape that loomed at the window. Then the thing was through and into the room in a scrabble of scales and claws, bringing with it a wave of heat and a choking metallic smell as though it had come from the heart of a foundry.

The Changer creature.

Its barbed tail moved round as swift as a whip, knocking Sorrow off balance. She fell hard, her head hitting one of the legs of the bed with an audible thud, the pistol dropping from her hand and skidding across the polished wooden floor. The creature paused a moment, watching to make sure she wasn't going to get up. Then it turned and stalked towards Elisse, blending into the shadows so completely that parts of it disappeared with each step it took. Only its eyes were constant, shining in the darkness; they tracked her every movement with a kind of mad intelligence.

Fear shooting up her spine in a cold rush, Elisse backed away on legs that felt as though they didn't belong to her. The hot scent of the creature filled her lungs, reminding her of the first time she had met Florentyn Nightshade. She should have run, back then. She should have escaped while she still had the chance.

'Go away!' she tried to shout, but her voice came out thin and cracked. 'Leave me alone!'

In response, the creature's neck arched. Fire bloomed in the night, a flare of it like the jet from a welding torch, dazzlingly bright. Elisse dodged as fast as she could, but her pregnancy made her heavy and awkward on her feet; the blaze scorched her cheek, a sting so hot it was almost freezing. She swallowed down a cry of pain, blinking back tears, and realised she was still gripping Serenna's cane in her sweat-slick hands. As the creature came closer she swung the stick with all her strength, but it shattered against the impenetrable scales and left her hands ringing with the impact. Then the creature reared up, lifting one clawed foot to rake at her, and agony ripped her arm from shoulder to elbow. She stumbled back and sat down with a bump, clutching the welling scratches with her other hand.

Get a grip, Elisse, she told herself. *It's no worse than grazing ya shins or catching ya finger in a piece o' machinery. Jus' find something ta fight back with.* But the truth was, there was nothing left. The creature had driven her into a corner of the room; there was no way out. She stared up at it and knew, with cold certainty, that she was looking at her death. Her insides contracted in another twinge of pure terror.

Then Sorrow was there, scrambling across the bed, landing light-footed between Elisse and the creature. She didn't waste time on talk. The pistol was in her hand, and as the creature reared ready to strike again she fired it. Elisse didn't see where the bullet struck, but it must have hit somewhere; the creature erupted in a low, bubbling hiss, retreating swiftly across the room in the direction of the window.

'Clipped it,' Sorrow muttered. 'Bloody pistol throws left. I was aiming for the throat.'

She advanced a few steps towards the creature, lifting the weapon as though she meant to fire it again, even though that wasn't possible until she reloaded. And it seemed the creature recognised the pistol as the one thing that could harm it. As Sorrow approached, it scrambled back through the window and disappeared into the night.

Panting with mingled fright and relief, Elisse dragged herself back to her feet, using the bed as a climbing aid. She would have expected her fear to subside now the creature was gone, but instead it was growing stronger, gripping her entire body. Her muscles clenched harder and harder with every breath she took; waves of tension washed up and down her body, all originating somewhere in her middle. She clung to the bedpost, a whimper of pain escaping her lips.

'Don't worry,' Sorrow said, banging the window shut. Her bravado couldn't quite hide the tremor in her voice. 'It won't come back.' She turned in Elisse's direction, concern flickering over her face. 'Are you hurt?'

'I'm not – it's not –' Elisse had to stop as another ripple overtook her. It was like a metal vice clamping down on her insides, squeezing her until her whole world was reduced to that one agonising, dragging sensation. Sweat had broken out on her forehead; she gasped in a breath of air, but it didn't feel like it was nearly enough.

'It's no' that,' she managed, forcing the words out through gritted teeth. 'I think – I think I'm going ta have the baby.'

And with that, as if to prove her right, she felt the warm gush as her waters broke.

As Sorrow scrubbed her hands under the tap, her mind was blank with fear. Though not all blank: the small part of it that always remained detached sat back and watched her response with interest. *So this is what I'm afraid of. Who knew?* She had fought men twice her size without her heart rate even increasing, but faced with a woman in the throes of labour, she was suddenly in a state of something close to panic.

Whilst Elisse paced the room as though she couldn't stay still, stopping at intervals to breathe through a renewed wave of pain, Sorrow had been making what preparations she could for what she assumed would be an extremely messy business. She'd stripped the covers off the bed and spread out several spare blankets from a high shelf in the wardrobe. She'd also dumped her leathers and all her weaponry to one side, and put on the simplest of Ayla's dresses she could find. That didn't exactly add to her enjoyment of the situation: last time she'd worn a dress, she'd been five years old and still tying pink ribbons in her hair. Still, it wasn't as if anyone was going to see her.

Turning away from the basin, she found that Elisse had clambered onto the bed and was lying on her side, hands resting on the curve of her stomach, eyes glazed and cheeks flushed. Sorrow walked over and stood looking down at her, wondering again whether she was doing the right thing. She'd expected the Helm to come running at the sound of the pistol going off earlier, but with Darkhaven's thick internal walls it had probably been more audible outside the tower – through the open window – than it had within. Not only that, but Ayla's room was in an isolated part of the building, so it was possible that no-one had heard. Whatever the reason, there wasn't anyone here but her, and she hadn't a damn clue what she was doing. She should probably fetch help.

But if she did, most likely she'd end up being arrested by the Helm.

On the other hand, if she didn't then it would be her fault if something went wrong and Elisse or the baby died ...

'I think I'd better go and find the physician,' she said, with an inward sigh. Elisse shook her head, clutching desperately at Sorrow's hand.

'No time. It's coming. It's coming now –'

Now turned out to be an exaggeration, but Sorrow was kept busy enough not to consider leaving the room again. She wasn't sure how long the process lasted; it felt like an eternity, but the night sky outside the window remained unchanged. Sometimes it seemed as though she and Elisse were caught in an endless struggle – as though they were labouring together to bring forth the world itself, and dawn would be held in abeyance until their work was done. Other times, she decided that exertion followed by the unfamiliar emotion of fear had combined to make her light-headed and silly. Either way, there finally came a time when Elisse hitched herself up on her hands and knees, her skirts all tangled around her waist, and spoke through gritted teeth.

'If Florentyn Nightshade wasn' dead I'd bloody well kill him myself for this.' She took in a long, trembling breath, then let it out slowly. 'It's going ta happen soon, Naeve. I can feel it –'

Her voice faded into a groan, her entire body shaking. Sorrow caught her breath as she saw the baby's head begin to emerge. She said something to Elisse, she wasn't even sure what, but the other woman was lost to everything except her own driving urges. A cry tore from her lips as the head passed fully through her stretched and delicate flesh, and Sorrow reached out to cradle the misshapen skull as the shoulders and the rest of the body followed. Then the baby was in her hands, tiny and whole and alive. She had never seen anything so completely fragile. She brought him close to her chest for warmth, heedless of the blood staining Ayla's dress.

'It's a boy,' she whispered.

'Clear his nose and mouth.' Elisse sounded tired but urgent. 'Make sure he can breathe properly.'

Sorrow did as she was told, using a finger to scoop away the sticky fluids that coated the child's face. She was rewarded with a weak, wavery cry as he found his lungs for the first time. Elisse lowered herself back down onto her side as though her arms and knees would no longer support her, one hand reaching out blindly. Understanding the wordless request, Sorrow brought the baby round to lie as far up the bed as possible, mother and child still tethered by the thick birthing cord. Elisse gathered him in against her breast, wrapping a clean fold of the topmost blanket over him for warmth.

'Should I cut the cord?' Sorrow asked doubtfully. Elisse shook her head, her hair plastered to her face in sweaty streaks.

'Not yet. There's more to come first.'

The *more to come*, when it happened, was messy but easy enough to cope with in comparison to the baby himself. After that, Sorrow cut and tied the birthing cord, then leaned against the bedpost and watched Elisse as she talked softly to the baby. She was suddenly exhausted. Perhaps that was why she felt as if she were about to cry. Shedding tears was something else she hadn't done for ages – not since she was ten years old and watching her mother being thoroughly beaten by her second husband. She and her mother had cried together, made plans to run away – and in the morning, Sorrow had watched in disbelief as everything went back to normal. That was when she'd learned the futility of grief.

The next time her stepfather beat her mother, and all the times that followed, she hadn't shed a single tear. But two years later, as soon as she was strong enough, she'd stabbed him while he slept and run away to Arkannen, a city where it was possible to become so thoroughly lost that no-one would ever find you. A city where it was possible to make a very good living by carrying out tasks that were unpleasant but necessary, just like her execution of her stepfather.

Perhaps her role in this baby's birth would go at least some way towards balancing all the deaths she had played a part in since then.

'How are you feeling?' she asked Elisse, trying to shake off her annoyingly self-examining thoughts. She'd never been one for navel-gazing.

'Knackered.' Elisse looked up, her lips curved in a wondering smile. 'But good. It feels –' she glanced down again, as if searching for an appropriate word in the baby's face – 'it feels right.'

'Can I fetch you anything?'

'A glass o' water would be nice.' Then, as Sorrow handed it to her, 'Thank ya, Naeve. And I don' jus' mean for the water.' Her hand gestured vaguely over her son's head. 'Thanks for – well, for all this.'

'No problem.'

They looked at each other for a long, silent moment. Then, feeling as though her legs were going to give up and let her fall, Sorrow dragged the chair over from the table to the bedside and sat down.

'In the morning I'll go and see Myrren,' she said. 'Tell him what happened here tonight.' She looked ruefully down at the dark stains that covered Ayla's dress from breasts to knees. 'But first I'd better change back into my own clothes. Otherwise he'll probably think I've murdered someone.'

'Ya don' think he'll arrest ya?' Elisse murmured, sounding sleepy.

'I hope not.' Sorrow gazed out at the night sky, the old shiver of opportunity seizing her once more. The familiarity of it was a relief. 'Since I've just helped to deliver his brother.'

TWENTY-SIX

As Caraway waited in line at a street vendor's stall, he scanned the sheet he had just bought in search of news. To start with he felt almost nervous with hope, but as he looked down the flimsy paper that quickly changed to disappointment. There was no mention of the capture of a rogue Changer, or the solving of Florentyn's murder, or indeed any word from Darkhaven at all. The entire news-sheet was given over to the description and analysis of a gang fight that had broken out in the Night Quarter the previous evening. Which meant that either Myrren had followed the same false scent they had, and the girl from the fourth ring – Elisse – was nothing to do with the attacks, or Caraway's suspicions had been right after all, and Myrren and the mysterious Elisse were working together.

With a sigh, Caraway folded the piece of paper and put it in his pocket. He wasn't going to enjoy breaking the news to Ayla. What was more, neither of the two possibilities they were faced with inspired him with much confidence that he would be able to help her any further. If Myrren and Elisse and the Helm were all working together, then as far as he could see, Ayla might as well flee the city for all the chance she stood of proving her innocence. And if the killer was still unknown and at large, then they were right back where they'd started, only this time without any favours to call in. Though he couldn't suppress a guilty pang of relief that Ayla wouldn't be leaving him today after all, it seemed almost certain he'd end up letting her down.

Accepting two slices of iced redfruit from the vendor, Caraway flicked the man a coin and turned away. He'd better get back to the apartment as soon as possible and let Ayla know where they stood. Maybe between them they'd be able to come up with a new plan of action.

As he approached the street where they were staying, the bright colours of a Helmsman's coat caught his eye. He ducked into a doorway, heart racing. They knew Ayla was with him, now, which meant he had to be extra careful not to lead them back to her. And this particular Helmsman, though standing at a busy crossroads without any attempt at concealment, didn't quite seem like a casual passer-by. His posture was relaxed enough, but his intent gaze scanned the face of each person who passed him.

If Caraway hadn't known better, he'd have sworn the man was a lookout.

For an instant he panicked, wondering if he'd been wrong about Lord Myrren after all. Wondering if by giving Ayla the opportunity to Change last night, he'd led Myrren and the Helm right to her.

No, he told himself. *Sorrow made it clear enough that Myrren knew no more about the pregnant girl – Elisse – than we do. He isn't working against Ayla, I'm sure of it. You're just being paranoid.* Yet all the same, his heart kept up its rapid beat as he used the cover of a wagon to slip past the Helmsman unseen and head for the street that held the corn mill.

When he reached it and saw another pair of striped coats on the corner, his unease solidified into something worse. Yes, these two men appeared to be having a heated conversation. Yes, neither of them was obviously looking for something, as the first man had been. And yet ...

And yet, even two sightings was too many to be a coincidence. He knew what it looked like when the Helm were preparing a raid, and it was something very like this. Of course, it was possible that the job they were on had nothing to do with Ayla. But if Caraway had learned one thing in life, it was always to assume the worst. So now he had to think of a way to get her out of the building before the trap closed.

Go back down to the cellar, said the well-trained part of him – the part that wasn't incoherent with anxiety. *They won't think to look there. And if they do, at least she'll have room to defend herself.*

He briefly joined a group of labourers to pass the Helmsmen on the corner, then broke into a jog. The street was busier than it had been when he left. Two men were unloading a cart outside the corn mill, and another man – perhaps a customer – was just dismounting from his horse. And opposite, drawn up at the door of Caraway's own building, was a carriage and pair. Caraway didn't recognise the device on the carriage, but all the same ...

Even as he quickened his pace further, the front door of the building opened and a man in a striped coat emerged, his arm wrapped tightly around a female figure in a hooded cloak. As Caraway watched, the woman drove an elbow into the Helmsman's ribs and made as if to run; the Helmsman caught her wrist, yanking her towards him, and her hood fell back to reveal her short dark hair.

They'd found her.

Caraway stumbled, the fruit in his hand sending sticky trails down his wrist. Then he flung it aside and started running in earnest. He saw the Helmsman aim a nervous glance in his direction, alerted by the slap of his soles on the paved street, then twist Ayla's arm up behind her back and shove her towards the carriage. Fury blazed through Caraway, darkening the edges of his vision until he could see nothing but the two of them ahead, a small illuminated picture surrounded by jagged shadows. He pushed himself harder, every muscle straining, but it wasn't fast enough. It could never be fast enough. Like running through a nightmare, the sheer weight and substance of his body held him back.

'Stop!' he shouted, though he knew he was only wasting his energy. If he could just keep running – if he could just hold them there until he reached them – but it was no use. With a terse command to the driver, the Helmsman bundled Ayla into the carriage and leapt in after her. Even as Caraway drew closer, his hands outstretched in a vain attempt to claw back what he had lost, the horses moved forward at a crack of the whip and the carriage juddered into motion. Caraway forced his legs to keep pumping, but already the gap between him and the vehicle was widening. In another few moments, it had reached the end of the street and turned out of sight.

I shouldn't have left her alone. I should never have left her alone. Caraway bent over, resting his elbows on his knees, fighting to catch his breath. Sweat was running down his forehead, stinging his eyes; he wiped it away with the back of his hand. His lungs were tight, his muscles seizing. If he hadn't spent the last five years drowning himself in alcohol then maybe he'd be in better shape. If he hadn't gone out by himself to fetch breakfast …

247

Forget all that, he told himself. *You have to get Ayla back before it's too late. Nothing else matters.*

As he straightened, he glanced over his shoulder: the two Helmsmen from the street corner were running towards him. In another few moments they'd be on him and his one chance to redeem himself would be lost. Staring wildly around, he spotted the horse that was now tethered outside the corn mill, the owner presumably having gone inside and left it under the eye of the two workmen. Caraway didn't hesitate. A few strides took him across the street; a slash from his broken blade severed the rope. Before the men unloading the cart could do more than stop and stare, Caraway was on the horse's back and urging it after the carriage.

It was a long time since he'd ridden a horse. The Helm didn't train on horseback – in the narrow streets of Arkannen, it was easier to fight on foot – but everyone who passed through the fifth ring learned at least the basics of mounted combat, and Caraway had grown up in a family that was just wealthy enough to teach its sons how to ride. All the same, to start with it was all he could do to stay in the saddle and keep the animal going in the right direction. It was like being in charge of a rather unstable machine that could set its will against his at any time and for which he only dimly remembered the instructions; his entire body was tense with the need to control it.

After a period of battling with himself and the horse he rediscovered the rhythm of their shared movements, and then he was free to focus on what he was doing. He hadn't lost the carriage, which was something. It was still a street length ahead of him, rattling and swaying around each corner just as he rounded the previous one. But the driver appeared to be aware that he was being chased; he was bowling along the roads of the first ring at a far greater speed than would usually be acceptable, throwing the occasional nervous glance over his shoulder. It dawned on Caraway that rather than taking the shortest route to the Gate of Flame and the higher rings, as he would have expected, the carriage was heading in the opposite direction: deeper into the industrial heart of the first ring, towards the Gate of Birth. Perhaps the Helm weren't taking Ayla back to Darkhaven after all. Perhaps they planned to leave the city altogether ... but he shrugged the question off. It made no difference. Wherever the carriage was going, he needed to catch up with it.

As if the driver had heard his resolve and was determined to counteract it, the carriage made a sharp right-hand turn in the direction of the canal. Caraway dug his heels into his horse's sides, spurring it on to greater speed. If he lost the carriage amid the maze of smaller streets and factories that lined the waterway, he'd never be able to find it again.

'Watch it, mister!' A mechanical cycle whirred across his path in a trail of steam, almost under the horse's feet; he swore, tightening his grip on the reins as the animal baulked, the muscles in his shoulders aching with the unaccustomed strain. Trying to soothe the horse with an unsteady hand on its neck, he encouraged it forward again, ducking as they veered beneath a low-hanging sign and around the corner into the narrower street.

Straight away the sound of the horse's hooves against the ground changed from a precise tap to a deafening clatter – some of the older streets of the first ring were still cobbled. Ahead the carriage was bouncing and shaking, ill prepared for a surface like this. Caraway permitted himself a grim smile and increased his pace. Maybe it had been an attempt at losing him, maybe a wrong turn by the driver; either way it would serve him well.

Hold on, Ayla, he told her silently. *I'm coming as fast as I can.*

By the time they reached the wider road lined with industrial yards that passed along the outermost edge of the first ring, Caraway had gained some ground. The noise of wheels and hooves alike faded as they returned to a smooth paved surface, to be replaced by the sounds of the nearby cotton mill: the hum of the looms, audible even through the walls, and the repetitive hiss of the atmospheric engine that lifted water out of the canal to drive the waterwheel. The carriage picked up speed again, racing along in the direction of the ironworks; Caraway could barely hold on to the advantage he had already gained, let alone close the gap further. He clung to the reins with stiff fingers, warehouses and factories passing in a blur to either side of him, identifiable only by the parade of different smells that came and went in quick succession: wood, sewage, lye.

Finally they reached a boatbuilder's yard, where both carriage and lone horse had to swerve around the hull of a merchant barge that was being hauled down the road towards them on a flat-bed cart by a team of oxen. The sudden turn set the carriage leaning at a crazy angle, its outer wheels skimming the gutter. Caraway chewed on the inside of his lip, fists tightening in helpless anticipation. It was going to tip over – it would crash, making him indirectly responsible for hounding Ayla to her death – but then it settled back into place, rocking on its springs, and kept going. Caraway was watching it so intently that he only just missed the barge himself, his mount shying and snorting at the sight of the oxen. Blinking away the sudden dizziness of relief, he gathered himself and urged the horse on, followed by the curses of the men driving the team.

Beyond the boatyard the road and the first-ring tramway converged, to run side by side before parting again at the ironworks. Caraway heard a low rumble and glanced up to see the square silhouette of a tram approaching, adding a lighter layer of steam to the smoke that already hung in the air. Several passengers were leaning out of the glassless windows, watching his pursuit with incurious faces. No doubt they'd seen many stranger things in their time than a wild-eyed man on a horse chasing a runaway carriage. One of them called out something that was lost in the throbbing of the tram's engine; it sounded uncomplimentary, but Caraway ignored it, keeping his gaze fixed on his target. The tram loomed beside him with a rhythmic rushing sound, before chugging on past in a swirl of coal-scented air. Ahead, the driver of the carriage was battling to control his pair of horses, which clearly weren't used to running for such extended periods through the city streets. Caraway leaned forward and murmured to his own horse. If he could just catch up somehow …

As they neared the roar and glow of the ironworks itself, he saw his opportunity. Ahead the road forged on between the ironworks and the outer wall of the city, with no room for turnings or branches until it left the industrial areas behind and began to enter the edges of the trading quarter. If he was quick, he could cut along the inner side of the ironworks and meet the carriage at the other end.

Waiting only long enough to be sure that the carriage was going straight on, Caraway hauled on the reins and steered his horse left, across the bridge that led over the tramway. The heavy tang of hot iron settled on him like a blanket as he sped past the red-brown metal skeleton that made up the ironworks, the rattle of the ore-carts as they were winched up the side of the furnace only adding to the general din. He kept going, coaxing the horse to move as fast as the cracked surface of the road allowed, until the noise of the ironworks began to recede behind them. Then he recrossed the tramway and turned down the nearest side street, aiming for a point at which his path and the carriage's would intersect. His route would return him to the main road just where it narrowed to pass under a grand archway into the mercantile quarter: perfect. He pulled up just before the narrow alley he was in rejoined the road, breathing hard and straining to listen. *Let me be in time. Let me not have missed them ...* Then he heard the sound of fast-approaching wheels.

As the pair of horses rounded the corner with the carriage that contained Ayla swaying behind them, Caraway forced his own mount out in front of them. He was broadside on to them; with no time to turn and too little space to pass him, the carriage would have to stop. For a terrifying moment it seemed he had left it too late – the oncoming horses showed no signs of slowing, their rolling eyes and foam-flecked cheeks heading straight for him as though they intended to barrel into him in a lethal tangle of hooves and limbs – but he gritted his teeth and held his nervous horse steady in the face of the onslaught. The driver was shouting at him, telling him to get out of the way or they'd both end up dead, and he kept on shouting right up until the pair of horses came to a halt in a flurry of snorting and stamping, close enough to Caraway that he could feel the heat radiating off them.

'You bloody idiot!' The driver's face was pallid and sweaty, his eyes showing the whites all the way round in much the same way as his horses'. 'A few lengths more and –'

'You're alive, aren't you?' Caraway dropped to the ground, catching himself with legs that suddenly felt much too wobbly.

Trying to conceal the weakness, he drew his broken blade as he advanced. 'And if you want to stay that way then you'd better run. This thing may not look like much, but I reckon it could still slit your throat.'

If possible, the man's eyes widened still further. Before Caraway could even contemplate climbing up onto the box, the driver had made a scrambling dismount on the opposite side of the carriage and fled down the street. Strange. The man hadn't been wearing the uniform of a Helmsman, but all the same Caraway would have expected him to put up more of a fight. Ayla Nightshade was in that carriage, after all. Why hadn't the Helm guarded her more securely? Owen Travers wasn't the sort of man to rely on a speedy getaway without having a bloodier and more violent backup plan.

The first uneasy tendrils of misgiving creeping through him, Caraway wrenched open the door of the carriage – and stopped dead, gaping at the two people huddled in the interior. One was a man wearing the striped coat of the Helm, and the other ... the other was a girl in a cloak, with the hood pulled up over her dyed black hair.

A girl, in fact, who wasn't Ayla.

She screamed as Caraway grabbed the Helmsman's shirt in two fists and pulled him out of the carriage, then threw a punch that sent him sprawling in the dirt of the street.

'Where is she?' he shouted. 'What have you done with her?'

'I – I don't know what you –'

'Ayla!' Caraway clenched his fists, fighting the urge to beat it out of the man. 'Where is she?'

The Helmsman shook his head, the back of one hand pressed to his bloodied mouth. He was only a boy, really; as young as Caraway himself had been when he first joined the Helm.

'I – I'm just obeying orders,' he stammered, blinking up at Caraway, making no attempt to get to his feet. 'Captain Travers –'

Fire and blood. Caraway took a step back, shaking his head, bitter understanding coming too late. How could he have been so damned stupid? The whole thing was a setup. Travers had got him out of the way as neatly as a rat in a trap, leaving him stranded pretty much as far as he could get from the Gate of Flame. And Ayla –

Leaving the staring Helmsman on the ground and the girl having hysterics in the carriage, he remounted his horse and turned it around, back towards the higher rings. Towards Darkhaven, where the Helm must have taken Ayla.

TWENTY-SEVEN

Serenna awoke with a shiver to an unfamiliar room that was bright with early morning sunlight. How she knew it was unfamiliar, she wasn't sure: the canopy above her looked exactly the same as Ayla's. It just felt different.

She turned her head and saw Myrren lying next to her, a small frown on his face as if he were trying to work something out in his sleep. Memory came flooding back to her in a hot rush and a sudden awareness of her own body. Last night she'd – they'd – oh, flaming *ashes*. The high priestess would have severe words to say about this.

She doesn't have to know, Serenna told herself, but somehow she couldn't believe it. She felt it must be written on her face for everyone to see. It was as though she had woken up in a world where everything had undergone a subtle change, meaning she didn't quite fit into it in the same way as before. *This can never happen again,* she'd said to Myrren, and she'd been in earnest. So why did she now feel she wanted it to?

Serenna shook her head. Giving in to physical desire had warped her faculty for logic, just as she'd been warned it would. She needed to get back to her own room – Ayla's room – and meditate for a time. Control the conflicting emotions that were racing through her veins and find the still, calm centre of herself once more. Only then would she be able to assess the effect that last night's actions would have on her life.

She sat up slowly and carefully, anxious not to disturb Myrren. She was still wearing her dress, though it was crumpled and wrinkled after her night's sleep. The window was wide open, she noticed; no wonder she was cold. The man certainly did like his fresh air. Or perhaps, like the bird in his painting, it was the closest he could get to freedom.

Stop it, she told herself sternly. *You're letting your judgement become clouded by sentiment. Just get out before he wakes.*

She slipped out of the bed and stole across the floor towards her discarded underclothes. She could feel the blood heating her face as she pulled them on, and hoped fervently that she wouldn't bump into anyone on the way back to her room. Having shaken out her skirts as best she could and pinned her veil with lopsided haste over her uncombed hair, she tiptoed towards the door, but before she could reach it she heard Myrren's voice behind her.

'Are you leaving?'

Serenna turned. He was sitting up in bed, blinking at her, an expression of concern on his face. Immediately she could feel the same tugging at her heart that had led her to reach out to him the night before, as though somehow he had attached a fine silk cord to it and could draw her back towards him with the slightest pull. It wasn't fair that he should have so much of an effect on her, even now.

'I've already stayed too long,' she told him. 'I need to go.'

Frowning, Myrren flung the covers aside and swung his legs out of the bed. With a shock, she realised he was naked.

She averted her gaze, a deeper blush spreading across her skin, but not before she'd caught sight of the dark purple bruise high up on his arm.

'How on earth did you get that bruise?' she asked as a way to distract herself, still not looking at him.

'What? Oh ... it must have been in the fight with Elisse's oddly named bodyguard yesterday.' Serenna heard a rustle of fabric; presumably he was clothing himself. She wished she could stop remembering the way she'd kissed him last night. The way she'd wrapped her legs around his waist.

'Did you sleep well?' she asked almost at random, still floating in a cloud of acute embarrassment.

'Not really,' Myrren said. 'I've been having a lot of bad dreams recently. They leave me feeling tired even when I've just been sleeping. Still, hopefully they'll go away when all this is over.' Then, with the hint of a smile in his voice, 'You can look at me now, Serenna.'

She did so. He was wearing a dark blue dressing gown trimmed with gold; there was both amusement and consternation in his eyes.

'Would you rather we pretended it never happened?' he asked her. 'Because if that's what you want ...'

Yes. No. Serenna bit her lip. 'I don't know. I need time to think.'

He nodded. 'I'll go along with whatever you decide. If you want to go back to your temple today, I won't try and stop you. But –' and here his voice took on a different tone, an edge of significance that cut through his careful neutrality like a rock in a stream – 'if you want to stay here for good, I would welcome that too.'

Serenna stared at him. She hadn't even considered that she might stay in Darkhaven. That Myrren might *want* her to stay in Darkhaven. He looked back at her, a self-deprecating cast to his mouth, as though he fully expected her to reject him outright. But the truth was, she didn't know what to say. She didn't know what she wanted, not any more.

In the taut silence that had fallen between them, a sudden flurry of knocks on the door made them both jump.

'Not again,' Myrren muttered. His face had lost all traces of colour. 'Didn't I tell you I had a nightmare? If this is another attack ...'

He strode to the door and opened it. Serenna stayed where she was, anxiety warring with the desire to keep out of sight, but soon anxiety won and she rose up on tiptoe to peer over Myrren's shoulder. It took her a moment to place the woman standing outside in the corridor, dressed as she was in a Helmsman's coat: Elisse's blonde bodyguard, Sorrow. There were dark shadows under her eyes, and she carried no weapons except for a single knife.

'You!' Myrren's hands curled into fists, and he glanced back into the room as though searching for something to defend himself with.

'I come in peace,' Sorrow drawled, offering him the knife hilt-first. 'This was just in case I met anyone I didn't like on the way. Will you let me in, my lord? I have some news I think you'll want to hear.'

Myrren took the knife and backed away far enough to let her through the door, but Serenna could tell he was frowning. 'I did warn you I'd have you locked up if I ever saw you again ...'

'I'm hoping you'll let me off,' Sorrow said. 'Since I've just saved Elisse's life and delivered your brother safely into the world.'

'What?' The word flew out before Serenna could stop it. Sorrow turned her head, apparently registering Serenna's

258

presence for the first time, and scanned her dress as if noting every crease and wrinkle. A knowing smirk touched her lips, but she made no comment.

'Explain yourself.' Myrren appeared oblivious to Serenna's awkward blushes; his gaze was fixed on Sorrow's face. 'Elisse has had her baby?'

'Correct,' Sorrow said. 'Elisse was visited by this rogue Changer creature of yours last night. I drove it off, but the shock sent Elisse into labour.' She offered a mocking grin. 'Next thing I knew, I was catching a baby in my bare hands.'

'So there was another attack,' Myrren whispered, before gathering himself together. 'That still doesn't explain what you're doing here in the first place, though. Or why you came to tell me about it.'

Sorrow shrugged. 'Turns out I do have some level of integrity, Lord Myrren. I came to you because Elisse needs a physician, and because she seems to believe you don't mean her any harm. Beyond that ...' She frowned, her eyes unfocusing briefly as though she were looking at something else. 'Travers thinks he can make me a scapegoat. And since I don't want both of you after me –' her lips set in a wry twist – 'I'm offering myself up to your mercy.'

That didn't make a whole lot of sense to Serenna, but Myrren was nodding as if he understood.

'All well and good, Sorrow, but I still need a full explanation of –'

'You'll get it,' Sorrow said. 'But first things first. Send the physician to Elisse. Then after that, we can talk.' She raised her eyebrows at him. 'Now, if I can just have my knife back?'

To Serenna's surprise, Myrren handed it over without demur.

'I'll send for the physician,' he said. 'Serenna and I will come to Elisse's room as soon as he's finished. I trust you'll be there?'

Sorrow's gaze travelled from him to Serenna and back again. 'You trust correctly.' She turned to leave the room, then added over her shoulder, 'And bring my pistol with you, will you? The one I stole from you throws left.'

As the door closed behind her, Myrren shook his head. 'You know, crazy as it sounds, I almost like her.'

Serenna frowned at him. 'Even though she did her very best to kill you last time you saw her?'

'She's just confirmed my suspicions,' Myrren said, still staring abstractedly at the door. 'Or at least, there is sufficient doubt over the matter to make it worthwhile questioning her before I call the Helm to cart her off to jail.'

Serenna rubbed the bridge of her nose, wondering if last night had dulled her wits as well as scrambling her emotions. 'What suspicions?'

'Captain Travers said that Sorrow overstepped her authority in what she did to protect Elisse.' Finally, Myrren turned to face her. 'But if there's one thing I know about sellswords, it's that they never do more than they're paid to do. It was always far more likely that Travers gave Sorrow permission to defend Elisse against anyone who stumbled across her, even if it happened to be a Nightshade.'

'Ah.' At last it made sense. 'So you believe Sorrow's account may provide you with enough evidence to have Travers demoted?'

'Exactly.' Myrren's teeth showed in a ferocious smile. 'Travers has been challenging my authority ever since my father died. Now, finally, I have something concrete to use against him. Added to the fact that I felt Ayla Change down in Arkannen last night, when he claimed she had left the city –'

'You felt Ayla Change?' Serenna echoed. She couldn't work out why Myrren appeared to be so happy about that. Surely, if Ayla had taken her other form on the same night that the rogue creature had attacked Elisse, that could only be seen as evidence against her ...

'I thought what you're thinking, to start with,' Myrren said. 'But in fact, it's the one piece of proof I needed that Ayla is innocent. I'd forgotten how familiar it feels, when she Changes. I didn't feel anything like that on the other nights when there were attacks. And though I know Travers wouldn't accept that as evidence, it's enough for me. Ayla is innocent, and I *will not* let her be convicted.'

His expression softening, he stepped close enough to Serenna to take her hands. 'Serenna ... you and I have things to talk about, I know that. But for now, I think it's important that we visit Elisse as soon as possible and find out what happened last night. There's still a killer on the loose; preventing any further attacks and finding the real culprit must be our foremost priority. That is, if you're still willing to help me.'

Flustered, Serenna gazed up at him. Part of her wanted to lean in towards him and kiss him as she had last night – to tell him she wanted nothing more than to stay with him in Darkhaven. Yet the rest of her knew she needed time to be alone and think things through. She was a priestess: she had dedicated her life to that. One impulsive night of pleasure couldn't be allowed to determine the course of her future.

'Of course I'm still willing to help you,' she said. 'But until these crimes are solved, my lord, it must be as though nothing ever happened between us.' Gently, she extricated her hands from his clasp. 'Otherwise it will be too hard.'

Myrren nodded. 'I understand. And after that?'

'After that ...' She hesitated. He was watching her with ill-concealed hope in his face; she didn't like to destroy it.

Yet she had to be honest. Promises were worth nothing if they were based on lies. 'After that, I don't know.'

In the silence that followed, she recalled that she still hadn't told him about her discoveries in the library. Yet again, it seemed the wrong time. She resolved to do it as soon as they had spoken to Elisse and Sorrow – as soon as they had moved away from this awkwardness between them, and back onto their previous businesslike footing.

'I'll leave you to get ready,' she said instead. 'Elisse is in Ayla's room, so I suppose this dress will have to do for me. In the meantime, shall I fetch the physician for you?'

'That would be very helpful.' Myrren inclined his head, giving her a controlled smile. Once again, he'd gathered up all his emotion and tucked it out of reach. Maybe sometime soon she'd be able to offer him the words that would mean he no longer had to hide what he was feeling. She ached to do that now, but she knew she owed it to herself to think it all through first.

'One good thing, at least,' she offered as a palliative. 'Didn't you say you'd often wished you had a brother?'

A kind of wonder crept into his eyes. 'You're right. Sorrow said it, but I didn't even think – you're right.' He gave her a grin that was childlike in its spontaneity, as though he'd rediscovered the ability to take joy in simple things. 'How remarkable. I have a brother.'

Serenna couldn't help herself. Stepping closer, she rested her hands on his arm to steady herself and kissed his cheek. Then, drawing her veil down over her face to hide her blushes, she retreated from the room and went to find the physician.

TWENTY-EIGHT

As soon as Caraway had left, Ayla walked into the middle of the room and took a deep breath. Right. It was time to investigate the communal bathing facilities.

With slightly flustered haste, she unfastened the dress she'd worn every day since she left Darkhaven and let it fall down around her ankles, then shuddered in release. This must be what a butterfly felt like when it emerged from its wrinkled and grubby cocoon. She wanted to burn the thing, but it was all she had to wear, so she contented herself with kicking it aside. Now what? Her wig would be no good if she wanted to wash herself thoroughly, so she pulled her cloak on over her shift and tugged the hood down until it touched her eyebrows. She'd only go in if there was no-one else around. She couldn't run the risk of being recognised.

Caraway had given her a square of towelling and a bar of grainy soap, both of which he'd purchased from the landlord the previous evening. She also tucked her knife into a pocket of her cloak; she didn't think there would be any abductors lurking in the bathing room, but it was better to be safe. Then, clutching the folds of thick fabric tightly around herself as though they could protect her from prying eyes, she slipped out through the door and along the corridor to her destination.

To her relief, the bathing room was deserted; even more to her relief, as well as the large communal tub in the centre of the floor there was a smaller tub set behind a battered screen. It was all rather cramped, but Ayla's standards had changed somewhat since she first entered the lower rings. She didn't let herself stop to think about how many other people had used the bath before her. She just set herself to carrying buckets of hot water over to it from the vast hissing cylinder that squatted in one corner of the room. When the bath was full enough, she flung cloak and towel over the screen, then stepped into the tub still wearing her shift – at least if anyone came in she wouldn't be caught naked. The temperature of the water verged on painful, yet she could feel it working its way through tensions she hadn't even realised she had. Who would have thought plain hot water could feel so good?

Yet once she was settled in place, the doubt that had been climbing up and down her spine all morning returned with full force. She hadn't told Caraway, because she hadn't wanted to crush her own modicum of hope, but she'd woken up again last night with the same cold shiver she'd felt on the night of her father's death and again a few nights ago: the shiver that meant a Change was taking place somewhere nearby. If it had been a true feeling, and not merely a nightmare, it indicated that the killer was still on the loose. Not wanting to consider the implications of that too closely, she was trying to avoid thinking about it at all until Caraway came back with a news-sheet. Until she saw the truth set out in blurred print, there was always the possibility that she had been wrong and that she'd be able to go back home today.

Unless, a small mean voice said inside her head, *Myrren is colluding with the Changer girl just as Caraway suggested, and calls you back to Darkhaven so he can convict you of murder, as he has planned all along.*

Shut up! Ayla told it. *Myrren wouldn't do that to me. He wouldn't!* But the doubt remained.

She took a deep breath and submerged herself fully in the water, letting it cover her head as though it could wash away all her uncertainty. Then she concentrated on working up a lather from the gritty soap and scrubbing her skin so hard it tingled. She'd find out the truth soon enough; until then there was no point in picking at it, no matter how it itched

She sought for another topic to distract her fran thoughts, and found herself remembering Caraway's illuminated by firelight. The understanding in his eyes, the way he had offered her his honesty. His tentative s after he'd given her the gift of last night's freedom. She to call up her mother's memory, to set Kati's vengeful between them, but somehow the pain wasn't there – was, it was no longer directed at him.

What are you doing? the same mean voice whispere *in love with the man who let your mother go to h*

'He didn't do it on purpose,' she answered her realising even as she said it that it was true, ar had known it for quite some time. 'And he's pai since.' Belatedly recalling which part of her o she should have been objecting to with greate added in a mutter, 'And I'm not in love with

Closing her eyes, she rinsed her hair aga thing was ridiculous. She'd just been coopec him too long: another reason to hope she'd to Darkhaven today. All the same, much idea, she supposed she ought at least to offer him an apology before she left. Choke back a bit of her cursed Nightshade pride, and thank him for what he'd done for her. She owed him that much.

He'd probably rather be given money, her thoughts said with a certain amount of snark. *He can't drink thanks.*

Though he hadn't had a single drink since she'd stumbled back into his life ...

Letting out an incoherent sound of frustration, Ayla plunged her head back under the water. She wasn't sure who she was more annoyed with, Caraway or herself. But since he wasn't there to take it out on, she had to be content with scrubbing herself all over one final time. By the end of it the water was cooling rapidly, so she stood up and wrung out as much of her shift as she could gather into two hands before applying the towel. Once she'd carried all her dirty bathwater, bucketful by bucketful, over to the drainage channel that ran along one side of the room, the thin fabric of the shift had more or less dried and her back was aching. She'd never appreciated before just how hard life must be for people who couldn't afford proper plumbing.

Wrapped in the cloak again, she left the bathing room and made it back to her own room without seeing a single person. She dropped the cloak on a chair, then looked with some distaste at the discarded dress. She ought to put it on right away – though her shift was decent enough, it was too flimsy even for summer wear – but the idea of climbing back into her shed skin sent a tremor of mild disgust through her. It so wonderful to be clean.

Rubbing ineffectually at her hair with the damp square of towelling, she crossed to the window and stood looking out at the busy street below. Where was Caraway? There had been plenty of time for him to fetch a news-sheet and be back by now.

'So here you are.' The voice was loud in the stillness of the room, making her jump.

'I was beginning to think something had happened to you,' she said – or started to say, because even as the first words left her lips she realised that the light, mocking tone was nothing to do with Caraway. Heart thudding, she turned. Owen Travers was standing in the doorway, watching her, the corners of his lips curled into a slight, satirical smile.

'How did you get in here?' Ayla forced as much anger as she could into her voice, though her knees were weak with fear. Travers stepped into the room, pushing the door closed behind him with his heel. One hand dangled a key in front of her.

'The landlord gave it to me. The law-abiding citizens of Arkannen are only too happy to aid the Helm in their enquiries.'

His gaze drifted over the thin fabric covering her body in a way that made her stomach plunge uncomfortably. She darted a quick surreptitious glance across the room towards her abandoned cloak. If she could just reach the knife in the pocket …

'What do you want, Captain Travers?' she asked, affecting cool unconcern. He gave her a sceptical look.

'You know what I want, Lady Ayla. I'm here to take you back to Darkhaven where you belong.'

'I see. Then if you'll just allow me to finish getting ready …'

She walked across the room to pick up the cloak. Travers made no effort to stop her; he just stood there, his amused gaze tracking her movements as though he knew exactly what she intended. There was a bandage peeking out from beneath the collar of his shirt, she noticed now, and another protruding from his left cuff.

'Have you been injured, captain?' she asked to distract him as she gathered the cloak into her arms. Again, his expression was frankly disbelieving.

'You should know.'

Ayla frowned. 'What does that mean?'

'You should know that, too.' He took a step towards her; she slid a hand into the cloak pocket, her pulse accelerating until it hissed in her ears. 'Enough dissembling, my dear. You're coming with me whether you like it or not.'

'Keep back!' Her hand closed around the hilt of the knife; she drew it out, brandishing it in his direction. 'I'm not afraid to stab you, Travers. I mean it. And when Caraway comes back –'

'Ah, yes, Caraway.' Travers didn't seem at all disconcerted, either by the weapon or by the prospect of Caraway's imminent arrival; on the contrary, the smile was back on his lips. 'I have to say, I'm shocked. I'd have thought you too proud to accept help from your mother's killer.'

'He didn't kill her,' she spat back at him. 'It was an accident. It wasn't his fault.'

'I know that, Lady Ayla. I'm just surprised you do.'

She stared at him. 'You know?'

'Of course.' Travers shrugged. 'Caraway wouldn't have had the guts for something like that. He was devoted to the woman.'

'Then why did you ruin his life?'

'Not me,' Travers said. 'It was your father who insisted he be punished for what happened. I was only following orders.' He smiled. 'Just as I'm doing now.'

There was a disquieting look in his eyes, a hint of something dark and deranged. Ayla backed away, lifting the knife between them as he advanced on her. *Please come back, Tomas. Come back soon.*

'You don't have to do this,' she whispered.

'I know I don't.' Travers grabbed her wrist, wrenching the blade aside, and kept coming. His other hand went into the inner pocket of his coat, drawing out a piece of cloth. 'But I want to.'

Only a handspan separated them now. She tried to resist him, but his grip was unbreakable and the knife dangled uselessly from her fingers. Gasping, she brought her knee up, angling it towards his groin; he blocked it with his hip, his leg pushing hers apart. Then she was caught between his body and the wall, and the darkness in his eyes was growing more intense. She had the strange sense that he didn't really see her any more – not as a person, anyway. Some idea had taken hold of him so strongly that there was no room for anything else.

'You shouldn't fight me, Ayla,' he whispered, so close to her lips that she could feel the shape of the words. In response, taking a tip from Caraway's fighting style, she lowered her head and drove it as hard as she could into his face. Yet no-one had ever taught her to defend herself; she had neither the power nor the accuracy she needed. Travers staggered back a step, blood staining his mouth, but even as she strained to get free he recovered himself and slammed her back against the wall. His fingers twisted viciously at her wrist, making her cry out in pain and drop the knife.

'I warned you.' He pressed still closer to her, fury glaring from his narrowed eyes. Fury and ... something else. Ayla's breath caught in her throat as she realised she could feel his excitement. He wasn't just following orders. Some of his interest in her was purely personal.

Energised by a new and sharper fear, she struggled even harder, but he was solid, muscular, immovable. She looked up into his face, and saw him smile. Then his lips were on hers, a brutal invasion. She tasted the bitter iron of his blood. She couldn't breathe. Her limbs strained against his, striving without success to push him away; her heart stuttered in her chest as though her entire body were crying out at what was being done to her. She nipped at his mouth and tongue with her teeth, trying to hurt him, but it only seemed to excite him further. A scream rose in her throat, but it had nowhere to go.

Finally Travers drew back from her a fraction, his passion-darkened eyes scanning her face with clear enjoyment. Then, as she took a shuddering breath, he clamped the cloth that was still in his hand over her mouth and nose. A sweet odour rose from it, penetrating deep into Ayla's lungs. Her eyes watered, tears spilling down her cheeks. She attempted to turn her face away, but his grip was inexorable. He was going to suffocate her. Panic rushed through her, a desperate longing for air. She tried not to take another breath, but her spinning head and the sharp pain in her chest left her no choice. Her lips parted in a ragged gasp, drawing in another cloying lungful. Only then did he lower the cloth, studying her as if to assess the results.

'What have you done to me?' she whispered. Her voice sounded hoarse and unfamiliar, like a stranger's. She tried to breathe normally, but no matter how much air she sucked in it wasn't enough. Something was circling in her head, a promise of darkness to come.

'Don't worry, sweet girl.' Travers smiled at her, lifting a hand to stroke her cheek with the backs of his fingers. 'You'll recover in good time.'

Ayla's vision was growing hazy, her limbs no longer able to support her. She sagged against Travers, feeling his arms come round her to hold her against his shoulder. That was wrong. She shouldn't be clinging to him like this, as though they were lovers, as though she wanted him to be there. But she didn't seem to have a choice.

'That's right,' he whispered in her ear. 'It will all be over soon.'

The last thing she felt before the shadows swallowed her was his lips touching her brow in a gentle caress.

TWENTY-NINE

Elisse looked down at the sleeping child in her arms. She was sore and exhausted, but most of all she was amazed. Amazed that she could have created something so perfect. Amazed that Florentyn's selfishness could have produced something so good. Above all, amazed at the love she already felt for the tiny life she was holding.

'Myrren and the priestess will be here any moment,' Sorrow said. She was sitting at Elisse's bedside, as she had been all through the physician's examination. The man had deplored the circumstances of the birth, but had been forced to admit that both mother and child were healthy. He'd added that Sorrow had done a good job – though with the sellsword herself watching his every move like a cat who'd spotted a bird with a bad leg, he'd probably been afraid to say otherwise.

She did do a good job, though. Elisse studied her son's crumpled features. His eyes were closed, but the patch of night-dark hair on the crown of his head – darker even than her own – proclaimed him a Nightshade beyond doubt. *If it wasn' for Naeve Sorrow, both o' us would be dead.*

'Have you decided what to call him yet?' Sorrow asked. Elisse looked up, blinking.

'Can I – I mean, is it up ta me ta –'

Sorrow gave her one of those flat stares. 'He's your son, Elisse. No-one has a better right to name him than you.'

Elisse ran a finger gently along the baby's downy cheek. 'Then I'll call him Corus. Tha' was my father's name.' She glanced uncertainly at Sorrow. 'Are ya – are ya going ta get inta trouble for being here?'

'Doesn't look like it.' Sorrow shrugged. 'Hopefully I'm going to drop Owen Travers in it instead. He's the one who got me into this mess.'

Elisse nodded and rocked the baby in her arms, saying nothing. She supposed that was all it had been, to Sorrow: a complete and utter mess. But she didn't know how she'd survive in Darkhaven without Sorrow. Now, more than ever, she didn't want to stay here. Myrren had said it would be safer, but Myrren had been wrong.

'Naeve …' she began slowly. 'If I wanted ta leave Darkhaven, me and the baby, where could we go?'

'You mean, run away from the Nightshade family altogether?' Sorrow frowned. 'They'd send the Helm after you, so I guess you'd have to leave Arkannen. Probably even Mirrorvale, to be safe.'

'Leave Mirrorvale?' Elisse had never even considered such a thing. Sorrow gave her a sardonic look.

'There are other countries, you know.'

'I know.' Which was true: she was well aware that Mirrorvale was surrounded on three sides by other countries. Yet they were only names to her, places on a map. They were less real than the legends she had grown up with as a child, which at least had the advantage of being rooted in something familiar. 'Which – which one's the nicest?'

'Depends what you want,' Sorrow said, her lips quirking

as though she found the question amusing. 'But like I told you before ... your son has royal blood. Changer blood. It will manifest itself in him one day, and when that happens I think you're going to need someone around who understands what it means.'

'I s'pose so.' Elisse scrutinised the baby's sleeping face once more, trying to imagine him as a man who looked like Florentyn or Myrren. A man who could turn himself at will into something strange and powerful. If Corus possessed the true Changer gift, he would have a claim to the throne of Darkhaven. Was that what she wanted for him? Would that be what he wanted for himself, when he was old enough to choose?

The silence was broken by a knock on the door, and Elisse straightened up as Myrren and Serenna walked into the room. She felt almost guilty, as though she had been thinking treasonous thoughts. But Corus was her son. She had a responsibility to do what was best for him, not what was best for anyone else.

'Elisse,' the current overlord of Darkhaven said. 'You are well?'

She shrugged. 'I'm all right.'

He crossed to her bedside and stood looking down at the child in her arms. 'And this must be my new brother.'

'His name's Corus.' The words came out defiant, but Myrren only nodded.

'A good name.' To Elisse's relief he made no move to take the baby from her, just stepped away again. 'Now, perhaps you or Sorrow could tell us what happened last night.'

'Tha' bloody Changer creature came through the window and attacked me, that's what.' Elisse indicated her burnt cheek, then pulled back her gown to reveal the start of the long scratches on her shoulder. The physician had put a few stitches into the two deepest, and they still stung like crazy, even with the ointment he'd given her. 'If it hadn' been for Sorrow then I prob'ly would o' been killed.'

'And what exactly did Sorrow do?' Myrren asked. Elisse glanced at Sorrow, not sure whether she was meant to mention the pistol – Sorrow had said she'd stolen it from Myrren, after all. But Sorrow just smirked and leaned back in her chair, crossing one ankle over the other knee.

'I shot it.'

Myrren frowned. 'You claim you actually hit the creature? Wounded it? No weapon can harm a Changer in creature form.'

'I hate to disillusion you, my lord, but it looks as though a pistol can.' Sorrow raised a mocking eyebrow. 'Like I told you earlier, the pistol I was using throws left. So my bullet only grazed the thing. Certainly not fatal – probably only left a nasty bruise – but it was enough to scare it off.'

During this conversation the priestess, Serenna, had been waiting quietly in the background. Now she stepped forward to stand beside Myrren, pushing her veil back from her face. 'Where did you say you hit the creature?'

Elisse stared at her: there was a disconcerting shadow of alarm in her grey eyes, and her skin beneath the freckles was pale. Sorrow seemed not to notice, answering with the same studied nonchalance she had used to answer Myrren.

'Right shoulder, I suppose you'd call it.'

'I see.' Serenna gazed blindly at Sorrow for a frozen instant, her face wiped clean of all emotion. Then she reached up with hands that trembled slightly and brought the veil back down into place. Only by listening very hard could Elisse decipher the words she murmured to Myrren.

'I'm sorry, my lord. I – I am not feeling well, all of a sudden. Please excuse me.'

Myrren turned to her with a frown of concern. 'Of course. Do you need me to fetch the physician again?'

'No, thank you.' Serenna had already started for the door; she didn't look back. 'I just need some fresh air. I'll return before too long.'

Without waiting for a reply, she left the room. Myrren watched her go, confusion and anxiety warring in his face. After a moment he turned back and forced a smile.

'So you shot the creature and it fled ...'

'Yep.' Sorrow grimaced. 'And that's when Elisse decided she was going to give birth.' Both feet came down on the floor as she leaned forward to fix him with an ironic stare across the bed. 'Maybe little Corus recognised his sister and came out to meet her.'

Elisse winced at the deliberate provocation, but Myrren just shook his head.

'Since Elisse only came to Darkhaven yesterday, Ayla couldn't possibly have known where to find her. If anything, this attack supports her innocence.' Then he leaned forward too, that hint of steel entering his voice that always reminded Elisse of his father. 'And if you think, Naeve Sorrow, that because you have performed my family a service, you can say whatever you like to me without fear of reprisal, you can think again. I've already allowed you far more of a free rein than Lord Florentyn would have, but there's still the matter of your treasonous attack in the fourth ring to consider.'

I've defeated you once, his fierce eyes said. *Don't think I won't do it a second time.*

There was silence, before Sorrow nodded. 'You're right, my lord. I'm sorry.' She actually managed to sound respectful.

'But on the matter of Lady Ayla ... I have to tell you that she and Caraway saw you leave the fourth ring with Elisse yesterday. I didn't tell Caraway who Elisse is or what she's doing in Arkannen, but no doubt he has his suspicions. So if Lady Ayla really is the attacker, she might have come to Darkhaven looking for Elisse after all.'

That was a blow to Myrren, Elisse could see. No matter how he tried to prove his sister's innocence, the evidence kept stacking up against her. Still, he managed to hide it well, the only sign of his inner perturbation the clipped tone of his voice.

'Then you've seen Ayla? With someone else, this ... Caraway?' He frowned. 'Surely not Tomas Caraway? The one my father had thrown out of the Helm when Kati died?'

'That's right,' Sorrow said, carefully neutral. 'Far as I can tell, he was asking questions on her behalf.'

'Tomas Caraway,' Myrren repeated. He looked totally bemused, as though the roses he'd planted had come up turnips. 'Why on earth would Ayla have been with him, of all people? She always thought the Helm had let her mother die on purpose. She'd never forgive the one man who was most clearly to blame.'

Sorrow shrugged. 'Don't ask me. But they were definitely together. Caraway had followed me to the fourth ring the previous day, and then yesterday he came back with Ayla.'

'Right.' Myrren considered the information for a moment, then seemed to dismiss it as inexplicable. 'Well, whatever the reason, she was still in the city yesterday. Both your evidence and my own sources confirm that – no matter what Captain Travers may claim.' His lips tightened. 'Which brings us back to the matter at hand, Sorrow. What exactly did Travers hire you to do?'

'He told me I should do whatever it took to protect Elisse, without being afraid that the Helm would come after me for it,' Sorrow said. 'He didn't precisely say it in so many words, but it was understood that you and Ayla were the greatest threats to her – that if you found out about her, you'd want her dead. And I was to stop that happening, by any means necessary short of killing you.'

'It's good to know that Travers drew the line at regicide,' Myrren murmured. 'His devotion to what he believes to be my father's wishes has already carried him far beyond the bounds of what is acceptable.'

Sorrow nodded. 'Of course, both Travers and I were working under the impression that it was Ayla we had to watch out for. Or rather, I should say, the creature that killed Florentyn Nightshade. That's why he hired me instead of anyone else. I have a reputation for being able to handle ... unusual situations.'

'As you demonstrated last night,' Myrren agreed. He had been leaning against one of the columns of the four-poster bed, but now he straightened up and began pacing the floor. Corus made a small sighing noise in his sleep; Elisse rocked him gently, and watched Sorrow watch Myrren. The blonde woman was lounging in her chair, trying to look casual, but her hazel eyes held a surprising amount of apprehension.

'So where does this leave me, my lord?' she asked finally. 'Do I have to make a run for it before you introduce me to the inside of your prison cells?'

'I should bloody hope not!' Elisse put in with some indignation, before Myrren could answer. 'If ya hadn' been here ta help me –'

Her arms had tightened involuntarily around her son; now his eyes fluttered open, his mouth turning down at the corners, and immediately everything else was forgotten.

Elisse hummed a snatch of an old lullaby to him under her breath, trying to convey a silent apology for waking him. It was no use: his whimper became a wail. Gritting her teeth, Elisse pulled her gown aside and put him to her breast. She wasn't going to let Myrren Nightshade embarrass her into not looking after her own child.

'Well, my lord?' she demanded over the soft sound of the baby sucking. 'Are ya going ta punish her for something that wasn' even her fault?'

'No, Elisse, I'm not.' To his credit, Myrren didn't seem at all perturbed by her actions; a rueful smile hovered on his lips as he looked from her to Sorrow. 'Since you didn't give me anything more than a few bruises, Sorrow, and since Elisse and Corus would have been lost without you last night, I'll overlook your actions in the fourth ring as well as the fact that you're very definitely not meant to be in Darkhaven right now. Just try not to accept any more treasonous commissions in future.' He reached into his coat pocket and drew out a pistol. 'Now, I believe you wanted this back?'

Sorrow's eyebrows had been climbing higher and higher with every word, until the expression of surprise on her face was almost comical. At the sight of the pistol, she seemed to recollect herself, sitting up straight and giving a quick nod.

'You can have it,' Myrren said. 'But I want the other one in return. I assume you took it from the armoury? And I want you to show me how to load it.'

'It's a deal.' Sorrow jumped to her feet, eyes bright with enthusiasm. 'If you just come over to the table by the window ...'

She certainly did love her pistol, Elisse thought as the blonde woman started her explanation. For her part, she couldn't see how anyone could get overly excited about a weapon. It was just a tool, like a spade was a tool.

As though drawn by an invisible cord, she looked down at Corus again. He had finished with her breast by now and was drifting back off to sleep. Elisse hummed another melody to him, wondering if it was normal for a newborn baby to sleep so much. Maybe Sorrow was right – maybe it was stupid of her to want to leave Darkhaven. She had no idea what was healthy in an ordinary baby, let alone what was healthy in a Nightshade baby: calves and foals were the limit of her experience. At least the physician here had some experience at raising Changer children.

Corus may not even be a Changer, she told herself. *He may jus' be an ordinary boy. And if that's the case, I don' want him feeling bad about it. He'd be better off growing up like every other child, and if he does have the gift – well, we'll deal with that when we come to it.*

She watched Myrren as he listened intently to Sorrow, wondering if she dared to broach the subject with him again. But she already knew what his answer would be. As far as he was concerned, every Nightshade child belonged in one place. It was as Florentyn had said, when he first moved her to Arkannen: *every child of Darkhaven should be under the eye of the Helm.* But what was the point, if a mad Changer creature could come through the window at will and attack anyone it chose? It didn't seem as though the Helm would be much use in that situation. No, the only person who could protect her and Corus properly was Naeve Sorrow, and she wouldn't be here for long – unless, Elisse thought with the sudden excitement of inspiration, Myrren could be persuaded to hire the woman as a special guard. After all, she'd already proved herself. And if Myrren asked her, maybe she'd agree to stay …

'That's the lot,' Sorrow said, turning away from the window and interrupting Elisse's plans. 'You now have a loaded pistol in your hands. When you want to fire it, just cock it and pull the trigger.'

'Thank you.' Myrren slipped the pistol into his pocket, that fierce look in his eyes again. 'I think it's time for me to pay Captain Travers another visit.'

Right. It was now or never. Elisse took a deep breath, ready to suggest her new idea – but Sorrow got in first.

'Lord Myrren?' The blonde woman's voice was coloured with some unfamiliar emotion; it took Elisse a moment to identify it as guilt. 'Before you go, there's one more thing you need to be aware of regarding my dealings with Owen Travers.'

Myrren frowned. 'Which is?'

Sorrow looked briefly down at the floor, as if searching for an answer in the grain of the wood, then raised her head to meet his gaze. 'He knows where Ayla is.'

THIRTY

As soon as the Gate of Steel came in sight, Caraway spurred his stolen horse on to greater effort. The animal's flanks were heaving, its breath coming in gasps, but if it could just carry him through the fifth ring –

'Come on, girl,' he murmured, leaning low on the horse's neck. 'Almost there. Please don't give up now.'

Ahead, the two watchmen on the gate had heard his approach; they stepped out into his path, drawing their swords and ordering him to stop. Gritting his teeth, Caraway kept urging the horse forward. He didn't have time to talk. Either they could get out of his way, or they could be trampled underfoot.

Wisely they chose the former, falling to either side as he pounded past them. Then he was passing under the archway, so close to the row of steel blades that one of them skimmed his hair. Familiar buildings loomed at the edges of his vision, practice floors and weaponries and barracks, but he kept his gaze fixed straight ahead, straining to catch his first glimpse of the Gate of Ice and the sixth ring. Behind him he could hear shouts and running footsteps as the two guards called for assistance.

Then, suddenly, there were people ahead of him, men and women of the fifth ring who must have heard the disturbance and come to investigate. Most of them were carrying weapons. Faced with their raised voices and their glinting steel, the horse skidded to a sudden stop, nearly throwing Caraway over its head. He tried to encourage it into speed again, cajoling and threatening alternately, but the horse was tired and nervous. Its ears were flat against its skull as it danced from side to side, snorting in alarm. Then, as one of the men stepped forward and lifted his sword in an attempt to drive Caraway back the way he had come, the horse reared.

Caraway felt his last chance of keeping his seat slip away as the horse bucked under him, and so he was ready for the fall, turning it into a roll and coming up in a crouch. Quickly he pivoted on the spot, assessing the situation. Already several people were working to calm and control the panicked horse; the rest of them, fierce-eyed and armed, had gathered in a tightening circle around him.

Caraway looked from one to the next, seeing men he recognised from the Helm, other men and women he had trained with when he was a new recruit, and still more he didn't know at all. Old faces and new, but they all had one thing in common: an expression that brimmed with contempt for him, Tomas Caraway. He was the thing they most despised, one of their own who had failed; they would sooner show mercy to a torturer or a rapist than they would to him. Caraway took a deep breath, his guts twisting with the sick knowledge. What had made him think he could possibly save Ayla from what awaited her? Of all the protectors she could have had, he was by far the worst. There was no way he could get anywhere near Darkhaven now, and Travers knew it.

All the same, he had to try.

283

'Please,' he said, spreading his hands to show his lack of weapons. 'You have to let me through. Lady Ayla –'

'You have no reason to be here, Breakblade.' It was one of the Helmsmen in the group who replied, a wiry man with a thick moustache. Caraway turned in his direction, addressing him directly.

'But you don't understand! Ayla is in danger –'

The man snorted. 'From what I hear, she's more dangerous than endangered. And even if that wasn't so, protecting the royal family is the job of the Helm.' He smirked. 'Which means it certainly isn't your concern.'

'It is if you're not doing your bloody job properly!' Caraway snapped. The Helmsman scowled, an angry flush darkening his face.

'And what the fuck would you know about doing a job properly? You don't have the first idea of what that means.' Spurred on by a murmur of agreement from the people around him, he kept going. 'You're a disgrace to the fifth ring, Breakblade. You gave us all a bad name when you stood back and watched Kati Nightshade die. So don't you dare talk to me about doing my job properly.'

'You're right,' Caraway said. 'I failed her. I failed you. I failed everyone in this damn city. But now I'm trying to make up for it.' He clenched his fists, willing them to listen to him. 'If I don't get up to Darkhaven, Kati's daughter will be convicted by the Helm for something she didn't do. And then there'll be two people's blood on my head.'

'Several things wrong with that story,' another man said. This one wasn't wearing the uniform of a Helmsman: a body-guard, perhaps, or a common soldier. 'One, none of us have seen Ayla Nightshade since she left Darkhaven several nights ago. Word is, she may have left the city altogether. Two, the whole purpose of the Helm is to protect the Nightshade line. They wouldn't convict anyone of that blood without good reason.' He paused. 'And three, even if what you just said is true, what makes you think *you* can do anything about it? What are you going to do, fight your way through the entire Helm with that fine example of a weapon you see fit to carry everywhere?'

Laughter rippled through the circle at this last sally, but Caraway barely heard it. His mind was fixed on the first point: that no-one had seen Ayla and her captors come this way. Perhaps he was wrong. Perhaps they'd taken her somewhere else entirely ... but no. It made no sense. The Helm must have her – the decoy had told him that – and there was nowhere for them to go except Darkhaven. If they'd kept it a secret, it only proved that there was something very wrong with what they were doing.

'Just give it up, Caraway,' one of the women said. 'Go home.'

He shook his head. 'I can't.'

'Fine.' Her face showed no hint of sympathy. 'Then you accept what's coming to you.' She glanced around the circle. 'Weapons away, lads.'

The sound of steel being sheathed rang through the air. Caraway scanned their grim faces and understood what was about to happen. They wouldn't afford him the dignity of swordplay, with its attendant rules and courtesies. How could they? He had no blade to speak of; it wouldn't be fair. So instead, they would maintain their code of practice by beating him up with their bare hands. The fact that there were twenty of them and just one of him had no bearing on the matter.

For an instant he considered giving up. If he begged their forgiveness now, if he promised to retreat into the lower rings and not cause any more trouble, they'd probably let him go.

He could return to his life, such as it was. Maybe he could even come up with a plan for getting to Ayla some other way. It wasn't possible for him to win here, after all. Even on his best days he'd only been able to keep two or three assailants back at once, and that was before he'd dulled his own fighting edge and allowed his physical fitness to slide. Against twenty, there could be only one outcome.

On the other hand, he was tired of running away. And he knew quite well that if he didn't reach Ayla today, he'd never reach her. She'd be locked in darkness, forced into obedience, never able to Change again, and he'd have to live the rest of his life knowing he'd failed her as badly as he'd failed her mother … he couldn't let that happen. No, he'd stay here and try to make them let him through, and he'd keep on trying until they had to kill him to stop him. Better to die quickly in pursuit of something worthwhile than to destroy himself slowly with alcohol and regret.

He lifted his fists into the guard position, knowing he would need to protect his face for as long as possible; and as if that was the signal they'd been waiting for, the circle of people around him began to close in. They were careful at first, taking it in turns to approach him, allowing him to block a punch here and a kick there, always leaving enough time for him to spin to face the next blow. Yet he knew they were only playing with him; like a gang of street bullies, they wanted him to realise the extent of their power over him before they finished him off.

Once or twice he tried to break out of the circle, to get into a position where he wasn't surrounded, but each time they closed ranks to drive him back. He was trapped. And gradually the attacks became harder and faster until there were two or three of them coming for him at once, making him twist and turn in a vain attempt to defend himself. After that, it wasn't long until the inevitable happened: one punch and then another broke past his guard, catching him just below the ribcage and on the side of the jaw, winding him and blurring his vision at the same time.

Caraway staggered, fists faltering. His teeth had sliced into the inside of his lip; he spat out a mouthful of blood. The faces around him merged into one, mocking smiles and determined frowns alike. He turned his head, searching for the single trace of compassion that would tell him he had a chance of succeeding. A couple of familiar faces swam out of the crowd, and he took a stumbling step towards them.

'Marco, Logan … you knew me once,' he mumbled. 'Please, just let me pass.'

Then several of them were on him, wrenching his arms behind his back, pushing him face-down on the ground. He turned his head to one side to avoid breaking his nose on the paving stones, and the gritty surface tore across his cheek with enough force to make his eyes water. One man was on his back, holding his wrists tightly together to prevent him from throwing a punch; another pinned down his flailing legs. A boot hit his ribcage like a hammer, and his entire body convulsed against the hands that were restraining him.

As the second kick caught his shin in another flare of agony, he closed his eyes. Sooner or later they'd kick him in the face – smash his nose or break his jaw or knock his teeth in – and that would be the end of it. He had no way of defending himself. His lungs were being compressed, making it difficult to breathe – he fought to take a gulp of air through the blood that was slowly filling his mouth, then lost it again as the toe of a boot prodded his head –

'What's going on here?' The shout reached him even through the clamour of pain that enclosed every one of his senses. The weight on his back eased slightly and the grip on his wrists loosened, allowing him to struggle up onto one elbow and spit out the mouthful of dirt and blood that had threatened to choke him.

'It's Tomas Caraway, sir,' another voice said somewhere above him. 'We think he's gone mad. He came riding into the fifth ring claiming he had to reach Darkhaven as soon as possible. Well, of course we couldn't let him get anywhere near Darkhaven, so –'

'And it takes this many of you to subdue him?' This time Caraway recognised Art Bryan's voice. 'I had no idea he was such a ferocious warrior.'

The words held no hint of satire, but they produced an awkward silence all the same. Caraway felt the man who was pinning him down relax his grip still further; immediately he pushed up on hands and knees, driving his head backwards into his captor's face, throwing the man off. Then he was on his feet, staggering a little, blocking a punch with more instinct than skill – a well-placed kick made him stumble and fall back to his knees – now someone had him in a headlock, squeezing hard, sending jagged blocks of darkness across his already blurred vision –

'Enough.' Again Bryan's voice cut through the ringing in his ears like a blade through a thread of silk. 'Let go of him.'

The pressure on Caraway's throat lessened. This time he stayed where he was, on his knees, gasping for air and trying to blink the spots out of his eyes. Dimly he was aware of Bryan walking towards him, stopping when he was only a short distance away.

'What's this all about, Caraway? I thought I told you never to show your face near the fifth ring again.'

Caraway looked up at him. The weaponmaster's face was set in stern lines; it was unlikely he'd show Caraway any more sympathy than the rest had. Still, there was no point giving up now.

'Ayla – they took her –' He couldn't catch his breath, and talking hurt, but he kept going. 'They tricked me – got to get to Darkhaven before it's too late –' He stopped as Bryan held up a hand.

'I'm not making any sense of this,' the weaponmaster said. 'Stand up properly, boyo, and get a grip on yourself.'

Damn him. Caraway dragged himself back to his feet, willing his head to stop spinning and his lungs to expand. One of his knees didn't feel quite right, and his cut cheek throbbed in time with his heartbeat.

'It's what I told you before,' he managed, forcing himself to look Bryan in the eye. 'Captain Travers and the Helm think Lady Ayla is a murderer. They're going to lock her up. I can't let that happen.'

One of Bryan's eyebrows lifted. 'I see. And did you think to arm yourself at all, before you rushed out on this vital mission?'

A muted snigger ran through the watchers. Caraway clenched his fists, anxiety and frustration flaring up inside him like a spark on powder.

'No, because I don't have any weapons!' he flung back at Bryan. 'I don't have any resources, I don't have any friends. I don't have anything except a broken blade and my own two hands. But I promised Ayla I'd help her, and I will not stand by and let her be condemned for something she didn't do!'

There was silence. Bryan studied his face, heavy brows knitted together in thought. Then he nodded. 'All right.'

Confused, Caraway blinked at him. 'All right?'

'You can go.' Bryan unbuckled his own sword from his hip, then held it out on his upturned palms. 'Though you may find this blade more serviceable than your own.'

Caraway accepted it tentatively, sure he must be misunderstanding. Around them there were mutters of discontent, and one voice protested, 'But –'

'But what?' Bryan turned on the gathered warriors, folding his arms across his massive chest. 'You want to argue with me? If any of you doubt my authority or my judgement, then I'm ready to debate the issue on the sparring floor, with or without a sword.'

'Then you're just going to let him walk into Darkhaven?'

'Why not?' Bryan shrugged. 'He'll probably go and get himself killed, and that will be an end to it. But this is between him and Captain Travers, and I see no reason to interfere. Travers is the one who threw him out of the Helm in the first place. Travers is the one who can deal with him.' A glower settled on his face. 'Not some jumped-up mob who think they have the right to mete out justice with their fists.'

There were further mumbles from around the circle, but it seemed no-one was willing to challenge the weaponmaster directly. Bryan turned back to Caraway, his face still contorted as though even he wasn't sure he was doing the right thing.

'Well? Why are you still here? Bugger off before I change my mind.'

'Thank you.' With unsteady fingers, Caraway buckled Bryan's sword belt on over his own, swivelling his own blade round to sit on the opposite side. The new weapon felt strange at his hip, heavy; it was years since he'd carried the weight of a whole sword.

'To be honest, I hope you're either deluded or lying,' Bryan said. 'Because whether you're telling the truth or not, I'm likely going to have to retrieve my sword from your cold dead hands.' His lips tightened briefly, as though keeping back a torrent of words. 'Good luck, Tomas. Maybe you weren't so very terrible a Helmsman after all.'

Unsure what to say, Caraway gave the weaponmaster something between a nod and a bow. Then he put his head down, ignoring his throbbing knee and his sore cheek and his aching lungs, and set off in the direction of the sixth gate.

THIRTY-ONE

Ayla's unconscious body draped over his shoulder, Travers walked into the incarceration room and shut the door behind him.

Finally. He had her here.

His heart already thudding with anticipation, he deposited her on the bed and unwrapped the cloak he'd bundled her up in. This room could only be locked from the outside, but he'd posted a guard at the top of the stairs. He wouldn't be disturbed. Still, not willing to take any chances, he pushed the room's one chair in front of the door and wedged it under the handle. That would give him plenty of warning if anyone tried to come in; long enough to hide anything he didn't want to be seen.

Once he'd done that he recrossed the room and looked down at Ayla, noting with satisfaction her unmarred features – he'd been right to drug her rather than knock her out and risk spoiling the perfection of her skin. As it was, in the glow from his lantern she simply looked as if she were sleeping. The short hair was a shame, but it didn't matter: she'd be here long enough for it to grow back to its proper length. The light fabric of her shift moulded to her form and tangled around her thighs, making his mouth dry. Before today, he'd never seen her less than fully clothed.

Sitting beside her, he traced the curve of her cheek with one finger, and noticed his hand was shaking. He needed to get a grip on himself. Maybe he should take what he wanted from her now, while she was still unconscious – maybe that would calm him long enough to make sure he was fully in control the next time, when she was awake. The thought stirred him. He stroked her cheek again, ran his fingers over the smooth paleness of her throat. Then, with the memory still vivid in his mind of what it had been like to kiss her, he leaned down to press his lips against hers ... and there was the problem. Her lips were warm, soft, pliant – everything he wanted them to be – but unresponsive. He would much rather feel her struggle beneath him, as she had before; at least that way he'd see the reaction in her eyes as he did all the things he wanted to do.

Yes, he definitely needed her conscious.

He took the second bottle from his pocket, shook a few drops of antidote onto the cloth he had used earlier, and held it to her nose and mouth. After a moment, her breath caught in her throat, becoming deeper and more ragged; a flush spread across her cheeks. Travers tucked bottle and cloth away, before dealing Ayla a single sharp slap.

'Wha—?' She startled bolt upright as though he had thrown cold water over her. As her eyes focused on his face, her expression changed from confusion to a mixture of anger and fear. 'Travers, what have you done to me? Where am I?'

He considered slapping her again – he had enjoyed the first one almost too much – but he was afraid that once he started hurting her, he wouldn't be able to stop. And he didn't want that. Not yet.

'Take a look around,' he invited her. In response, her gaze moved from his face to the four walls of the small room that surrounded them. When she looked back at him, the fear was more prominent.

'This is Darkhaven.' It was a bare whisper. 'Are we –?'

'In the incarceration room?' he finished for her. 'Yes. I'm carrying out your sentence, just as Lord Florentyn ordered.'

'But I didn't attack that priestess.' The reply was automatic; he shrugged it off.

'The evidence says otherwise, Ayla. What's more, it also says you killed your father and attacked me. You have to be locked up, for the safety of everyone around you.'

'Travers.' Her voice was laced with hysteria now. 'I'm telling you, I didn't do it.'

He leaned closer to her. 'But who else is there, sweet girl? Who else in this city can Change, apart from you?'

Ayla backed away from him, into the corner, hugging her knees to her chest. 'Does Myrren know about this?'

'Of course.' Travers moved after her, trapping her in position. 'He thinks you did it too.'

She flinched at that, then shook her head. 'You're lying.'

'You're all alone, Ayla. And if you think your alcoholic friend Caraway will save you, you can think again. He'll never get anywhere near Darkhaven without being cut down.'

A tremor shook her body, but she lifted her chin defiantly. 'Let me go, Travers. You have no right to keep me here.'

She was altogether too arrogant, too sure of herself. It was time to show her a little of what the future held. With swift precision, Travers reached out and grabbed a handful of her hair, forcing her head back against the wall. His other hand moved slowly down over her exposed throat, feeling her pulse leap beneath his fingers.

'I have the only right that matters,' he murmured. 'This room will be your home for as long as I see fit, and the key is in my pocket.'

He saw the flicker in her eyes an instant before her feet lashed out at him, and so he was ready for the impact. All the same, it sent him reeling backwards, allowing her enough space to scramble off the bed and make for the door. She got as far as reaching out to move the chair before he caught her around the waist and dragged her kicking and struggling back across the room. One flailing foot struck his shin, making his eyes water – her head caught him a glancing blow on the cheek – then his knife was in his hand, the blade pressed lightly under her chin. Immediately she froze, holding herself stiff and still.

'Quite so,' Travers said. 'I'm glad we sorted out that little misunderstanding.'

He walked her back to the bed, pushing down on her shoulder to get her to sit. It was a good thing he had the knife. Before he'd gone out into the city to fetch her, he'd visited Darkhaven's armoury with the intention of taking the pistol from the cabinet of illegal weaponry, but it had been missing; most likely Naeve Sorrow had something to do with it. At the time he'd been furious at the realisation that not only had Sorrow felled three of his men and managed to evade arrest, she had also stolen the most effective means of controlling his captive. Now, however, he was relieved. A pistol was a lethal sort of weapon, inclined to go off at the slightest provocation – and the last thing he wanted to do to Ayla was kill her.

'Now, my lady,' he said, sitting back down beside her on the bed. 'I told you before that you shouldn't fight me. If you do anything like that again, I may have to hurt you.'

'What are you going to do to me?' Ayla's voice was faint, but she faced him as though she didn't realise or didn't care that she was afraid. It was that spirit Travers had always liked in her; it would be a shame if she lost it too soon. He smiled.

'I think you know the answer to that.'

She flinched, but held his gaze. Her eyes had glazed over slightly, yet he had no doubt that behind the vacant stare she was thinking as hard as she could of ways to distract him. Amused, Travers didn't reach for her again straight away. Let her think she had a chance of keeping him at a distance, armed only with words and her quick wit. She'd learn her mistake soon enough.

'Who was the girl?' she asked. 'The one being guarded by your sellsword in the Ametrine Quarter?'

'What, Elisse?' He threw her a glance, unimpressed by her first line of attack. 'Nobody. Just a girl from the country.' Still watching Ayla's face, he added, 'But the child she's carrying is of the Nightshade line. Your half brother or sister.'

'Oh.' Ayla was silent a moment, considering this. 'Caraway seemed to think you'd hired Sorrow to kill my father and implicate me in the crime.'

Bloody Tomas Caraway! Travers narrowed his eyes. He still couldn't believe Ayla had gone to Caraway for help, after everything that lay in their shared past. Then he realised the truth: she was trying to change the focus of his attention, and she'd almost succeeded.

'No doubt Caraway thinks many things,' he said lightly. 'Who knows what goes on in the mind of a disgraced alcoholic? He probably sees conspiracy in every corner.'

'He will come after me, you know.' Even Ayla seemed to recognise how remote a possibility that was; her voice quivered as she said it. Travers shrugged.

'I hope he does. I look forward to hearing of his defeat at the hands of the Helm – that is, assuming he gets that far. He's got the whole of the fifth ring to claw his way through first.' He gave her a pitying smile. 'You know, my dear, if you wanted someone to watch your back, almost any beggar off the street would have done better than Tomas Caraway. At least the average beggar wouldn't have offended the entire fighting population of Arkannen by the simple fact of being an incompetent fool.'

'He didn't strike me as incompetent.' Ayla had recovered her composure; the look she gave him held a hint of mockery. 'At least, not when he defeated four of your men in the first ring.'

'Competence and luck are not the same thing,' Travers snapped, then heard the edge in his own voice and softened it. 'He wasn't a total disaster on the duelling ground. I daresay he's retained some of the skills that every Helmsman has. But he'll need more than that to get past all the people who despise him for his failure.'

Ayla's eyebrows arched. 'Why do you hate him so much?'

Because you used to watch his every move like a lovesick puppy. Travers shook his head. 'I don't hate him. He doesn't mean enough to me for that.'

At her disbelieving stare, he felt anger touch the back of his throat again. Ayla must have read the emotion in his face; she lowered her gaze, studying her clasped hands.

'I'm sorry,' she said softly. 'I didn't mean to question you.'

She was learning. Or was it another tactic? Travers concealed a smirk. He wasn't so blind to reason that he had forgotten how she'd behaved towards him only a few moments ago. She was like a warrior on the training field, trying one weapon and then another to see which cut the keenest. It seemed almost a shame she'd have to find out that ultimately, all her blades were useless.

'But if you dislike Caraway because I turned to him for help,' Ayla went on, oblivious to his cynicism, 'then you should know it was only because there was no-one else.' She looked up, wide eyes searching his face. 'I would have come to you, if I'd thought you would have believed me.'

Despite himself, Travers responded to the note of appeal in her voice. 'You would?'

'Of course. You're the Captain of the Helm. The one person who my family can always rely on.' She reached out a pleading hand. 'Owen, isn't it possible that we've both got it wrong? That I've been suspecting you and you've been suspecting me, while all this time the real killer is free in Arkannen?'

She was so intent on trying to convince him, she actually leaned forward – and she'd called him by his first name. Travers frowned at her, hearing the ring of truth in her words. Was it possible that she was innocent? Was it possible that she didn't deserve to be locked up? She was looking at him now as if he were her one remaining chance of salvation. It was all he'd ever wanted, for her to look at him as though she really saw him. He could justify that look. He could open the door, and stand aside, and let her go free.

'Owen?' Ayla whispered again, her breath warm against his skin, and his body stirred in response. Yes. He'd do it – he'd let her go. Just as soon as he'd kissed her goodbye.

Closing the remaining gap between them, he pressed his lips hard against hers. Immediately she flinched back, the fear returning to her eyes. Travers stared at her, and felt the anger rising swift and hot in him once more. She'd nearly done it. She'd nearly fooled him. He'd nearly forgotten why she deserved to be here.

'Enough games,' he snarled, grabbing her upper arms.

'I'm telling you, you've got it wrong!' Ayla pounded at his shoulders with both fists as he pushed her inexorably backwards until she was horizontal on the bed. She strained against the weight of his body, trying with all her strength to push him off, but it only excited him further. The truth was, he didn't care if she was innocent or guilty – not any more. His brief moment of doubt had passed, leaving his mind smooth and clear, like a blade cleaned of all blood.

'Travers, get off me!' Her voice rose to a shriek. He stopped it by covering her mouth with his own, forcing his tongue between her reluctant lips. She bit and scratched at him, all teeth and claws like a trapped wild thing; he bit her back, hard enough to break through the soft skin of her lower lip. Her blood tasted richer and sweeter than his own, the power of it tingling through him. He had to have her. He had to have her now or he'd explode.

Catching one of her thrashing wrists, he forced it up and back until he found the open manacle at the corner of the bed. There had been a Nightshade or two in Darkhaven's history who had been mad enough to need restraining, one or two more who'd needed it by the time they'd been locked in this room for months or even years; what he was doing now was just the latest in a long line of violent deeds housed by these four walls. As he clicked the manacle into place around Ayla's wrist, she gave a low moan as though she knew exactly what it meant. Her eyes were dark holes, the pupils blurring into the shadowy blue of the irises so that he was no longer sure whether she saw him or something completely different.

'I'll keep fighting you,' she whispered. 'I won't stop until I'm dead.'

Baring his teeth in a savage grin, Travers slammed her other wrist into place. Her resulting whimper pleased him: after all, wasn't she being punished? And if it didn't hurt then it could hardly be called a punishment.

'How long do you think you can fight for, Ayla?' he asked. 'Because unless you can will yourself into death, you've got most of your life ahead of you.'

She shook her head, wordlessly denying it. Travers smoothed the rumpled hair back from her forehead and tucked it tenderly behind her ears.

'Be patient, my love,' he murmured. 'And who knows? Maybe one day our children will rule Darkhaven.'

Ignoring the curses she hurled at him, he turned to her ankles, making sure both were fixed as securely as her wrists. By the time he had finished, Ayla lay quiescent as though she had lost both the ability and the will to defy him; there were tearstains on her cheeks. As Travers looked at her, he knew in a flash of pure clarity that whatever happened afterwards, this was the one perfect moment of his life.

'Scream as loud as you like, sweet girl,' he told her, leaning down to wipe the blood off her mouth with his thumb. 'There's no-one here to hear you.'

THIRTY-TWO

Myrren stared at Sorrow, slow fury uncoiling itself like a snake in his chest, taut and hissing. The headache he'd had when he woke up that morning began to creep back into place, as if something were gnawing gently and relentlessly at the backs of his eyes.

'Travers knows where Ayla is,' he repeated, his voice coming out flat.

'I told you I saw Ayla yesterday.' Sorrow sounded wary. 'After that, I followed her and Caraway back to their lodgings. I made a deal with Travers that I'd tell him where Ayla was if he gave me the freedom of Darkhaven.'

'For what?' Myrren didn't even try to restrain his frustration. 'So you could get your bloody pistol back?'

'My lord ...' Sorrow lifted her hands in a conciliatory gesture, but her jaw was set. 'I'd heard nothing to convince me of Ayla's innocence. I had no reason to protect her. It was my belief that if the Helm were so anxious to find her, they must have good cause.'

Myrren shook his head. 'The truth is, you used the information to your own advantage, to get what you wanted from Travers. Just as you have sought this morning to get what you want from me.' He took a deep breath, fighting the urge to shake her. 'Well, enough. I've pardoned you for your previous actions, and that pardon still holds. But I don't ever want to see your face again. You will leave Darkhaven today, and you won't come back.'

'But –' Elisse began, then shrank back against her pillows as he turned on her.

'But nothing! This woman isn't fit company for you, Elisse, and she certainly isn't fit company for my brother. She's done her job. She's protected you. Now let that be an end to it!'

There was silence. Myrren lifted a hand to massage between his eyes, wishing he could think more clearly through what was fast becoming a blinding pain. Travers would have wasted no time in taking Ayla into custody. And the lie he had told about Ayla leaving the city suggested he had no intention of informing Myrren about it. It was possible, therefore, that he had gone in search of Ayla first thing that morning. It was possible that she was already in Darkhaven …

The thought drove Myrren a few paces towards the door, before dizziness overtook him and left him reeling. He really should see the physician about these migraines. Tomorrow. Later. He had more important things to attend to first. He needed to find Serenna. He needed to find Travers. Most of all, he needed to find Ayla.

'Lord Myrren?' He dimly recognised Elisse's voice. 'Are ya all right?'

'Fine,' he mumbled. It would pass in a few moments; it always did. Yet he didn't seem able to tame the snake of fury inside him. It spiralled up and up, into his throat, until he could hardly breathe. He felt as though he were trapped inside one of his own nightmares – as though his whole self were slowly dissolving into a dark cloud of lethal intent. He wanted to kill Travers, he realised. He wanted to rip him apart with his bare hands.

Stay calm, he told himself. *Stay in control.* Yet he couldn't suppress the emotion that was rising, always rising. He took a few more stumbling steps in the direction of the door, then stopped again. Everything around him appeared slightly off-kilter, as if he had crossed into a different reality without realising it. He rubbed his face, but the sensation didn't fade. Clumsy, he reached out one hand to grasp the door handle, the other fumbling at his pocket to make sure the loaded pistol was still there. He had to find Serenna. He had to find Travers and make him release Ayla.

The door swung open, revealing the corridor beyond. It seemed to be breaking up, swirling into dancing spots wherever Myrren looked. The pressure was building inside his head, crushing his thoughts. He couldn't resist it any longer.

With a sigh, though whether of relief or regret he wasn't sure, he succumbed to the darkness inside him.

Serenna burst into the library and ran straight to the desk, where the book called *Changer Myths and Truths* was lying as she had left it. Once there, she shoved the veil back from her face again and stared at it, her heart pounding so hard she thought she might faint. She didn't want to open it. She didn't want to find the confirmation she knew it contained. But she had to know the truth.

Feverishly, she leafed through the pages until she came to the one she was looking for, the account of the previous attacks that had taken place in Arkannen. And there it was. It had been there all along, only she hadn't seen it. *There were nine Changers in Darkhaven, as well as one who it was rumoured had been born without the gift ... a spate of murders in the city ... obvious a Changer was the perpetrator ... the Nightshades closed ranks and denied responsibility.* What if they had denied responsibility because they hadn't realised one of their own was responsible? What if the girl who was kept hidden in the tower, unable to Change, had in fact possessed a much darker version of the Nightshade gift?

If a Changer could have the ability to Change into a second creature form without realising it, couldn't he have that same condition with just a single form?

Wasn't it possible that a man could be a Changer and not even know it?

Serenna buried her face in her hands as the truth swept over her in a shivery wave. She didn't want to believe it, yet it all made a ghastly kind of sense. Lord Florentyn had threatened to incarcerate Ayla, and Myrren had acted to defend his sister. Serenna was sure it was that, and not his own disinheritance, which had been his motivation. He loved Ayla. And to make sure Florentyn couldn't hurt her, he had killed him. He had killed his own father, and awoken the next morning without any more memory of doing so than a vague, uneasy nightmare.

Then Myrren had discovered the address in the Ametrine Quarter, and that very night Travers had been attacked there. Flaming ashes! Myrren had even questioned the coincidence himself, and she had dismissed it. And he knew the layout of Darkhaven intimately, well enough to locate both Florentyn's window and the window to Ayla's room: the room where he went looking for Elisse and was hurt by Sorrow's pistol, enough to leave a bruise when he returned to human form. Serenna wasn't sure why Myrren had attacked Elisse. Perhaps it was because her testimony implicated Ayla yet again. Perhaps it was because his creature-self was much more ruthless than he was, and knew quite well that Elisse's unborn child was a threat to him – or, more likely, to Ayla. Yes. He had no care for himself; everything he had done had been to protect Ayla.

As for the attack on Serenna herself, the one that had started it all ... who knew? She'd said to Myrren, the first time she met him, that she thought the creature had been lost. That it hadn't meant to hurt her. *It didn't know its own strength*. Maybe that had been true of all these attacks. Maybe the creature-Myrren had searched for people in order to frighten them, trying to make them see the truth he knew better than anyone: that Ayla wasn't guilty. Or maybe after Florentyn's death he'd gained a taste for blood. Whatever he had intended, he had left only destruction behind him.

Elements. She wiped her eyes with the heels of her hands. Her heartbeat was a throbbing ache inside her. *What do I do now? How do I tell him the truth?*

They'll lock him up! a voice in her mind was screaming. *They'll lock him up and throw away the key!*

She took a deep breath, trying to compose herself. But the ability she'd developed over many years serving the Altar of Flame, to detach herself from the fears and tribulations of the world, had vanished in the few short days she'd spent in Darkhaven. She was a woman burdened with a truth like a burning coal in her hand, and she was afraid for the man she loved. Faced with that, she was as shaken and panicky as she had been when her parents walked away from the temple and left her there for good. No, more so: because this time it was up to her to do the leaving. She couldn't let any more people be injured or killed. And so she had to tell Myrren the truth about himself, before walking away and leaving him alone in the dark with only the four blank walls of the incarceration room for company.

It doesn't have to be like that, she told herself. *Maybe there's some way you can help him. But before you do anything else, you have to go back. You have to go back and face him with it.*

She left the library and set off as fast as she could, back the way she had come. She hadn't replaced the veil over her face, but that was just tough; she needed to see the world, not be separated from it by a piece of cloth. Her throat was sore with the desire to shout or scream or do something – anything – to let out the turmoil of emotion that was building up inside her.

Keep going, Serenna, she ordered. *He needs you to be practical, so that's what you'll be. Time enough for grieving later.*

Her ankle was aching, and she couldn't run as quickly as she would have liked; she wanted her cane, but she didn't know where it was. She hadn't taken it with her last night when she went to see Myrren – pure vanity, she admitted to herself now – which meant it was probably somewhere in Ayla's room. Its absence left her limping along, cursing herself for stupidity and feeling that every step was too slow.

She arrived at one end of the final corridor just as Myrren emerged from Ayla's room halfway along, leaving the door swinging open behind him. Relief shuddered through her, and she forced herself to move faster. Yet even as she opened her mouth to call out to him, his body began to shimmer. It was as if she were seeing him through a heat haze, a quivering of the air between them. Then, before her eyes, he blurred into a cloud of what looked like black smoke or dust, a formless substance that swirled and changed from one shape to another, patterns forming and then dissolving again like a flock of birds in the evening sky. His clothes dropped to the floor to lie still and empty, a sloughed skin.

She was too late.

She stood perfectly still, barely remembering to breathe, as the cloud of smoke expanded and began to solidify again, taking on a shape that was much larger and stranger than the one before it. Gradually texture and colour coalesced out of darkness until there it was: the creature that had killed Florentyn and injured three others.

Myrren.

In animal form he matched, in every respect, the illustration of the Wyvern she had seen in the book. There were the long neck and powerful jaw, there the gleaming black scales. The wings were folded tightly across the back, rustling with every movement; the barbed tail and two clawed feet scraped across the smooth-worn stone. In an average room the creature's head would have brushed the ceiling, even with neck bent, but Darkhaven was built on more generous lines. Even with her heart beating so hard that it threatened to break out of her chest, Serenna couldn't help marvelling at how well Myrren-as-Wyvern fitted his surroundings. For the first time, the imposing blackstone walls of Darkhaven made sense to her as a setting for what they contained. Perhaps, once, the overlords of Mirrorvale had spent as much time in creature form as they had in human form ...

Concentrate, she told herself. *You have to bring him back.* The trouble was, she had absolutely no idea how to do it. She didn't know whether Myrren would even recognise her when he was in this form.

As far as she could tell, he hadn't noticed her yet. She took a stealthy step towards him; almost at exactly the same moment, he turned and ran in the other direction. Serenna swore, desperation rising in her throat and threatening to choke her. She swallowed it down. She couldn't ask Elisse for help, not with a new baby, and she didn't trust Sorrow. As for the Helm, she hadn't seen a single one of them in Darkhaven's corridors since leaving Ayla's room. So that only left her. Perhaps if she caught up with him in time, she could persuade Myrren to Change back before anyone else saw him. After that, maybe, they could work out how to stop it happening again.

Crouching down beside his shed clothing, she gathered as much of it as she could carry into her arms; the boots would have to wait. Then, gritting her teeth, she set off after him.

She just hoped she could reach him before it was too late.

THIRTY-THREE

By the time Caraway reached Darkhaven, he was ready to collapse. He hadn't eaten anything since yesterday, and all his energy had been used on the chase through the first ring and the futile fight in the fifth; he was running on willpower alone. Still, it would be enough. It would have to be enough.

He'd got through the Gates of Ice and Death by the simple expedient of waving Bryan's sword and shouting something about urgent Helm business. Either the guards had assumed he must be allowed through if he'd already got up so high, or they'd taken one look at the desperation in his face and decided he was a blade-wielding madman better dealt with by the Helm than by them. Whichever it was, he didn't think Darkhaven itself would be as easy to get into. The Helm would be on their guard – or at least, a subset of them would be. It seemed Travers was treating the whole thing as a covert operation, which meant only some of his men would know what was going on. Caraway's one meagre hope was that he could use that to his advantage.

As always during the daytime, the postern gate was open and a handful of Helmsmen were patrolling, two at the gate itself and another three at intervals around the tower. Catching sight of Caraway as he came panting up the hill towards them, they converged in a cluster and waited for him. He kept Bryan's sword sheathed; there was no way he could cut a path through the entire Helm, and he didn't want to give the impression he was going to try. As a result, these five didn't all draw their weapons and slice him to pieces as soon as he reached them. Instead, they simply formed a barrier between him and the gate.

'Breakblade,' one of them said. 'How did you get in here?'

'Art Bryan let me in.' Caraway scanned their faces: three he recognised from his own time in the Helm, two he didn't. 'Where's Ayla?'

The speaker snorted. Caraway hadn't seen the man in years, but his name floated up from the recesses of memory: *Soren*. The most senior of the five. 'You tell us.'

'Captain Travers had her brought in today.' Caraway kept a tight grip on his urgency, though he longed to shake the information out of them. 'Where is she?'

'Haven't seen her,' Soren said. 'And even if I had, bringing her in's what we're meant to be doing. Lady Ayla is wanted for her father's murder. Everyone knows that.'

Caraway frowned. 'Wait – so none of you have seen Ayla today?'

'Not that it's any of your business, but no. We haven't.'

'Well, take it from me, she's somewhere in the tower.' Exasperated, Caraway scrubbed his hands through his hair. 'And doesn't that strike you as a little odd? If she really is guilty and she really should be locked up, then why has it been done in secret?'

The five men exchanged glances, but no-one replied.

'If I'm right, then Travers has brought her here without telling anyone,' Caraway persisted. 'And that's against every protocol of the Helm. You know it is.'

'Captain Travers left Darkhaven early this morning in a closed carriage,' one of the new recruits put in, oblivious to the glowers of the three older men. 'He returned about a half-bell ago and headed in the direction of the Nightshade family vault.'

'There, you see? That's where the incarceration room is.' Fear burned in Caraway's throat: a half-bell ago. Was he too late? 'I'll bet you anything he's taken Ayla down there.'

Again there was no reply. Images swam in front of Caraway's eyes, each worse than the one before it. What was Travers doing to Ayla? What was so important to him that he'd keep it a secret from most of his men?

'Look, just let me go to the incarceration room.' He couldn't help the panic that suffused his voice. 'If I'm right, you'll have helped to avert a miscarriage of justice. If I'm wrong, you can execute me for all I care.'

Again the Helmsmen looked at each other doubtfully.

'Fine,' Soren said at last. 'We'll take you down there. But I swear, Breakblade, if this is a load of bollocks, I'll lock you in that damn room myself and throw away the key.'

Caraway shrugged. 'If Ayla isn't there, you can do what you like.'

The route from the postern gate to the incarceration room led across the central square and past the mess hall, then down into the foundations of the tower. It wasn't far, but to Caraway every step felt like wading through treacle, slow and cumbersome. The Helmsmen clearly didn't trust him at all; they'd locked the gate as they did at nightfall, leaving all five of them free to march him through Darkhaven as though they were taking him to his execution – which, perhaps, they were. One of them peeled off as they passed the guardroom, no doubt to fetch reinforcements. If Caraway didn't find

Ayla where he expected to find her, and maybe even if he did, he'd have the entire Helm standing between him and the exit. Still, what did it matter? He only wanted to get in. He didn't much care about getting out.

When they reached the antechamber in which Florentyn Nightshade's body lay, they found another Helmsman on guard at the top of the stairs that led down to the incarceration room. Caraway's pulse speeded up still further. He'd been right. He'd been right all along.

'What do you want?' the guard asked, frowning at his colleagues and then more deeply at Caraway, as though he'd just encountered a rare and potentially dangerous animal in the midst of a herd of cattle.

'We're looking for Captain Travers,' Soren said rather uncertainly. The guard shook his head.

'He's not to be disturbed. Important Helm business.'

For fuck's sake. Caraway shifted restlessly on the balls of his feet. 'He's got Ayla in there, hasn't he? Let us through before she gets hurt.'

'Any man who goes down there will be thrown out of the Helm.' The guard scowled. 'As for you, the captain 'ud probably have you killed.'

They didn't have time for this. They didn't have bloody *time*. Seeing the indecision on the faces around him, Caraway seized his opportunity. Before any of his escort could react, he drew Bryan's sword and slashed it across the guard's leg in one swift movement. Then, as the man fell back against the wall, he threw himself down the stairs towards the incarceration room.

He knew he wouldn't be able to break the door down – it was made of reinforced metal – but there wasn't any way it could be locked, either. The only lock was on the outside;

something must be blocking the door from within. Caraway hurled himself against it again and again, ignoring the fresh bruises it gave him, until finally it sprang open under his shoulder. The sudden lack of resistance sent him stumbling forward into the room, only to be brought up short by the point of a sword at his throat. He froze, his gaze travelling slowly along the length of the blade until it reached Travers' intent face.

'Drop your weapon and step over to the wall.' The captain's voice held a strung intensity. 'Keep your hands where I can see them.'

Caraway obeyed. As he moved, he risked a quick glance beyond Travers and saw Ayla on the bed, wrists and ankles locked in place, terror and relief mingled in her eyes. Anger surged up in him, but he gritted his teeth and forced it down. Impaling himself on the end of a sword would do her no good whatsoever.

'I have to admit, this is a surprise.' Travers had kicked the door shut and shoved the chair back under the handle, then jammed the point of Bryan's sword under the door as an added precaution, all without letting his own sword point fall. Now he stood there frowning at Caraway as though trying to understand a difficult problem. 'I didn't expect you to get this far.' His gaze flicked to the sword at the door. 'You even got a real weapon from somewhere. What did you do, steal it?'

'Let her go, Travers.' Caraway kept his voice calm and even, but Travers only sneered at him.

'I don't think you're in a position to be giving orders, Breakblade. The only reason you're not dead already is that I want to know how you made it into Darkhaven without being cut down by one of the many people who despise you.'

'Maybe I'm the rogue Changer,' Caraway said flippantly, at the same time scanning the room for anything he could possibly use against Travers – but there was nothing. Still, he hadn't come all this way just to give up because one more person held a blade to his throat. 'Ever think of that?'

'In a way I'm glad you're here,' Travers went on, ignoring him. 'It gives me the chance to deal with you myself. I thought you'd faded into the oblivion you deserve, but over the last few days you've turned out to be a real pain in my arse. Concealing fugitives, beating up my men, interfering with Helm business –'

Caraway looked from him to the trembling girl on the bed, and gave a tiny shake of the head – anything more vigorous would have resulted in terminal injury. 'Whatever this is, Travers, it isn't Helm business. In fact there are several Helmsmen outside who would really like to know what's going on in here.'

'Then I'll just have to kill you, won't I?' Travers retorted. 'That way none of them ever have to know the truth.'

Caraway stared at him. 'You must be mad. There's no way you can conceal Ayla's presence down here forever. Sooner or later someone is bound to find out.'

'The Helm do what I tell them.' Travers punctuated his words with a flex of his fingers; Caraway felt the cold sting of steel in the hollow of his throat, then a trickle of warm blood running over his collarbone. 'And if I tell them to look the other way, they'll look the other way. They know as well as I do that Ayla is guilty. Do you really suppose they care what happens to her?'

'How do you think I got in here?' Caraway flung back at him. 'The Helm may be good at following orders, Travers, but they also believe in protecting the Nightshade line. That's what they're for.'

As if to prove his point, there was a rattle at the door handle, followed by a hollow thud as one of the men outside set his shoulder to the door. They were shouting something, but the words were indistinguishable through the metal. In reality Caraway didn't know if their concern was for Ayla or for their captain, but it didn't matter either way. If he could just hold out long enough for them to force their way in ... He glanced at the door, but sword and chair together were holding firm. He had to keep Travers' attention on him until the Helm broke through. He couldn't run the risk that Travers would decide to finish him off and start on Ayla while he still had the chance.

'They don't want to see Ayla wrongfully imprisoned,' he said, in pursuit of that end. 'If there's to be a trial, at least let it be a fair one.'

'No trial necessary,' Travers snarled. 'Florentyn Nightshade convicted his daughter of a crime, and now she's going to be punished for it. Just as you were punished for letting her mother die. That's the way the world works.' His shoulders lifted in a shrug. 'Though, clearly, one punishment wasn't enough for you.'

Caraway caught the flicker in Travers' eyes and threw himself aside, meaning the blade didn't pierce his throat but his right shoulder. Pain rushed through him in a white-hot wave, dissolving his vision in a swirl of lurid colours. Yet the move had got him into a slightly better position. As Travers wrenched the sword back out of Caraway's flesh, sending a fresh gush of blood spilling down his chest, Caraway hurled himself bodily at the other man. The room was too small for Travers to step back out of the way and bring his sword round for a second attack, as he would have done on the practice ground; the two of them slammed against the far

315

wall, staggering and spitting curses at each other. The impact jarred Caraway's shoulder, ripping his nerves apart in another flash of agony. Yet Travers had also flinched, his face turning pale. There were bandages at his neck and wrists, Caraway realised dimly. He must be wounded.

Before Travers could tighten his grip on his wavering sword, Caraway brought his left forearm down as hard as he could on the closest wound, at the join between shoulder and neck. Travers swore as his weapon fell from his hand. His fingers gouged at Caraway's eyes, trying to drive him off. Caraway pushed his arm away and brought his own knee up into the other man's groin. Grunting, Travers retaliated with a blow just below the ribcage that left Caraway gasping. Then they were locked together, each trying to force the other to the floor, using elbows and fists and boots without discrimination –

Another loud bang at the door distracted them both, if only for a moment. Travers was the first to recover. He caught Caraway's forearm, wrenching it back to open the wound at his shoulder still further, then landed a precise punch on the affected area. The pain was so intense that Caraway blacked out for a moment, his guts clenching with the desire to vomit. He reeled backwards, trying to blink the world back into existence. Even as it rematerialised around him Travers was on him, pinning him against the wall, his eyes bright with hatred as he rained down blow after blow. Caraway's head swam, his world contracting to a dark-edged circle of agony. He wasn't sure where he was any more. Perhaps back in an inn in the first ring, being held in place while Travers beat him up. Perhaps he had just learned the news about Florentyn Nightshade's death. About Florentyn, and Ayla …

Ayla.

Then, somehow, his broken blade was in his good left hand. As Travers drew back his arm in preparation for a final knockout punch, Caraway brought the length of jagged steel that was all that was left of his Helmsman's sword slashing up between them. Travers fell back with an almost inhuman cry of agony, his hands trying without success to staunch the flow of scarlet from his groin. Pushing himself off the wall, Caraway grabbed the captain's hair in his faltering right fingers and forced his head back. The blade in his other hand came round again, slicing open Travers' exposed throat in a spray of blood.

There was a horrific gurgle, then silence.

Caraway let the broken blade fall to the floor beside what had been Owen Travers. Dizziness was climbing in his head, and the urge to vomit was back. He leant his elbows on his knees, eyes closed, and breathed deeply until it passed. The Helm were still pounding on the door; he supposed he ought to let them in, but first things first. Wiping his face with his sleeve, he stumbled to Ayla's side. Her expression was taut with the strain of being trapped in place while battle raged around her, but she managed a shaky smile as she looked up at him.

'Is he dead?'

'Yes.'

Her lower lip trembled. 'I'm glad.'

With that, she burst into tears. As soon as Caraway had found and opened the catches on the manacles that were holding her wrists in place, she sat up and flung her arms around him. She was saying something, but it was so muffled against his chest that he couldn't make it out. Aware of her dislike of being touched, he held her as lightly as he could and tried not to think about how close he'd come to being too late. What Travers had done to her would leave a scar, but it could have been far worse.

'You're hurt,' she said finally, drawing away from him, though her body still shook with sporadic sobs. 'We need to find the physician.'

Caraway had almost forgotten his wounded shoulder, but her words drew it back to his attention. Immediately he could feel it throbbing away in time to his heartbeat. He lifted a hand to it: his shirt was sticky with blood, both Travers' and his own. Still, he wasn't about to keel over.

'Lord Myrren first,' he said. 'He needs to know what's been going on. Then the physician.'

He moved to Ayla's ankles to unlock the second pair of manacles.

'I'm sorry,' he added as he released her feet. 'I've bled all over you.'

She glanced down at the dark stains smeared across her shift, then back at his face. 'Tomas ... you have no need to apologise to me. For anything.'

'Sorry,' he mumbled again, automatically. 'Are you ready to go?'

'I mean it!' Her voice sounded unusually intense. 'Just ... you saved my life, all right? So stop being so humble.'

He frowned at her. She had drawn her knees in to her chest, hugging them to herself as though he was making her uncomfortable. In a flash, it dawned on him: she didn't like being indebted to him. She didn't want to have been rescued by her mother's killer. *Of all the people in the world, Tomas Caraway, you're the very last one I'd want to help me.*

'Fine.' The word was sharp in his own ears; she looked up in surprise. 'But we need to go, now. The sooner we find your brother, the better – and we'll have to deal with the Helm first.'

'All right.' Ayla lowered her bare feet to the floor and stood up, carefully not looking at the body in the middle of the room. Caraway picked up the cloak that had been discarded on the bed and wrapped it around her shoulders; she gave him a quick, tight smile. 'Ready.'

Stepping around Travers, Caraway crossed to the door and wrenched the sword out from underneath it, then shoved the chair aside. Immediately the door flew open, revealing a large group of Helmsmen gathered in the narrow stairwell.

'Tomas Caraway,' the foremost of them said. 'You are under arrest for injuring a member of the Helm.' His gaze travelled past Caraway to the body on the floor, and his eyes widened. 'And – and for killing Captain Travers.'

THIRTY-FOUR

As soon as the creature that had been Myrren disappeared out of sight, Sorrow jumped to her feet and began stuffing all her loose weaponry into her bag. The baby was crying; she hunched her shoulders and did her best to block it out. *This is what happens when you get mixed up with Changers, Naeve Sorrow,* she told herself, observing with vague interest that her hands were shaking. *It never ends well.*

'Naeve?' Elisse's voice held a tremor. 'What are ya doing?'

'You heard him.' Sorrow didn't look up from her task. 'He told me to leave Darkhaven. And after what we just saw, I'm sure as shit not going to disobey. In fact, I think I might go a little further than just leaving the tower. I might leave Arkannen for a while. Screw it, I might even leave Mirrorvale.'

Picking up the full bag, she turned to look at Elisse. The dark-haired girl was still sitting in bed, rocking the bawling Corus in her arms, the expression on her face one of almost painful hope.

'Will ya take me with ya?'

'No chance,' Sorrow said, sternly suppressing the small part of her that leapt with joy at the idea. 'The Helm would be after us before we had time to blink.'

'Most o' the Helm don' even know I exist,' Elisse pointed out. The baby was quietening in her arms, his momentary panic gone as quickly as it had arrived. 'And if Myrren kills Travers –'

'Then we'll have an enraged Changer creature after us instead.' Sorrow shook her head. 'Whoever's left standing at the end of this, Elisse, they're going to want you back. More specifically, they're going to want Corus back. And I don't want to end up taking the blame for kidnapping a child of Darkhaven. Both Myrren and the Helm would be glad enough of an excuse to have me executed.'

'But they can't follow ya across the border,' Elisse said, blue eyes pleading. 'Once ya leave the country, ya safe.' She looked down at the baby's tearstained face, then back up at Sorrow. 'This is the only chance I'll get, Naeve. The only chance ta give my son a normal life. So whether ya help me or not, I'm leaving.' She bit her lip. 'It's jus' – I think I'll get a whole lot further if I have ya with me.'

Sorrow stared at her. She knew she should cut her losses. When a job went bad, you disassociated yourself from it as swiftly and painlessly as you could – and a job that involved a murderous Changer and an obsessive Captain of the Helm was about as bad as it got. She should give Elisse a firm negative and get out as soon as possible. If she made all haste to her apartment in the first ring – a visit to which was necessary in order to retrieve the considerable amount of money in her safe – she could be on an airship before the sun set. Another day, and she'd be too far away from Darkhaven for anyone to track her.

And yet … and yet …

'Are you sure you're in a fit state to travel?' she asked Elisse, in a final attempt to convince her to stay put. 'You only finished giving birth a couple of bells ago.'

'I'll be fine.' Perhaps sensing that Sorrow was weakening, Elisse leaned forward and spoke eagerly. 'Sore and tired, o' course, but I'll feel a lot worse if I stay here.'

Sorrow hesitated a moment longer, then capitulated. 'All right. I'll take you across the border, and after that we'll see.'

Elisse responded with a radiant smile that Sorrow couldn't help returning. At the same time her heart seemed to stutter in her chest, which explained a lot. Ever since meeting Elisse, she had been listening to her heart much more than to her head. It was a disturbing phenomenon. She couldn't remember the last time – if there ever had been one – when her heart had been involved in making any of her decisions.

'Have you got everything you need?' she asked brusquely, and Elisse shrugged.

'Din't have anything when I came here, 'cept Corus, o' course.'

'Well, you can't just walk out of Darkhaven with him in your arms.' Sorrow frowned at her a moment, then went to the wardrobe to fetch one of the richly embroidered cloaks she remembered seeing in there. 'This will have to do to cover you. At least it's got a hood. As for the baby –' she scanned the room before grabbing one of the clean blankets from the bed – 'I think we'd better make a kind of sling ...'

Once she'd tied Corus safely across Elisse's chest, she draped the cloak around Elisse's shoulders and fastened it in front. As she'd hoped, the thick folds of fabric made it hard to tell that Elisse was carrying a baby – and with the hood up, Elisse's distinctive colouring was much less obvious. Sorrow nodded.

'I think you'll do. Are you ready?'

'Ready as I'll ever be.' Elisse paused, her eyes searching Sorrow's face, then added softly, 'Thanks, Naeve.'

Sorrow shook her head, though her heart was behaving erratically again. She supposed she'd have to live with it from now on. 'Thank me when we're safely across the border. Until then …' She shrugged. 'Just hope we make it.'

When she saw how slowly Elisse walked, though, it seemed a vain hope. The woman was doing the best she could, but she was clearly still in pain from her exertions the previous night. As Sorrow led her through Darkhaven towards the postern gate, the only way out for those who couldn't fly, she was convinced that at any moment they would be stopped by one of the Helm – or worse, by Myrren-as-creature returning. Yet it seemed luck was on their side. The tower was more or less deserted, with the occasional Helmsman who crossed their path in too much of a hurry even to notice them. Better still, when they reached the gate they found it locked but unguarded. The Helm had sealed Darkhaven off from the outside world, but they weren't watching to make sure no-one left. Why should they?

'I 'spect they've all gone chasing after Myrren,' Elisse murmured. 'It's hard ta believe he was the one who attacked me and killed Florentyn.'

'Anything's possible when it comes to Changers.' Sorrow was concentrating on the lock. It was a tough one, but eventually she managed to cajole it into opening. She ushered Elisse through, before following and pulling it shut behind her. There. The hardest part was done. Now down the hill to the Gate of Death – the city watch would take no notice of what would appear to be a Helmsman escorting his lover back to the lower rings – and they'd be away.

'Time to pick up the pace,' she told Elisse. 'The quicker we get out of sight of the tower, the better.'

Elisse obeyed with barely a wince, one arm cradling Corus under her cloak as though he gave her strength.

'Where are we going?' she panted as they hurried down the slope, and Sorrow gave her a grin of pure satisfaction.

'Airship. We'll be out of the country before they even notice we're gone.'

'I'd keep back if I were you,' Caraway said to the Helmsmen outside the incarceration room. His broken blade was in his hand again, Ayla realised as he lifted it to point at the foremost man. 'Unless you want to go the same way as Travers.'

The man's eyes widened incredulously. 'You're threatening us?'

'Damn right I am.' Ayla had never heard Caraway sound so vehement. 'The whole lot of you are a disgrace to the Helm. Your captain brings a member of the Nightshade line – a woman you are *sworn to protect* – down here against her will and threatens to assault her, and you just let him get on with it. Seems to me the Nightshade line needs protecting from the Helm more than it does from anyone else.' His voice dropped to a low murmur that was somehow more threatening than a shout; the jagged, bloodstained blade remained perfectly steady in his hand. 'So I suggest you step back out of our way before I slit all your throats for failing in your duty.'

'Let me get this straight,' the man said. 'You, Tomas Caraway, are lecturing me about failing in my duty?'

There was an uneasy ripple of laughter, which ceased as soon as Caraway replied.

'Yes!' His voice was so ferocious that the man took an involuntary step back. 'Because what you've done is worse! I would have suffered anything rather than let Kati Nightshade be hurt. I've paid for her death for five years. But *you* ... you're content to sit back and turn a blind eye while her daughter is punished for a crime she didn't commit. Can you honestly claim to be any better than me?'

A tense silence fell. Then the Helmsman turned his head and said, 'Better let 'em up, lads. At least as far as the antechamber. No point trying to sort anything out down here.'

Without looking at her, Caraway held out his free hand to Ayla. She took it. She could feel the suppressed tension trembling through him, yet despite that, the strength of his fingers around hers was a comfort. Her whole being was still shaken by how close Travers had come to raping her. She wanted to retreat into a small hole somewhere and hide; better yet, she wanted to Change and fly as far away from Darkhaven as possible. Her entire body felt sullied by the experience. Yet she knew that if it hadn't been for Caraway, things could have been much, much worse. For that reason, his hand on hers felt surprisingly like the only thing that could keep her on her feet.

In some disorder, the Helm retreated back up the stairwell, and Caraway and Ayla followed them. More Helmsmen had gathered in the antechamber, some grouped around a man with a bloodstained uniform who must be the one Caraway had wounded, others apparently waiting to find out what was happening. In the middle of the room was a raised marble slab that held Florentyn Nightshade's body. Ayla hadn't seen her father since his death; the sight struck her like a blow to the stomach, making her gasp. She turned her face aside, swallowing, glad she wasn't close enough to see his wounds in detail; but she thought she could still smell the faint sweet scent of decay.

'Captain Travers is dead.' Caraway's voice was harsh as he made the announcement. Ayla was dimly aware that he was drawing her closer in beside him, as though he feared something might happen to her if she got too far away.

'How?' one man asked amid a general rumble of shock and discontentment.

'I killed him,' Caraway said, and the rumble grew louder. Hearing the danger in it, Ayla rubbed the tears from her eyes, forcing herself to concentrate on what was happening around her. She and Caraway were now standing beside the wall a short distance from the staircase that led to the incarceration room; two of the Helm were already climbing the steps, carrying their captain's covered body between them.

'You'll pay for this, Breakblade!' one of the assembled men shouted, and at that all Ayla's fear and fury came spilling out of her.

'Don't you dare call him that!' she snapped, turning on the speaker. 'Tomas Caraway is the only one of you with any guts at all. If it hadn't been for him, your precious Captain Travers would have violated me down there, and not one of you would have lifted a finger to stop him.'

'How are we to know you're telling the truth?' another of the Helm called out. 'How are we to know you didn't kill your father and Captain Travers as well?'

'Lady Ayla is not a murderer,' Caraway said, soft and low. 'I don't know what Travers told you, but his preoccupation with catching her appears to have stemmed more from his own personal obsession than from any evidence against her.'

Doubting glances were exchanged, and mutters of denial. Did they really think so little of her that they were reluctant to stop believing the worst? Were they truly so anxious to see the half-blood discredited? The thought drove Ayla to step forward, wrenching her hand out of Caraway's grasp.

'Do you require proof?' she demanded in a voice that sounded grating even to her own ears. 'Fine. I'll give you proof.'

She took a deep breath, preparing to Change. To show them all her other form, to make it clear once and for all that she wasn't and never had been dangerous. But before she could do it, the main doors to the antechamber were battered from their hinges in a shower of wooden fragments to reveal something else entirely: a creature of rustling wings and black scales, a creature that was nothing like her own creature-self. Ayla stared at it, pulse jumping in her throat. So it was true. There was another Changer in Arkannen.

In the long, confused moment that followed, several Helmsmen looked from the creature to Ayla as if they were wondering how she had managed the trick. Yet the creature itself left them little time for doubt. Lowering its head, it sent a long gust of flame over the nearest man, leaving him rolling on the floor and screaming as fire ate through his clothing to the naked skin beneath. Without hesitation, the creature stalked further into the room, its barbed tail swiping aside another Helmsman who tried to approach it from behind. Its jaws gripped a third man and shook him vigorously, then flung him down. Some of the Helm fled through the broken doors; others were braver and tried to stand their ground, but their swords simply shattered or bounced off the impervious Changer hide. The room filled with the cries of wounded men and the stench of blood and burning flesh. And still the creature advanced through the room, coming closer and closer to the far end where Ayla and Caraway stood as if petrified.

When it was almost on them, Caraway moved. His hand shot out to grab Ayla's wrist, pulling her back until she was behind him. The other hand lifted his broken blade in a symbolic but ultimately useless gesture of defiance.

'If you want her,' he said steadily, 'you'll have to go through me.'

The creature didn't appear to consider that a problem. Its hot, mad eyes studied him as though it were trying to decide how best to kill him. Ayla pressed her back against the wall to keep her rebellious knees from giving way and understood, for the first time, what it was like to be an ordinary person confronted with a Changer. There was simply nothing she could do to defend either Caraway or herself. She could Change, but she didn't think her creature-self would stand a chance against this beast. So she just stood there, her insides quivering with a melting fear that left her with no strength even to run, and watched in impotent misery as the blunt-nosed head hurtled towards Caraway with bloodstained teeth bared ready to strike.

Then, suddenly, a woman wearing a flung-back veil that imperfectly covered her red hair was running through the room. She bundled whatever she was carrying into the arms of the nearest Helmsman left standing, before interposing herself between the creature and Caraway in what was surely a suicidal act of bravery.

'Stop,' she said, her voice breaking with sorrow rather than fear. Her hands lifted, imploring the creature to listen. 'Please, stop.'

To Ayla's amazement, the creature wavered. The bloodlust in its eyes dimmed, to be replaced by confusion.

'Please,' the woman said again. The creature retreated a few steps, head swinging from side to side as if it were battling with itself. Then, in a swirl of black dust, it Changed.

As the vast bulk of the creature became an amorphous cloud and then began to reshape itself into a new form, the veiled woman returned to the staring Helmsman and took back what she had given him. Her face was pale and her hands shook, as though she hadn't been at all sure that her risk would pay off, but she stood her ground and watched the Change take place. Her lips were pressed together in a tight line, but whether it was anger or grief she was holding back, Ayla couldn't tell.

Finally, the dust cleared to reveal a naked man lying on the stone floor. Ayla took an involuntary half-step forward, her nails digging into her palms. Shock so intense that it was painful shot through her core, leaving her feeling as if she had been ripped apart by Caraway's broken blade.

The man lying in front of her was her brother Myrren.

THIRTY-FIVE

Myrren opened his eyes. He was lying on his back, looking up at a shadowed stone ceiling. It faded into an indistinct blur beside the series of vivid memories that were playing through his mind: a set of searing emotions that felt remote, alien, but that he knew beyond doubt were part of him. Burning anger, a keen sense of betrayal, a desire to tear apart everything that stood in his way. Satisfaction as the Helm scattered before him like sparrows before a hawk. Swift fury when one of the men pushed Ayla behind him – blood on his blade and on their clothing – he must be threatening her – preparing to strike – and then the woman with hair like flame, stepping in front of them. *Serenna*. Sudden fear upon seeing her, a horror of hurting her, a desire to protect her that overcame every other instinct … yes, he remembered it all.

And because he remembered it all, he knew what the truth must be.

I am a murderer. I killed my own father. He tried the words, experimentally, examining each one for truth. He expected them to bring him pain, but the pain he was already feeling was so vast that he was numb to it. If he let himself feel it, he would surely lose his mind again, and with it any chance he had left of controlling the creature that lurked inside him. He could feel it there, a strong fierce presence without compassion or conscience. His new awareness of it had brought it closer to the surface; if he relaxed his grip on it, even for a moment, it would rise up and take over. That was how it would be, now: the two of them locked in a desperate struggle until the day he died.

'Myrren.' A face appeared above him, ragged dark hair and blue eyes washed with tears. She was kneeling beside him, gazing at him with an expression that held no accusation, only a deep sorrow. He lifted a hand to touch her cheek.

'Ayla.'

She was holding a cloak, which she handed to him. He realised he was naked and took it gratefully, struggling into a seated position despite the dizzy pounding of his head. The roughness of the thick fabric around his shoulders brought him a strange kind of comfort.

'Are you all right?' he asked Ayla, seeing the bloodstains on her clothing with renewed anxiety. 'Travers –'

'Travers is dead.' She took his hands in her own. 'Tomas killed him for me. And I'm fine. I'm not even hurt.'

They looked at each other. There were so many things Myrren wanted to ask her, and so many things he wanted to say, but in the end he just said, 'I didn't know I could do this, Ayla. I – I don't want you to think this was some kind of plot against you.'

She shook her head. 'I don't.'

His fingers tightened on hers. Then Serenna was beside them, leaning down, his discarded clothes in her arms.

'My lord, I have your clothes.'

Letting go of Ayla's hands, he took the bundle from her. 'Thank you.'

'No, thank you,' she said. 'For turning back.'

He studied her face, the freckles stark against the paleness of her skin. 'I did all of it, didn't I? I killed my father. I wounded Travers and Elisse – and you.' She was silent, but he could read the answer in the misery of her grey eyes. He nodded, accepting it as truth because he had to. 'When did you work it out, Serenna?'

'Only today,' she whispered. 'The bruise on your arm ... but I couldn't tell you, Myrren. I couldn't.'

'No.' He understood that. There could have been no easy way to tell him he was a murderer. That the nightmares he had been suffering from were, in fact, the sole intimation of the truth. He wondered how long it would have continued, if events hadn't brought him to this point. Perhaps he might have gone on for years, Changing only in his sleep, never knowing what he was doing. Taking out his hidden anger on anyone who posed the slightest threat to him or to Ayla.

He knew what he had to do next.

'Thank you, both of you,' he said, looking from Serenna to Ayla. Saying farewell in his heart to the only two people he really loved. 'Now, I'd better address the Helm.'

The two of them backed away as he clambered to his feet, keeping the cloak wrapped tightly around him, still clutching the clothes Serenna had given him. He found he was standing beside the marble slab that held his father's body. Around the walls of the antechamber, the Helmsmen he had just terrorised stood in groups of two or three, some of them nursing injuries of varying degrees, all of them watching him with wary eyes. They didn't know what to do, he could tell. He had just rampaged through the corridors of Darkhaven and done his best to wipe them from his path. It must be obvious to them that it was he and not Ayla they should have been pursuing all this time. Yet he was also their over-lord, the pure-blood heir to the Changer throne – and more importantly, he had the Nightshade gift after all, even if it was of the hybrid form his father had so despised in Ayla. If he asked it of them, he sensed they would accept him as their ruler and carry out his commands. Even if he was mad. Even if he had no control over his gift. Even if he ordered them to kill Ayla and Corus and everyone else who might possibly threaten his position.

That was why he had to do what he was going to do.

'I must apologise to you all,' he said. 'But I hope you will agree this is evidence that my sister is innocent of any wrongdoing.' He glanced around, a wry smile on his face, and heard a few uneasy chuckles. 'For that reason, I believe the decision my father made before his death still stands. I hereby renounce the throne of Darkhaven in Ayla's favour.'

There was a pause. Then one man, bolder than the rest, spoke up. 'But my lord, you have the gift –'

'Yes, as it turns out, I do have the gift,' Myrren said. 'But not in a form I could ever consent to let loose in the world. For a Changer who has no control over when or where he Changes – particularly a Changer who has killed as a result of it – there is only one possible option.' Though his throat ached with the fear of what he was about to say, he kept his voice firm and even as he added, 'And I hope that when I step into the incarceration room, one of you will obey my final command and turn the key.'

In the shocked silence that followed, he couldn't look at Ayla or Serenna in case seeing their faces weakened his resolve. Instead he looked at his father's body, at the horrific wounds he himself had inflicted without even knowing it. He thought of everything Florentyn had done in an attempt to awaken the Changer gift in his pure-blood son. And he remembered his nightmare, the morning he woke up to learn of the attack on Travers: trapped alive in a metal coffin. That would be his fate, now. That would be his reality. The law stated that a mad or murderous Changer must be incarcerated for good, and that was what he was.

His hands tightened on the small pile of clothes, and he felt the shape of the pistol in his pocket.

He's going to lock himself up. Serenna knew it before Myrren even said the words. For that reason, she had a tight enough grip on herself not to react when he made it clear to everyone else. She just watched his face, the back of one hand pressed against her mouth to stop herself screaming, and wondered how the whole flaming world could be so unfair as to let this happen to him. Ayla, standing next to her, was not so restrained; a small cry of protest escaped her lips before she choked it back. Yet Myrren didn't look her way, but stared around at the Helm as if seeking obedience to his will. Even though he was dressed in nothing but a cloak, he had never looked more regal – or more sure of himself.

Only when he was apparently satisfied that the Helm would do their duty did he turn back to his sister. To begin with he said nothing, just stood there gazing at her as though his heart held too much to put into words; she looked back at him with equal reticence, her lower lip quivering. Her profile was close to a mirror image of Myrren's: same strong nose, softened only slightly for a woman; same finely moulded mouth; same sweeping hairline and well-shaped jaw. Looking at the two of them, Serenna couldn't doubt that in losing Myrren, Ayla was losing a part of herself.

'You have a new brother now,' Myrren said finally. It

seemed he meant the words to be light, but an underlying note of strain spoke of effort. 'He will need teaching about us, about what it means to be a Nightshade ... you can do that, Ayla. I know you can.'

'Myrren ...' Ayla stood straight and proud, though her eyes were brimming over. 'You don't have to do this. We can find out how to stop it happening. We can help you control it ...'

'Hush, little sister.' Myrren lifted a hand to brush a tear from her cheek, and the sorrow in his smile made Serenna's heart ache. 'This is how it has to be. I killed our father. I hurt several more people. I can't trust myself not to do it again.'

'I'm not going to give up.' Ayla's voice broke. 'I'll keep searching until I find the answer. And then I'll come and let you out.'

Myrren didn't reply. He just put his free arm around her shoulders, drawing her close; for an instant his cheek rested against the top of her head, his dark hair blending into hers so that it seemed they were becoming one. Then Myrren stepped back, and Ayla retreated with a sob into the arms of the man she had called Tomas, hiding her face against his chest. He held her gently, as though she were something rare and precious; over her head, he and Myrren exchanged a long look of wordless communication.

Take care of her.

I will. I promise.

Finally Myrren nodded, and turned towards Serenna.

She watched him approach with her heart beating fast, forcing herself to hold her head high. She wanted to hurl herself at him, to cling to him and beg him not to leave her alone. But she understood him well enough by now to know that his sense of honour wouldn't allow him to do anything other than what he intended. He had found his father's murderer, and now he was going to punish him. She had no right to make it any harder for him than it already was.

'Sister Serenna.' He stopped in front of her, looking at her with the same grave expression he'd worn the day she met him. His free hand gestured at her right ankle. 'I am truly sorry. For what it seems I did to you.'

She managed a smile. 'It is nothing, my lord. Really.'

'Thank you for all the help you have given me.' As he had so many times before, Myrren lifted the back of her hand to his lips. 'And for making these past few days so unexpectedly bright.'

'It was my pleasure,' she whispered.

'I hope you will go back to your temple, now.' He didn't seem able to let go of her hand. 'Go back to your temple and get on with your life.'

'Yes ...' She wanted to be strong, but she couldn't hold back the tears that were overflowing from her eyes. Her fingers tightened on his as she added fiercely, 'But I will be here as often as I can, helping Ayla with her research. I know my way around your library by now.'

He shook his head; the set of his mouth was rueful. 'I should tell you to forget about me. But I have to admit ...' A momentary anguish flashed across his face, but then it was gone and he was smiling sadly at her. 'I have to admit, I hope you will remember me from time to time. Most of all things, I find it is hard to leave you behind.'

Unable to bear his pain any longer, Serenna stood on tiptoe and pressed her lips against his. He returned the kiss with urgency, tasting her as if he sought to imprint the shape of her mouth in his memory. Then he pulled away, to look deep into her eyes. His pupils were wide and dark, as though he could already see the four walls of the incarceration room around him.

'Have courage, Myrren,' she told him, soft and intent. 'We'll find the answer soon enough.'

He ran a strand of her hair through his fingers, then tucked it back into place beneath her veil. 'Goodbye, Serenna.'

Then, gathering the clothes more tightly to his chest, he turned and walked away. Serenna watched him duck under the low archway beside the door to the vault and disappear out of sight down the stairs. She longed to run after him, feeling his kiss still tingling on her lips, but she held herself back. Instead she glanced at Ayla; the girl was gazing after her brother from the circle of her young man's arms, the same bereavement in her face that Serenna felt in her heart.

In the silence, they all heard the small explosion that was the pistol going off.

THIRTY-SIX

A mute stream of anguish and bitter love flowing through her, Ayla knelt beside her brother and clutched his cold hand in hers as though she could somehow bring him back if she tried hard enough. She was in the incarceration room, where Myrren would lie for a traditional seven-day period of his own before being moved into the vault beside his father. He was dead, she was sure of that; the shattered portion of his skull left no room for doubt. The physician had said death was almost instantaneous. Yet Ayla felt she owed it to him to keep a vigil beside him, for a while at least.

I told you I'd help you, she said to him silently, over and over. *Why couldn't you just hold on long enough for me to find an answer?* But in reality, she understood. He had wanted her and Serenna and the rest of them to get on with their lives. She, Ayla, was overlord of Darkhaven now. She couldn't fulfil her duties if all her time was spent searching for her brother's cure. And besides, even if she and Serenna could have worked out the rules of his gift and how to control it, it wouldn't have taken away his guilt. Whether he had meant to do it or not, he'd killed his own father and wounded two other people; the law said he had to be locked up for it, and Myrren wouldn't have dreamed of trying to make a special case for himself. She remembered how she'd felt at the prospect of permanent incarceration: she'd been determined to claim the right to die at her own hand rather than live forever in a cage. Myrren, too, had prized freedom above all things. And he had seen only one way he could hold on to it.

Ayla understood, but it didn't make her feel any better.

Getting up from her kneeling position, she staggered as frozen muscles flared back into life. It must be dark outside by now; she'd been down here for at least two bells. Much as she hated to go, there were other things she should be doing. After one last whispered farewell, she touched Myrren's face gently and turned away. Earlier she had feared being locked alone in this room until she died; now she was leaving her brother here, and it hurt just as much as if she were the one staying. She was frightened and heartsick and full of uncertainty, and she could think of only one thing that would make the pain a little more bearable.

She found Caraway in the main hall, at the centre of a buzz of activity. His right shoulder had finally been bandaged; in addition, the physician had diagnosed him with two cracked ribs and a sprained knee, as well as multiple smaller cuts and bruises. One of his eyes had swollen almost shut, notwithstanding the earlier application of a cold compress. Despite all that, however, he greeted her with a sympathetic smile and said something to the Helmsman beside him. Then he led her to a nearby window seat, where they sat side by side without touching.

'How are you feeling?' he asked her softly, and she shook her head. She was feeling many things, but she didn't want to talk about them. Not now.

'I'm all right,' she said. 'More to the point, how are you?'

He gave a shrug that turned rapidly into a wince. 'Takes me back to my days in the fifth ring. Which reminds me, I must give Art Bryan his sword back. It'll be worth it just to see the look on his face when he realises I'm still alive.'

Ayla nodded. 'And Serenna?'

'Upstairs. The physician gave her a sedative. She'll return to her temple tomorrow.' Caraway paused. 'You know, she blames herself for what happened.'

Ayla pressed her lips together to avoid saying anything. She couldn't help blaming Serenna a little bit, too, for handing Myrren an armful of clothes that included the pistol that killed him.

'I told her no-one could possibly think it was her fault,' Caraway went on carefully. 'If it hadn't been the pistol then it would have been a knife or a sword. There were plenty of them around.'

The look in his eyes seemed to ask something of her. Ayla sighed. This was one of the many reasons why she needed him here.

'I don't really blame her,' she muttered. 'She loved Myrren, didn't she? And I think he loved her too. The way they kissed …' She stopped, blushing, and then blushing more because she was blushing. Hurriedly she moved on to her next question. 'And is there any word of Elisse?'

'No-one saw her or the baby leave Darkhaven,' Caraway said. 'They must have gone down into the city, but after that …' He made a resigned gesture. 'I've sent some of the Helm out looking for them, but if Sorrow is helping Elisse then there's a good chance they won't find anything. I'm sorry.'

So her new brother – the sole living member of the Nightshade line apart from her – was out in the world somewhere with only his mother and a notorious sellsword for protection. Ayla knew that should be a concern, but her mind was so blurred with emotion that she couldn't take it in.

'Elisse can't hide forever,' she said, trying to comfort herself. 'She looks too much like one of us …' Her voice trailed away as Caraway's words belatedly registered in her overloaded brain. *I've sent some of the Helm out.* And he had appeared to be at the heart of the hall when she entered it … She frowned. 'The Helm are taking orders from you now?'

'Seems like it.' Caraway sighed. 'They feel they've failed, you see. I'm the only person in Darkhaven who even came close to protecting the Nightshade line today. And with Travers dead … well, none of them really know what to do next. They're lost. So I thought I'd better take charge, just for now.' He gave her a sidelong glance. 'Quite a difference from five years ago.'

Ayla nodded. They sat in silence for a few moments, and she wondered if he was thinking – as she was – about everything that had happened to bring them to this point. Finally she turned to him, just as he turned to her.

'Tomas –'

'Ayla –'

She bit her lip, both frustrated and relieved at the reprieve. 'You first.'

'Well …' He looked down at the floor. 'I thought – that is, I hoped you might consider letting me rejoin the Helm.'

'What?' After everything he'd done for her, surely that wasn't all he wanted. But he gave her a self-deprecating glance and continued.

'I just thought it might be useful for you to have me around. At least to start with. Then maybe I can get another job –'

'No.'

'Oh. Then –' even more hesitantly – 'perhaps I could work here in some other capacity ...'

'I don't want to employ you at all, Tomas.' *Wait. That didn't come out right.* 'I mean ... I wondered if ...'

Now it was her turn to be hesitant. She stared at him, willing him to read what she wanted to say in her eyes, but he still wasn't looking in her direction.

'I thought you might stay here,' she said, forcing the words out. 'Not to work. Just ... with me.'

Then he did lift his head. His expression wasn't at all what she had hoped; it was sad, but determined.

'I don't need your charity, Lady Ayla.'

'It's not charity. I mean, it ... um.' Now she was blushing again. She'd never blushed this much in her life. 'It would be for my benefit too.'

'I'm sorry,' Tomas said. 'It's been a long day, and I'm probably not – what are you saying?'

Come on, Ayla. You're making an utter mess of this.

'It's just ... Darkhaven can't go blithely on as it always has.' Sudden, renewed misery leapt inside her; she looked away, into the night outside the window, fighting to control her tears. 'My father was obsessed with the purity of the Nightshade line, and look where that's brought us. I intend things to be different from now on.'

She stole a glance at Caraway, but he still wore a confused frown. Hardly surprising. She was doing a wonderful job of not getting to the point.

'Make my own choices,' she stumbled on. 'Marry who I want. Isn't that what you said? Darkhaven needs children. A new future. And so I thought perhaps, one day, you and I ...'

Silence. Dead silence. When it became too much to bear, she turned to face him. The confusion in his eyes had melted back into sadness.

'I don't think so, Ayla,' he said gently.

Shock swept through her, leaving her feeling as though she had nothing to hold on to – as though the ground beneath her and the walls around her were as insubstantial as air. She hadn't realised quite how much she was relying on his continued presence. More than that: how much she wanted it.

'You don't understand,' she said, her voice shaking. 'Darkhaven needs you. I need you.'

'Maybe if it was the other way round,' he muttered. She frowned, unsure whether or not she was meant to have heard.

'What do you mean?'

'It doesn't matter.' He looked down at his hands again, clasped so tightly the knuckles showed white. 'Lady Ayla, I'm willing to stay here and serve you in whatever professional capacity you choose. But as for this other thing you've dreamt up … I can't imagine what made you think it would be a good idea, but my answer has to be no. For both our sakes.'

'What do you mean?' she said again, stupidly.

'Well …' His shoulders hunched in embarrassment. 'For that kind of thing to work, the two people involved at least have to like each other.'

Oh. Ayla stared at him, unable to find any coherent words through the pain that tore at her heart. He'd offered her help when she was lost and alone – put up with every mood she'd thrown at him – come running to rescue her from Travers, been there to comfort her when she learned the truth about Myrren – and yet he didn't even *like* her?

'Right,' she managed at last. 'Yes. Of course you're right.'

They gazed at each other in silence. Tears prickled behind Ayla's eyes, and she turned her face away.

'In fact, it's probably best if you leave now. Don't you think? I mean –' she swallowed over the constriction in her throat – 'since we've established we don't actually like each other, seeing each other every day would be too ...' *Painful. Embarrassing.* 'Awkward.'

'Awkward,' he echoed. 'Of course. I understand.'

Ayla felt rather than saw him get up from the window seat. She dug her nails into her palms to keep herself from clutching at his arm. *You've made enough of a fool of yourself already. Don't make it worse. Don't –*

'Ayla,' he said, and despite herself she looked up. His expression was sombre. 'I wish you all the very best. And –' He hesitated, then said all in a rush, as if he doubted the wisdom of it, 'If you ever want anything, you know where I am.'

I don't need your charity, she almost flung back at him – but didn't. Instead, she gave him a stiff nod. 'Thank you.'

His hand touched hers, ever so lightly, as it had the night before. And then he was gone, walking at a brisk pace out of the hall. Only when he was out of sight did she cover her face with her hands and let the tears flow: for Myrren, for her father, but also a little for herself.

As soon as the first light of dawn broke on the horizon, the airship's engine ramped up from a murmur to a growl. Elisse glanced down at Corus, strapped to her chest, but the noise didn't seem to bother him; he just slept peacefully on. Given that his first day in the world had been full of panic and confusion, he was a remarkably well-behaved child.

'Born traveller, that one,' Sorrow remarked.

'Yeah.' Elisse peered over the side of the gondola as the airship began to rise above the third ring, then sat back in her seat and swallowed hard. 'Not sure I am, though.'

'It's pretty smooth once it gets going,' Sorrow said. 'It's the smell of the coal that usually affects people, but after a while you get used to it.'

Sorrow had arranged the flight with someone she knew. Elisse wasn't sure how she'd managed to organise it in a single evening as well as packing up everything in her life that was essential to her, but that was what she had done. She'd claimed the owner of this particular small airship owed her a favour, but Elisse suspected she'd just threatened him until he'd have done anything to get her as far away as possible. Either way, the three of them were now in the air above the city, and Darkhaven – she risked another glance over the side, then leaned back with a sigh of relief. Darkhaven was behind them, and receding all the time.

Now that she wasn't on edge with expecting the Helm to leap out of the shadows and drag her and her baby back to the tower, Elisse realised how tired she was. She tipped her head back against her seat, closing her eyes. The motion of the airship was surprisingly soothing, a slow and gentle rocking – perhaps that was why Corus liked it so much. Even the noise had become bearable now she was used to it. She wondered briefly what had happened to Myrren, who'd turned out to be the Changer he'd been seeking all along, but then decided it didn't matter to her. Her association with the Nightshades was over. It was in the past, just like her life at home on the farm. The future was just her and Corus and Sorrow, riding in an airship to –

Elisse sat bolt upright. Thus far she had followed Sorrow's instructions without question, knowing it was her best chance of leaving Arkannen without getting caught. For that reason, it was only now that it occurred to her to ask the obvious.

'Where are we going?' she called over the throb of the engine. Sorrow grinned at her, cheeks flushed bright by the breeze.

'Sol Kardis.'

Sol Kardis. Elisse repeated the name to herself, tasting its strangeness. *Where Naeve's pistol came from. The Helm will never find us there.*

'Ya hear that, Corus?' she murmured to the sleeping baby. 'We're going ta a new country.' Ever so gently, she ran a finger across the wispy Nightshade hair on his head. 'And ya don' have ta be a Changer unless ya wan' ta be.'

THIRTY-SEVEN

Serenna stood in the middle of the small room she had left just seven days before and looked around. It was the same, she could see that at a glance. Nothing had changed. Yet it felt completely different.

She had left Darkhaven that morning at first light, declining Ayla's offer of an escort and simply walking down the hill to the sixth ring. She had returned to the Altar of Flame sure that everything she had seen and done must show in her face. Surely the emotions that filled her lungs with hot lead and her belly with a stone must have left some external mark. Yet the few priestesses and acolytes she had encountered between the entrance and her own room had greeted her with barely a pause. After all, she hadn't been away that long. To them, one week in Darkhaven was nothing compared to the nine years she had spent as a priestess. She was the only one who realised that in fact it was the other way round.

Now she stared at the walls and heard, over and over, the sound of a pistol being fired.

No. She had to stop thinking about it.

She picked up the small bag she had taken with her to Darkhaven and began unpacking the contents, concentrating on returning each item to its place. When she'd finished, her face was wet with tears. This was ridiculous. Even if yesterday's events had never taken place, she was a priestess. She couldn't really have stayed with Myrren, not without breaking the vows that made her who she was. On some level she'd always known that, despite how the idea had tempted her. So what was the difference?

Of course, she knew the answer to that. The difference was, he'd still be alive.

'You should never have come here,' she said fiercely to the empty room. 'You had no right to tear my life apart like this.'

But there was no answer. There never would be an answer, only memory and regret.

I hope you will remember me from time to time.

Serenna sat down on the edge of the bed as more slow tears fell. This would fade, she knew it would. Weeks and months and years would pass, and she would gradually fit back into her old life. She would become what she once had been, only with the weight of experience behind her. *Experience is growth*, her father had always said; she would cling to that, and wait for something good to come out of what had happened.

She just wished it didn't have to hurt so much in the meantime.

Caraway sat at the table, palms face down on either side of the bottle of taransey, and stared at the unbroken seal on the lid. He'd made the right decision. He knew he had. So why did he feel so bloody miserable?

He'd bought the taransey with the money Ayla had sent after him yesterday. A servant had come running with it, catching him before he was halfway down the hill to the seventh gate. A small fortune in mixed coins, enough to pay his rent for months and give him plenty of time to find work – good work, permanent work, not just a series of casual jobs. He'd understood that Ayla was repaying her debt to him; that she had realised what a mistake she'd almost made, and this was her way of expressing gratitude at his rejection of her proposal. As a result, he'd gone right ahead and spent most of the money on vintage liquor. He'd vowed to drink the lot and the future be damned. Yet night had shaded into dawn and here he was, sitting with the bottle unopened in front of him.

You were desperate for this a few days ago, he told himself. *Just drink the stuff, and go back to being who you were.* But he couldn't. Something had changed in him – a door had slammed shut, never to be reopened – and now he couldn't even seek solace in his own weakness.

Pushing the bottle aside, he stood up and began pacing the room. He'd done the right thing. Ayla despised him; she soon would have regretted asking him what she had, and that would have been worse – to see the mute dislike in her face as she struggled through a life with him by her side, an inescapable burden. At least this way the pain was clean. At least this way he didn't have to fight every day with the knowledge that his love for her – the love he'd always felt – was unwelcome and unwanted.

I'll leave Arkannen. The resolution came out of nowhere, like a gift from a higher power. *Better out of the city.*

He'd unpacked his few belongings when he and Ayla first arrived in their new rooms; now he fell to his knees and began feverishly stuffing them back into his bag, ignoring the pain in his wounded shoulder. He'd go to the Kardise border, become a patrolman. They were always short of men out there, so they didn't ask too many questions of anyone who came seeking a new life – and besides, he'd heard there had been a few skirmishes with Sol Kardis recently, raids designed to test Mirrorvalese strength. If there was going to be war, his weaponry training could find no better place. He could still be of use to his country, and to the Nightshade line. He could still be of use to her ...

'I always liked you, you know.'

The voice made him start. Dropping the last item into his bag, he turned. Ayla was standing in the doorway, her face very pale, her hands curled tight at her sides. Caraway got to his feet, making a half-formed gesture of rejection, though his heart was suddenly beating faster in painful hope.

'You shouldn't be here, Lady Ayla.'

'You never treated me as if I was inferior,' she went on, ignoring his admonition. 'The rest of the Helm saw me as tainted by my mother's blood, but not you. That's why it hurt so much when I thought – when I thought you'd killed her.'

He nodded. 'I understand that.'

'I don't think you do.' She took a few steps into the room; one hand lifted as though she wanted to touch him, then fell again. 'When you came after me in the city, it brought all that pain back. I hated you for it, and I made that clear. But even after I realised it wasn't your fault, I was too proud or too stubborn to admit it. To tell you I was wrong.'

Not knowing what to say, Caraway said nothing. As the silence stretched out, Ayla wrapped her arms around herself, shivering.

'So that's why I'm here. To apologise for how I behaved towards you. And to tell you ... to tell you I still like you.'

That sent a trickle of warmth through him, but he knew he couldn't succumb to it. She was lonely; she was bound to be lonely, with Myrren gone. That didn't alter the facts.

'Ayla ...' He tried to find the right words. 'Things change. People change. I'm not the boy who used to worship you.'

'No,' she said quickly. 'No, I know you're not. But I hoped –'

He held up a hand to stop her, his heart aching with renewed anguish. 'And I really don't think this is the right time for this to happen.'

'Oh.' There was pain in her eyes; seeing it, he stumbled on. 'I mean, I'm leaving for the border. Today. I was just packing ...'

Her gaze settled briefly on his bag, then returned to his face. 'And if I ask you to stay? If I ask you please to stay with me?'

'It would be wrong of me to agree.' Caraway forced himself to say it, though the appeal was hard to resist when all he really wanted to do was take her in his arms and never let go. 'You've been through so much, your father and now your brother – I don't want you to cling to me because you feel I'm all you've got left. And I don't want you to feel you owe me anything, either ...'

The hurt had gone from her expression; he could no longer tell what she was thinking. 'I see,' she said, drawing every word out with deliberate emphasis. 'So you think I'm here – that I *offered* myself to you – because I'm scared, or remorseful, or because I feel *grateful* towards you?'

'Well –'

'Tomas Caraway,' she said, smiling now, 'you really are a complete idiot.' And then she wound her arms around his neck and kissed him.

To begin with it was gentle, an awkward touching of the lips. But then he drew her body closer to his, and she tilted her head and allowed the kiss to deepen, and after that he wasn't aware of anything else for a long time.

When they finally drew apart, Caraway looked down into Ayla's face and felt a weight he hadn't even realised he was carrying fall away. Suddenly light-hearted, he grinned at her; a little breathless, she smiled back.

'I wasn't expecting that.' She made a credible attempt to sound nonchalant, but her wide eyes gave her away. 'When I think of all those wasted nights we spent sleeping in the same room without even touching ...'

'Plenty more nights to come,' Caraway said cheerfully. 'That is, on one condition.'

A hint of the old constraint returned to her face. 'Which is?'

'You let me see your other form.' Then, as she hesitated, 'If this is to work between us, Ayla, I need to know both sides of you.'

'You won't judge me?'

'What?' He frowned at her in confusion; then realisation struck. 'Oh ... love, I wouldn't know one of the correct Changer forms if it flew past my nose. If you hadn't just reminded me, I wouldn't even have remembered that your creature-self is different. And besides –' he took one of her hands in his – 'we're making a new future, remember?'

'Yes ...' She looked down at their interlinked fingers, biting her lip. Then the smile returned to her face, and she gave him a decisive nod. 'All right. Let's go home. And Tomas ...' With her free hand, she gestured towards the hilt of the broken sword at his belt. 'I think you can probably leave that behind. Don't you?'

Epilogue

One month later

She really should leave. Sorrow knew it, yet still she stayed.

Trouble was, there was always a reason to put off her departure for another day. First there'd been finding Elisse and the baby a cottage on the outskirts of a small village, and reassuring Elisse that the Kardise language wasn't that different from Mirrorvalese once you got used to a few basic twists. Then there'd been preparing the little vegetable garden and a couple of chickens so Elisse could be self-sufficient, and long discussions about how best to trade for other necessary supplies. And after that Corus had taken ill for a few days and needed constant attention. Before Sorrow knew what had happened, several weeks had passed. She'd told herself she couldn't go back to Arkannen and so this place was as good as any. Yet she knew that wasn't true. She couldn't stay out here in the middle of nowhere. Her kind of work needed people, and for people she needed a city. The sooner she started building up her reputation again, the better. She had money, but it wouldn't last forever.

Now she stood at the front window of the cottage and watched the sun as it crept down the sky, thinking again about leaving. And suddenly she knew that if she didn't leave now, she never would. She'd stay here: growing vegetables, taking care of Corus, and hoping that one day Elisse would feel more for her than just friendship. Yet that wasn't her style. She had never been satisfied with less than enough, and she didn't intend to start now.

She turned away from the window, to find Elisse standing in the doorway with the baby in her arms, watching her.

'I have to go,' Sorrow said. The words came out in a rush. 'You've got everything you need, and I have to start sorting my own life out.'

'I understand.' Elisse moved further into the room, her eyes searching Sorrow's face. 'But I wish ya'd stay.'

'Why?' Frustration made Sorrow's voice sharp. 'I can't always be here to dig your garden and fetch your firewood and –'

She stopped as Elisse took another step closer and leaned towards her. Their lips touched for a brief, heart-stopping moment, a kiss as fleeting as summer and as light as a butterfly's wings. Then Elisse stepped back, her cheeks flushed but her eyes bright with certainty.

'Naeve,' she whispered. 'Corus and me … we need ya.'

Need. Sorrow smiled wryly to herself. It wasn't love, but maybe it was enough for now.

'All right,' she said. 'I'll stay a few more weeks. Just until you're properly settled in.' She reached out for the baby, and Elisse relinquished him into her arms. 'Now, how about we put this little bruiser to bed?'

Serenna sat in her chair by the window, gazing without really seeing at the pink-streaked evening sky beyond. A flame sunset, the other priestesses called it: a time when the sun's power spilled over into the heavens, setting the very sky on fire. A perfect time for meditation. Yet although she knew she should fetch the appropriate tools, she remained seated and motionless, her hands folded in her lap. Her whole body resonated with an emptiness that was more terrible than pain.

It will pass, the high priestess had told her once she'd poured out her confession. Once she'd admitted how seriously she'd considered taking up Myrren's offer to remain in Darkhaven; how deeply she mourned him, even though their lives had been entwined for no longer than the flicker of a candle flame. *You will come through it, and your commitment to our life here will be stronger than ever. In the meantime, let your current suffering serve as penance for your transgression.*

Yet she hadn't told the high priestess everything.

It had been a few weeks, now, since she left Darkhaven. Not a long time, but long enough. Long enough to feel the changes in her body. Long enough to recognise the truth. A physician would call it early days yet, but she was certain. Certain with every breath she took and with every pulse of her blood through her veins. Something had taken root in her, a seed finding its way into fertile soil as blindly as any green shoot that thrust upwards through the earth in search of the sun.

She was carrying Myrren Nightshade's child.

Serenna touched the flat curve of her stomach beneath her demure dress, but she could feel the new life inside her no more than she could see it. Yet she knew it was there – and it terrified her. The entire course of her existence had been altered by one short night, a night that should never have happened. *Would* never have happened, if she hadn't been so weak as to forget her vows. And now she would have to leave the Altar of Flame. She would have to raise the child alone, or – and she didn't know which idea filled her with more dread – take it to Darkhaven to be raised there. Most frightening of all, she knew it might have inherited its father's hidden and lethal gift.

Yet despite all that, a tiny and impractical corner of her heart rejoiced that some part of Myrren would live on, even if it was at the cost of everything she had.

She bowed her head, hoping without knowing what to hope for, while outside the sky faded from pink to purple to the blue shadows of night.

The evening sun was setting. Its light spilled in through the windows in layers of rose and crimson, bringing Ayla's pale skin to flushed life as she stood naked in the centre of the room, turning in a circle to watch the colours slide across her body. Her dress hung like a discarded chrysalis from the hook on the wall, boots underneath, underclothes folded neatly to one side. This room, with its wide walls and high windows, was Darkhaven's transformation room: a place where a Nightshade could go to Change in private and leave her clothes waiting for her return. Ayla had come here before, but always it had been with the weight of her father's disapproval on her shoulders. He had disliked her creature-self, and so she had grown to think of it as something furtive and shameful.

Now, for the first time, she was going to reveal her true nature to someone else.

Closing her eyes, she took a deep breath through her nose and released it slowly through her mouth. For the first time in weeks she felt at peace. Her grief and shock were still part of her, and Myrren's absence was a permanent ache in her chest, but they no longer threatened to build into something so painful it could kill her. And Tomas ... a helpless smile curved her lips as she thought of Tomas. It had taken the two of them a while to get there, but the past few nights had been ... surprising. And yet it was more than that. Every time he took her hand or brushed a stray strand of hair from her face, she felt safe. She forgot the things that hurt. When he was around, she remembered how to laugh.

Of course, they had plenty of problems to deal with. There was still no sign of Elisse; the most reliable accounts indicated that she and the baby had left Mirrorvale altogether. And Tomas certainly had his hands full with reshaping the Helm, not to mention the threat of trouble on the southern border. But the point was, it was all possible. For the first time in her life, she felt as though anything was possible.

She turned in one final, deliberate circle, then gathered her strength and summoned the Change.

As the sensation of pins and needles all over her body faded, she snorted a sigh of relief. It had been a long time since she entered this form openly and unafraid: too long. She pirouetted a moment, relearning the feeling of her four legs beneath her, furling and unfurling her wings. Then she put her head down and pushed her way through the vast double doors at the end of the room, out into the world.

Her mate was waiting outside in the square. She stepped towards him, arching her neck, and he reached out a tentative hand to stroke her feathers.

'Ayla,' he whispered. 'You're beautiful.'

She tossed her head, catching the last of the sunlight on her spiral horn; correctly interpreting her intention, he stepped aside. The powerful muscles along her back bunched, lifting the wide expanse of her wings before bringing them down in a stroke that stirred the dusty soil. She caught a glimpse of her mate's face, and the pride and joy she saw in it made her heart leap.

Then she was flying free, past the stark walls and empty windows of the blackstone tower, into the sky above Darkhaven.

Acknowledgements

First and foremost, I would like to thank Mr Smith. Because if there's one thing harder than being a writer with a full-time job and two young children, it's being married to that writer.

Mr Smith rarely reads, because he's too busy keeping the household going while I swear at my computer screen. But Mr Smith, if you ever get this far: thank you. I love you. And I'm sorry for what I did to the character who looks like you.

Thanks to my parents, for bringing me up on a diet of Tolkien and Lewis and Le Guin, Wynne Jones and McCaffrey and Pratchett. One of you has read this book already. One of you never had the chance. Both of you are the reason I'm here today.

Thanks also to Harriet and Sam, the Alliance of Worldbuilders, and all the many other fellow authors who have helped and supported me over the years. None of you have read more than a few pages of this book (I hope you enjoy it!) but you have read other things I've written, and given me encouragement and criticism and sympathy and jokes and everything else an author needs. I'm proud to call you all my friends, even if I've never met most of you.

Of course, this list wouldn't be complete without thanking the wonderful team at Voyager: Natasha Bardon, who took a chance on me in the first place; Rachel Winterbottom, who made the book so much better (and has an apparently inexhaustible supply of patience for my hundreds of emails!); Simon Fox, who did a fabulous copyediting job; and Alexandra Allden, who designed the beautiful cover. You've helped me fulfil a lifelong dream.

And finally, I want to thank you, the reader. None of this would have any purpose without you. I really hope you loved reading about these characters as much as I loved writing about them.